TH

Mac spoke u _____ vent down to see what he was doing there. He set a forge by the doors. That building is built with rock from the quarry, and it's just like a cave. Galt didn't have any lights on, just the light from the forge and the sunlight that comes in through the window and doors."

"I walked right past the doors, and the heat hit me like a fist. It seemed to me that Galt had opened a vent to hell, and I was smelling fire and brimstone. At night you can only see that forge. He's just a black shape, moving around the glow of the fire."

Mac pulled his eyes up to Frank and Thompson. "Sometimes when I see him I think he's the devil, warming himself at the fires of hell."

"That's Jack Galt, all right," Thompson said. "And I'm sorry as hell I set him on you, Frank. Sorry as hell."

Independence Public Library

Books by Gary Svee

Spirit Wolf
Showdown at Buffalo Jump
The Peacemaker's Vengeance
Sanctuary
Single Tree

Available from Pocket Books

THE
PEACEMAKER'S VENGEANCE

GARY SVEE

Independence Public Library
Independence, Oregon 97351
Phone (503) 838-1811
2880 5346

POCKET STAR BOOKS
New York   London   Toronto   Sydney   Singapore

The sale of this book without its cover is unauthorized. If you purchased this book without a cover, you should be aware that it was reported to the publisher as "unsold and destroyed." Neither the author nor the publisher has received payment for the sale of this "stripped book."

This book is a work of fiction. Names, characters, places and incidents are products of the author's imagination or are used fictitiously. Any resemblance to actual events or locales or persons, living or dead, is entirely coincidental.

An *Original* Publication of POCKET BOOKS

 A Pocket Star Book published by
POCKET BOOKS, a division of Simon & Schuster, Inc.
1230 Avenue of the Americas, New York, NY 10020

Copyright © 2003 by Gary Svee

All rights reserved, including the right to reproduce this book or portions thereof in any form whatsoever. For information address Pocket Books, 1230 Avenue of the Americas, New York, NY 10020

ISBN: 0-7434-6346-3

First Pocket Books printing June 2003

10 9 8 7 6 5 4 3 2 1

POCKET STAR BOOKS and colophon are registered trademarks of Simon & Schuster, Inc.

For information regarding special discounts for bulk purchases, please contact Simon & Schuster Special Sales at 1-800-456-6798 or business@simonandschuster.com

Front cover illustration by Tim Tanner

Printed in the U.S.A.

I dedicate this book to my sister, Shirley, and her husband, Oscar, who sold their home and pulled up their roots to help my mother through the last days of her life. My brothers, Bob and Rod, and I are eternally grateful to them.

Author's Note

The Peacemaker's Vengeance is a fictional account of a haunting incident that occurred in 1912 in Columbus, Montana. There is little physical evidence remaining from that summer, only newspaper accounts and a tombstone near the center of the Mountain View Cemetery. Fictional characters carved *The Peacemaker's Vengeance* from those shards of the past, just as the headstone was carved from a quarry north of Columbus. The reality of what is buried beneath that stone remains for others to ponder, as I have.

THE
PEACEMAKER'S
VENGEANCE

1

Damn wind! Mac McPherson wanted to hide from it, drop behind a tombstone and wrap himself in his arms and legs for warmth. It stung his eyes with dust and his body with cold.

If they didn't get Deak underground soon, they'd have to bury Mac, too. Most likely they wouldn't even haul him home. They'd just toss him in a hole and cover him up. His ma would come out later, when the wind had died down. "He was just fourteen," she would say. "Just fourteen, and he gave his life to report old Deak's funeral. Ben Simpkins said he'd be a fine newsman some day if he weren't so damn wordy."

But his ma wouldn't say *damn*. *Damn* wasn't in her lexicon any more than the Reverend Eli Peabody had a short sermon in him.

A quarter, Ben Simpkins had said, a quarter to report old Deak's funeral. A quarter to stand in this wind and let the cold take Mac McPherson's life away.

Mac peered through the blowing dust at Sheriff Frank Drinkwalter. Call an end to this sham, Sheriff! Say good-bye to Deak, so they all could say good-bye to this windblown graveyard.

Sheriff Drinkwalter leaned away from the grave at his feet to stare at the slate-gray sky. The wind was strong, strong enough to shake his six-foot frame, strong enough to blow the sunshine away.

Deak wouldn't be sorry he missed a day like this. He had been a tidy man, body and mind, and he couldn't understand why Mother Nature would sweep the dust off a parcel of prairie one day and sweep it back the next. No, John Deakins wouldn't be sorry he missed a day like this.

The sheriff stared down at the pine box at his feet, watched it disappear behind a tear torn from his eye by a gust of wind. Damn wind.

The scent of raw earth filled the sheriff's nose, and he wondered if it came from the gaping wound dug into the gumbo at his feet or from the swirling dust. Nothing seemed content to stay in its place in this country. Not dirt, not water, not air—not even Deak. The sheriff sighed.

Drinkwalter had seen it coming. Hell, Deak had, too. He spent the winter withering away. Said he didn't have much of an appetite, but there was more to it than that. The sheriff could see the pain Deak tried to hide when a spasm caught him mid-step and left him braced against the back of a chair.

The old man had come to him a month ago—no five weeks, it was—and told him what Doc Johnson had said. They had sat in the sheriff's office, not wanting to look each other in the eye.

Deak had hidden his pain behind that bottle of laudanum. He hated that. Drinkwalter could see the old man's revulsion every time he downed a teaspoonful of the foul-tasting liquid. But Deak had started his journey through life seventy-three years ago, and he was too worn to carry the pain alone.

Another gust of wind shook the sheriff as though to get his attention. His eyes skipped across the cemetery, stopping for a moment at the ornate tombstones carved from sandstone quarried north of town. He peered at the angelic figures through eyes squinted almost shut against the wind. Seraphs or cherubim, he supposed, not knowing what either looked like and wondering how the artist did.

He almost mistook Mac McPherson for one of the stones. The boy was dressed drab as sandstone, and he stood as still, leaning into the wind. Tall for his age he was, but skinny as a rail. The wind shuffled and reshuffled the leaves of the boy's notepad like a gambler absently shuffling a deck of cards, waiting for a rube to step through a saloon door.

The wind stopped to catch its breath, and Peabody's words filled the vacuum: "Dust to dust and ashes to ashes." The sheriff wondered how many times that litany was being repeated into bitter winds around the world. The dust stinging his nose might be from some other John Deakins long dead, doomed to blow about forever in this damnable wind.

Peabody's droning stopped. The sheriff nodded to the other pallbearers. Including the sheriff, there were three on either side of the coffin. They reached down, each taking the ends of three ropes set at regular intervals beneath the coffin. The pallbearers leaned back, the muscles of their shoulders and necks straining with the weight of the coffin and the earthly remains of John Deakins.

"Easy boys. Don't dump old Deak."

The pallbearers shuffled along until the coffin hung over the grave. Drinkwalter nodded, and the pallbearers let the ropes slip slowly between their fingers, letting John Deakins settle into his final resting place.

The coffin had hardly settled when Shorty the grave-digger began raining dirt down on the old man. Drinkwalter's jaw clenched and then eased. He couldn't blame Shorty for wanting to get out of the wind.

The sheriff nodded once more to his old friend, and then turned to the black carriage the undertaker threw in with even the pine-box funerals. He saw the boy turn, too, taking his first steps toward the long walk back to town.

"Mac!" The word fluttered and died in the wind. "M-a-a-c!"

The boy turned, and Drinkwalter motioned him back. The boy came, shoulders turned in, arms pulled tight against his chest for warmth. He was shaking with the cold, his teeth clamped shut to keep them from rattling. The widow McPherson did the best she could for the boy, but it wasn't easy to be a grass widow in Eagles Nest.

"Might as well ride with us, Mac. Got a blanket in the carriage. Get out of this damn wind."

The boy wavered, and then his jaw set. "Walked out here."

"Doesn't mean you have to walk back."

McPherson shook his head. He hadn't asked for any help, and he didn't need any. The boy turned his back to the wind, setting cold stiffened muscles to the task of carrying him back.

The sheriff shook his head, watching for a moment as the boy urged his muscles into a mile-eating jog. *Tough little nut.* Drinkwalter climbed into the carriage, the leather springs creaking with his weight.

◦ ◦ ◦

The sheriff sat in his office, more a cubbyhole really, in the county jail. A barrel-bellied stove was working overtime by the door, but the building was built of the same sandstone hewn into tombstones at the cemetery. It always seemed cold and damp, as though the Italian stonecutter had carved a cave and set it next to the courthouse. Come August, the sheriff would appreciate the coolness. But he could do without the ever-abiding chill in the cold months.

Drinkwalter tried to resist, but his eyes were pulled again to the envelope. For three days the letter had lain unopened on the desk. *Damn it, Deak, you left me in such a hell of a mess.*

Drinkwalter took his handkerchief from his back pocket and polished a little circle of clear glass in the window. The sky was one huge gray cloud stretching from horizon to horizon. It seemed cut from stone, too, allowing no warmth to fall on the Earth. Miserable damn time of year.

The sheriff sighed, and turned. It wasn't the weather. Hell, if you didn't like the weather in Montana, you just had to wait fifteen minutes for it to change. It wasn't the weather.

His mind drifted back to the cemetery, and the sound of the dirt clods hitting Deak's pine box. Another image crowded into Drinkwalter's mind: Mac McPherson leaning into that god-awful wind.

Maybe Mac could replace Deak. The thought flickered into his mind. No, he was only a boy. But then the sheriff glanced at the letter on his desk. Maybe. No doubt the boy could use the money. Nobody who could afford a coat would have stepped into this day without one. Mac was a loner, too. The sheriff had never seen him with his classmates. He wouldn't have any special friends with whom to share special secrets. That was the real test: Could Mac be trusted with the contents of that letter?

Drinkwalter's back stiffened. He had little choice. Desperate situations drove men to desperate acts. He stalked to the door, pulling his jacket from the coat tree Old Deak had carved from bits and pieces of wood he picked up in the hills. Pretty it was, and anything left hanging there took on the sweet, clean scent of cedar.

The sheriff slipped on his coat, turning up the fleece-lined collar as armor against the cold wind waiting outside. As he stepped out the door, the wind howled its delight at having the sheriff within its grasp, shaking him as a parent might shake a child to get his attention.

The wind sneaked under the sheriff's collar, sending a chill down his back. *Damn wind.*

The sheriff turned south, each step sending up a puff of dust that disappeared like smoke. He hid in his coat and his thoughts, surprised when he came to the gravel roadbed of the Northern Pacific Railroad. Even in the wind he could smell the creosote guarding oak ties from Montana weather. Even in this wind he couldn't resist looking down the tracks to where they came together somewhere near the west hill, wondering if they could carry him somewhere, anywhere, without a soul-scouring wind.

He didn't go directly to the McPherson place, standing instead a hundred yards away in a copse of cottonwoods near the bank of the Yellowstone River. The McPherson house didn't hold much promise—more tar-paper shack than home. There was no grace in the structure, no lines to catch the eye, no porch to sit on summer afternoons, languishing in the scent of mint and wild rose. The building sat flush with the ground, with no foundation to protect the walls and floor, no foundation for the people living there. The roof was cut into a shallow half-moon, the builder apparently having neither the time nor the will to build a proper roof.

Still, Mrs. McPherson had done the best she could with the little she had. The yard, little more than a clearing cut in the brush, had a sense of orderliness about it, not like most of the shacks along the river. A pump stood outside the home, near the path that led to the cabin's door. A flower bed, brown still with winter and outlined with river rock, waited beside the front door for warmer days. Through the trees to the back, Drinkwalter could see the graying wood of the outhouse.

The sheriff ducked behind a tree when Mac McPherson appeared. Not much chance Drinkwalter would be noticed this far from the cabin, but he didn't want to be seen skulking about a widow's cabin. People might get the wrong idea.

Mac was carrying a burlap sack stained black with coal spilled along the railroad. The boy seemed hopelessly tired, each step an effort. He leaned against the weight of the sack and the wind. The boy opened the door, and the sheriff saw a huge range inside. They needed a range like that to heat the shack, to heat the water that Mrs. McPherson—*Was her name Mary?*— used for the washing she took in. It was a hard life for the two, living alone as they did.

The door closed, leaving the sheriff outside, slouched against the wind. Drinkwalter turned his attention to the cottonwoods. The trees' branches were bare, gray arms reaching in supplication toward the gray sky. They awaited the life-giving warmth of a spring sun so they could rise from their slumber and dress themselves in the soft green leaves of spring.

The sheriff awaited spring, too. There had been so many winters, so many gray, windy days.

Drinkwalter's feet found a deer trail following the bank of the river. The Yellowstone ran cold and black, a flash of white rising occasionally as the wind beat the water into froth.

He lost his thoughts in the depths of the river where hellgrammites lingered under rocks, awaiting warmer water and their brief flights of procreation and death.

A cottonwood log blocked the sheriff's path and his thoughts. The years had stripped the tree of its branches and bark, leaving just its bones. Bones, everywhere bones. His chin dropped to his chest in frustration, exposing his neck to the wind. A shudder tried to chase the chill away.

Resolve straightened the sheriff's shoulders. Mac was his best chance, if he could be trusted. The sheriff rose and turned back toward the McPherson cabin. He stepped along the trail with resolve, Diogenes seeking truth under the Big Sky.

The heat, the smell of lye soap, the steam rising from the tub on the stove hit Mac full in the face as he stepped through the door. His mother glanced up and smiled, her dark hair knotted against her brow.

Mac stepped up to the stove, absorbing the heat into his thin body, trying to drive the cold from his bones.

"Sold another story to Ben Simpkins."

His mother turned to him and beamed, "Oh, Mac, I am so proud of you."

Mac reached into his pocket and pulled out two dimes. They rattled against the bottom of a tin can his mother kept near the stove. "Just the twenty cents," Mac said. "He promised me a quarter, but he only gave me twenty cents. Said I was too wordy. He always tells me that I should use as much description and as many names as I can. Names sell newspapers, he says. But when I do that, he docks me a nickel."

The boy's forehead wrinkled as he looked at his mother.

"It doesn't matter," she said. "What matters is that you have another story in the paper."

She smiled at him, the weariness that marked her face disappearing for a moment. Then she reached again into the tub, rubbing the clothes over a scrub board. She paused for a moment to move her neck from side to side, and Mac knew his mother's back was aching.

"We will have to hang these inside," she said, more to herself than to Mac. "I like to hang them outside to pick up the scent of the sun, but with that wind and the dust . . ."

She stretched again and peered at her son. "You didn't wear your coat again today."

"Wasn't so cold this morning. Wind came up while I was at school."

Mary McPherson sighed. "Mac, I know the coat is patched and it doesn't look like much, but you have to have something between you and this wind."

Mac nodded, but the nod was a lie. He wouldn't

wear the coat. He hadn't worn it since he saw Sally Old-ham pointing at him and whispering to Nancy Goodall. Both girls giggled. Scarecrow, they called him, skinny as a stick and dressed in rags. Scarecrow.

Mac had never felt very much at home with the other children, but now the gulf was widening. Most of the poor kids were dropping out of school, called to help their parents scratch a living from an unaccommo-dating land. They left, eyes dead with the realization of the rest of their lives. As the others left, Mac became more and more a curiosity to poke with dagger-like words. Giggles hurt the most, stabbing him deeply enough to almost draw tears to his eyes.

Mac's jaw gritted shut. Nobody was going to make him cry. Not those rattle-brained kids at school. Not the girls who pointed at him and laughed. Not Ben Simp-kins who sent him into cold winds to report a story and then shorted him a nickel. Nobody would make Mac McPherson cry.

Still, the sharpness of the scent of soap made Mac's eyes blurry for a moment, and Mac turned away from his mother so she wouldn't see.

"When I took Mrs. Thompson's clothes to her, she asked if you could stop by. She'd like to have you spade her garden this weekend."

That was good. Good for a dollar. The garden was huge, and spading it would take most of the day, but maybe the spring sun would come back to Montana by then. Maybe he could use part of the dollar to buy his mother an ice-cream cone. Vanilla it would be, sweet and creamy and maybe with a maraschino cherry on top. Mac could almost taste the treat and rubbed his tongue against the roof of his mouth to savor the essence of it. But the effort brought reality, not the sweetness of vanilla.

"Best get cleaned up, Mac. The soup is done, and I'll have these clothes rinsed and hung up in just a bit."

Mac took the dipper from its nail beside the stove, panning hot water from the boiler that sat always on the stove's surface and mixing it in a washbasin with cold water from a bucket. He dropped a washcloth into the mix, letting it soak before rubbing it against a bar of soap. He scrubbed the washcloth across his face and neck, willing it to rid him of the dust that seemed to have invaded the very pores of his body. As the water touched his arms, he was reminded again of how cold it was outside, how drafty inside the McPherson home.

Mary McPherson was wringing the clothing dry, pinning shirts and trousers and dresses on cords strung just under the open rafters in the cabin, her thoughts drifting again to the hand wringer she had seen in the window of the Eagle Hardware. The wringer would make her work so much easier, but if her work were any easier, the women of the town would do their own washing. Where would she and Mac be then?

Blessings came in strange wrappings, she thought, but they were blessings all the same.

Mac was already sitting at the table, his fresh-scrubbed face glowing slightly red, perhaps from the harsh soap, or perhaps with relief from shedding the dust. He was a handsome boy, Mary thought, wide-set blue eyes under a shock of auburn hair. His face sat on a chin that he would likely poke into the world the same way his father's had. Mac would be a handsome man like his father, but not so ready with a laugh. The boy was as serious as he was thin.

He had been such a happy child. But she had been happier then, too, before Ephraim disappeared. Perhaps his happiness then reflected her own. Perhaps, now . . . she shook her head at the thought and took her seat at the tiny table. She reached across to take his hands in her own, and then she nodded. Mac bowed his head.

"Dear Lord, bless this food to our use, and us to thy loving service. Amen."

Mac reached for his spoon. The soup was mostly potatoes and carrots left over from last year's garden and stored in a tiny root cellar behind the shack. His mother had added canned tomatoes—there were only a few more jars on the shelves in the root cellar—and a couple strips of bacon for flavor. Mac had seen people eat bacon for breakfast, and he could hardly imagine that extravagance. A couple strips of bacon could last a family a week in stew or salad or bean soup.

For all its simplicity, the meal was good, especially with his mother's bread, first for dunking in the hot soup and then for cleaning up the bowl. The food took the edge off Mac's hunger, but only the edge. Always, he seemed hungry.

"Thanks, Ma. That was good."

His mother smiled at him. "You could have more."

"Let's save it for tomorrow night. I'll have something to look forward to."

Mary McPherson smiled again. "I'll do the dishes. You finish your homework. You can't let your grades slip."

Mac scraped his chair around the table, so the light from the cabin's only lantern shone directly on his books. He would do math first and then science and geography. He would save English for last. His English class was reading a book by Herman Melville, a book of the sea, which had not, in Miss Pinkham's opinion, been given the attention it deserved.

Books gave Mac wings to fly away from Eagles Nest. He was enthralled with Melville's description of life on the sea, imagined standing on a rolling deck, a salty wind long spent of dust blowing his face, his eyes seeking the edge of the earth and the white whale. For a moment the dishes his mother was rattling in the basin on the stove became the rattle and groan of a ship en route to destiny. A rapping at the door broke through Mac's reverie. The sound persisted, and Mary, brow knotted into a question mark, stepped to the door. Mrs. Thompson couldn't expect her washing so soon. Mary had just picked up the clothing that morning.

She opened the door just a crack—Sheriff Drinkwalter. What could the sheriff want at this time of night? Her eyes darted back to Mac. Surely Mac had done nothing wrong. Not Mac.

2

Mac sat frozen in his chair. The sheriff must know about the five-dollar gold piece. Frank Drinkwalter had come to tell Mac's mother that her son was a thief, and Mac knew he would die of shame.

The day of his dishonor had come earlier that spring in the time when it snows one day and melts the next, leaving everything muddy and dirty. He was walking the alley behind the Absaloka Saloon when the half eagle winked at him. He picked it up, rubbing the mud from it until it shone like sin.

Never before had Mac held a gold coin. It shined so he could see a new dress for his mother reflected there. He couldn't remember her ever having a new dress. Perhaps there was enough in that coin for a coat for himself. Maybe if he had a new coat, the children at school would stop laughing at him. Maybe God had put the coin there.

Mac had shaken his head at his blasphemy. God wouldn't tempt him so.

Temptation won. The thought of having five dollars was stronger than his conscience. Mac had sneaked down the alley, expecting with each step to be impaled with a shouted accusation. "Thief!" Guilt grew until he staggered under its weight.

The devil had rushed to his side. He couldn't return the coin. The first person he saw would claim it for his own and retire to the saloon to celebrate Mac's gullibility and his own good fortune. Mac's conscience countered that claim: Not knowing to whom it belonged didn't make it his own.

The farther Mac had walked, the heavier the gold piece became. He couldn't spend it. Storekeepers would read larceny on the boy's face if he appeared with a five-dollar gold piece. He couldn't tell his mother about it. She would make him return it; turn it in to Pete Pfeister at the Absaloka.

But then the dragon in his belly rumbled into the argument, shoving his conscience and the devil aside. The pain wasn't much, just a twitch, a reminder of harder times. Mac had grown up believing if he didn't feed the dragon, the creature would gnaw on his gut, spasms of pain marking each bite. Mac could debate with the devil and his conscience, but he couldn't fight the dragon in his belly. He hid the coin in a hole he dug behind the cabin. If the dragon came again and the pain was beyond his ability to bear it, he would "find" the gold piece and share it with his mother.

But now the sheriff was standing in the doorway. Now his mother would learn of her son's thievery. Guilt washed over Mac. Someone must have seen him pick up that coin. They would brand him thief and he would carry that mark for the rest of his life.

Mac's eyes squinted shut. His mother had told him once that nobody could take their honesty from them. Now the sheriff had come to take that, too.

Mary stood guard at the door, barring entrance to the cold and the dust from the clothing she had washed that day. The sheriff's face was buffed red, the spring wind carving it as craggy as the sandstone cliffs overlooking

Eagles Nest. The sheriff was handsome. That thought rattled Mary. She hadn't thought of men as handsome or plain since her husband left that day so many years ago. Her hands fluttered to her hair, and she jerked them away in embarrassment, clasping them together in front of her, red and rough still from the wash.

The poverty of her home crowded into Mary's consciousness. Two mismatched ladder-back chairs graced either side of a tiny table. A curtain separated the two single beds on the far wall, but there were in full view of the visitor. A man shouldn't be looking at a woman's bed. The sheriff shouldn't be in a married woman's bedroom.

Resentment swept over her. She resented the sheriff for shaking her composure. She was angry with herself for thinking that the humbleness of her home made her somehow less than her visitor. Her chin went up then, and she looked the sheriff full in the eye.

"Please come in, Sheriff."

"Thank you. I won't keep you long, I just wanted to ask you a question."

Mary nodded.

The sheriff fidgeted, shifting his weight from one foot to the other, clearing his throat before he spoke. "Milo Phillips came to see me the other day. Seems that a herd of antelope has pretty well taken over his hayfields. He was wondering if I'd like to take some."

The sheriff scratched his forehead, willing the words to come. "Now, some say that antelope aren't much to eat, but taken unsuspecting from a hayfield, before they have a chance to run and work up a sweat . . . Well, I consider antelope taken like that to be fine eating. I was wondering if you—"

Mac's fear roared into anger. "No!" The boy stood so fast his chair tipped and fell *Crack!* to the floor. "No! We don't need any help. Not from you or anybody else. Ma and me do just fine by ourselves."

Mac stomped across the room to stand chin to chest with the sheriff. The force of the boy's approach so surprised Drinkwalter that he stepped back. Mac followed him.

"We don't need charity."

"Mac, I didn't mean—"

"No!"

Mary McPherson stepped forward and grasped Mac's shoulder. "Mac, that's no way to talk to the sheriff. There's no need to—"

"No!"

"Mac, will you hear me out before you make up—"

"No!"

"Mac, that's enough!" Mary shook the boy's shoulder.

Mac shrugged his mother's hands off his shoulders. He stared at the sheriff, his face white with the heat of his anger, muscles knotted along his chin as he ground his teeth together.

Frank Drinkwalter shook his head, gathering his senses. "I didn't mean charity. It's just that it's too warm to keep the meat. I was just wondering if maybe you could can it, and we'd split it."

He turned toward Mary. "I didn't mean to insult you. Old Deak had a bunch of canning jars, and I just thought . . ."

Mary's voice followed a long sigh. "We're not insulted, Sheriff. It would be wonderful to have some canned antelope later this summer. Mac?"

Mac's anger crumbled, his face breaking down in

bits and pieces. For a moment the sheriff thought the boy might cry.

"Mac, I'm here to ask for help, not the other way around. I was hoping you might come along with me. Thought you might give me a hand with the hunting and cutting up the meat."

The boy's face stiffened, leaving it as cold as the wind outside. "What's that worth?"

"Mac! Stop that! I will not have you insult a kindness. Do you understand me?"

Mac glared at his mother.

The sheriff's voice was soft, speculative. "Let's put it this way. Two of you and one of me, so you get two-thirds of the meat. But I'm pitching in the jars, the horses, the rifles, and the ammunition. So you help me butcher the animals."

Horses and rifles and hunting? Mac's face softened and then hardened again.

"Don't know how."

"Not much to it. If I can do it, anyone can."

"We'll do it together?"

Drinkwalter nodded. "Fair?"

"Fair," Mac said.

"Saturday?"

"Can't go Saturday. I'm going to spade Mrs. Thompson's garden."

"Sunday?"

"Got church in the morning—but maybe just this once?" Mac turned to his mother.

"Sunday would be fine," Mrs. McPherson said. "Just this once."

"Good," the sheriff said. "If we get a decent day this week, maybe we could go out after school so you could fire a few rounds, get accustomed to the rifle."

A smile teased the corners of Mac's mouth. "Tomorrow, maybe?"

"Tomorrow it is. As long at this infernal wind has eased up. Wind like this would blow a bullet right back at you."

Mary winced.

The sheriff grimaced. "Ma'am, I'm sorry. Don't know why I said that. You don't have to worry. I've been around firearms all of my life. They're safe enough if you follow the rules."

Mary smiled, but the sheriff could see that the expression was forced.

"I won't let anything happen to him. Mac will be just fine."

Mary McPherson nodded, and Drinkwalter turned to Mac. "How about you meet me at the office right after school; Something comes up so I can't be there, I'll tell Bert. That suit you?"

Mac nodded. That would suit him just fine.

Sheriff Drinkwalter fidgeted. A second letter with the same ornate handwriting lay on his desk. Two pages, gauging from the weight and thickness, most likely written on both sides. Not long as letters go, but the sheriff's life was squeezed on those pages.

Drinkwalter stood, placing the envelope on the shelf with the other. He couldn't sit alone with his thoughts any longer. He stepped through his office, catching Deputy Bert Edgar with his feet on his desk, reading a magazine.

"Going out to make the rounds."

"Need any help?" Edgar asked, boots thumping to the floor.

"You better stay here in case something happens."

Edgar nodded, his feet thumping back on the desk, his attention returning to the magazine in his lap.

The wind had died down, leaving a chill in the air. The sheriff shivered and wondered whether he should go back for his jacket. No, most of the night he'd be in one of Eagles Nest three watering holes. He'd be warm enough.

The sheriff's stride lengthened as he walked toward the smithy and livery downtown. Seemed wasteful to pay Ben Stromnes twenty dollars a month to keep the horses. The county could pasture them down by the river for little or nothing. Of course, that didn't matter. What mattered was that Stromnes was one of the county commissioners' brothers.

The sheriff stepped through the unlocked side door of the blacksmith shop. Stromnes was too trusting. Some people would feel no compunction about helping themselves to the smithy's tools and feed.

Stromnes's shop was less than snug, wind whistling through the building's board siding, but the forge was still warm, and the sheriff stood in its heat for a moment to drive the chill from his bones.

The livery proper was better built than the forge and heated with the warmth of the horses' bodies. The sheriff took it as a measure of a man that he would be more concerned about those in his care than in himself.

Drinkwalter reached up to turn up the light from the kerosene lantern hanging from a rafter above. The sheriff didn't need the light to know where he was. Stromnes shoveled out the livery every evening and morning, but the scent of horses and their leavings permeated every splinter of the rough wood building.

The bay nickered her welcome from the shadows of a stall. The sheriff ran his hands along the mare's sleek neck. She nuzzled him, asking for the oats he usually brought her. The sheriff slipped a carrot from his pocket and gave it to the horse.

He waited a moment before slipping the bit between the mare's teeth and pulling the bridle over her head. He led the horse from her stall then, draping the harness over her back, telling her that all was well in the world.

"Nothing special tonight, old girl. Railroad pension came in, so we'll have to give Tippins a ride, but after the wind this afternoon, most folks will hold close to home. It'll be a quiet night, and I think we can spare some oats later."

Electric lamps wore themselves out attempting to shed light on the Absaloka Saloon. The carved rosewood bar collected shadows as handily as it collected drunks. Overhead, trophy moose and deer and elk and bear and mountain lions stared glassy eyed at glassy-eyed men at the bar.

The Absaloka was a dark church presided over by high priest Pete Pfeister. Pfeister glanced at the sheriff and grinned. He held up a shot glass he was polishing behind the bar. The sheriff smiled, but shook his head.

"Not tonight, Pete. Thanks, anyway."

The sheriff's eyes roved up the bar, taking roll. Same bunch. No real troublemakers.

He turned to Pfeister.

"Heard the railroad pensions came in."

Pfeister nodded. "Tippins's in the back room watching the poker game. Drummer's been taking on all comers. Slicked-down black hair, derby hat, and gray suit. He's been winning a hell of a lot of money."

"Check him out?"

"Didn't see anything. Thought I caught him going for a card up his sleeve, but he just pulled out a handkerchief."

"Hell of a place for a handkerchief."

"Suppose he fancies himself a dandy."

"Who's playing?"

"The regulars, and Jimmy Tillot. That boy's been spending a lot of time in here."

"And money?"

"And money, too."

"Jimmy's got a boy now, doesn't he?"

"And one on the way if I'm any judge."

"Think I'll go back and check it out."

"Might as well."

Only a shoulder-high wall separated the back "room" of the Absaloka from the front. Drinkwalter stepped past the wing doors and into a pall of smoke. Some of the poker players looked up and nodded as the sheriff approached. Jimmy Tillot was too busy chewing his lip and sneaking peeks at his hole card to notice the sheriff.

The drummer, his back to the sheriff, said, "Raised you a dollar. You in or out?"

Jimmy had a pair of sixes showing, the drummer a pair of eights. He rubbed his hand over his forehead, and then across his neck.

"It's all I've got, the three dollars. . . ."

"You need only the one dollar to see the next card."

Jimmy stared at the drummer's hand. Nothing big showed. No possible straight or flush, just the pair of eights, and the drummer didn't know about Jimmy's ace in the hole.

Jimmy picked up a silver dollar and held it clenched in his hand. He pitched the dollar into the pot and jerked back.

"Pot's right," the drummer said. "I declare, I thought you Montana boys would take a little to the cold. I haven't been in a room this hot since I was in that Grecian bath down in Denver. Pretty ladies, passing out towels to all the gentlemen. Whooee, now that was hot."

The drummer winked at Jimmy and reached up his sleeve for his handkerchief.

Drinkwalter caught the drummer's hand in a grip that made the drummer wince. "What the hell?"

The sheriff reached over with his other hand and dealt the top card on the deck to Jimmy—an ace. Jimmy's eyes widened, and he tried to hide his grin. Then the sheriff took the top card from the deck and added it to the drummer's hand—a four.

"Jimmy, this man is so certain he's going to win that he's willing to bet his entire holdings against yours."

"Now, you just wait one damn minute," the drummer growled, struggling to rise.

The sheriff growled back. "That's the bet, unless you want me to pull that handkerchief from your sleeve."

The drummer sagged in his chair.

"Clyde, you turn over the drummer's hand."

Clyde Thompson flipped over the cards. "Pair of eights."

"Jimmy, show us what you've got."

"Aces and sixes!" Jimmy whooped. "Boys, the drinks are on me."

"No, they aren't, Jimmy. You go over to the bar and talk to Pete. Rest of you better break out a new deck. I suspect this one is short a card or two. Eight of diamonds and hearts would be my guess.

"And drummer, you're going out on the westbound. Leaves in fifteen minutes. Don't expect your travels will bring you back to Eagles Nest. Is that a safe bet, drummer?"

The drummer, wincing from the pressure on his wrist, nodded. "I sure as hell don't want to see this one-horse burg again. It's a hell of a thing when an honest citizen is waylaid by a crooked . . ."

The drummer winced with the increased pressure on his wrist.

"Much as I'd like to talk to you," Drinkwalter said, "you'd best be getting for the depot. Wouldn't like you to miss the train. Wouldn't like that at all."

Drinkwalter released the drummer's hand. The card cheat straightened, attempting to regain his composure. "You will hear from my attorneys on this matter."

"Best be on your way, drummer. I can hear that train coming."

The drummer fled.

Drinkwalter left the men at the card table and stepped up to the bar. Jimmy Tillot was in a deep conversation with Pete Pfeister. When the sheriff appeared, the young man looked up, his face red and splotchy.

"I'd best be going home, Sheriff."

"Yup, you'd best be going home."

As Jimmy disappeared through the front door,

Drinkwalter leaned over the bar toward Pfeister. "You sure as hell had his attention. What did you tell him?"

"Told him there wasn't anybody in this bar who wouldn't rather be going home to that pretty wife and that little boy of his than sittin' here. Told him he was a fool to leave his wife alone, like that. Said he'd go home one of these nights, and she'd be gone."

"You're a hell of a preacher, Pete."

"Well, I told him, too, that if he didn't stop coming in here every night, I'd have him blackballed. No booze, no cards—"

"And no job," the sheriff said.

"Yeah, no job."

"What'd he say?"

"Nothing. He looked like I'd hit him with a stick. His dad was quite a rounder, you know, 'til he stepped in front of that train. That straightened him out."

"Jimmy straightened out?"

Pfeister shrugged. "Have to ask him."

"Well, if it worked, you did a fine night's work."

"I've got enough drunks. Don't need another one. See Tippins back there?"

"No."

"He had a few drinks and started muttering about that damn watch, so I gave him a bottle and sent him to the back room. Probably passed out by now."

Tippins was sprawled over a table across the room from the poker table. Dressed in a conservative dark blue suit and vest, he seemed like nothing so much as a broken manikin in the back room of a men's clothing store. His shoes, while not new, shone as though they were polished each day and left on the shelf for the old man's one night out on the town.

"Tippins? Tippins. Tippins!"

The old man lay without stirring. Drinkwalter draped him over his shoulder and stepped toward the door with tiny hurried steps.

"Check back in about an hour or so?" he called over his shoulder.

"Ah, it's a slow night. You might as well get some sleep."

The sheriff nodded and carried Tippins into the dark of an Eagles Nest night.

3

Tippins sat in the chair beside Sheriff Frank Drinkwalter's desk. The old man's suit was wrinkled, his hair awry and skin pasty white. His dishevelment belied a cultivation acquired during fifty years of service in Northern Pacific Railroad's finest dining cars.

"Why didn't you take me home?"

"Cold last night. I was afraid you might wander off."

Tippins nodded. "I suppose I should go home now."

"I suppose."

The old man stood, bracing himself, hands on knees. He took a deep breath, straightening his back and tucking his shirt into his pants. Everything in place, Tippins stepped toward the door, touching the wall to steady himself. At the door he turned and looked at the sheriff.

"Thank you."

"No thanks needed. I am pleased to be of service."

As the old man left, Mac McPherson poked into the doorway, his thin body an exclamation mark.

"Sheriff?"

Drinkwalter smiled. "You're early."

Mac's face fell. "Sorry."

The boy turned to leave.

"Now, wait a minute, Mac. I don't want you to leave."

27

When Mac turned, his face was set. He had learned to hide his disappointment behind anger. The transition came easily to him. His voice was gruff, challenging.

"That's what it sounds like to me."

The sheriff leaned back in his chair, tipping it up on its hind legs. "Mac, I've got no call to say this, but if we're going to be working together, we should get one thing straight. Everybody's got a little feisty in him. You and me have got more than our share, so maybe we could try to rein it in a little."

Mac glared at the sheriff and then sighed. "Sorry."

"Good. Let's get this show on the road."

The sheriff stepped to a steel gun case bolted to the jail's wall. An assortment of rifles and shotguns waited there, chained together and locked with a padlock far too big for the job. The sheriff opened the padlock and threaded the chain through the trigger guard of each weapon, careful not to scratch the finish.

He pulled a lever-action rifle from the cabinet, opened the action, and peered into the chamber. Then, to make sure that his eyes had not deceived him, he pushed his little finger into the action, making sure that the chamber was empty.

"Always do this, Mac. Sometimes your eyes will lie to you, but your fingers can generally be trusted."

Mac's forehead knotted again. "I know enough to make sure—"

"Mac." The sheriff's voice stepped up almost indiscernibly in volume, but it had a rumble to it that jerked the boy up short. When Drinkwalter spoke again, his voice was softer than usual.

"Mac, this rifle is made to kill. If you hunt with me, I

want to be sure that you know how to use it. That's the rule. You understand?"

Mac stared at Drinkwalter for a full minute before he spoke again. "I didn't mean anything. It's just that . . ."

Drinkwalter nodded and handed the rifle to Mac, action open, muzzle pointed to the ceiling. Mac took it as though he had been given a treasure. The rifle must be new. The barrel gleamed, a light coat of oil over bluing that had never known a scratch. The stock and forearm were walnut, carved and polished to perfection.

Mac checked the chamber as the sheriff had, first with his eye and then with his finger. He yanked his hand back as though he had touched something very hot. His eyes jerked to the sheriff. "It's loaded. It's got a shell in the chamber."

Drinkwalter smiled, his face softening. "Good, Mac. You did it just right. Don't ever assume that a rifle is empty just because somebody says it is. Always check it for yourself."

"You could have killed one of us. What if I hadn't checked? What if I had just pulled the trigger?"

The sheriff took the rifle back and pried the cartridge loose from the chamber. He held it up for Mac to see.

"It's been fired."

Drinkwalter grinned again. "Not everybody is as smart as you, Mac. So when I play that trick, I don't do it with a live round."

Mac grinned, and the sheriff handed him the rifle.

"This was Deak's. It's one of Winchester's new calibers, a .25-35. Doesn't put out much of a slug, but she is one sweet shooting piece of work.

"That's what you'll be using. I'll take ol' blue." The sheriff pulled a Sharps from the cabinet and leaned it carefully into a corner. He talked as he threaded the chain through the trigger guards of the weapons remaining in the cabinet. "The Sharps is old-fashioned—still shoots black powder same as that pistol of mine. But that's what I learned to shoot, and I don't see much reason to change."

The sheriff picked up his rifle and took two boxes of cartridges from a shelf by the cabinet. "Mac, we're armed and dangerous. Let's go get those horses."

"Horses?"

"Mac, if a couple of desperadoes like us were to walk through town armed to the teeth, someone would likely call the sheriff. What a fix we would be in then."

A smile winked on Mac's face, breaking through the serious set of his expression as the sun had broken through the clouds outside.

The day was magic, as only spring days in Montana can be. The sun leaned down to gently kiss the Earth as though they were lovers too long apart. Meadowlarks sang, and the air carried the tune as gently as a mother carries her baby.

Sheriff Drinkwalter had hobbled the two horses, leaving them downstream to graze on the soft spring grasses, to glory in the spring sun. He and Mac were following the twists and turns of Keyser Creek north. Gray clay walls loomed over both sides of the creek, cutting off the view upstream and down. The creek defined the world into bends and whorls, opening new vistas and closing off others. At each turn the sheriff paused, measuring distance, light, and shadow between where he stood and the next clay bank. The two walked until the rifle felt more like a digging bar than a weapon to Mac. His arm was beginning to ache with the unaccustomed weight when the sheriff stopped.

"This is good enough."

"What makes this any better than every other loop we've passed?" Mac asked, exasperation creeping into his voice.

Drinkwalter turned to stare at the boy, cocking his head. But he didn't answer the question.

"I suspect that clay wall would stop a cannonball, but why don't you run over there and see what's on top."

Mac's eyes squinted almost shut, and the muscles in his jaw tightened into little knots.

"I've never shot a rifle, but there's no way I would ever miss that clay bank. If you think I'll miss that clay bank, how in the . . . world do you ever think I'll take an antelope?"

"Mac, a bullet can hit a rock and ricochet and only God knows where it's going to wind up. It's always best to be sure, just like checking the chamber with your finger. So climb up that bank just so we know there are no cattle up there."

Mac started to speak, but he clamped his jaws shut and walked up the creek, looking for a place where the water ran deep and narrow or a log hung over the edge so he might jump to the safety of the grassy bank on the other side. Not enough water in the creek to worry about, but he could sink knee-deep in that gumbo mud. Might as well be caught in a trap as that.

The creek narrowed, and he jumped, balancing one-legged for a moment while his body decided whether his momentum would carry him on or he would fall backward into the cold water.

Momentum won, and he walked along the gray wall lining the creek until he came to a cut leading to the top. The years had gentled the cut, easing the slope. Grass had taken root there, and prickly pear. Here and there silver sage graced that emerald setting. Over the years the cut had become a path down from the prairie above. The soft soil of the creek was marked with the tracks of deer and the clawed prints of a coyote. Most likely the coyote was mousing in the deep grasses along the creek, en route to the ground squirrel towns that dotted the region.

Mac topped out, stepping into the full face of the sun and the glory of the day. A meadowlark called, and Mac answered, the three descending notes followed by an arpeggio that reached back to the beginning. The meadowlark's song must be learned, one male passing it along to the younger of the species. Mac tried again, and the meadowlark gently corrected him.

Wouldn't it be wonderful to be corrected only by song, Mac thought, but he shook the whimsy from his mind, pulling his attention back to the task at hand. To the west lay sandstone-topped hills blanketed with ponderosa pine, and to the south the Beartooth Mountains stood clothed in a blue so deep it could only have been rubbed from a Montana sky.

The valley was free of cattle to the west. Mac's job was done, but he was pulled deeper into the meadow by the sun and the scent of fresh grass.

The lilies caught his eye and stole his breath. He

dropped to his knees beside one, bending his head in the reverence that beauty always summons. The flowers' waxy white petals blushed purple at the base. A gold star burst from the purple as a scepter from a throne. Stigma, he remembered from his biology class—the golden stars were stigma—but no one could attach so sullied a word to anything so glorious. He tried to put words to the feelings the flowers invoked, but the effort fell flat. Beauty cannot be defined, only appreciated.

Mac stood, breathing deeply of air scoured clean by spring winds and the sun. He might have stayed there an hour, but the sheriff was waiting beside the creek. The thought chafed at him for a moment. Montanans shouldn't be called out of the spring sun.

Mac turned away from the flowers, stopping a few moments later to look back. Someday he would paint this picture with oils or words, sharing the lilies, the soft green of spring and the white-capped Beartooths with those not fortunate enough to know Montana. Someday he would do that.

The boy turned back toward the creek, his eyes searching the grass for the color of spring. As he stepped down the cut, he heard the thump of the sheriff pounding stakes into the creek bottom's soft earth. The sheriff bent over his work, affixing a piece of stiff white paper to the stake. Mac joined him a moment later and the two walked toward the shooting place where they had left their rifles.

"What did you see?" Drinkwalter asked.

"No cattle."

"What did you see?"

For a moment Mac considered telling the sheriff

about the lilies, about the Beartooths rising to the south, and the magic of a spring sun. But he couldn't. To do that was to open his soul to someone little more than a stranger. To do that was to risk being impaled on a sneer.

"Nothing."

"You must have seen something."

"Didn't see any cattle."

"Lot of country up there. You must have seen something."

Mac hesitated. "Saw some flowers."

"You saw the lilies? I thought they would be out now."

Mac glanced at the sheriff. "Yeah."

"They're sego lilies, Mac. Some places near the desert, they grow flame red. They must be beautiful."

Mac stiffened. "White is pretty enough."

The sheriff's smile brought a scowl to Mac's face.

"No, I'm pleased, Mac. Pleased that you really saw the lilies. Did you pick any?"

"No, how could anyone . . . ?"

Drinkwalter smiled. "You'll do, Mac. You'll do." The two were silent then as they walked back to the shooting place.

Sheriff Drinkwalter drew a V in the soft, silty soil lining the creek. "Lot of different ways to do this, Mac. Some people center the front sight in the V, and then line up the top of the front sight with the top of the rear sight. Then they set the top of the sight on whatever they want to shoot.

"That's got some advantages. You can see a little better in low light, but it's always seemed to me that you're juggling too many things to count on getting a shot off before a deer or antelope dies of old age. So I center the top of the front sight fine as I can in the bottom of the V. Then I set the front sight on the target.

"The rear sight will seem fuzzy when you're looking down the barrel, but you'll see it clearly enough. Understand what I'm saying?"

Mac nodded.

"A lot of people think that shooting is in the eye, but it's really in the mind. You have to focus on what you're doing. When everything lines up, you squeeze the trigger, slow and easy. If you're doing it right, you won't even know when the rifle is going to go off. You'll be as surprised as whatever you're shooting at.

"Sometimes it seems that the front sight is jumping around like a kid walking barefoot across a bunch of sharp rocks. But you just keep squeezing the trigger and keep the sight as close as you can. It will all come to you."

Mac cocked his head and stared at the sheriff. "Are you going to talk all day or are we going to shoot?"

Drinkwalter grimaced. "Just one more thing. Some people slip a round into the chamber and put their rifles on safety so they'll be quicker to shoot. I would rather not shoot something I wanted to than shoot something I didn't want to. Understand?"

Mac nodded.

Drinkwalter handed the boy two wads of cotton. "Stuff these in your ears."

"So you can go on talking, and I don't have to listen?"

Drinkwalter cocked his head. "When I shoot off at the mouth, I always hit my target. Let's see what you

can do. First, we'll do some dry firing just get you familiar with the rifle."

"Dry firing?"

"No ammunition. Okay?"

Mac nodded.

"Good. See that white spot on the clay bank across
there?"

"Yeah."

"That's your target. Lie down on your belly. Hold the
rifle tight to your shoulder, but not too tight. Keep your
elbows solid with the ground, two legs of a tripod,
elbows and shoulder, to hold the rifle steady.

"Now just pull back the hammer, line up your sights,
and squeeze the trigger, just like you would if there
were a bullet in the chamber. Just relax and squeeze the
trigger."

"Crack!"

Mac jerked back as the rifle banged into his shoulder. The weapon skittered away from him on the grass
as he jumped to his feet.

The boy's face was taut and white. "You loaded it.
You sent me up on that hill so you could load that rifle."
Mac's head shook with his fury. "Sheriff, you are one
gold-plated son of a bitch! You can keep your damn
rifle and your deer and your antelope. I'm going
home!"

Drinkwalter reached out to take Mac by the shoulder. Mac shrugged off the sheriff's hand and stomped
down the creek.

"Funny," Drinkwalter called after him. "I didn't figure you for a quitter."

Mac turned, his eyes glaring at the sheriff.

"Two things, Mac. Didn't I tell you to always check

to make sure that a weapon isn't loaded before you pick it up?"

Mac glowered at the sheriff.

"Mac, didn't you say that you would do that?"

Mac's shoulders slumped. "Yes, I said I would do that."

"Do you suppose you will ever pick up a rifle again without checking the chamber?"

"No, I don't suppose I will." Mac sighed. "What's the second thing?"

"You know that white spot you were shooting at on the clay bank?"

Mac's eyes jerked to the bank. "It's not there."

"Helluva a shot, Mac. That bank must be 150 yards away. You aced it, Mac. You're a natural."

The corners of Mac's mouth twitched. "I must have jumped a mile and a half."

"Son, if the moon had been out, you'd have gone clear over it."

Their laughter roared into the creek bottom then, chasing the last reverberations of the shot clear of Keyser Creek.

"Nice shooting, Mac. You really are a natural."

"How would you know?"

The sheriff cocked his head, the question plain on his face, and Mac replied, "That cannon you shoot. Every time you shot, that whole clay bank shuddered and sloughed off into the creek. No way to know where you were hitting."

A rumble crept into the sheriff's voice. "You casting disparaging remarks about old blue?"

Mac shook his head. "No. It's a helluva rifle if you

want to knock down a clay bank. It just lacks a little finesse."

"Sounds like someone I know."

Mac grinned, and Drinkwalter chuckled.

"We'd best be getting back. I want to show you how to clean these weapons. Have to do that every time you shoot, or you'll ruin the barrel."

Mac nodded. "Suppose we could stop by the house so Ma knows I'm all right?"

Drinkwalter nodded, and Mac tried very hard to conceal his grin. He wanted his mother to see him on horseback and armed and with Stillwater County Sheriff Frank Drinkwalter.

She would step from the cabin door the moment she heard his voice, wiping her hands with the towel she kept beside the washing tubs. Pride would spread across her face as she looked up at Mac. He would tip his hat to her, and she would smile. Mac would wheel his horse then, and he and the sheriff would ride through the trees of the river bottom to the streets of Eagles Nest.

Mac knew what it was to be the center of attention, to be dressed in rags and skinny as a rail. Most of the time he would hide. Even in the midst of a crowd, he would hide.

But this day he would ride back straight as a lodgepole pine. His eyes would stare straight ahead, not deigning to look to either side. But their eyes, the eyes of those who looked at a boy and saw only a scarecrow, their eyes would follow him as he rode through town with Sheriff Drinkwalter.

Shrouded in mystery, the riders would be, and tongues would wag in speculation. No scarecrow astride that horse. No scarecrow with a back straight as a lodgepole pine and eyes straight ahead.

The image was so strong Mac forgot how hungry he was. There weren't many times then when he forgot hunger. He pulled himself back to the scene beside Keyser Creek. Drinkwalter was looking at him and smiling, and Mac wondered if the sheriff could read his mind.

4

Mac lay in bed, waiting for the sun. No sleep and his eyes felt scratchy, but he had been too excited to sleep. He hadn't really slept since the day they sighted in the rifles.

Mac sighed and sat up, swinging his legs over the edge of the bed, his hand groping for the clothing he had arranged the night before on a bedside chair. On top of the pile were his socks. Putting bare feet on a cold floor was no way to start a new day.

He slipped into his shirt and trousers, shivering as he tugged his suspenders over his shoulders. He stopped to hug himself with his arms, but there was more cold than arms. He bent over to squeeze his feet into shoes a size too small, his fingers guiding laces into eyelets stretched beyond their limits.

Mac shuffled to the stove, feet maintaining contact with the floor so he wouldn't stumble over something he couldn't see in the dark. The stove, a huge range hugging one wall of the cabin, was warm still, but only that. Mac reached into a bucket beside the stove to take out a handful of kindling he had split the night before. He opened the lid, built a little pile of sticks around a wad of old paper, and touched a match to it. The paper flared, lighting the boy's face in its yellow light, leaving a ghostly apparition in the midst of total darkness.

His mother stirred. "Mac?"

"Just lighting the fire, Ma."

"What are you doing up so early?"

Mac could hear his mother rustling in her bed-clothes as she waited for her mind to catch up with the morning. "Oh, yes, you're going hunting with the sheriff. Wait a minute, and I'll fix you some breakfast."

"No, Ma. You stay in bed. Wait until the fire warms up the cabin a bit. It's Sunday, your day of rest."

"God gave himself to rest on the seventh day," his mother replied. "That wasn't given to us."

"This morning. This once it is. I took a dime from the dollar I got from Mrs. Thompson yesterday. I got six eggs and some side pork. You just stay cozy and warm in bed this morning, Ma. It's my turn to fix breakfast."

"Mac, you're going to make some woman very happy someday."

Mac cleared his throat, but he didn't say the first thought that came to his mind: It is not given to scarecrows to make women happy.

"Want to make you happy, Ma. Just you."

Mary McPherson snuggled into her covers, listening to the sounds Mac made as he stirred around the stove.

"Better light the lamp, Mac. Don't want you burning that side pork or those eggs."

"It won't bother you?"

"No, it won't bother me. I was going to get up anyway to see you off."

"When do you suppose he'll get here?"

"It will take you a while to ride to the Phillips place, close to an hour. And he will probably want to get there before daylight. He could be coming any time, now."

Mary McPherson realized then that she didn't want to be in bed when the sheriff came for Mac. She sat up, swinging her feet over the edge, stretching to set her muscles and mind to working.

Mac heard the stirring. "Ma, I told you that you could sleep in this morning. I'll fix breakfast."

"That's nice, Mac, but I can't sleep anyway. I don't want anyone to think me a sloth. What kind of a mother would I be to have my favorite son fixing me breakfast, and me not even up to admire his work?"

"Ah, Ma."

"Ah, Mac."

They both chuckled, and Mary slipped into her robe. She carried water, tepid now from the boiler on the stove, to the little table. She scrubbed her face and arms with a washcloth, feeling more fit for humanity as she finished. She ran a comb through her long black hair, shaking her head to spread the tresses over her shoulders. She stepped back into her cloth-draped cubicle then, to slip into her Sunday dress. The dress was too big, her flesh having abandoned her just as her husband had. She straightened it as best she could, hoping that people would concentrate on God during church and not how she was dressed.

Being a widow woman in a town like Eagles Nest was not easy. If she tried to make herself attractive, wives would think that she intended to steal their husbands away. It was better to be thought of as a laundry woman than a widow. This dress—the only Sunday dress she had—would fit that image.

Mary stepped into darkness. Dawn lay some distance to the east, stars dying though in the predawn light. Her feet followed the familiar path to the outhouse, nose wrinkling in distaste as she neared the little building. It was time to dump more quick lime into the hole, to ease the reality of it. But quick lime cost money. Everything cost money. She emerged a moment later, frantic to step into fresh air and starlight.

She stood outside the cabin door, willing her nose to remember the scent of the roses she planted beside the step. The scent teased her memory, and then it came to her, soft, subtle and beautiful. The roses were an extravagance for a family that could afford no extras, but every life needed a bit of color and beauty in it.

Mary sipped the memory of the roses' scent once more and then stepped through the door and into the warm glow of the stove and the soft yellow light from the kerosene lantern. Mac stood in front of the stove, stirring side pork in the large steel frying pan. He looked up as she neared the stove, the question plain on his face.

"You're doing fine, Mac. It smells delicious."

The boy smiled and went back to his work, fretting over the side pork as he fretted over everything, seeking perfection in an imperfect world.

"Did you use salt and pepper?"

Mac threw his head back in chagrin. Mary brought the shakers and handed them to the boy. He sprinkled the meat liberally with both. The quarter-inch slices of side pork were dissolving into grease and meat, and the smell of it yanked at the boy's stomach. Meat was a rare commodity in the McPherson household, something to be savored.

"Ma?"

"Ah, it's just perfect, Mac, just the way I like it. Here, put the side pork on this plate. We'll drain most of the grease into this cup, and then do the eggs. Maybe later, we can use the grease for some cookies. We'll stretch the bounty as long as we can."

Bounty. Mac smiled. They had a bountiful table. It was the first time he had tied that word to his home.

"How many eggs, Ma?"

"All six."

"All six?"

"Yes, we'll have enough to share with the sheriff, if he comes in time. If he doesn't, we'll eat them ourselves."

"I hope he's late."

"Mac!"

"I didn't mean it," the boy said, but the words lacked conviction.

Mac cracked the eggs against the side of the frying pan and eased them sputtering into the grease. He couldn't remember the last time he had eaten an egg. He couldn't even remember their taste. No, that wasn't true. He could remember the taste. The taste was warm and moist on his tongue when he had stopped yesterday at Eli Jenkins's house to ask how many eggs he could buy for a nickel. The taste followed him into the chicken house as Jenkins checked the birds' hiding places. Six warm, wonderful eggs for a nickel. That was the price for Mac and his mother, Jenkins said.

The edges of the eggs were bubbling up. Mary took a knife and slipped it between eggs and pan. "Just to be sure that they don't stick," she said. She went back to folding the wash then. It was not right to labor on the seventh day, but not right to look at unfolded clothing, either.

She had just finished when they heard the jangle of a bridle outside.

"Sheriff's here, Mac."

Mac's face twisted into a knot. He had looked forward to breakfast, one meal when he could eat everything he wanted. He had thought about breakfast almost as much as he had thought about hunting.

Mac's mother glanced at the disappointment written on Mac's face. "We have a boiled potato left over from last night. I'll make some hash browns. There'll be plenty for all of us."

Mac tried to smile, but the effort died miserably. He reached the door just as the sheriff knocked. Drinkwalter was standing on the step, hat in hand.

"You ready, Mac?"

"Sheriff, we would be pleased to have you for breakfast."

"That's fine, Mac, but I don't want to put you to any trouble."

Mary called from inside the cabin. "No trouble, Sheriff. Mac has fixed a feast for us. Please share it with us."

When the sheriff stepped into the little cabin, a wave of warm air from the stove hit him. The little table was set with three mismatched plates and forks, knives, and spoons. There were no extras in that room, nothing that wasn't needed to get along. The two chairs were simple, straight-backed, and bare wood. People didn't really need cushions, not if they weren't accustomed to them. Plates were plates and no matter that the roses clashed with the lilacs, and the silverware was no closer to silver than the copper penny in the sheriff's pocket. Still the room generated warmth, put there with loving care.

The sheriff's eyes drifted to Mary. She stood expectantly behind her chair at the table, long, black hair cascading down her back. She was a pretty woman, attractive on the outside but prettier still on the inside. Some people were like that. They shone through their skin, mocking the fallacy that beauty is only skin deep.

Drinkwalter stepped behind Mary's chair. "Ma'am," he said, dipping his head in respect. She blushed then, a faint tinge of pink spreading upward from her neck, and Drinkwalter felt the strangest need to touch that blush, to feel the warmth of her skin. He guided her chair to the table.

Once Mary McPherson was in place, Drinkwalter nodded to Mac and they both sat—he on the other chair and Mac on an apple crate Mary used as a hamper. Mary and Mac joined hands, reaching with their free hands toward the sheriff, making a circle around the table. Drinkwalter's strong hands held Mary's rough laundered skin and Mac's tentative grip.

Mary led them in prayer:

"Dear Lord, we are thankful for the bounty You have heaped upon us, for the time You have given us together. Please set us on the paths You have chosen for us. Let our feet celebrate the joy of going Your way. And please, dear Lord, bless Mac's and Sheriff Drinkwalter's hunt so that they may come back safely."

"That was very nice, Mrs. McPherson."

"Thank you, Sheriff."

Mary served the side pork from an old chipped plate. She had no serving dishes, hadn't really thought about that until this morning. She started to give the sheriff a third piece of the meat, her piece, but he shook his head. She felt slightly guilty about not giving him more than she would have.

She glanced across the table at Mac. He was a good

boy. He had never done anything but make her proud—and sad. Mac's teacher, Miss Pinkham, said Mac was bright and should go to college. But Mary could barely afford to keep him in high school. He was such a ragamuffin and so thin that sometimes she thought a high wind might come along and blow him away. Then she would lose him, too, just as she had lost his father.

The thought of her husband carried Mary away from the table. Always in the evenings she pictured him staring into the sunset. He had talked of the high country to the west as though the sun stored the day's beauty there, waiting to unveil it the next morning as a bride lifts the veil from her face.

"It must be a wondrous place out there," he would say. "Wondrous."

One day in South Dakota she had awakened and he was gone. She and Mac had followed, taking the little money they had to travel west, asking in each town if anyone had seen a tall man with brown hair that turned reddish in the sun. He always seemed to be smiling, she had told them, and if they looked close, they could see sunsets burned into his face. Always those people had turned away, unwilling to share her search, unwilling to share her pain.

Max and Mary ran out of money and hope in Eagles Nest. She remembered still the hollowness she felt, as though something inside her had been wrenched out. She had written home to tell her parents that she and Mac were in a cabin along the Yellowstone River. If her husband came looking for them, would they please tell him to come to Eagles Nest? But he hadn't come looking.

She thought that first summer that she had found the place where the sun stored its beauty. The colors of sunsets could be found in the river's greens, in the pastel pinks of the wild roses and the bright yellows of the sunflower. The Beartooths thrust so far into heaven that she wondered each day how the sun managed to pass over them. Perhaps those tall mountains scraped the colors from the sky, painting their flanks a sapphire blue.

Her husband would have spent some time in this place, nourishing his soul with its beauty, but he would have moved on, wondering if something even more beautiful waited around the next corner. She thought he would move west until he reached the Pacific Ocean. He would strip his clothing then and leave it strewn there on the beach. Tanned he would be on the arms and neck and face, the rest of him pale as the belly of a fish. He would swim then into the Pacific, diving finally through the black waters to find the resting place of the sun.

Mary shook the image from her eyes, focusing on the side pork growing cold on her plate. She cut off a piece with her knife and tasted it. "It's very good," she said to Mac. "Perhaps you will be a great chef someday, serving the crowned heads of Europe."

"Side pork," Mac said, grinning. "Do you suppose they will like my specialty?"

"They will if they have any sense, Mac," the sheriff said. "They will if they have any sense."

5

Mac stumbled as he eased off the cabin step to the ground. He paused, willing his eyes to forget the soft yellow light of the cabin's kerosene lamp so they could pierce the darkness.

"Dark," the sheriff said.

"Never saw it so dark," Mac replied.

"Always darkest just before the dawn."

"Must be just about dawn?"

"Must be."

"I led your horse over, so he's probably just behind mine."

"Where's yours?"

"Just ahead of yours."

Mac snickered.

Mac could feel the horses' warmth before he saw them. In the soft, motionless morning air, their distinctive odor and the more modest aroma of grass hay hung close to the animals. But as Mac and the sheriff stepped closer, their eyes began to clear, discerning the horses as shadows against shadows.

"I see 'em," Mac said.

"Which one do you see, yours or mine?"

"Depends on whether we're coming up on them head on or from behind."

Sheriff Drinkwalter chuckled. "I hope we can figure it out. I would hate to have it said that the Stillwater

49

County Sheriff didn't know the front end of a horse from the back."

"I've been told that one end bites and the other kicks."

"That's a helluva a thing to say, boy, when we're walking up on two horses in the dark. Maybe it would help if you sang to them."

"Be better if you did. They know your voice."

"You ever hear me sing, boy, you'd rather be horse bit or kicked."

Mac laughed, the sound muted in the darkness. For the first time, he was joking with someone not his mother.

Mac stepped under his horse's jaw and ran his hand down her neck and shoulders. She shivered a bit under his touch. The sheriff had tied the reins to the saddle horn. Mac held the reins and untied the lead rope from the horse's neck. He found the stirrup and pulled himself into the saddle. He could feel the bulge of the rifle scabbard under his right knee, the stock slick as satin against his pant leg. Settled, he heard the sheriff's saddle creak as Drinkwalter climbed aboard. Mac saw movement, but only that.

"How are we going to find our way in this?"

"We'll follow the railroad track west. By the time we get to the west hill, it should lighten up a bit. We'll cross the river up there."

"I don't know how to swim."

"Well, you'd best not fall off your horse, then."

Drinkwalter kicked his horse north toward the Northern Pacific railroad track, guiding himself by the smell of creosote. As they neared the track, he could see the shine of steel polished daily by passing trains.

Stars winked secrets at the track, and the track winked back.

The roadbed was wider than the gravel and ties that bore the track, so there was a ready-made trail on either side, easy walking for a horse. Drinkwalter turned the gelding west, settling into the horse's easy gait. When he was sure that Mac's horse was following, he set his thoughts on the secret. Today, he would decide if he could trust Mac.

The gray light of false dawn lay upon the land. The Yellowstone was shiny black, the west hill a dark gray marked with the darker shapes of juniper and yucca. The day untouched yet by the sun was cold, and Sheriff Drinkwalter hunched his shoulders, pulling his neck into the warmth of his jacket. A moment later he pulled his gelding to a halt, turning in his saddle.

Mac was riding with his arms pulled up to his chest. Even in the gray light, the sheriff could see that the boy was shivering.

"Mac, there's an extra jacket in your saddlebag, left side. Put it on."

"Don't need it." Mac's words came between squeezed teeth. The boy was trying very hard to stop his teeth from chattering.

"Put it on, Mac. There's no sense being cold."

"It'll warm up pretty quick, when the sun comes up. I'll be fine."

"Put it on, Mac."

"Don't need it!" Although the words were whispered, an edge was creeping into the boy's voice.

"Mac, from this point on, we're hunting. No way in the world you can hit an antelope, shaking like that."

Mac stared at the sheriff for a moment. Then he nodded, reaching behind him to pull the jacket from the saddlebag. Wool lined it was, with a cotton shell in the style of the dusters that so many cowboys wear. The jacket was soft and warm and smelled of laundry soap and the sun. For a moment, Mac wished that he had a jacket like that, but he pulled his thoughts from such fancy, an oft-repeated litany forming in his mind: "Dear Lord, please forgive me for wanting things that I am not meant to have."

The sheriff rode west past a cattail-filled slough that marked a long-dead channel of the Yellowstone. He pulled his horse into a stand of trees shading the river bottom from the early morning light. A band of river rock, white with dead moss and the silt of last year's high water, lay between the trees and black water. Wide the river was, slick water that hid its depths from anyone who dared venture into it. A ridge tiptoed into the river on the far side, keeping the bank steep, too steep, Mac thought, for a horse to scramble up. Too steep, anyway, for a novice rider like Mac to stay on the animal's back as it struggled for purchase.

"It's not as bad as it looks," Drinkwalter said. "Only way you can get into trouble is to slip off the downstream side of the ford. It's deep there and fast. If you go over, let the horse have her head. She'll go for whatever bank she figures she can make. You stay with the horse, and she'll get you through. Hang on to the saddle, or the mane, or the tail, or anything else you can get your hands on, but don't leave the horse, Mac.

"I'll be going ahead of you. So you just follow me, but if I go over, you just let me be. Won't be anything you can do, anyway. You understand me, Mac?"

"Can't swim."

"Don't have to. Anything goes wrong, your horse will take care of you."

Mac stared wide-eyed at the river.

"Mac, just keep your head about you, and everything will be just fine. The ford is the tail end of that ridge. Just keep the horse headed toward that ridge, and you'll do fine. You ready?"

"Can't swim. I told you I can't swim."

The sheriff shook his head and sighed. "I made this sound worse than it is. I didn't mean to do that. It's just that it's always a good idea to hope for the best and prepare for the worst. We'll do just fine crossing this river, and once we get across, we'll shoot some antelope.

"You ready to cross with me, Mac?"

Mac nodded.

Sheriff Drinkwalter nudged his horse into the river just as the sun cracked the eastern horizon. The bright light turned the morning air clear and crisp. Colors appeared where only shadows existed a moment before, and the river, black as obsidian in the darkness, turned green as an emerald, the slanting rays of the sun lighting its depths.

The horses clattered across the rocks and into the water. For a moment, Mac saw the crossing. It was as the sheriff had said it would be, a natural roadway leading across the river. But as the horses edged into deeper water, the path disappeared into the darker green of the depths. The boy involuntarily sucked in his breath, holding it as though he were already immersed in the river, as though he were already drowning.

The water was lapping at Mac's feet, seeping through the holes in the soles of his shoes. The river seemed eager to reach the boy, eager to claim him for its own. Mac jerked his feet up, and the horse, feeling the tap of her rider's feet, surged ahead. Mac almost panicked, but he eased back on the reins, willing the horse to walk.

The water was over his ankles, the river welling on the upstream side, raging against the arrogance of this four-legged creature and its rider. Rocks, ledges, mountains had fallen to the river in its eons of existence, each yielding to the power and majesty of the Yellowstone. It was pure folly for a four-legged to resist its flow.

Mac could hear the river's warning in the rush of the water. He had spoken with the river before. The boy had been down on the banks of the Yellowstone, watching trout leap from its emerald depths, silver spraying from their twisting, writhing bodies. He had thrust his head beneath the surface to see what frightened the trout so.

He had expected the river to be quiet, but the water was filled with a great clatter as the current rearranged its bottom, moving one rock here and another there. Perhaps the trout were fleeing the rocks that the river was throwing at them.

The mare stumbled, and Mac wondered if the river had hurled a boulder at her steel-shod feet. He wondered if the river would pick this moment to shift in her bed and send the boy and the horse flailing helplessly against the current and the depths downstream.

Mac tried to pull his thoughts away from the rocks bouncing past his horse's feet. The far bank was nearer now; they were nearly halfway across. But the water was deeper here, nearly up to the boy's knees, and he could feel the horse scrambling for footing on the rocky bottom. He wondered what would happen if the horse refused to go on. If he tried to turn back, she would be swept over the edge. So they wouldn't be able to go on, and they wouldn't be able to go back. They would stand in the middle of those dark green waters like a four-legged boulder until the cold of the water took away their strength, and then they would surrender to the Yellowstone.

The mare was leaping now, fighting for footing. Mac was hanging on to the saddle horn, afraid he would be thrown off. He looked up just as the sheriff's gelding slipped over the edge. The sheriff's horse screamed, eyes rolling in terror, as he threw his head back to keep his nose above the water.

The current was faster than Mac had imagined. The sheriff's gelding was swept downstream, fighting to keep its head up, to breathe the air that would fuel its fight with the river. Mac's mare turned to follow, but Mac jerked her head around. *"Hyah, hyah."* The boy urged her into the current, away from the edge that carried the sheriff away. Too far they went, the horse stepping into the deep water upstream, but just as the sheriff had said, the current carried her back to the ford. She lunged up on the gravel, seeking footing, seeking safety.

Mac's eyes desperately searched the opposite shore, looking for the end of the crossing. There, just where the ridge stepped into the water. Safety lay there.

"Hyah, hyah." The mare lunged toward the shore, the current carrying away her wake, the only evidence of their passing. *"Hyah, hyah."* Mac was slapping the mare with the reins, urging her on, and then the water was back down to his knees, and then his shoes. Only

then did Mac seek the sheriff. The current had carried the horse and rider nearly a quarter mile downstream. But they seemed no closer to the bank. The gelding, head held back in fright, was flailing the water with his hooves, making little progress.

Mac's mare was only knee-deep in the water now. Without the river to restrain her, she lunged toward the safety of the bank, nearly throwing Mac off. She reached the bank, dancing out her fear in the shallow water.

No time for dancing. A trail led up from the river, just as the sheriff said it would. Mac pointed the mare's nose toward the break in the willows and chokecherry bushes. A moment later, he broke out on a meadow. He wheeled the mare downstream and kicked her into a gallop. She ran as though to free herself forever from the green waters of the Yellowstone. Mac held to his saddle horn, giving the horse her head. He had to help the sheriff. If he didn't get there in time . . . Mac drove the thought from his mind as he drove his heels into the mare's belly.

6

The sheriff's gelding was fighting the river. If the horse could have gotten his feet under him, he would have reared, bucked against the indignation of being dumped into the cold water. But there was nothing beneath his feet to offer purchase. So he ran for his life, feet flailing.

Sheriff Drinkwalter leaned forward in the saddle, face near the horse's neck. "You can make it, boy. We're almost there. You can do it. Good hoss. Good hoss. Just run, boy, just keep running, and we'll make it."

The gelding's ears flicked back at the sound of the sheriff's voice, and Drinkwalter sensed a strengthening of resolve. The horse was swimming now, pulling away from the panic that had been pulling the animal into the depths of the river.

"Good hoss. We'll make it across. I won't let anything happen to you. We'll make it."

And then a *click*, steel against stone: one of the horse's hoofs had struck a boulder beneath the water. That was good and bad: good because it meant that they were entering shallower water; bad because the bottom might be littered with boulders, traps for a horse's thrashing feet. A trapped hoof could snap a leg or hold the horse captive while the relentless surge of the river pushed him to the bottom. Either case meant death for the horse and perhaps for the sheriff.

"Good hoss. We've almost made it now. We're coming up on the bank. It's not so steep here that we can't climb out. Good hoss. Good hoss."

The gelding surged on, encouraged by the sharp scent of willow buds about to burst into leaves, encouraged by the scent of new life. *Click!* Another rock and then a clatter as the horse charged toward the bank.

The gelding pulled free of the river and danced out his freedom. The sheriff pulled back on the reins, speaking softly to the horse. "Easy, now. Easy."

The sheriff's eyes searched the crossing above. Mac wasn't in the crossing. The boy had made it across. But then another thought pierced the sheriff's consciousness. The boy could have slipped over the crossing just after the sheriff did. If he couldn't turn the mare toward the shore, if the horse took the easiest path and swam downstream, he could be . . . The sheriff's eyes jerked downstream. The river made a wide bend to the north there. Could he already be around the bend? There was something in the water there, dark against the darkness of the water.

The bank was too steep and high here to climb to the meadow above. Drinkwalter pointed the gelding downstream, the sheriff's eyes probing the bank for a path leading to the top, probing the river for a sign of the boy.

He had traveled nearly two hundred yards downstream before he found a game trail leading to the top. At each step the sheriff's dread had grown. He reined the gelding over to the trail, and the horse took easily to the climb, anything to free himself from the dark waters of the river.

As the sheriff breached the top, a smile spread

across his face. Mac was sitting on last year's grass, leaning against the trunk of a cottonwood.

Mac glared at the sheriff.

"Good to see you, Mac. I was worried about you."

The muscles at the back of Mac's jaw bulged. One eyebrow crept up the sheriff's forehead. He would probe with words the source of the boy's anger as delicately as a surgeon's scalpel probes for a malignant growth.

"Helluva ride, wasn't it? Something to tell your mother about."

Nothing. The sheriff took a deep breath and eased it out.

"Well, we better get up on top if we're going to catch those antelope in the pastures. Won't be long before they move off. No need to dry our clothes. The sun will dry us off soon enough."

Mac spoke, his words seasoned with deadly resolve. "I'm not going hunting with you. Not now, not ever. Just waited to tell you that. I'm going to take the road back to town. I'll leave the rifle at the livery."

The boy stood, stepping toward his mare on legs shaky with rage.

"Mac, wait a minute. What the hell's wrong with you?"

"What the hell's wrong with you?"

"What do you mean?"

"Go to hell."

"Mac, at least tell me what rankles you so. You owe me that."

"I owe you nothing!"

Mac had removed the mare's bridle and loosened the saddle's cinch. He took the bridle now from the low branch where he had hung it, slipped the bit into the mare's mouth and the bridle over her head. He stepped up to the horse then, tugging against the cinch to tighten it. But the mare had taken a deep breath; Mac couldn't pull the cinch tight.

The sheriff's words came softly: "Kick her in the belly, Mac. Then she'll let you tighten the cinch."

"Yeah, kick her in the belly. What'd she do, fail one of your stupid damn tests?"

"Mac, your mother wouldn't like you using language like that."

Mac stormed away from the horse toward the sheriff. "Who the hell are you to tell me what my ma wouldn't like?"

The sheriff sighed. "You're right, Mac. I don't know what your mother would say. I don't know what put the burr under your saddle, either, but I sure as hell would like to."

Mac's face pinched together and for a moment it seemed that the boy might burst into tears. But Mac McPherson wouldn't be brought to tears: not by anything, not by anybody.

"I told you I couldn't swim, but you dragged me into the river anyway. And then you pulled off that fool stunt."

"What stunt?"

The muscles in Mac's jaw tightened, and his eyes cut like razors.

"You went over the edge. I've never seen a horse terrified before, but that's what your horse was. His eyes rolled back like the devil had him by the lead rope. I thought I was going over then, too."

Mac glared at the sheriff. "All I could think about

was what it would be like to be laying on the bottom of that river and not being able to breathe. And finally I'd take a breath and get a lung full of water and cough myself to death down there. I couldn't breathe just thinking about it. I didn't take a breath till I got to shore.

"Then all I could think about was you being out in that river. I thought about all the things that could be happening to you."

Mac's face grimaced. "So I ran down here, first place I could get to the river and I watched you, watched you swim that horse to shore. You know what?"

Drinkwalter's face wrinkled. "What?"

"Not one time did you look over your shoulder to see how I was doing, to see if I made it across the river or not. Not once did you even look back!"

Mac's jaw clamped shut, and only the force of his anger could squeeze the words between his teeth. "At first I thought you didn't give a damn if I drowned or not. At first I thought you were one cowardly son of a bitch who wouldn't pitch in to help someone . . . someone who didn't know how to swim.

"But then you started looking around for me. You looked upstream. You looked upstream because you knew I would make it across. You knew that because you knew that you could have made it across! You went into that river on purpose."

Mac stood and stomped around the little clearing, his feet raising little puffs of dust. He turned to face the sheriff.

"This was another of your stupid damn tests. Just like the test to see if I would check the chamber of the rifle before firing it. Only this test could have killed me!"

Mac's voice roared now, as a fire roars with a gust of wind. "You were willing to see me dead just to see if you could 'trust' me to do what you told me to do. Well, I passed the test. I did exactly what you told me, and I got across the river.

"But I'll tell you something, Sheriff. You failed my test. There is no way I can trust you. Don't you ever come around me and Ma's cabin again, Sheriff. If I don't ever see you again, it'll be too damn soon."

Drinkwalter's face blanched white. "Mac . . ."

The sheriff's mouth opened and closed silently, as though he were a fish waiting for the current to carry him air to breathe, and then his thoughts caught up to the moment.

"Mac, we're here. We might as well take some meat back with us. We might as well."

"You go to hell, Sheriff! You get any meat, you don't bring it to us. We don't need you. I told you at the beginning. We don't need your damn charity. We don't need it now. We don't need it ever!"

Mac stepped back and kicked the mare in the belly, using his rage to tighten the cinch. The boy twisted the stirrup, stepped into it and pulled himself into the saddle. He was reining the horse around when the sheriff's voice, flat as a homesteader's dreams, came to him.

"Mac, it's true. I did that to see if I could trust you. Truth is I need your help. I probably should have come to you straight on, but I didn't do that."

The sheriff's chin sunk toward his chest.

"Mac, you keep that rifle. It was Deak's. I know he'd be pleased that you have it. Maybe you can get a deer down on the river bottom by your place.

"I . . ." The sheriff sighed. He shook his head and

dropped his eyes to the ground. He waved, a last, flickering gesture, without looking up. "I'm sorry."

The sheriff seemed to have aged decades in the last few moments, and Mac's anger fled as quickly as it had raged.

"I couldn't keep the rifle."

"Keep it. I don't need it. Shame to have it go to waste."

Silence stretched until Mac's words tiptoed out. "Why did you do that?"

The sheriff took off his hat and stared south toward the Beartooths as though he expected to find the words he needed written there, but that page was blank, too.

"Look, Mac, I had Tilly over at the Stockman make me some beef sandwiches. She makes 'em better than anyone. Well, I'm hungrier than a bear right now. If you'd like, maybe we could eat, and I'll tell you about it. How does that sound?"

Mac was hungry, always he was hungry, but it wasn't the sandwiches that pulled him off his horse. Scarecrows don't have many friends. It would be a shame to waste the ones they had.

"Told you Tilly makes the best sandwiches."

Mac nodded, his mouth full of beef and home-baked bread.

"I've got a couple cans of peaches, too, but I thought we would have those later . . . when we were hunting."

Mac nodded again.

Drinkwalter sighed. "I've been thinking about this for a week, how I was going to tell you, but none of it seems to make any sense."

The sheriff scuffed graffiti into a soft patch of silt

with an uprooted willow, long dead and gray from the sun. He sighed, and then the words began:

"Secrets are hard to keep, Mac. Hard to keep when they are our own and harder still when they belong to someone else. I have secrets I used to share with Ol' Deak. . . . I need someone else to share those secrets with now, Mac.

"So I'm asking you straight out, Mac. No more stupid tests. Can I trust you to keep my secrets?"

Mac nodded.

The sheriff scuffed the dirt with his boot. "Mac, I can't read or write."

Mac's brow wrinkled. "Lots of people can't read or write."

"Not many sheriffs can't."

Mac nodded. "I could teach you. . . ."

"No, Mac, I can't learn it. It's not that I'm stupid. It's just that there's something wrong with the way that I see letters. They're all in a jumble, and I can't make them out the way most folks can. I've been to a lot of doctors. They say I'm dyslexic. It can't be cured, and I can't read or write. So Deak did all my reading and writing for me. He read all the notes from the commissioners and all the wanted posters and some of the stories in the newspapers. He wrote the reports and kept the books.

"Mac, I'd like you to do that for me."

"Why not one of the deputies?"

Sheriff Drinkwalter shook his head. "There's more to it than that, Mac. When I was growing up, I thought I was stupid. I went to school like everybody else, but I couldn't learn to read. I was learning my lessons, though, one lesson, anyway. The other kids would 'read' that lesson to me. 'Frank Drinkwalter is the dumbest kid ever to enter grade school. He's too dumb to read and too dumb to learn anything.'

"You know what it's like to be singled out like that, don't you, Mac?"

Mac picked up a piece of driftwood and scratched at the ground. "Yeah, I know."

"I did a little teaching, too, with my fists, so they would know what it was like to hurt, the way they were hurting me. But they'd gang up on me, and I'd get the worst of it. I got kicked out of school.

"I worked around the farm until I was fifteen, my mother teaching me everything she could. I'm not dumb, Mac. I can do more math in my head than most people can do with a paper and pencil, but I can't read.

"I left home, but it was no better. I took a job on the railroad. They liked the way I swung a hammer, but it was clear to me that was all I could hope for.

"That's when I started drinking and fighting. I either had a shot of Old Crow in front of me or I was beating the hell out of someone I didn't even know. The gandies would cheer me on then, as long as the blood was flowing.

"Then I heard about a doctor in Cincinnati, Ohio, so I went up to see him. He ran some tests on me. Said I was smart, smarter than most people. Said there were others like me. But he couldn't help me learn to read. What the hell good does it do to be smart if you can't read?"

Drinkwalter stared into Mac's eyes. "I was thinking about going into a tough bar and picking a fight with three or four toughs. People would be cheering me on while the toughs beat me to death. I thought that was what I ought to do, go out with a cheer.

"It was April, and I was walking past this park on the way to the bad side of town. It was all greened up, leaves coming out on the trees fresh as a tiny baby. I don't know what made me sit down on that bench. Maybe I just wanted a little peace before . . .

"I sat there thinking about a lot of things, about Ma, about how she would feel when she found out what happened to me. I was thinking that it was a hell of a poor way to pay her back for everything she had done for me.

"Then I caught the scent of roses. I looked around and this young woman was standing behind me. She had her back to the sun, and it set her hair afire, like a shining halo. I couldn't see her face; it was all in shadow. I thought God had sent me an angel.

"Mac, you remember when I sent you up on top of the bank at Keyser Creek, and you found the sego lilies?"

Mac nodded.

"You remember how beautiful they are? Too beautiful to put into words. You can only feel their beauty deep down in your soul?"

Mac whispered, "Yes."

"That's how beautiful she is. I can only draw lines around her with words. She shines, Mac. From some inner beauty, she shines. She is . . ."

The sheriff shook his head in the wonder of that moment.

"Anyhow, she said, 'My name is Catherine Lang.'

"I couldn't speak. I could barely breathe. She reached out and took my hand. We stood then and walked together through the park, hand in hand. We must have walked, because I can vaguely remember the trees stepping past us, but I can't remember my feet touching the earth.

"We didn't speak until we reached an ice-cream parlor. We both had strawberry sodas. I didn't even ask her what she wanted. I just knew. . . . I told her everything, Mac. Things I hadn't been able to tell anyone else, not even my mother. She hung on each word as though it were a diamond, and she was measuring its clarity and brilliance. And when I finished, she told me about herself. Her father had owned a freighting business when she was a child. He worked himself to death, leaving enough money to keep Catherine and her mother . . . comfortably.

"Her mother is very ill, has been for years. So Catherine has been caring for her, spending her life caring for her mother as her father did. I met her mother, Mac. Even after years of illness, you can still see her beauty. I've since wondered if Catherine's father didn't work himself so hard just so that he might feel more worthy of her."

The sheriff shook his head. "Wouldn't that be something? Throwing away your life so you would feel worthy to spend it with someone special?"

The sheriff shrugged. "I stayed in Cincinnati for a month, and then I decided to move West. I thought I could find something out here that I couldn't find there, something that would make my life worthy enough to offer to her.

"So I settled into this job. I knew most of what it was like to be on the other side, so I'm especially well trained for it. People think of sheriffs as legal ruffians who stalk miscreants, daring them to break the king's law. But it isn't like that, not in Eagles Nest, anyway. We are arbiters, peacemakers. That's a worthy life to offer a woman, Mac.

"It was ten years ago that I left Cincinnati. Catherine and I haven't seen each other since. I teamed up with Deak not long after I came to this country. He was my. . ."

Drinkwalter scuffed at the dirt at his feet with his boots.

"Mac, did you ever read *Cyrano de Bergerac?*"

Mac shook his head.

"I saw the play a couple of times. It's a story about a tongue-tied young man who wants to court the beautiful Roxanne. He recruits Cyrano de Bergerac to plight his troth from the shadows as the young man stands before Roxanne's balcony. Cyrano is in love with Roxanne, too, but he won't court her because he possesses a 'great nose.' He makes light of that. One of his lines is: 'A great nose indicates a great man—genial, courteous, intellectual, virile, courageous.'

"So Cyrano speaks of his love for Roxanne and in so doing allows the young man to win her hand. Deak was my Cyrano, Mac. I have been courting Catherine with words. Deak put my words on the pages, and he has been reading me her letters. Since Deak died . . . I know she's worried about me, but . . ."

The sheriff scuffed at the ground with his boot. "Mac, the most private things a man has to say are between him and the woman he loves. Do you understand, now, why I put you through the tests I did?"

It was Mac's turn to scuff in the dust with his boots. "Yes," he whispered.

"Mac, I need somebody around the office who can be my eyes and voice. I need someone who can read the notes from the commissioners and stories from the paper so I know what's going on. But mostly, I need someone to play Cyrano to Catherine.

"I told the commissioners I needed someone to fill in for Deak. They agreed to give me five dollars a week. If you want the job, it's yours. You'll have to come around the jail every night after school. Sometimes I might need you on weekends, but not often.

"Would you do that for me, Mac, and never talk to anyone about what I've told you today, never tell anyone about what's in those letters?"

Mac cleared his throat. "I'd do that for nothing if you want."

"No, Mac. The letters from Catherine are my life. Certainly, my life is worth five dollars a week."

The horses danced as they neared the McPherson shack. The raw meat on their backs made them edgy. Let them dance, Mac thought as the hunters drifted through the trees. Let them dance, and I will dance with them. I will climb down from the saddle and dance in celebration of God's bounty.

The door to the cabin opened the moment the horses pulled to a stop, and Mac's mother stepped out on the porch, her hand shading her eyes as though it were still day and not evening.

And then she saw Mac, and a smile spread across her face, and she danced a little, sending the horses again into a dance of their own.

They hung the antelope in the root cellar, lined still with winter ice. Drinkwalter turned to Mary.

"Ma'am, I've got no call to ask you this, but if I were to cut some butterfly steaks from one of these animals, and if you had some flour and pepper and salt . . ."

Mac's excitement was contagious, and Mary was almost giddy with it.

"Didn't you hear me when I invited you to dinner to share the great bounty two hunters have brought to me?"

Drinkwalter grinned. "I guess I missed that."

"Well, sir, you will not miss dinner. If you will give me those steaks, you and Mac can attend to your ablutions while I attend to the feast."

"Ma'am, we are of like mind."

"Yes, sir, we are."

"Are you of one mind, Mac?" Drinkwalter asked.

"More of half a mind," Mac said, "if I am to believe what I am told."

The three laughed then, giddy with the moment.

7

Mac stood across the street from the school, pretending to be examining the tiny buds on the lilac bushes beside the stucco one-story building where Doc Johnson practiced medicine. Mac wondered momentarily why medicine is always practiced, whether doctors ever get it right. But the whimsy flittered in and out of his mind, his attention pulled back to the crowd of girls and boys across the street.

They were chattering with one another. Even from across the street, he could hear the ebb and flow of their conversations. Two stood off by themselves at the corner of the building. That would be Sally Gingrich and Ben Haraldson. They seemed always to walk in a little sphere that had room only for them.

Mac didn't hear the bell, but it must have sounded. The little cliques broke into swirls of color that disappeared into the maw of the school. He waited a moment more and then stepped into the street. He thought he saw a flicker of movement in the window of the Salisbury house. Mrs. Salisbury was probably watching him. Everybody would be watching him. He stood out like a boil on a beautiful girl's nose.

He didn't want the clothes. He had told his mother and Sheriff Drinkwalter that. He didn't want Deakins's clothes. But his mother had said that it would be a waste not to take the sheriff's offering, and there was no room for waste in their lives. So they had picked through the sheriff's beneficence, his mother washing each piece with care, hanging each to dry in the cabin.

The collection included new boots, woolen pants and a blue plaid shirt. When he had dressed that morning, his mother had smiled.

"A handsome lad, that Mac McPherson," she said with a grin. "A handsome lad, and a fine dresser."

But Mac didn't feel like a handsome lad or a fine dresser. He was wearing a dead man's clothes. Surely someone would see that. Someone would remember seeing this shirt or those trousers on Old Deak. They wouldn't call him a scarecrow then. They would call him a grave robber or a ghoul. They would ask him what it felt like to have a dead man's shirt clinging to his skin, if he could smell the dirt of the grave.

Mac stepped up to the school door, peering through the window into the dark hall within. It was empty. The other students would already be in class. He would have to walk past the whole classroom to take his seat in the rear of the room. They would all see him, then. They would all see the clothes that he was wearing.

Mac stepped up to the classroom door. He swallowed once and stepped through, keeping his eyes on the back wall of the classroom so that no one could catch his eye, so Scarecrow wouldn't have to look at any of the other children.

He was still staring at the wall when Matt Stilson tripped him, when he dropped his books and fell headlong into a desk and then on the floor. The eyes of everyone in the classroom jerked around to focus on him, to see the blood gushing from his nose. That was good, Mac thought as he held a handkerchief up to catch the blood. As long as he was bleeding, they wouldn't notice that he was wearing a dead man's clothes.

Sheriff Frank Drinkwalter sat behind the closed door to his tiny office, wastepaper basket propped between his knees. He was whittling a stick into a pile of shavings in the basket. If he were looking for something in the branch, the face of a long dead friend, a mule deer's arching neck, he would have been disappointed. There was no art in the branch, only solace.

A pocket knife the sheriff kept honed to a fine edge stripped the branch into long smooth shavings. It was art only in that it occupied enough of his mind to keep it from skipping back to the letters lying now in the top drawer on his desk.

He had the regular correspondence on his desk: a letter from the commissioners, some officious-looking documents from the Yellowstone County Sheriff's Department in Billings. Mac would zip through those. But the two letters in his desk drawer : . .

Drinkwalter could see the concern guiding Catherine's fine hand in the second letter. He couldn't read the words, but he could see the tension in her hand. He remembered her hands, fine boned, soft, and beautiful. The sheriff had heard a college professor talking once about hands.

The professor said that it was a common misconception that the superiority of man's brain separated him from the other animals. But the brain was the tail end of the evolutionary scale, he said. Hands were such wonderful instruments with so many uses that the brain had developed simply in order to better use them.

The knife slipped, sending the razor-sharp blade

toward the fingers of the sheriff's left hand. He jerked back. Best not to let the mind wander too far when one is whittling, the sheriff thought.

A soft rap at the door: Mac had come to read the secrets between Frank Drinkwalter and the woman he loved. The sheriff clicked the knife's blade shut and scooted the wastepaper basket beneath his desk, the dead branch poking from one corner.

"Come in, Mac," the sheriff whispered. The door latch clicked and the scarred oaken door swung open. Mac stood framed in the door. The boy's clothes were wrinkled and soiled. His nose was red and looked sore to the touch. A bruise glowed under one eye.

Sheriff Drinkwalter's face wrinkled into a question. "What the hell happened to you, boy?"

"Nothing."

"Mac, if this is nothing, you better head for the hospital when something happens. Now, what happened?"

"Matt Stilson tripped me in class. Hit my nose on one of the desks as I was going down. I ran him down after class."

"That Matt Stilson must be one hell of a tough kid."

"He wasn't so tough. Not the second one, either. But then they came at me all in a bunch."

"Yes," the sheriff whispered. "All in a bunch. You can't beat them all, Mac. I tried that when I was not much older than you. You can't beat them all."

Mac's back stiffened. "They can't beat me. Not one of them. Not all of them. They can't beat me."

"You feel like working today?"

Mac nodded, grimacing at the jolt of pain that followed the movement.

"I'm ready."

"We've got some warm water on the stove, and some washcloths. Why don't you go out and clean up before we start?"

"Don't need to."

"Maybe you don't, but I need you to. I don't want to sit here looking at you like that."

Mac started to nod, but anchored his head in place with the first shot of pain. "Okay."

"Mac, put some cold water on that blood on your shirt. It'll keep it from staining."

"Doesn't matter. Won't be wearing them anymore."

"Just try it."

Mac turned and walked stiff-legged from the room, his head and neck stiff, as though he were balancing a book on it.

Sheriff Frank Drinkwalter leaned back in his chair, remembering what it was to be different, to lash out with his fists at the injustices. Mac shouldn't have to go through that. No one should.

A moment later Mac stepped into the office again, his face clean, his shirt wet from the cold water. "Looks like the blood came out," he said.

"Good. You feel up to going through the mail?"

"Yeah."

"Why don't you close the door? Bert will be coming back any minute, now."

"Okay."

"First, the commissioners." Drinkwalter handed Mac a letter bearing the county seal, and an ornate letter opener from his drawer. Mac opened the envelope. "It's the minutes of their last meeting," Mac said.

"No sense reading it all. Anything in there about the sheriff's office or me?"

Mac scanned through the letter. "The board approved an expenditure of five dollars a week for temporary help to fill in for Mr. Deakins, deceased."

"That's you, Mac."

"Temporary?"

"Don't worry about that. Usually, I would be in there asking for a new deputy. I'd pay him five dollars a week until I knew that he would work out. But if the commissioners can get temporary help for five dollars a week, they won't complain."

Mac set the letter and envelope aside and reached for another.

"Mac, after we get done, you should file that in the cabinet over there under COMMISSIONERS."

Mac nodded.

"This one's from the Yellowstone County Sheriff's office."

"What's Big Jim up to?"

Mac looked up.

"James Thompson, Yellowstone County Sheriff."

"Oh." Mac nodded and winced, closing one eye and opening it slowly. "Do you want me to read it to you?"

"Yeah."

Mac stared at the letter. "Well, where the salutation should be, it says 'One sorry son of a bitch to another.' "

Drinkwalter grinned. "Well, what's that sorry son of a bitch got to say?"

" 'You catch the bait and have Tilly at the Stockman's make some of her sandwiches. I'll take three. Get a bucket of brew from Pete Pfeister. Do that, and I will grace you with my preeminent self and show you how an expert catches the wily trout. Train schedule says six-thirty A.M. Saturday, so you can figure about seven-fifteen.'

" 'What do you say, you sorry son of a bitch?' "

Drinkwalter grinned. He reached into his top desk drawer and pulled out a tablet of paper, a pen, and a bottle of ink, unscrewing the lid for Mac.

"You write what I tell you, okay?"

"Don't write very fast."

"Don't talk very fast."

Mac nodded, and the sheriff began his letter.

"Dear sorry son of a bitch:'

" 'I supply the bait, the food, the beer, and the fishing hole. In return, you bless me with your presence. I don't see how I can go wrong with a deal like that.' "

The sheriff paused. "Mac, would you like to go fishing Saturday?"

"I think I'll have to work."

"Take a day off. I'd like you to come."

"You catch the bait?"

Drinkwalter nodded.

"You get me one of Tilly's sandwiches?"

Drinkwalter grinned and nodded.

"I don't have a pole."

"I've got an extra one."

"Deak's?"

"Yours if you want it."

Mac grinned. "All right, I'll grace you with my pre-eminence."

"One sorry son of a bitch to another?"

"One sorry son of a bitch to another."

Drinkwalter grinned, "Okay, finish the letter with: 'I'll introduce you to my newest deputy. He is young yet, but he has all the makings of one sorry son of a bitch.'

"Sign it, 'Yours truly, S.S.O.B.' "

Mac finished the letter and the sheriff took it.

"Looks fine to me," he said, holding it up to the light.

Drinkwalter took the pen from Mac then, and signed the letter with a fine flourish, handing it back to Mac.

Mac looked suspiciously at the sheriff. "I thought you couldn't write."

"I can't, Mac. Catherine showed me how to write my name. It's the same to me as drawing a picture of a horse. I don't write my name: I draw it."

Mac cocked his head. "Maybe I could teach you to draw other words?"

The sheriff leaned back in his chair. "Maybe you could, Mac. Maybe you could. The Chinese write with pictures, you know."

Mac shook his head. He didn't know.

"Anyhow, let's get on with this."

Drinkwalter took a deep breath. He cocked his head and stared at Mac for a moment, before reaching into the top drawer of his desk. He pulled out two letters, placing them on the desk. He chose one, working as much by feel as sight and held it to his nose.

"Some women perfume their letters," the sheriff said. "Catherine doesn't, but I swear they take on her scent. Sometimes it's wild rose or fresh mint. In the spring I smell apple blossoms, subtle but very, very sweet. There are apple trees in that park where we met, and in the spring I can tell when she has gone there to sit in the sun."

The sheriff handed the envelope to Mac. "Shut your eyes, Mac, and hold the letter up to your nose. What scent does it carry?"

Mac shut his eyes. At first he smelled nothing. Then he picked up what seemed to be the slightly sharp scent of paper, the slightly alcoholic scent of ink. He didn't really smell the apple blossoms so much as sense them. He seemed to be carried back to a time when his mother had carried him through an orchard in spring. The blossoms were everywhere, shimmering in a warm spring breeze.

"Mac?"

Mac opened his eyes; the sheriff was staring at him.

"For a minute there, boy, it looked as though you had gone somewhere else."

"I . . . I did. To an apple orchard."

Drinkwalter smiled. "Yes, an apple orchard. Open it, Mac."

Mac slipped the point of the letter opener beneath the envelope's seal, the blade hissing against the paper as it opened the letter's secrets.

The letter was written in blue ink, in the same flowery hand as on the envelope.

" 'Beloved.' It begins with beloved."

"Yes," the sheriff whispered. "Well, read it slowly, Mac, so I can feel the words."

"Beloved:

"We are nearing the end of another spring apart. No matter what I am doing, I cannot pull the moment of our meeting from my mind. I will be at the bank, tallying a column of figures, and my mind will pull me away and put me again in that park, our park.

"Even after all these years, I don't know what led me to our park that day. I remember only seeing you on that bench. You seemed so sad, but it was not your sadness that pulled me to you. It was

something else. Something I don't understand.

"It was your sadness, however, that caused me to take your hand. I felt a need to reach out to you, to tell you that you were not alone, not so alone anyway as you seemed to think you were.

"Until you took my hand, I had not realized how alone I had been. I had my work, and the caring for my mother. Those tasks kept me busy, but they didn't make me whole.

"Isn't it strange how two specks could swirl about in the cosmos and on coming together find that each is a perfect match for the other?

"Yesterday was a fine spring day, and I returned to our bench in our park. I sat there with the warmth of the sun caressing my neck and thought of you. There was a young couple strolling by, and they had the look of rapture on their faces. I thought then that the park may hold magic for young lovers—and for those who are no longer so young.

"Mother is slipping. It distresses me so to see her failing. She has given me nothing but love. And yet, sometimes, I resent that my life is given to the caring for her. I feel terrible then, guilty that I would think such awful thoughts. And then I think of you, and how much I would like to be there with you and . . .

"I am such a wretched soul. I need to be made whole, my beloved, but that is impossible at this time.

"I am writing this as I prepare for bed, but I know that I will not sleep. I will think of you through the darkness until the sun kisses the east-

*ern window in my bedroom. I will dream then
that the sun's warmth is your own.*

> *"Good night, my beloved.*
> *"Catherine"*

*"Deak, I remember that you have a birthday
coming. I will send you a box of cookies along with
my love. Please take care of my husband to be."*

There was a long silence, and then Mac whispered,
"That's all."

"Yes. Mac would you get me a cup of coffee before
we begin the second letter?"

Mac nodded, reaching for the cup on the sheriff's
desk. The cup was caked with the residue of coffee long
gone. Mac looked at the cup with distaste. "You ought
to clean this thing up."

"Son, it took me years to get that cup tamed the way
I want it. I would no more wash that cup than a pipe
smoker would scrub out his favorite pipe."

Mac's face wrinkled with distaste, and he left the
room holding the cup with two fingers at arm's length.

Drinkwalter smiled, and then held the letter again to
his nose, wondering at that day in the park. Drinkwalter
remembered every moment of their first meeting. He
had sat on the park bench for nearly an hour before she
stepped up behind him. He hadn't seen the beauty of
the park in that terrible hour, only the bleakness, the
hopelessness of his own life. And then she appeared
behind him, wearing a soft green dress the color of the
leaves emerging from the park's trees. . . .

Mac stepped through the door, coffee cup held at
arm's length. The sheriff lay the letter on the desk,

embarrassed to have been caught in such an intimate moment.

"Had to scour that cup. It might as well have been painted brown."

The sheriff looked into the cup and scowled. "You ruined it! You ruined my cup. How could you have taken it upon yourself to ruin my cup? I've had that cup since I left Cincinnati, and now you've gone and ruined it."

"Probably saved you from scurvy or leprosy or something like that. You ought to be grateful."

"Grateful? I ought to be grateful? You mutilated my cup."

The sheriff stared at the cup as though it were the body of a good friend, stricken down in the midst of a conversation.

Mac, unrepentant, urged the sheriff along. "Want me to read the second letter?"

The sheriff nodded, setting the cup gingerly on the desk, as though it might crack without the strong glue of old caffeine to hold it together.

"*Beloved:*

"*For what seems to be a century now, I have gone to my mailbox to find a letter waiting there for me. It is almost as though you are waiting there for me, and I treasure those meetings. They hold my life together.*

"*But today the mailbox was empty but for the new Sears Roebuck catalog. On most days, receiving the catalog would please me. I sometimes spend evenings poring over that book, seeing what's new in fashion. Mrs. Glynnis tries to keep* up, and always her store's front window is full of color and style. But hers is the only store I see walking to work in the morning. So the catalog gives me something to compare with her choices.

"I peruse the men's clothing, too, imagining you in this hat and that suit. I found one in the current catalog that I believe would fit you perfectly. It is cut for tall, rangy men like you, and it comes in a light blue that would bring out the color of your eyes. It would be wonderfully appropriate for our day, and I thought about ordering it, having it sent to you for whatever alterations it might need, but then I thought that it might be out of style when finally we are wed. That thought tore at me so.

"I manage to make it through my days by thinking about what it will be like when we are together. And then I think of all the things that might happen that would keep us from fulfilling our lives.

"Your descriptions of Montana make it seem so grand—and so terrible. Your words take me to the mountains and the green rivers and the bright sun and the soft shadows. But I have felt the pain of winter blizzards in your words, too.

"It seems that the land is written so large there that it can't help stepping on mankind now and again as I worry about you, think of all the things that could take you from me, and leave me with . . . nothing. I would die then. I would die in the hope that we might find ourselves in the cosmos as we found ourselves in that park.

"Whatever danger has kept you from writing, I

*pray it is finished, now, and that I will find your
letters in my mailbox with a note from Postmaster
Jackson, saying he is sorry for the inconvenience,
that your letters had slipped his attention in some
shadow or another.*

*"Know, my beloved, that my prayers follow
this letter and my love. Always my love.*
                                        "Catherine"

Sheriff Drinkwalter turned to stare out the window
at his back. He watched the leaves of the lilac bushes
north of the jail cut silver slivers from the golden sun in
an alchemy known only to them. He turned then to
face Mac.

"Do you see, now, why I tested you before I offered
you this job?"

"Yes," Mac whispered.

Drinkwalter nodded. He reached into his desk,
pulling stationery and pen from the drawer. "Would
you write a letter for me, now?"

Mac nodded.

"Dearly Beloved:
*"As you can see, my handwriting has changed.
Our good friend Deak, chronicler of my love for
you, has died. We buried him on a windy, blus-
tery day. I thought that I heard his voice in the
wind, protesting his leaving this earth before he
met you.*

*"How many times have I seen you stepping
from that train, parasol over your shoulder, and
the conductor watching you with adoring eyes? I*

know he will be doing that because to be near you is to fall in love with you.

"I knew that you would be worried, and I have spent more than one sleepless night trying to decide how to remain in touch with you. You can't imagine—or perhaps you can—what it was to have two of your letters here and not be able to hear your words.

"I saw a swami in a carnival once. He would ask someone in the audience to write a note and seal it in an envelope. He would hold the envelope to his forehead then, and tell the audience what was written there. I've been doing that with your letters, holding them to my face as though the words could flow straight from your pen into my heart. But I haven't the swami's gift.

"I have asked Mac McPherson to play my Cyrano de Bergerac. He is fourteen, and a good student at the high school. He reminds me of myself at that age, independent and more than a little curmudgeonly.

"I suspect that Mac will be leaving here in three or four years, bound for some university or another. But perhaps by then, we can be together, and this cruel separation will be ended.

"I love you more than life.

"Frank"

"Did you get that, Mac?"

Mac nodded.

"I want you to say something to Catherine, now. You will come to know her through our letters, but she has to come to know you, too."

"Is this a test?"

"Yes, I suppose you might say that. She will be putting a lot of trust in you, and she's never met you."

Mac bent over the page, carefully writing the words.

"What did you write, Mac?"

Mac set straight up in his chair, holding the letter in both hands. " 'I will read your words truly. The words I write for the sheriff will be his.' "

Mac looked up at the sheriff.

"Is that all, Mac?"

"No." The boy looked the sheriff in the eyes. "I also wrote: 'I can't wait to see you step down from the train with a parasol over your shoulder.' "

The sheriff smiled. "That's fine, Mac. That's just fine."

8

Sheriff Frank Drinkwalter was staring out his office window when he heard the tentative knock. He turned to an empty doorway and said, "Yes?"

Mac edged around the door to the desk. He stood there at attention, stiff as an army cadet at an inspection. He swallowed twice and then the words came in a rush.

"I was wondering if I could work full-time. I would sweep floors, clean up around here. I'd do anything you needed me to do, and I wouldn't backtalk you the way I do sometimes."

"What about school? I don't think your mother would take kindly to your leaving school."

Mac looked up, his face pale and barren as an alkali flat. "They kicked me out of school."

The words seemed to cut the boy's underpinnings. He sagged, but he made an effort to pull himself straight, to say the words that needed to be said.

"I haven't told Ma yet. She's always said that education is something they can't take away from you. But Ma was wrong. They took it away from me."

The boy pulled his eyes up to look at the sheriff, willing him to understand.

"I wanted to please Ma, to give her something for all the things she does for me, but I can't go to school anymore, so I'll have to find a job. I'd like to work for you, if you'd let me. I can do the reading and writing for you, and I'm more than a little handy with numbers.

Mr. Aiperspach says he never saw anybody so good at math as I am, so I can do your figuring for you. I won't let you down. I make it a point not to let anybody down, but now . . . Ma . . ."

Mac shut his eyes. The sheriff could see the muscles bulge in the boy's jaw as he gritted his teeth, fighting the tears that welled up behind his eyelids.

"Why did they kick you out, Mac?"

Mac squeezed the words between gritted teeth. "Because I picked a fight with Matt Stilson. They don't allow ruffians in school. They said not to come back."

"They talk to you in the superintendent's office?"

Mac nodded.

"Who was there?"

"Superintendent Gibbs and Miss Pinkham and Major Stilson."

"Yes, Major Stilson." Drinkwalter leaned back in his chair. "Do you think they are still there?"

"Probably. They told me to leave. They said they had some things to talk about."

"Most likely they're patting themselves on the back for their prompt action in ridding the school of a ruffian."

Mac stared at the floor at his feet.

Drinkwalter stood, "Come on, Mac, we're going to go talk to that unholy trio."

Mac shook his head. "No, I'm not going back."

The sheriff strode past Mac, catching the boy by the arm. "Yes, you are, Mac. We're going to go over to the school and give those good ol' boys a little education."

Martha Jenkins's eyes widened as Sheriff Frank Drinkwalter swept past her desk toward Superintendent Gibbs's office, Mac McPherson in tow.

"I . . . he . . ."

"Don't you worry yourself about it, Mrs. Jenkins. I'm sure that Mr. Gibbs will be pleased to see me."

Gibbs, a portly man with pork-chop sideburns and impeccable suit, sat at a corner of his dark oak desk. He and Major Stilson were huddled over a sheaf of papers. As the sheriff appeared, Gibbs swept the papers into the top drawer of his desk.

Drinkwalter tipped his hat: "Mr. Gibbs. Freddy."

Major Stilson bristled. No one called him Freddy anymore. He was Major Stilson, a man who served with the Rough Riders in Cuba. Freddy was a diminutive, a belittling of the honor and respect the major had won fighting for his country in the jungles of that plague-ridden backwater. To belittle Major Stilson was to belittle the red, white, and blue, and he would not put up with that, not from this penny-ante public servant.

"Sheriff, I find your breaking into this office totally—"

"Yes," Drinkwalter said. "I'm pleased that you will give me a moment of your time. I understand that you have expelled this young man from your school for assaulting another student. I'm here to investigate that charge."

Stilson stared at the sheriff through squinted eyes. This might work out better than he had thought. A charge of assault against the McPherson boy would be a mark of stature for the Stilson family. Mess with one of the Stilsons, and you would likely find yourself in court.

"Yes, an investigation is called for," Stilson said. "This bully blackened my Matt's eye. He attacked Matt without provocation and without warning. Only through Matt's physical prowess was he able to give this boy the thrashing he deserved. Yes, I believe the incident deserves further investigation. Perhaps charges of assault should be filed."

Mac blanched. He hadn't wanted to come back to the school, and now the sheriff was selling him out. Stilson was one of Eagles Nest's community leaders. The sheriff, an elected official, wouldn't want to cross swords with him. Mac glowered: He should have conducted some tests of his own before agreeing to work for Drinkwalter.

"Will Miss Pinkham still be in her classroom?"

Superintendent Gibbs smiled smugly at the sheriff. "Of course she is. I believe in giving the taxpayers of this great district an hours' work for an hours' pay. She remains at her desk eight hours every day."

"Even though the students she teaches have gone home?"

"Students," Gibbs sneered, "are only a small part of a teacher's duty. She must keep her room straightened and cleaned. Her records must be up to date and without error. I grade my teachers, Mr. Drinkwalter, and I do not grade on a curve."

"Perhaps, then, you gentlemen would show me to Miss Pinkham's room."

Gibbs stood, pulling down his coat to straighten any wrinkles. He nodded to Stilson and led the procession toward the hall and Miss Pinkham's classroom. The door was shut, and Gibbs stormed through without knocking. Teachers in his school learned early on that classrooms were not their private domains. Gibbs might pop in at any moment. That kept his employees on their toes. That was the way Gibbs liked his employees—on their toes.

Miss Pinkham was standing with her back to the door, straightening books, rocks, and shells that lined a shelf just beneath the windows on the wall opposite the door. She turned at the sound of the door opening. When Mac stepped through the door, her face pinched together. The teacher's eyes were red, her cheeks stained with tears. "Mac, I—"

Gibbs interrupted, "The sheriff's here to investigate Mac McPherson's assault on Matt Stilson for the purpose of filing criminal charges."

Miss Pinkham stepped back, steadying herself with a hand on the shelf behind her. "Assault charges? But—"

The sheriff stepped up to Miss Pinkham, taking her by the elbow. "This won't take very long. I just want to establish what happened yesterday, during class and afterward."

"What's school got to do with the assault on Matt?" Stilson demanded. "Let's get to the case in point and stop this dawdling."

Drinkwalter fixed the school board chairman with a stare. "Allow me to continue."

"But you are obviously not investigating the assault on Matt."

"I said I was investigating an assault. I didn't say who I was investigating."

Stilson sucked in his breath through clenched teeth. "I demand you stop this charade!"

"You can't demand the end of any investigation, Freddy. That's against the law, and I don't think either you or Mr. Gibbs would like to break the law. You wouldn't want to break the law, would you, Freddy?"

"The good people of Eagles Nest are accustomed to calling me Major. I expect no less of you, Sheriff. Perhaps if you had served with the Rough Riders in Cuba, you would have a little more respect for those of us who did."

"I do have respect for those who served with the Rough Riders, Freddy. I intend to talk to you about that in just a few minutes. In the meantime, you stay out of my investigation."

There was a quiet assurance in the sheriff's voice, and one eyebrow crawled up Stilson's forehead. He stepped back.

The sheriff continued. "Miss Pinkham, were you teaching here yesterday?"

"Yes."

"Did anything unusual happen . . . shortly after the first bell rang?"

Miss Pinkham's eyes darted to Superintendent Gibbs. She wilted under his glare.

"I . . ."

"Miss Pinkham, you can't get in trouble for telling the truth. Surely, you know that."

Her back stiffened, and she continued. "It was right after the bell rang. Mac came in after the other children. Usually he's here before anybody else, but yesterday he came in last. All the children were already seated, and—"

Gibbs broke in: "Late, the little bastard . . . He was late. He's been a problem for as long as he's been going to school here. We simply won't put up with it anymore."

Miss Pinkham stiffened. "No, Mac's never been any trouble. He's never caused—"

"Miss Pinkham are you calling me a liar?" Gibbs snarled. "If you are so discontent with your work here, I'm sure we can find a replacement for you."

Stilson nodded.

"That's enough of that," the sheriff said. "Intimidating a witness is a felony offense. If I hear a word from either of you, I'll put you both in jail. Do you understand that?"

Stilson stepped forward to be impaled again by the sheriff's eyes.

"Do you understand that, Freddy?"

"Yes."

The sheriff turned to Miss Pinkham, his voice softening. "What happened when Mac came into the room?"

"Well, he was walking toward his desk, and he tripped and fell."

"Was he hurt?"

"Yes, he fell face first into a desk, and his nose was bleeding something awful."

"What was the reaction from the rest of the class?"

"They were all laughing."

"What was Matt Stilson's reaction?"

Stilson butted in. "Sheriff, I've had enough of this! My boy was probably laughing like the rest of the class, wasn't he, Miss Pinkham?"

"Freddy, intimidation is a felony offense. Another word and you'll await Judge Jimison's next visit in jail."

"You can't . . . I won't . . ."

"Freddy . . ." The words crawled low and ugly from the sheriff's throat.

Stilson blanched.

"Miss Pinkham, I'll repeat the question: What did Matt Stilson do when Mac fell and bloodied his nose?"

"He raised one arm—you know, the way that prize-fighters do when they win a match."

"What did the other boys do?"

"Some of them patted him on the back."

"Why do you suppose they did that?"

"Because he . . ."

The teacher's eyes turned to Stilson. He glared at her.

"Miss Pinkham, the truth."

Miss Pinkham looked back at the sheriff. "Because he tripped Mac."

"Now, see here!" The superintendent's interruption was cut short by the sheriff's glare.

"And what did you do about that?"

"I got a cold compress for Mac's nose."

"What did you do about Matt?"

"I didn't know what to do."

"So you did nothing?"

"Yes." Tears spilled from the teacher's eyes, and sobs racked her words. "Yes, I did nothing."

"And what were you doing after class?"

"Straightening and cleaning the shelves."

"Did you see the fight?"

"Yes. First, Mac fought with Matt. When Matt got a bloody nose, he ran for home. Then Jimmy Bronson hit Mac from behind, and Mac knocked him down, and then they all started hitting Mac. They were hitting him and kicking him, and he went down and they didn't stop. They just kept hitting and kicking him."

"And what did you do?"

"I went in and told Mr. Gibbs, but he said let them handle it. But I couldn't stand it, so I went out there and told them to stop."

Tears were flowing freely down Miss Pinkham's cheeks. "I couldn't sleep last night. All I could think about was all those boys hitting and kicking Mac. Every time I shut my eyes . . ."

Mac stepped over to his teacher. "There wasn't anything you could do. It's always been that way."

A growl crept into the sheriff's voice. "So we do have an assault charge here. Matt Stilson and those other boys obviously assaulted Mac. And we have an accomplice, Mr. Gibbs, who was aware that the beating was going on, but failed to do anything about it."

Major Stilson was shaking with rage. "No, what we have is an overwrought woman who is obviously not suited to be a teacher in the Eagles Nest school district. I admit some of the blame in that. I approved Mr. Gibbs's recommendation, but now that we've found out what a mistake we made, I'm sure that we can correct it immediately."

Gibbs nodded, a little smile turning in a sneer that he directed at the sheriff.

The sheriff's voice came so softly that the two conspirators had to strain to hear it.

"Major, it would be in your best interest if you stepped into the hall with me for a moment."

"I have no intention . . ."

The sheriff reached out as though to shake Stilson's hand. Stilson was a glad-hander, a politician in the making, and he could no more resist an offer of a handshake than a child could resist an ice-cream cone. But there was no ice cream in the sheriff's grip, only a tremendous pressure that bent the school-board chairman's wrist back in agonizing pain.

"Would you have a word with me in the hall, Freddy?"

Stilson, eyes wide, nodded. The sheriff stepped

toward the hall, then, and Stilson followed hand in hand, stiff-legged with the pain.

The sheriff closed the door to the classroom with his toe. He shoved the school-board chairman against the wall with a *thump* that could be heard inside the classroom. The sheriff edged up to Stilson, then, until their noses were about two inches apart.

"Went on a vacation last year to Denver, didn't you, Freddy?"

"No, not a vacation, not really. I was working on—"

Drinkwalter twisted Stilson's wrist. "Uh, yes, I guess you could call it a vacation."

"And you met a young woman at the Denver Club?"

"Uh, no, uh, yes, I believe I did."

"You impressed that young lady, Freddy, with the tales of your valor in the war. She was taken with your tale of woe about how you had played a key role in the Charge of the San Juan Hill and never received any recognition for your bravery.

"Well, that young lady's father is a general, Freddy, and she made him promise to set the record straight. I got a letter from the Department of War. They said they had no record of a Major Stilson. They did have a record of a Frederich J. Stilson who listed his address as Eagles Nest. That's you, isn't it, Freddy?"

Stilson nodded.

"But Frederich J. Stilson was a private in the quartermaster corps. Seems that Private Frederich J. Stilson didn't see any action at San Juan Hill or anywhere else. Have you been stringing us along all these years, Freddy, waving this nation's flag in the face of anyone who disagreed with you?"

Stilson's chin dropped to his chest, and his "yes" was

more the wind escaping his chest than the spoken word.

Drinkwalter released Stilson's wrist, and the school-board chairman grimaced, massaging the wrist with his left hand.

"I told the War Department that I had no knowledge of a Major Stilson, Freddy. I didn't see why I should intrude on your little play, because it didn't seem to be hurting anyone. I figured that you would grow out of it. But you started to believe your own lie, Freddy, and now you're trying to bully that boy. I won't allow that, Freddy."

The sheriff rubbed his hands down his cheeks, settling his chin in the cup the heels of his palms created. "Now, I'll tell you what I think is a reasonable solution to this affair, and if you agree, this will be the end of it.

"This is what I would like you to do. . . ."

Stilson slouched into the classroom, face white. The man had been stripped of his arrogance, and there was little left. He stepped up to Miss Pinkham.

"I apologize. Like most fathers, I like to believe that my son always tells the truth. I see now that is a false assumption."

Mr. Gibbs stepped forward, "Now, see here. . . ."

Stilson shook his head, "No, I was wrong. Matt was picking on Mac. He got what he deserved. When I get home, he will get what he deserves from me."

Stilson looked at his friend. "Mr. Gibbs, I would very much appreciate your calling all the boys concerned into your office tomorrow morning. I would like you to tell them what a cowardly thing they did. Each of them must stand up in Miss Pinkham's classroom and admit their cowardice and apologize to Mac."

"No!" Mac was shaking his head. "No, don't make them do that."

Mac was accustomed to hiding in the class, seeking corners and shadows so that no one would laugh at the scarecrow. Being the center of the room's attention was more than Mac could bear.

Drinkwalter put his hand on Mac's shoulder. "It's got to stop, Mac. You've put up with it for so long that you think it's your fault. You helped create those bullies by doing nothing. You have to help undo that, Mac. You owe them that."

Mac's face wrinkled into a question mark. "Yes," he whispered. "Yes, I guess I do."

The sheriff looked up. "I think the three of you owe Mac an apology, too."

Stripped of his arrogance, there seemed little left of Major Stilson. He apologized to Mac and Superintendent Gibbs and Miss Pinkham. They left the room in a chorus of apologies to walk back to the courthouse.

For the first time in Mac's life, someone besides his mother had stood up for him. He glanced at Drinkwalter occasionally as they walked. He must be about the best man who ever walked the face of the earth.

Mac thought about his father, then, and guilt edged into his mind. But he hardly remembered his father. He had only the picture of his ma and pa at home to remind him. His ma had changed from the image in the photo, but his pa stayed always the same. He didn't seem real to Mac anymore. Not real, anyway, the way the sheriff was.

9

Yellowstone County Sheriff James Thompson rattled toward the east hill just outside of Eagles Nest, watching the countryside jolt past the train's smoke-stained windows.

Milk run! Hell, they ought to call this the butter run. Cream from Guernsey cows fat with river grass would turn into thick, rich butter after a pounding like this. Add a little salt and this train could serve up butter fit for a king.

He imagined one of Tilly's sandwiches slavered with that butter. Beef, it would be, lean beef sliced thin with Tilly's secret mix of salt and pepper and some other spices and roasted to perfection.

The sheriff swallowed at the thought. Anyone who could get Tilly's recipe would make a fortune, have enough money to eat like a king. Course, anyone who had Tilly's recipe wouldn't have to be rich to eat like a king.

Sheriff Thompson growled: Life was nothing but a bunch of damn paradoxes.

Thompson hadn't eaten breakfast before leaving Billings, and the thought of those sandwiches made his mouth water. Drinkwalter better make good on his promise to have three of Tilly's sandwiches ready for this fishing trip, or there would be hell to pay in Eagles Nest, Montana.

The Yellowstone County sheriff fidgeted, trying to

stretch his legs, but the coach's seats were better suited for children. Of course, no mother worth her salt would ever put her child aboard this bone-rattling, butter-churning excuse for a railroad train.

Thompson hunched his six and a half feet of self down in his seat to peer out the window at the Yellowstone. The Northern Pacific had built a wall of dark basaltic rock here to keep the river from washing out the railroad's roadbed. The wall was built at an angle of about forty-five degrees and hell to walk on, but if Sheriff Thompson knew anything about fish, they would be lined up for their turn to take a fisherman's fly.

The river swirled by in eddies, pulling hoppers and freshly hatched nymphs into the depths and offering a veritable buffet for any bull trout big enough to rule his piece of this river. Rainbows and lochs, the fish would be. No cutthroat lived this far away from Yellowstone Park.

The sun had chased the sheriff all the way from Billings, and now its rays slanted down into the green waters of the Yellowstone. If this damn train wasn't so damn rough, he could probably see fish out there as they rose from the depths to snatch a passing fly.

Damn! Look at that!

The train had been hugging a narrow bridge of land between the river and the hills on the north edge of the valley. Farther west, the river ran along the valley's south side, but just at the east hill, it swung north to crash against the hill and the railway.

Low and fast the river ran, dodging a rock here and there. It was an assault team storming an enemy strong-hold.

But Thompson's attention was focused on eddies swirling along the bank. Had to be trout in those eddies, trout big enough to resist the rush of the river. They would be lying on the edges of the current, leaving it to the river to serve them oxygen for their gills and food for their gullets.

Thompson could feel their fierce pull on his fishing line in their dance with death. Damn, what a river this was!

The sheriff scooted back in his seat, willing his body to fit. Might as well be trapped in a cave as stuck in this seat. The sheriff climbed stiff-legged from the seat, hunching his head to his shoulders to avoid the coach's low ceiling. In the aisle, he leaned forward, bracing himself against the backs of two empty seats, leaning down so he could see out of the train's windows. The valley opened up here, cottonwoods following the course of the river to the south and ponderosa pine, sage, yucca, and juniper dotting the hills to the north. Directly north of town, a sandstone-rimmed plateau stood vigil.

Thompson leaned down to see the sandstone quarry, but it was too far west, hidden behind the confines of this damn milk train.

What the hell? A boy, five or six, was tapping Thompson's leg as though it were a door he wanted to open. The boy's mother was sitting in the back of the car, pretending the child was a stranger to her.

Johnson stepped aside. "Sorry, son. Didn't mean to block your way."

But the boy didn't move. He cricked his head back to look up at the sheriff, one brown eye squinted shut as he studied the lawman.

"You a giant?" the boy asked.

Thompson grinned. "I suppose you might say that, compared to some, anyway."

"Like Goliath?"

"I suppose."

The boy nodded,

"How long will it be before we get there?"

"To Eagles Nest?"

"Yeah."

"Just a few minutes."

The boy nodded, his mind obviously on greater matters. He walked back to his mother then, and she smiled feebly at the sheriff. He smiled back. Cute kid and smart as a button.

The train was slowing now, coming into the station. Drinkwalter was standing there with his new deputy. Hell, he wasn't a deputy, nothing more than a kid. Frank had picked up another stray. He collected people like Mrs. Codgins collected stray cats.

Nice-looking kid, but a little stiff. That wouldn't do, not if the kid wanted to be a sorry son of a bitch.

The train shuddered to a stop, and Thompson leaned down to collect his fishing rod and gear. Drinkwalter best have some of Tilly's sandwiches. He'd best have the three sandwiches that Yellowstone County Sheriff James Thompson ordered or there would be hell to pay, one sorry son of a bitch to another. Thompson grinned and shuffled for the door.

Mac McPherson stood on the depot's wooden plank dock, waiting for the Yellowstone County Sheriff. The train was late. The train was always late, Sheriff Drinkwalter said, but Drinkwalter didn't seem to be concerned about it. He stood, leaning on one hip, the way horses do sometimes. It didn't seem to bother him that they had been standing motionless for nearly half an hour. Mac envied him that. Standing still was an anathema to him. He had to be doing something. When he mentioned that to the sheriff, Drinkwalter said they were doing something, waiting for the train.

Mac was excited about the fishing trip, but a little nervous, too. He had fished the Yellowstone before with a makeshift rod he cut from a willow patch in early spring, peeling the bark from it. It was suspended from nails along a rafter in the cabin now, drying and seasoning. Light, it was, and smooth to the touch, but growing brittle with age.

At its best, the willow was nothing like Deak's old rod. Mac had been studying the rod since the sheriff picked him up that morning. Split bamboo, the sheriff called it. It trembled in his hands, eager to go fishing.

Mac's eyes swept over his new possessions. A wicker fishing basket with a leather strap lay in the wagon box against his new rod's reel. Inside the basket was a book of hand-tied flies and leader and hooks. When the sheriff gave the outfit to Mac, he said that they would fish with hoppers this day so that Mac could learn to read the water, so he would be less likely to miss a strike when it came. Another day he would teach Mac how to cast a dry fly with a split bamboo rod, the sheriff said in a voice that suggested he was a wizard about to pass along a magical potion to his apprentice.

Mac was intrigued with that, but apprehensive, too. What could someone learn from watching someone else fish? Sounded like another damn test.

The train screeched to a stop, wheezing steam as

though it were catching its breath from the long run from Billings. The conductor stepped down from the coach, looking up and down the track.

He leaned down, then, and placed a step on the depot platform. First from the train was a boy of five or six. He jumped to the platform, ignoring the step. Next came the boy's mother. She seemed tired, nervously tired, as though the early hour and her son's energy had worn her down to nerve and muscle.

And finally Sheriff James Thompson stepped down from the train. The man was huge, almost eye-to-eye with the conductor standing on the train step. The sheriff was wearing a flannel shirt, cotton pants, boots, and a hat. He carried a case that Mac knew must hold the sheriff's fishing rod, and a wicker basket much like the one the sheriff had given him that morning. The sheriff hitched up his pants and strode over to Mac and Drinkwalter. *Strode* was the only word for the sheriff's determined gait, Mac decided. No other word would fit.

Thompson grinned as he reached out to envelop Drinkwalter's fist in his own. "Good to see you, Frank. Been a while."

"It has indeed."

"Haven't changed much."

"Just for the better. Everyone tells me I've changed for the better."

Thompson cocked his head. "Well, I don't know if I'd go that far, but . . ." *Whack!* A rock bounced off the sheriff's forehead and fell, skittering off the platform. The sheriff's eyes turned, and Mac could see a storm cloud centering on the knot glowing red and white on the sheriff's forehead.

The little boy was bent over near the depot, apparently looking for another rock. He found one and *whiz*, the stone zipped past the sheriff's head. Thompson stood for a moment and then crooked his finger. The boy skipped over to face his nemesis.

"Son," the sheriff said, his voice rumbling like a prairie thunderstorm. "Why did you chuck that rock at me?"

The boy offered his hand for the sheriff to shake. Thompson looked at the boy as though he had been offered a rattlesnake, but he reached out to take the boy's hand between his thumb and forefinger.

"Name's David," the boy said.

"It's nice that you're David, but why in the . . . why'd you throw that rock at me?"

"Didn't have a sling."

Thompson's eyes squeezed shut. "From the train," he said. "On the train you asked if I was Goliath."

The boy nodded, "And I'm David."

"So you set about to slew me with a rock?"

"Yeah. Did I do it?"

"Slew me?"

"Yeah."

"No."

"Would have if I'd had a sling. The other David had a sling."

The boy's mother stepped up. "Is there something wrong?"

Thompson started to shake his head, but the growing knot on his forehead restricted the movement. "No ma'am. The boy was just giving me a Bible lesson."

"Ma says you should do whatever the Bible says."

Sheriff Thompson's mouth started to open, but then his teeth audibly ground shut. His words came softly. "Always good to know the Bible," he whispered.

"You sure he hasn't caused you any trouble."

"No trouble."

"Tried to slew him, Ma."

"You what?"

"Tried to slew him."

"David Patrick Monahan, I swear, sometimes you don't make any sense at all."

"But I do what the Bible says."

"Yes, you do what the Bible says."

The two started to bustle off. The boy turned to shout: "Bye, Goliath."

The mother took three steps, jolting to a stop. She turned to look at the growing knot on Sheriff Thompson's forehead. "You tried to slew him?"

"Yeah, Ma."

The mother reached out and grabbed the boy by the ear, dragging him wailing toward her luggage. "David Patrick Monahan, when your father comes home from work, you are going to learn another lesson from the Bible: Spare the rod and spoil the child."

Only the boy's retreating wail remained as the two turned the corner of the depot and disappeared.

Sheriff Thompson reached up to explore the knot on his forehead with tentative fingers. "Hell of a town you have here, Frank."

"We're a Bible-believing bunch."

"You"—Thompson stared squinty-eyed at Mac—"your name isn't David, is it?"

"Nope. Your name isn't Goliath, is it?"

A smile twitched at the corners of the sheriff's mouth. He held out his hand. "James Thompson. Some call me Big Jim."

"Mac McPherson. Some call me one sorry son of a bitch."

Thompson grinned, turning toward Drinkwalter. "He'll do."

Drinkwalter was staring at the corner where the Monahans had disappeared.

"You know that kid's got a helluva arm on him for his age. We might have a major league pitcher on our hands, here."

"Nah," Thompson said. "He'll never live that long. Don't suppose you brought a horse."

"Thompson, there isn't a horse in Montana big enough to carry you, but I did bring a wagon."

"Spring wagon. I don't like to be jostled about. I was jostled a lot on that milk run, and I don't want to be jostled anymore. Spring wagon?"

"Yeah."

"Tilly's sandwiches?"

"Beef."

"Three for me?"

"Nope. Got you six. You always ask for three, but you always eat six, and I don't get any."

"Six?" Thompson grinned. "Drinkwalter, you are one sorry son of a bitch."

One of Thompson's eyes squeezed almost shut. "Get bait?"

"Fresh this morning."

"Beer?"

"Sitting on ice in the wagon."

"Then what the hell are we waiting for?"

"For you, Big Jim."

"You mocking me?"

"Yeah."

"Just so I know."

The three stepped toward the waiting wagon. "You know, as long as you got six of Tilly's sandwiches for me, I might as well have one now. No sense saving them all for lunch."

Drinkwalter nudged Mac. "Grab your sandwich and run for your life. It always starts out like this."

"Most of the time you cast blind. You don't know if there's a fish out there or not. So you drop that hopper in a place where fish are likely to be. Now, later in the day, they'll start rising, eating hatches on the surface. You'll know where they are then. Then it's the question of getting the right fly to them in the right way."

Sheriff Frank Drinkwalter and Mac McPherson were edging toward the river through a bank of willows that threatened to tangle their lines and steal their rods. "We'll come into the river along the bottom of the hole. It's always best to fish upstream when you can. A trout's attention is always fixed on what's ahead and above, so you come up below and behind him. You come downstream, and he'll see you or your shadow. That will spook him, at least spook him enough not to take your fly or your hopper if it comes past him in the leastways wrong."

The sheriff stopped, caught for a moment in the rustle of the willows, leaves dappling his face in light and shadow. "There's poetry in fishing, Mac, pure poetry. I can't read Shelley or Keats, but I can read poetry in a fly line carving soft loops into the big sky. I see a poem flashing from a rainbow's side as it dances across the water. You understand that, Mac?"

Mac shook his head.

"Well, you will if I've got anything to say about it. Anyhow, we'll come in on the bottom of this hole. Not much space between the willows and the water, so we won't be making any long casts, just flipping the hoppers along the bank. Let them drift down and watch for a bite. Don't jerk too fast, Mac. Just set the hook, and bring them in. I'll walk up and fish the top of the hole. Along the way I'll likely scare some hoppers into the water, ring the dinner bell for some of these bull trout."

"No bull trout here. Never heard of anyone taking a bull trout from this river."

"Bull trout, rainbows, and lochs big and mean enough to call a hole their own."

"Oh."

"You get into a big one and need some help, you let out a shout, and I'll come running."

"Isn't Mr. Thompson going to fish this hole?"

"Well . . ." Drinkwalter stared at the top of the hills on the south side of the river. "Well, I mentioned that it was getting along toward noon. Told him it wouldn't be long until we could have some of Tilly's sandwiches and a little beer."

Mac cocked his head and looked at the sheriff. Drinkwalter rubbed his chin. "You see, Mac, Thompson can't do anything else when his mind is on Tilly's sandwiches. He had to go back to the wagon and have one. Might be, he'll have a beer, too. So we'll have this hole to ourselves."

Mac's forehead curled into a question mark. "You don't want him to fish?"

"Mac, if Thompson catches the biggest fish, he will

be one impossible son of a bitch. I've seen some humongous trout in here, Mac. If he caught one of those, and we didn't, well . . ."

"You really are one sorry son of a bitch, aren't you?"

"I'm not the guilty one here. He didn't have to go back to the wagon for the sandwiches and beer. That was his decision. Besides, he isn't above pulling a fast one if he can. One time he sent me back to town. Said one of my deputies had dropped by to tell me there was a letter from Catherine marked 'urgent.' I ran all the way back to town. There wasn't any letter. Deputy hadn't set foot out of the office. By the time I got back to the river, Thompson had eaten all the sandwiches, drunk all the beer, and caught two rainbow that would make tears come to the eyes of a normal man. He's one sorry son of a bitch.

"Now, you won't say anything about this, will you?"

"One sorry son of a bitch to another?"

Drinkwalter grinned. "One sorry son of a bitch to another."

Mac grinned, too. "Let's get some bull trout out of this hole before Thompson figures out what's going on."

"Mac, we could clean this whole river of trout before Thompson figures out what's going on—so long as we had enough of Tilly's sandwiches to keep him busy."

"Well," Mac said, "you take the high road and I'll take the low road, and we'll get the big trout. He might be eating Tilly's sandwiches now, but when he sees the fish we've caught, he'll be eating crow."

Drinkwalter chuckled. "You'll do, Mac. You'll do."

The sheriff drifted off through the willows, protecting his face and his rod from their clinging grasp, and

Mac was left beside the river. Frank Drinkwalter was one sorry son of a bitch, and Mac McPherson was proud to call him friend.

Mac stood in the shadows of the willows, only his fishing rod giving any indication where he was. He had been working his way up the bank just as Drinkwalter had said he should, lobbing a hopper ahead of him, watching it float down toward him, bobbing and weaving in the eddies along the bank. More than once, trout had risen to the bait, but Mac was always a little too slow or a little too fast. He had put five new hoppers on during the trip up the bank, replacing the ones trout had taken.

Mac had been casting blind, tossing the hoppers to places where fish should be, but this was different, breathtakingly different. Something huge was feeding under the bank at his feet.

Mac had stepped back into the cover of the willows when he first saw the movement. He jerked the tattered remnants of one hopper off the hook and eased open the top of a Bull Durham sack the sheriff had given him. A hopper made his bid for freedom, a yellow-bellied hopper of the kind that Drinkwalter said trout liked best.

The sheriff had talked about the role that fate played in fishing. Was it fate that this particular hopper poked his head out of the sack to take the hook? Was that huge trout waiting for this specific hopper to come down the river, feebly kicking its way toward shore?

One cast: He would only get one cast. It had to come at just the right time, when the fish's attention was focused at just the point of the river where the hopper was carried by the current. Casting upstream could leave coils of fish-frightening line on the water. Mac would have to mend the line, keep the coils at his feet and not on the river. But the line couldn't be too tight. Then the hopper's drift would be unnatural, and he would spook away from the bait, probably leave the hole altogether.

Mac almost wished that he hadn't seen the fish. He might have caught it anyway, working along the bank as he was. He might have caught it unconsciously, without all the tension he was feeling now. Then again, he might have frightened the fish to deeper water without ever having seen it. That would have been all right, too. You can't feel bad about not catching a fish that you haven't seen. He must have spooked a dozen fish on his walk up the river.

But he knew that this fish was lying under the bank. He knew this fish was huge, and Mac knew he was frightened to death that he would mess this up, be left with nothing more than a fish story to be told around campfires.

Mac swallowed once and took a deep breath. No sense waiting anymore. Might as well take his chance. Might never have another chance like this. He let out a little line and swung the hopper back and forth from the end of the rod as though it were a child on a swing. When the swing picked up a little momentum, he let out a little line. Soon, the hopper was almost touching the water on the bottom of the swing. And then, as the hopper almost reached the top of the swing on the upstream side, Mac let the hopper go. It sailed upstream as though that were the only purpose in its swiftly waning life. The hopper landed with a little *splot* and started its downstream journey toward Mac. Mac held the rod tip high. When that monster fish took the hopper, he would need the full length of the rod to absorb the shock of the strike.

Mac's hands were trembling slightly as he watched the hopper enter the swirl that the bull trout called his own. The hopper, caught in a little eddy, turned circles on the water, and Mac could see a dark shape rising from the depths. The fish held a foot below the surface, watching the hopper dancing above his nose, and then sank back into the depths.

Mac's chin fell to his chest, and he almost cried out his despair. At that moment the rod was almost wrenched from his hands. The big fish had come back, and the bull trout was hooked solidly.

"Yahoo!" Mac whooped. "Yahoo!"

The boy could hear Sheriff Drinkwalter yelling something from upstream, but he lost the words to his excitement and the rush of the river. The boy held the rod tip high, letting the line slip through his fingers to ease the fish's power against the pole, line, leader and hook.

The fish was running now, downstream, and the line was cutting into the boy's thumb and forefinger. Mac ran downstream, too, stumbling along the bank, crashing through willows, always the rod tip held high, always his attention on the fish and not on the branches cutting past his face.

The fish came out of the water as it tried to shed itself of the hook. Mac stood stiff-legged and wide-eyed. The fish was even bigger than he had thought, bigger than any fish he had ever seen. The fish fell back into the water with a *SPLOOSH!*—the same sound a big rock dropped off the bridge might make.

The fish was whipping its head back and forth, and each time the split-bamboo rod throbbed with the power of the creature. No one could land this fish—no one. It was too strong and too set in its ways to allow a fourteen-year-old boy, a puny rod, and a flimsy line to stop it.

Once again the fish rose from the water as though it meant to fight this creature that dared to challenge it. Bull trout it was: ruler of the deep green stretches of the Yellowstone River; eater of nymphs and flies and any other fish that dared move into its path. Bull trout it was, all muscle and power and meanness.

SPLOOSH! The fish crashed into the water, sending up a spray that painted the sun pink and blue and red, like the colors that flashed from its flank. A magic fish this was, magic enough to paint the waters, magic enough to set a fourteen-year-old boy to dancing on the bank.

"Whooee!"

Mac looked up. Sheriff Drinkwalter was standing beside him, smile wide as the river.

"Boy, you got yourself into the bull trout of all bull trout. *Whooee!* Look at that fish jump. You're doing great. Keep that rod tip up. Let him have his head until he tires, and then point him toward the bank. Let him run now, boy, and run with him. If he isn't exhausted, you'll never get him on the bank. *Whooee!*

"He's headed upstream, boy. Go with him, but keep the pressure on him. Always keep that line tight or he'll spit that hopper at you like a bullet. Beaver cache up at the head of this island. Keep him away from that. He gets into that tangle of branches, you might as well kiss him good-bye. *Whooee!*"

Up the river the two ran, the sheriff ahead, breaking the way through the willows, and Mac behind, seeing only the fish, nothing but the fish. And then when it seemed that neither Mac's arms nor the rod and line had the power to keep the fish away from the beaver cache, a tangle of limbs the animals stored for winter forage, the fish jumped again, but not so high and no so wildly.

"He's tiring, Mac!" the sheriff shouted as the fish turned again downriver. "But he isn't whipped yet, not by a long shot. This is when they slip loose, when they've been on a long time. Sometimes a leader will wear through, or a hook will pull straight.

"You have to keep the pressure on, Mac, but not too much. You've got this bull trout damn near broke to lead, Mac. Come on, Mac. He's running, boy. You've got him on the run."

Down the river they ran, willows slashing at their faces as they passed. And always there was the line, the line, a telegraph between the two-leggeds and the bull trout.

Near the tail of the island where the river had eaten away some of the land, leaving only the bones of river rocks to bleach in the sun, the fish turned toward the bank, no longer fighting the line or fate.

"You've got him coming, boy. He's coming in. All you have to do is keep his head pointed toward the bank, and that's where he has to go. He can't swim backward, so he'll come right up on the bank. But when he first sees us, he'll spook. He'll head back for deep water, so keep the pressure on him, but not too tight. He's coming."

Only an avalanche could have pulled the two's attention from the trout, and that's what happened. Big Jim

Thompson was running across the gravel bar, rocks skittering away from his boots, as though he were a giant boulder crashing down a talus slope in the Beartooths.

"Don't lose him, boy. I seen him. That's the bull trout, granddaddy of all trout. Hang on to him, boy."

The avalanche slowed to a walk about twenty feet from the two, Thompson walking softly the rest of the way so he wouldn't frighten the fish.

"That's it boy," Thompson said. "Ease him toward the bank, just keep him pointed this way, and he'll come right to you. Now, when he first see you, he'll . . ."

. The trout showed himself ten feet out in about three feet of water. At least thirty inches long, maybe more, with a back green as river moss. His body was thick, ending at one end with a hooked jaw and at the other in a tail that seemed bit as a canoe paddle. His sides flashed silver as he swam into the current, gill cover opening and closing.

"Damn," Thompson whispered reverently. "Damn, what a fish."

"Bull trout of all bull trout," Drinkwalter said. "Biggest fish I've ever seen."

"Or heard of."

"Or heard of."

"Better get him in."

"Yeah. Mac, just ease him in toward the shore. You get him into that shallow water. We've got him then."

The fish came in as though he'd been broken to lead, spent all of his life at a fisherman's beck and call, but when his belly touched the rocks, he made one last desperate lurch for deep water and safety—and the hook popped from this fish's mouth.

The trout skittered through the shallows, trying to find swimming depths. With great whoops, Drinkwalter and Thompson took chase, water spraying from each step. But now they were in the fish's environment, and with a thrust of his great tail, he slid over the shallows and into the green waters.

Both men stopped, not willing to believe that they had lost the giant fish.

Thompson looked up at Drinkwalter: "We are two sorry sons of bitches."

"Three," Mac whispered. "There are three of us. I'm one sorry son of a bitch, too."

Independence Public Library

10

"He was a helluva fish, one helluva fish."

Sheriff James Thompson sat on the wagon bed, legs swinging as he watched Sheriff Frank Drinkwalter and Mac McPherson eat their roast beef sandwiches, Tilly's specialty at the Stockman Café in Eagles Nest.

Drinkwalter would take large bites from the sandwich and then savor the explosion of flavor that followed his teeth's assault on beef and bread. Mac was taking tiny bites, nibbling away at the sandwich as a squirrel might, if squirrels ever had a chance to eat one of Tilly's sandwiches.

Thompson decided that Mac's style was more aggravating. The boy seemed to be doing nothing so much as teasing the Yellowstone County sheriff. Big Jim's eyes squinted nearly shut. A boy should respect his elders, not tease them with one of Tilly's beef sandwiches, seasoned and roasted to perfection.

"He was one helluva fish," Thompson said, trying to pull his thoughts away from Tilly's sandwiches.

"Aren't you going to have a sandwich, Big Jim?"

Thompson glared at Drinkwalter. "You trying to be funny?"

"You didn't really eat all six of your sandwiches while Mac and I were fishing, did you? I only got you six as a kind of joke. I didn't really expect you to eat them."

Thompson's eyes squeezed almost shut. "You're going to go too far, Frank Drinkwalter. I won't be responsible, if you keep up that chatter."

"You responsible? Someone who eats six of Tilly's sandwiches and doesn't have anything left for lunch? Now, that's not very responsible, Big Jim. That's not really very responsible at all."

Thompson growled, a low rumbling that made both Drinkwalter and Mac look for dark clouds on the horizon.

"Sounds like rain," Mac said.

"Yes, it does," Drinkwalter answered.

"No clouds."

"Just the few, but they don't look like rain."

"Doesn't feel like rain."

"No, it doesn't."

"Don't think it's going to rain."

"Don't think so, either."

"What do you think, Big Jim? Think it'll rain?"

"I'm about to rain on your parade, you sorry son of a bitch."

"Oh, a discouraging word. I just hate discouraging words. Don't you, Mac?"

"Just hate 'em, but I can't talk now. I'm whittling away on one of Tilly's sandwiches. I think she got an especially good do on this batch."

"I believe you're right, boy, an especially good batch. I'd like to say they're good to the last drop, but that would remind me that Big Jim drank all the beer. Drank a whole bucket of beer this morning. I think the man needs help."

"I'd say he does," Mac agreed, nodding.

Thompson jumped stiff-legged from the wagon box,

and Mac swore the earth recoiled from the force of the sheriff's weight.

"The hell with the both of you. I'm going fishing. It'll be a cold day in hell before you see the likes of me up here again. I sure as hell wouldn't treat anyone the way you've treated me, Drinkwalter. Be damned if I'll buy you dinner at the Golden Belle the next time you come to Billings."

Thompson grabbed his fishing rod and creel and took three stomping steps toward the river.

"Uh, before you go, Thompson," Drinkwalter said, "would you mind getting something for me? Mac and I are awful tired from our morning of fishing."

Thompson's eyes squeezed almost shut, and the giant man took one step toward Drinkwalter. Then he sighed. "What do you want?"

"See that toolbox under the seat?"

"Yeah."

"Would you open it?"

"Open it yourself, you . . . you . . ."

"One sorry son of a bitch for another?"

"Ah, hell." Thompson jerked the box from beneath the seat and twisted off the wire holding the latch shut. He popped open the lid, and a grin crept slowly across his face. "Tilly's sandwiches. You got me some of Tilly's sandwiches."

"And another bucket of beer."

"And another bucket of beer. Drinkwalter, you are truly one sorry son of a bitch."

"You, too, Thompson."

"Me, too," Mac said.

All three broke into guffaws. This was one beautiful day on the banks of the Yellowstone River, just outside of Eagles Nest, Montana. But that was about to change.

Sheriff James Thompson pulled a handkerchief from his back pocket and dabbed his lips. "Ah, hell," he said. "I think I've died and gone to heaven."

"It's nice enough to be in heaven, isn't it?" Sheriff Frank Drinkwalter said.

Nice enough it was. The trees had the soft green leaves of early spring. The air was soft and clean, and the sun kissed the earth as gently as a mother kisses her sleeping child.

Thompson stuck one of his huge fingers into his mouth, his fingernail working at dislodging a bit of beef stuck between his teeth.

"Water's coming up. Won't be long before it's muddy with the runoff. That will take care of most of July. No sense fishing in August. Fish just find a deep pool and cool water and hibernate, so I probably won't be coming back until September."

Thompson leaned back, studying the flash and glitter of the sun off the trembling cottonwood trees. "You did the right thing coming up here, Frank. Nice place to spend a life." Thompson shifted a bit, making room in his pockets for his hands. He pulled out an envelope. "Kind of hate to do this. Feel like the serpent in the Garden of Eden must have felt." Thompson nodded toward Mac. "Maybe it would be better if we waited until Mac went fishing."

"Mac's all right. He reads all of the reports in my office."

"This isn't like any of the reports in your office."

"Go ahead, Jim."

Thompson cocked his head and looked at Mac. "Well,

Sam Fiddler was out on patrol this past spring. You remember him, don't you, Frank? Damn fine officer. Not so big, but wiry and smart. Good man to have around."

Drinkwalter nodded.

"Anyway, he was patrolling down by the uh . . . cribs, a couple weeks ago. Just a normal patrol. Men get a snootful of booze and decide they'd best go down and . . . uh, visit the girls down there. Often as not, they get robbed. Sometimes some pimp . . . uh . . . Frank, you sure it's all right to talk in front of the boy like this?"

"Go ahead, Jim."

"Well, it was quiet that night and black as a banker's heart. Fiddler saw something oozing out from under the door of one of those cribs. Sam knew what it was. Once you get the smell of that in your nose, there's no way you can mistake it for something else.

"So Sam knocked. It was just a formality. He didn't expect anyone to answer, but then he heard the window break at the back of the crib. So he put his shoulder to the door. The latch broke, but the door held. He thought somebody was pushing back, trying to keep him out. He shoved and the door opened, and he saw what was blocking it. He said later that it was almost like that woman didn't want to be seen in the condition she was in.

"Fiddler is a tough cop. He's been on that beat for years seeing the worst that humanity has to offer. But when he saw what that man did to that woman, he went down on his hands and knees and vomited. By the time he got around the crib, the killer was almost a block away, running from shadow to shadow.

"Sam, he kept as close as he could, and the killer led him straight toward a little one-room cabin. Jack Galt's place," Thompson said, leaning over to spit in disgust. "Didn't surprise Sam at all. Galt was pimping her, and he had put his boots to that woman before. He has a god-awful rage in him that . . ."

Thompson shook his head and spat again on the grass.

"Anyhow, Galt had a little shed out back of his place. There was light shining out of the shed when Fiddler ran up, so he stepped over and peeked in the window.

"Galt had been keeping a calf, fattening it on grain he found along the railroad track. Well, the calf was too young to butcher, but Galt had cut its throat, and he'd done a hell of a poor job of it. Blood all over the shed. Galt was blood head to toe.

"That sly son of a bitch. He covered himself with the blood from the calf so the policeman couldn't see the woman's blood on him. Galt said he didn't know anything about the woman. Said he had heard someone running by just before Fiddler got there. And all the time he was grinning, grinning like he'd played some kind of joke.

"We found a patch of Galt's shirt at the crib. It matched perfectly with a tear in the shirt he was wearing when Fiddler caught him. We took what we had to the county attorney, but he said it wasn't enough. With Galt hanging around that woman the way he was, that shirt could have been torn anytime.

"Galt beat her up more than once, but down around the cribs, somebody's always beating up someone. It's like they all hate being there, hate themselves for what they're doing. So the pimps beat up the drunks, and the drunks beat up the women.

"There's something about . . . that profession that hurts everyone. The woman loses her dignity at the door. She lets herself be pawed by drunks, and the man feels cheapened because he has to resort to ladies of the night. It's as though a woman couldn't stand being around him if he didn't pay her. So fists fly. We see that all the time.

"But the woman wouldn't settle for what Galt was doing to her. She had been planning to go back home, someplace in the Midwest. We found the railway ticket in the room, all stained with blood.

"Hell! Isn't any justice for some people. She was no different from Gertie, but Gertie plays her parlor games with the mayor and some of the other leading citizens of Billings. Had Galt done that to Gertie, it would have been different. But it was Sally Higgins, poor little Sally Higgins, and nobody gave a damn about her when she was alive and nobody gave a damn about her when she was dead.

"Anyhow, there wasn't anything legal I could do about Sally, so I had Galt hauled in for questioning. I took him back to a cell in the jail and told the jailer to go have a cup of coffee. Galt was smiling at me the same way he was smiling at Fiddler that night.

"He wasn't smiling when he left that cell, Frank. He didn't have a mark on him, but he was hurting something terrible. I told him that he didn't look well. I told him it would be a lot better for his health if he went somewhere else."

Thompson leaned back and locked his huge fingers behind his neck. "Wasn't anything new to him. He'd been run out of Glendive not much before that. Woman died down there, but nothing could be proved. There are other rumors, too, but . . ."

Thompson leaned forward, putting his hands on his knees and staring into Drinkwalter's eyes.

"I should have killed him, Frank. I should have beaten him to death so he had a chance to feel sorry for what he had done. But I've been in the law a long time, and I couldn't bring myself to do it. I just couldn't. I thought I was shut of him, but a problem doesn't go away just because you hide it upriver."

Thompson sighed. "Frank, Galt's living in Eagles Nest, now, running a smithy."

Thompson stood and walked over to where Drinkwalter was sitting. He leaned down to look into his friend's eyes.

"I think you ought to kill him, Frank. I think you ought to kill him and haul him out somewhere in the country and drop a clay bank on him. That's what you ought to do, Frank."

Thompson shook his head and stomped back to his seat on the wagon box. "But you won't do that. You won't do that any more than I could beat him to death, and we'll all be the sorrier for it. He'll put that god-awful knife to some woman, and we'll all be the sorrier for it."

Mac poked into the conversation. "He took Milt Jenkins's place. You know, the wheelwright.

"When Galt moved in, I went down to see what he was doing there. He set a forge by those double doors. That building is built with rock from the quarry, and it's just like a cave. Galt didn't have any lights on, just the light from the forge and the sunlight that comes in through the windows and doors.

"I walked past the doors, and the heat hit me like a

fist. It seemed to me that Galt had opened a vent to hell, and I was smelling fire and brimstone. At night you can only see that forge. He's just a black shape, moving around the glow of the fire."

Mac pulled his eyes up to look at Thompson. "Sometimes when I saw him I'd think he was the devil, warming himself at the fires of hell."

"That's Jack Galt, all right," Thompson said. "I'm sorry as hell I set him on you, Frank. Sorry as hell."

11

Nelly Frobisher sat at a table in her tiny office, separated from the front room of her establishment by a heavy green velvet curtain. She could do her bookwork behind the curtain and still hear anyone coming through the establishment's front door. Nelly liked to think of her house as an establishment and herself as an entrepreneur.

She kept immaculate books, knowing to the penny how much each of her three women produced. Of course, the total didn't count any tips their clients might leave them. Tips in this country of cowboys and penny-ante businessmen were rare. Nelly held that her women were entitled to any tips for extra services they offered their clients. The women appreciated the little extra they had each month.

The business was all there on the desk in front of her: income, expenses for heating and lighting and food and liquor and monthly examinations by Doc Soliloquy. That wasn't his real name, of course. Most people called him by his proper name, Dr. L. C. Higgins. But Nelly had studied for the theater before she became . . . before she entered her current form of employment, and Higgins's mutterings as he treated his patients reminded her of the soliloquies of the stage.

Nelly buried those thoughts in her ledger, written in her own tight hand. To think about those early years was to think about what she might have been—and what she was. Nelly didn't like to think about that.

Like all businesspeople, she pondered each week how she might cut expenses and increase profits. She ran her finger down the page to an entry marked LIQUOR. Liquor wasn't a big moneymaker for her, not even after she had mixed the booze half and half with water. Most of her clients appeared at the door drunk as lords, more than a few of them too drunk to do what they came to do. It was not rare that one of the men would pass out before they partook of the establishment's offerings. In decent weather she would drag the clients outside and prop them against the back wall so they wouldn't clutter the front room. When the drunks awoke and staggered back inside, Nelly would tell him how shocked her girls were at his "manliness." She would whisper into the drunk's ear: "Bridget said you were an animal. You ought to come around here more often, Henry . . . or George . . . or Philip." And Henry or George or Philip would go home with a little spring in his step, as much spring, at any rate, as the alcohol allowed.

Nelly peered back at her books in the soft yellow light of a kerosene lamp. She might have had the pantry/office wired for electric lights, but for reasons she didn't really understand, she didn't like the idea of doing her books in their harsh white glare.

March had been a good month, the longer days of spring bringing out the sap in men just as it did in the cottonwoods along the Yellowstone River. The heating bill was down considerably, and the light bill, too. Everything was going along quite nicely.

Nelly sat in the soft yellow light, feeling content, as content at any rate as she could. A nagging emptiness drove her from her solitude whenever her mind pulled her away from her books and left her alone. She was about to stand when it began. "Uh, uh, uh, oh, oh, oh, o-o-o-o-h, e-e-e-e-e-e-e-e-e-e!" The squeal reached a crescendo that seemed to endanger the very windows of Nelly Frobisher's little house on the west edge of Eagles Nest.

Nelly grimaced. She didn't like being reminded of what went on in her rooms. She didn't like to be reminded that while she was, indeed, a businesswoman, the business was so venal. Still, Beulah's enthusiasm was good for business. Beulah earned nearly as much as both other women combined, and when the men asked for a woman by name, they usually asked for her.

Beulah was an anachronism, a lady of the night who sought the trade from sheer enjoyment. Most of the men liked that. It seemed, then, that their . . . activity . . . was something more than a simple business transaction.

Nelly had wondered often about Beulah's squealing. Surely, it was forced, bred of business sense and not physical passion. Sometime, when the house was quiet and Beulah was alone, Nelly intended to talk to her about that matter—discreetly, of course.

The front door scuffed open. The rare humidity occasioned by melting winter snows had swelled the door, set it rubbing against its step. Ole had promised to take the door down and plane it smooth, but the season belonged to the wind, and leaving a door open to its icy blast was simply not acceptable.

Nelly smoothed her dress, a sequined blue silk that she had found years ago in St. Louis, and stepped outside into the front room.

Sheriff Frank Drinkwalter was standing there, and when Nelly appeared, the sheriff took off his hat, running the brim through his fingers. Courtesy was a rare commodity in a house of ill repute, and Nelly blushed at the gesture.

The sheriff was a handsome man, tall and lean. His face showed strength and serenity, a thoughtfulness that Nelly didn't often see in her business.

"Why, I haven't seen you in a month of Sundays."

Nelly remembered then who she was and who the sheriff was, and the smile fled her face. "There isn't any trouble, is there? I'm very strict about the girls. They don't take anything that doesn't belong to them. I run an honest establishment here, and I wouldn't allow any stealing no matter what anyone says."

"No, Nelly, it isn't anything like that. I was just wondering if I could speak to you for a moment?"

"Certainly, Sheriff, I'd be pleased to buy you a drink. I have some fine bottled in bond . . ."

"No, Nelly. Coffee if you have it made. Maybe we could talk in the kitchen."

Color fled Nelly's face. Of course the sheriff wouldn't want to be seen in her parlor. If someone came in and saw him in her parlor, they would think he was . . .

Nelly's defenses crumbled. She could take the stabbing looks she suffered in Eagles Nest. She understood mothers shuffling their children to the other side of the street whenever she appeared. Even the gutter language of her clients didn't pierce her armor, but the sheriff with his soft words and his courteous ways had skewered her soul, left her pinned to the door of her own profession.

Sheriff Drinkwalter didn't want to be seen with her, and she a businesswoman who paid taxes and salaries just like any of those stuffed shirts on Main Street. Well, she wouldn't put up with his high-handed ways.

She wouldn't allow the sheriff free rein to her feelings. Nelly's back stiffened, and her face hardened.

"My parlor is not so abhorrent to my customers."

"No, it isn't, Nelly. But I might be."

Understanding spread across Nelly's face—and then embarrassment. "Yes, you're right. I don't know what I was thinking of."

Nelly's hands fluttered down her dress to smooth the material over her hips, and then she realized what she was doing and a blush spread up from her neck. How could he fluster her so? Why did he make her feel like a child?

She drove those thoughts from her mind and managed to say, "Would you like some tea, Sheriff?"

"Coffee if you've got it. Don't make any on my account, but a cup of coffee would be nice to take off the chill."

"Yes, it is chilly tonight. It's the wind, I believe."

"Yes, the wind."

Nelly opened the door and showed the sheriff into her kitchen. While the parlor was decorated in what might be described as lavish decadence, the kitchen was nothing if not utilitarian. The wooden floor was scrubbed and waxed until it shone. A simple table painted white stood in the middle of the room, contrasting with the huge, black range and water tank that dominated the opposite wall. A sink with a hand pump framed a window looking over the river. Spotless: Everything in the room was freshly painted or scrubbed.

Drinkwalter stepped over and examined the cupboard doors. Squarely in the center of each was an intricate painting of flowers and leaves, highly stylized, and each identical to the other.

"These are beautiful, Nelly. Did you . . . ?"

Nelly smiled. "No, I haven't got that in me. Never been able to draw or paint. I've always been oriented toward . . . business. Ole Stinsdahl did that for me. I didn't know he was doing it, I just came down to fix dinner, and he was putting on the final touches.

"He said the kitchen reminded him of his parents' home in Norway, so he painted those flowers on the cupboards. He called them *fjell flora*. I made him keep repeating it until I could pronounce it. I look at them in the winter, when it's cold outside and this is the only warm room in the house. They remind me that behind every winter, there is a spring."

Nelly couldn't imagine why she told the sheriff that. She hadn't told anyone else. Her hand darted to her face then, and when she realized what she was doing, she buried her hand in her lap, tying her fingers together to control a nervousness she didn't understand.

"I never would have thought that Ole had those flowers in him," Drinkwalter said.

"The flowers don't really look like that. He painted them not so much as they are as how he sees them. Wouldn't it be a wonderful thing to see the world though Ole Stinsdahl's eyes?"

Nelly clapped her hand over her mouth. What was it about this man that flustered her so? She was a professional businesswoman, and she was chattering childish things to the sheriff. She resented the sheriff, then. Resented his intrusion. Resented the effect he was having on her. She began to rebuild the wall around herself with words.

"Here I am boring you, when you want a cup of coffee. That's what we women are for: to give you men what you want. Sometimes I forget that, Sheriff."

"The flowers are beautiful, Nelly."

Nelly's jaw clenched. "Let's get down to business. You didn't come here to drink my coffee or look at my kitchen."

"No, although I am pleased to be doing both."

Nelly looked at the sheriff then, and the hard shell of her faced cracked, just a little bit, but it cracked nonetheless.

"Nelly, I've got some bad news."

Nelly jumped from her chair and stalked to the window over the sink, starring through it into a black wall of night. "Is there any other kind? What is it? Did the good ladies of Eagles Nest decide that I am a scourge on their community?"

She turned then to glare at the sheriff. "Or did some of the community leaders come to you and ask you to run me and my establishment out of town? Is that what you're here for, Sheriff, to run me out of town?"

Sheriff Drinkwalter shook his head. "No, Nelly, I'm not here about anything like that, but I do have bad news, really bad news for the both of us."

Nelly's face softened. "For both of us?"

"Yes. We'll have to work together on this."

"You need my help?"

"Yes."

"What is it, money? You need some money to give to someone to keep the do-gooders off both our backs. Is that it?"

"Sit down, Nelly. Sit down, and drink a cup of your coffee. Listen to what I say, and then tell me what you think we can do. Is that so much?"

Nelly Frobisher shook her head and sat at the table.

What was it about the sheriff that made her emotions bounce around like a stick on a river riffle?

"I'm sorry."

Drinkwalter shook his head. "No reason to be sorry about that."

Now it was the sheriff's turn to fidget in his chair. He hesitated and then looked across the table. "Nelly, a woman was killed in Billings a month ago. A man cut her up something awful with a knife. She was ... uh, she was living in one of those cribs down by the railroad track."

The color drained from Nelly's face. "What was her name, Sheriff? Do you remember what her name was?"

"The Yellowstone County sheriff said her name was Sally Higgins."

Nelly's hands curled into fists and jumped to her face as though she meant to hide behind them. Her eyes opened wide with shock.

"Not Sally," Nelly said, shaking her head. "Not Sally."

"You knew her, Nelly?"

Nelly pressed her fists into to her face, trying to hold in her emotions, trying to meld her face into some semblance of normality, but the effort failed. Tears gushed from her eyes, leaving a glistening path across her face, and then the sobs broke through her fists as a river breaks through a line of boulders.

Nelly fled to the window, staring out into the blackness, her shoulders shaking. The sheriff rose, stepped to the window, taking Nelly in his arms. She didn't attempt to stop the crying, then. She laid her head on his shoulder and sobbed, her tears wetting his shoulder.

And just when the sobbing began to ebb, the door to the kitchen crashed open. Beulah stormed through. Her substantial body, constrained only by the robe she wore, rolled, bobbed, shimmered and shook with each determined step. Her eyes shone with the fierceness of a woman warrior, and her blond hair seemed afire with the heat of her fury.

But Sheriff Frank Drinkwalter's attention was focused on the double-barrel Parker shotgun, carried with both hammers at full cock. Her words came in a snarl. "You son of a bitch, you leave Nelly alone or so help me God, I'll splatter your guts all the way back to . . ."

And then a question crawled across Beulah's face. "Sheriff?"

Nelly stepped toward her protector, a tentative smile belying the tears that still ran down the woman's face. "No, Beulah, it isn't anything like that. The sheriff brought me some bad news, about Sally. A man killed her, carved her up with a knife." The words turned into a wail.

The butt of the shotgun thumped against the floor as the woman warrior propped the weapon against the wall by the door. Beulah's face cracked into tears, then, and the two women embraced, sobbing.

When the sobbing eased, the sheriff intruded. "I apologize. I didn't know that you knew Sally. I would have—"

Nelly turned toward the sheriff, sniffling. "No way you would have known. Beulah, you go up and tell the girls everything is all right. No sense scaring them over something they can't do anything about. If someone comes in, you . . . uh, handle it, would you? The sheriff will tell me what happened to Sally, and I'll pass it along. Is that all right?"

Beulah nodded and stepped toward the door, leaning down to pick up the shotgun by the barrel as she passed through.

Drinkwalter watched the door for several seconds after it closed. "You know, she shouldn't be carrying that shotgun around with both hammers at full cock."

Nelly smiled wanly at the sheriff. "She has such little hands, and not much power in them, and that old shotgun needs a good cleaning and oiling. So the hammers are stiff, hard for her to pull back. She doesn't want to be struggling to tug back the hammers when she needs the gun, so she carries it around like that."

"I wouldn't want to be on Beulah's bad side."

"She doesn't have a bad side. She's just sweet as can be. It's just that we . . . well, we have to stick up for each other out here. There are so many men, who . . ."

Nelly stepped to the cupboard and took out two cups. She filled them with coffee, trying to put her thoughts in order before she joined the sheriff at the table. She cleared her throat and began, "Beulah was indentured to a family somewhere near Boston, and the master of the house was using her in ways a man shouldn't use a child. So when she saw the newspaper advertisement about a man in Montana wanting a wife, she wrote, and he wrote back with train tickets. He was a pig farmer out of Springtime. First night, he found out she was 'used goods.' "

Nelly was wringing her hands together, staring at them as though they were Christ's bleeding hands.

"They were married. Not much he could do about that. But he made her life a living hell. He built her a little shack out by the pigpen and locked her in there. He fed her table scraps and brought her out to work during the day."

Nelly looked across the table at the sheriff. "He beat her, the way a man might beat a horse that wouldn't let him tighten a cinch. It's one thing for a man to lose his temper. But he just beat her like it was one of the chores he had to do. There's something wrong with a man like that, Sheriff."

Drinkwalter nodded.

"Well, he had an accident one day and fell into the pen with the hogs. I guess those hogs went crazy. Wasn't anything left of him, but some bones.

"Wasn't anything to hold Beulah to the pig farm, so she came down here. Only thing she brought with her was the shotgun."

The sheriff whispered, "Is that how it happened, Nelly? Did he just fall into the sty?"

Nelly's eyes flashed. "That's how it was told to me, Sheriff. I've got no reason not to believe it."

Drinkwalter nodded. "And Sally?"

Nelly leaned back in her chair, her eyes on the darkened window. "I got up one morning and came down here to start the stove. Ole hadn't left kindling in the bucket—that's so unlike him. He takes care of us so well. But he forgot to put kindling in the bucket that one morning, so I opened the door to go out to the shed. Early spring it was, like March or April, and I saw what I thought was a bundle of rags beside the door.

"But when I stepped out, Sally looked up at me. Poor child, she was almost frozen. Her face was white as snow and eyes black as two pieces of coal. She didn't say a word to me, just huddled down there shivering, so I gave her my hand and helped her into the house.

"She just sat there on the chair shaking. I didn't know if she was frightened or cold or just worn out, or what. Well, the other ladies were getting up by then, and they started mothering her like she was a stray cat or something.

"By then I had a fire going, and fixed her some eggs and bacon and toast, and you'd swear that she had never eaten before, she was so hungry. Once we got her warmed up and fed, we gave her a bath. Her hair was dirty and stuck together with cockle burrs, but it combed out real nice. Black, it was, and shiny, and if she hadn't been so afraid, she would have been pretty, really pretty.

"She was about the same size as Betsy, and Betsy had some clothes left over from . . . before she took up the life. Betsy was pleased to give them to Sally. Said she would never have any use for them."

Nelly's face wrinkled into a map of pain. "That's the thing, Sheriff. Once you take up the life, there's no going back. There's no forgiveness for a woman who has taken up the life."

Nelly sighed, reaching up to rub the back of her neck. "Anyhow, Sally told us she'd been married to this man . . ."

Nelly's face worked as though she meant to spit. Her eyes softened then, and she turned to face the sheriff.

"It's the same with all of us. Just the same."

Nelly jumped to her feet and stepped to the stove, bringing a blue enamel coffeepot to fill the sheriff's cup and her own.

"She just got tired of the beatings."

Nelly took her seat, dropped one elbow to the table, and propped up her cheek as though she no longer had the strength to hold up her head. "What is it about women that makes men want to beat us? What makes big, strong men take their fists to us?"

Drinkwalter shook his head.

"You wouldn't hit a woman, would you?"

"No, but tell me about Sally."

Nelly nodded. "She and her husband had been living up near Whitehall. One day she just started running. She caught a ride with a teamster, and he . . . had his way with her and then kicked her out of the wagon. So she walked the rest of the way. All the way down here. She knew what this place is, but she thought she might be safe here."

"We all took to Sally. She was a real lady. She stayed here for a while and cooked for us. We had real sit-down dinners, and she showed the ladies how to hold their forks and pass biscuits. But she wanted to go back to Chicago, where her folks were."

Nelly paused for a moment. "That's all any of us want, to go someplace else and get started where nobody knows us or what we are. You don't know what it's like to walk down the street and have men say things they do."

Nelly shook her head. "We all want out, Sheriff. We all hope that someone will come along and look past what we are to see what we can be.

"Sally was that for us. She was everything we wanted to be. We wanted her to go home and to find a good life with a good man. We took up a collection for her. She took the train to Billings and found a job there. She wrote us every week, telling us how everything was. I'd read the letter aloud, and while I was reading, we were carried away from this."

Nelly's arm swept around the room.

"And then she started writing about this man who kept following her. Every time she looked up he was standing there. He frightened her. It was his eyes, she said. They were flat and dead as though he were hollow.

"The letters stopped, but she still scribbled us notes whenever she could. That man had put her on the street. He said all women were . . . whores . . . and she might as well be taking money for it. He kept all the money, Sheriff. He kept everything. But she started hiding money, saving up. She was going to get away on the train and go as far as her money would take her."

A tear threaded its way down Nelly's cheek. "And then we didn't hear anything. We kept hoping she had gotten away. We would talk about where she might be, what she might be doing, but now . . ."

A sob racked Nelly's body. "But now you tell us she's been killed."

"Nelly, did she mention the man's name in any of her letters?"

"Yes, it was . . . Jack. Jack something."

"Jack Galt?"

"Yes, that's it—Jack Galt."

"Nelly, they ran Galt out of Billings, and he's come here. He's living here now, Nelly. That's what I came here tonight to tell you."

A long, keening wail as primitive as a Montana wind escaped Nelly's lips.

"He's coming, isn't he, Sheriff?"

"Yes, Nelly, he's coming."

12

Nelly Frobisher hadn't dreamed the dream for years, but it came back to her that night. She twisted and turned in sweat-drenched sheets, watching the scene play darkly through her mind in grays and blacks. There was no light in this dream.

It was dark, dark as the belly of Jonas' whale. She huddled in the coal bin in the basement, smearing coal dust on her face to hide in the darkness. She knew he would be coming, and that thought seared her eight-year-old soul.

It was Saturday, and on Saturday her mother volunteered to clean the church for Sunday services. It was Saturday, and he would be coming for her. She had asked her mother to take her to church. She was old enough to work. She would work really, really hard if her mother would take her to church.

But her mother said Saturday was a gift for her little girl, a respite from rising early for school during the week and for church on Sunday. The little girl had screamed in her mind then. She didn't want to sleep in on Saturday. If she slept in on Saturday, he would be coming for her, he and that terrible thing of his. But while she was screaming that in her mind, she was saying, "Yes, Mother," as though her mother had given her a great gift.

Her mother was always giving gifts. The Woman's Christian Temperance Union met weekly in her home, and each time she served them cookies and cake as they spoke of the evils of demon rum. She made clothing for families "in need," and always she was the first to bring dinner to a bereaved family.

And sometimes the little girl thought she was a gift that her mother gave to him on Saturday mornings. Sid, she might say, I have a gift for you hiding somewhere in the house. This is my gift to you, Sid, for working so hard all week to provide for us.

He was awake. She had heard the floor creak under his weight. He would go first to the kitchen and drink a cup of coffee. And then he would come looking for her.

He seemed to think that it was a game, calling to her in a little child's voice as though he were playing with her. The little girl didn't want to play. She wanted to run away, but that would make her mother sad.

She didn't want to make her mother sad. Her mother gave her warm breakfasts and sent her to school in clothing that smelled of the sun. She didn't want to hurt her mother, and that's why she didn't tell her mother what her father was doing to her.

"You don't want to make your mother feel sad, do you?" he would say. "You don't want to make her feel bad."

And always the little girl would shake her head. No, she didn't want to make her mother feel sad. Feeling sad hurt so much. It hurt almost as much as when he took his thing and . . . No, she didn't want to hurt her mother.

She heard a cupboard door close in the kitchen, and a whimper primitive as life tore from her throat. She grabbed her mouth, digging her fingernails into her flesh, willing her mouth to be silent, to not give voice to the terror that crept about in the little girl's mind.

She followed the soft sound of bare feet to her bedroom door, and she heard the door scuff open. She could hear him murmuring then, a singsong child's voice. She couldn't hear the words, but she knew them by rote.

"Hey, little piggy, no sense to hide,
Papa's coming to take his bride."

Nonsense words sung over and over and over.

She whimpered again, and tears ran down her face, cutting rivulets through the coal dust. The steps stopped, and she could feel his ears searching the house, trying to find her. She took a deep breath, holding it so that he wouldn't even be able to hear her breathe.

"Hey, little piggy, no sense to hide,
Papa's coming to take his bride."

The door to the basement opened then, and a shaft of light stabbed into the darkness.

"I hear you," he said, taking the first step down the stairs. "I hear you, my little pumpkin. Now, let's see where she might be hiding. Could she be hiding in the corner? No, she's not in the corner. Could she be hiding under those burlaps sacks? Nope, she's not there.

"Do you suppose she might be in the coal bin? I'll bet she's hiding in the coal bin.

"Hey, little piggy, no sense to hide,
Papa's coming to take his bride."

The little girl screamed then. She screamed and screamed and screamed.

"Nelly, what's wrong. Nelly, wake up. You've just had a bad dream. Wake up, Nelly." And Nelly Frobisher, Eagles Nest businesswoman, awoke sobbing. She hugged Beulah to her. "He's coming, Beulah. He's coming," she sobbed.

Mac stepped around the door to the sheriff's office. Sheriff Frank Drinkwalter was standing, back to the door, and staring through the window to the blue sky. The sun had scrubbed all the clouds away, leaving the sky azure. He turned smiling when he heard Mac's heels on the floor. "Now, there's one sorry son of a bitch," the sheriff said.

"Takes one to know one." Mac grinned.

"How'd school go today?"

Mac's face wrinkled into a question mark. "It was good. Everyone was . . . nice to me."

"Well, there's no accounting for taste."

Mac grinned again.

"I have one letter from the commissioners."

Mac's face wrinkled into a question.

"Been here long enough to recognize the stationery," the sheriff answered.

Max nodded, taking the envelope. He opened it with a wooden letter opener lying on the desk and began reading:

"Dear Sheriff Frank Drinkwalter:
"It has come to our attention that you have hired the son of the widow McPherson as your

part-time deputy. As you are aware, we approved your plan to hire a part-time deputy, but your choice is simply unacceptable. Deputies must be full adults if they are to provide the taxpayers full value for their dollars. We have asked around town and have found a suitable replacement for the McPherson boy. Sonny Ingram is a strapping youth, and while employed daily at the Emporium, he would be more than willing to spend his evenings in the county's service.

"To expedite this matter, we have already spoken with Sonny Ingram. He will report to you this Wednesday next.

"We are pleased to have been able to help you in this matter."

Mac's eyes jerked to the sheriff's face. The boy was stricken, as though he had learned of a death in the family.

Drinkwalter shook his head. "Don't worry about it, Mac. Sonny is Sam Goodman's nephew. I suspect he's about to lose his job at the Emporium. I heard Hank Brittle complaining about him the other day. Sam just wants to find Sonny a new job before he gets fired. He did the same thing to get Sonny a job at the Emporium."

"Can he do that?"

"Take your job and give it to Sonny?"

"Yeah."

"No. I'm the elected sheriff. I can hire and fire anyone I choose. The commission cannot interfere with the operation of my office, except at budget time, and by the time that rolls around, Sonny will already have been fired and Sam will have had to find him another job.

"Nobody is going to fire you, Mac. That's my word, one sorry son of a bitch to another."

Mac tried to grin, but the effort failed. He hadn't realized how much his job meant to him.

Drinkwalter read the expression on the boy's face.

"Don't worry about it, Mac. We have enough on our plates. Don't have time to worry about something that isn't going to happen."

The sheriff turned and took the envelope from the shelf, offering it to Mac. The boy took the letter and held it to his nose, closing his eyes so that he could concentrate on the scent. Nearly a minute had passed before he said, "Roses. It smells of roses."

Sheriff Drinkwalter smiled. "Yes, roses. I suspect she's been working in her rose garden. I wish I could be there with her."

The sheriff sat silently for a moment. "Mac, have you ever thought about an apple pie?"

Mac cocked his head, trying to see around the corner the conversation had taken. But the sheriff didn't say anything, so the boy answered, "Sure, every time I walk past Charley Goodman's apple tree. I think about the apple pies Ma used to make when . . . we had an apple tree out back. Ma's apple pies were always so good. The crust was flaky and the apples just right and—"

"That's right, Mac. Apple pies are built of apples and flour and shortening and cinnamon and sugar and the heat of an oven and your mother's special touch.

"But the thing of it is that if you laid all those things out on the table, they wouldn't be much to look at, would they?"

Mac shook his head.

"It's only when they come together in the right proportions under the direction of someone like your mother that an apple pie is made, a really delicious, warm apple pie."

Mac swallowed. "Yes."

"That's the way I feel when I look into Catherine's eyes, Mac. Being with her makes me something more than I am by myself. Do you know what I mean?"

"No."

"I thought you had something of the poet in you."

"That's dumb. Comparing a woman to an apple pie."

"I don't know how to say it any better, Mac. I know what I want to say, but I can't put words to it. I guess that's your job, to put words to it. But how can you do that if I can't make you understand?"

Mac hesitated, and when he spoke it was barely more than a whisper. "I know what you mean. When Pa left, we thought he would come home, but when he didn't, it seemed as though I had been torn apart. I hurt so bad that I went into my room and took off my shirt to see if I was bleeding.

"I didn't think I would ever be me again, not what I was before . . . and I'm not. I'm not the same. But Ma and me . . . we make an apple pie together, too."

Mac turned to stare into Drinkwalter's eyes. "It's hard to go to school when I know that the kids are going to laugh at me. I couldn't do that if it wasn't for Ma. I know it would hurt her if I didn't go, and that would hurt me, too.

"Sometimes when she has spent a long day over the washtub, I can feel her back hurting. She puts her hand on her hip and throws her head back like she's reading something on the ceiling when it's really bad. My back hurts then, too."

Sheriff Drinkwalter smiled. "Sometimes, Mac, I don't know if you are fourteen or eighty-four."

"I'm fourteen, skinny as a rail, and dressed like a scarecrow."

"Not anymore."

"Still skinny as a rail."

"Yes. Would you read the letter now?"

Max opened the letter. He performed the task carefully, placing the letter opener exactly where it had been on the desk, slipping the letter from the envelope as though he were celebrating Eucharist.

" 'Dear beloved,' " Mac said. "She opened it with 'Dear beloved.' "

Drinkwalter nodded.

"I received your latest letter with great dread. I was so accustomed to Mr. Deakins's hand that I had come to think of it as your own. After the long break in your letter writing—two weeks is a terribly long time, isn't it?—I thought someone was writing to tell me something terrible had happened to you. I couldn't see how that might have happened without my knowing. Even though we are so far apart, we are still together.

"Sometimes as I am walking down the street, I smile for no reason. I think then that you are experiencing something pleasant or funny and that I am sharing that experience with you. Saturday last, I was so taken with the trees' tender shades of green that I thought you must have been sharing that thought.

"I'm terribly sorry about Mr. Deakins's death. He had so become a part of our lives. I have his photograph draped in black on the mantel in my mother's home.

"Perhaps you remember the picture. He had just taken you trout fishing. You are holding one end of a string of beautiful trout and he the other.

"I am taken with how young you look in that picture, and I wonder how you and I have changed. Perhaps when we come together after all these years, you won't remember me, and I, with age-weakened eyes, will walk past you on the station platform, wondering whatever kept you from me.

"I know those thoughts are whimsy. Although the years have stretched on interminably, I suppose that having been apart for ten years is not so terribly long. But how different the calendar and the heart.

"Sometimes, I think you are a fantasy, something I created in my mind to carry me through these difficult years of caring for my mother. But then I feel the touch of your hand or recall your laugh. I realize then that the creation of someone like you is too grand for me. If I could work my feelings toward you into bronze or canvas or stone, people would come from miles around to marvel at it.

"I have been having a terrible dream lately. I am trapped inside a place so dark that I cannot see, in air so thick I can barely breathe. I want to run, to you, to have you rescue me, but I don't *know which direction will take me closer to you, and which will take me farther apart. It is a terrible dream, and it ends my night's sleep. I toss and turn, unable even to find comfort in the book of poems you sent me."*

Mac stopped reading and ran his finger over the wrinkled edge of the page. "She cried here," he whispered. "You can see where her tears fell on the page."

He handed the letter to the sheriff. "See, there where that one word is blurred."

Sheriff Drinkwalter stared at the page as though his thoughts could wring her tears from the paper. Then he handed the letter back to Mac without raising his eyes from his desk.

"Please read on, Mac."

"The rose garden is doing wonderfully well. I work there, amazed at its beauty, pleased that God allows us the privilege of polishing one facet of his creation. The roses are such a relief after spending a week at the bank, spring locked out and me locked in. Beauty fills the corners of the soul, and I feel so privileged to share in it.

"I'm sorry that I ramble so.

"I bought you a hat. I don't know what possessed me to do it, but I was walking past the haberdashery and happened to look into the window. It is a soft brown, which depicts the ease and comfort I always feel when I think of you. The brim is relatively wide to shield your face from

*the Montana sun and to hide it in shadow from
the women I always fear will be gazing at you
from the corners of their eyes.*

*"Mac, I charge you with keeping an eye on
Sheriff Frank Drinkwalter. Guard him for me
from the many lovely ladies who must inhabit
Eagles Nest. In the last letter you told me little
about yourself. Please help fill the gaps in my
imagination.*

*"I must go, now, to await your next missive as
roses await the rising sun. I love you Frank
Drinkwalter, and I miss you terribly."*

"She signed the letter 'Catherine,'" Mac said, handing the letter to Drinkwalter.

He stared at the sheets of paper, seeking her hand in
the swirls of blue ink, stopping to stare at the page
wrinkled with her tears.

"Mac, could you please get me a cup of coffee,"
Drinkwalter said, handing the boy his cup. "No need to
hurry. I need a little time to gather my thoughts."

Mac nodded and stepped out of the office toward
the coffeepot, taking care not to awaken Deputy Bert
Edgar, who was gently snoring in his chair.

When he returned to the office, Drinkwalter looked
up and smiled, but the smile was too weak to cover the
emotions he was feeling.

Drinkwalter took a sip of the coffee, grimacing.
"About this time of day, coffee's strong enough to etch
glass."

Another weak smile crossed his face. "Is Bert sleeping?"

Mac nodded.

"Good, he was up late last night. Some drunk was out howling at the moon."

The sheriff leaned over his desk, cupping his chin in his hands. "You ready to take a letter, Mac?"

Mac nodded.

"Well, let's get started."

"Dear beloved?" Mac asked.

"Yes," Drinkwalter said. "Let's start it with 'Dear beloved.'"

13

The wind scoured Eagles Nest streets, carrying off dust and ashes to some hiding place. Sheriff Frank Drinkwalter was swept along with the wind, too, shoved toward a woman-killer's hiding place.

Gandy dancers were at work on the railroad crossing, doing something with the steel track that must be done, but something too subtle for passersbys' eyes to define. One of the men looked up as the sheriff passed, nodding to Drinkwalter. He tapped the shoulder of his companion. He looked up and waved.

Hard work, the sheriff thought as he passed. Hard work whether in August, when the tracks buckled with heat, or in January, when the hard steel of the track turned brittle with cold. The men made games of their work, betting who could drive spikes into oaken ties with the fewest swings of their special hammers, watching as one man carried the weight assigned to two. They tested their young muscles against the heat and cold and each other, and the winner bought the beer after work.

Smoke was rising from the blacksmith's shop, seen more in the distortion the heat painted on distant trees along the river. Jack Galt was an experienced blacksmith. He kept his fires burning hot, hot enough to bend metal to his will, hot enough to distort distant trees with the heat rising from the chimney.

The smithy was built of rock cut straight and square from the quarry. The building seemed nothing so much as a rock itself, squat and brown beside the road, the windows and door on the west side dark with shadow. But inside the forge burned red, and the sheriff wondered if he were looking at the door to hell.

He crossed the road leading south toward the Beartooth Mountains, pausing for a moment before stepping through the door. The building was dark, enlightened only by a shaft of sunlight to dance with the heat and the smoke of the forge. The eye goes naturally to light, leaving the remainder of the room dark as the bottom of a well on a cloudy night.

It was several moments before the sheriff saw movement, a shadow darker even than the darkness of the smithy. Jack Galt stepped then into the shaft of the light, his arm pumping air into the fire on the forge, each pump of the bellows followed by a roar of the fire and the glow of the coals.

But Galt's eyes were not on the forge. At least Sheriff Drinkwalter thought they were not. In the dim light, he could see Galt's face only in light and shadow, and the blacksmith's eyes were nothing more than a glitter in the deep shadow beneath the man's brow. The effect was skeletal, as though the sheriff were staring at a skull, and the skull were staring back at him.

The sheriff stepped up to Galt, his eyes squinting to see this killer of women.

"Sheriff Drinkwalter," the sheriff said.

The only reply was the *whoosh, whoosh, whoosh* of the bellows.

"Want to talk to you for a minute."

Whoosh. Whoosh. Whoosh.

"Sheriff James Thompson was down this weekend. Your name came up."

Jack Galt's arm hesitated for a moment and then continued. *Whoosh. Whoosh. Whoosh.*

Drinkwalter leaned into the shaft of light, his face only inches away from Galt's.

"How about you stopping that? Give me a minute of your time."

"Got work to do." Galt's words came out flat, their passing marked not at all on his skeletal face.

"I've got work to do, too," Drinkwalter said.

"No matter to me. I didn't invite you down here. Don't much give a damn what you've got to say."

"Sheriff Thompson said I should shoot you, haul you out into the country, and dump a clay bank on you. I see what he meant."

Galt turned to peer into the darkness over the sheriff's shoulder. "Hear that, Leaks? Sheriff is threatening to kill me and hide my body."

"Yeah, I heard him."

Drinkwalter turned, staring into the darkness. "Donnan?"

"Yeah."

Drinkwalter knew Donnan well. He was always on the top of the usual suspects list when a drunk was rolled, or a house burglarized. Always he worked as he was working this day, from the darkness behind a man's back.

"You want him in on this," Drinkwalter said, pointing his thumb toward the darkness.

"My experience is that you need a witness to keep the law on the straight and narrow."

Drinkwalter nodded. "Thompson told me about the woman. Told me how you cut her up."

"Damn lie. Didn't touch her."

"What about the woman in Glendive?"

"Don't know anything about that."

"Glendive sheriff said you did. He passed the word to Thompson, just like Thompson passed word to me.

"What are you doing, Galt, working your way west one woman at a time?"

Whoosh. Whoosh. Whoosh.

Galt stopped, took his arm off the bellows, and stepped into the light from the door. "I knew you'd be here, sheriff. I knew you'd be coming to see me. That's the way it always is."

Galt shook his head. "I've never been charged with a crime, not pilfering or assault or drunkenness. I sure as hell am not guilty of murder.

"The Glendive sheriff thought I killed a woman down there. He didn't have one bit of evidence that I had, but he figured I did it. So he gets two of his deputies and they beat the hell out of me and tell me to get out of town.

"So I pack up my gear and sell my shop for half of what it cost me."

Galt stopped to look Drinkwalter in the eye. "You know who bought my shop, Sheriff? The Glendive sheriff's brother bought it for next to nothing. So the sheriff's suspicions turned into a nice profit for his family. Did Thompson tell you about that?"

Drinkwalter shook his head.

"I didn't think so. The Glendive sheriff wouldn't want Big Jim Thompson to know what a slick deal he pulled. But he wanted Thompson to think that I had killed that woman in Glendive, so he passes his *evidence* on to Thompson.

"Then Sally gets killed. Doesn't make any difference

that I was butchering a calf that night. Doesn't make any difference that whores get killed every day. All that matters is that Thompson has *evidence* from the Glendive sheriff that I kill women.

"I suspect Thompson didn't tell you this, but he took me back to a cell in the Yellowstone County Jail. That man beat me until I thought I would die, until I hoped I would. I pissed blood for two weeks after he beat me. There's no law in this country, nothing but law dogs and their suspicions. That's the way it's been, Sheriff, and now you're here to tell me that's the way it will be."

Drinkwalter whispered, "Sally had a job in an office. She wanted to go back home to her parents, but then you dragged her out on the street."

Whoosh! Whoosh! Whoosh!

"God makes whores, not me."

"How many of these 'whores' have there been, Galt?"

Whoosh. Whoosh. Whoosh.

"Well, I came to tell you that it stops here, Galt. This is the end of it."

Whoosh. Whoosh. Whoosh.

Galt looked up. "I sure as hell hope this is the end of it. I sure as hell hope that there is some justice in this county that doesn't come from law dogs' fists.

"I'll tell you, Sheriff, I'm tired of being harassed by the law. It's got to stop. I'll take you to court, and when the people of Eagles Nest find out what kind of a man you are, maybe they'll beat you and send you up the road."

Whoosh. Whoosh. Whoosh.

Galt turned to stare into the darkness. "Remember, Leaks, the . . . good sheriff threatened to kill me. Remember that so you can testify at the trial."

"I'll remember, Jack. Won't forget that."

"You want something to remember," Drinkwalter said. "Remember that it stops here."

Galt turned to grab a pair of heavy iron tongs behind him. He reached into the coals and pulled a long piece of steel free from the heat. He held it up then, between his face and Drinkwalter's, and in the dull red light of nearly molten steel, Drinkwalter could see that the skull was smiling, teeth red.

Galt shoved the steel into the coals. Sparks fleeing the force of his thrust, rising to be carried out the chimney like the prayers of the damned.

Whoosh. Whoosh. Whoosh.

Drinkwalter stepped toward the door of the building in a heat that rivaled any August sun. But the sheriff felt a chill cold as a winter wind cross his back, and a shudder swept through him as he stepped through the door.

He walked toward his office then, followed up the road by the sound of the bellows.

Whoosh. Whoosh. Whoosh.

It was warm in the little cabin, almost cheerful. The McPhersons had eaten a wonderful dinner, chicken and noodles. Mary McPherson had bought and butchered the chicken that afternoon. The thought of fried chicken had made her almost giddy, but this was a retired laying hen, too tough to fry. If Mac kept his job at the sheriff's office and nothing disastrous happened, perhaps they could have fried chicken that summer when the pullets matured.

The two were washing dishes, Mac scrubbing the plates clean and Mary rinsing and drying them. Life was good in the McPherson home, better than it had been for years. Mac's money made the difference between going hungry each week and being able to step beyond staples for their evening meals.

Mac was a good boy: Pride swept across Mary's face. He didn't complain about putting all of his money into the coffee can on the shelf above the stove. He didn't know that Mary was taking half of that and putting it into an envelope she hid in a torn corner of her mattress. The money wouldn't be enough to allow Mac to go to college, but if everything went well, he would have a bonus to take with him to school.

Mac was drying his hands on his pants, and Mary shook her head. Deputy or not, he was still a boy.

Mac looked up at his mother. "Ma, do you suppose that we could play some cribbage?"

"Do you have your homework done?"

"Yes."

"Then I would like to play some cards."

The two pulled up their chairs to the table, Mary putting a worn, dog-eared deck of cards in the center. Mac cut the deck, drawing a seven of diamonds. Mary drew a nine of spades.

"Your crib, Mac."

The boy nodded, rubbing his hands over the rough top of the table as his mother shuffled the cards. Something was bothering the boy, but Mary supposed that he would talk to her when he was ready to.

They played out the hand, and Mac miscounted his points. Mary reached across the table, putting the back of her hand against Mac's forehead. Mac absentmindedly brushed her hand away, before realizing what he was doing.

"Are you feeling all right, Mac?"

Mac's face twisted into a question mark. "What? No . . . I mean, yes, I'm feeling fine."

"Is something bothering you?"

"What?"

Mac looked up at his mother, cocking his head to one side as he did when he was perplexed by something. "No, it's nothing. I was just . . ." Mac reached up and scratched his face. "Ma, what was it like when you met Pa?"

It was Mary's turn to cock her head, wondering at the question. Then she smiled as she thought about that time that seemed so long ago.

"It was summer, early summer," she said. "That time when the air is warm and the moisture from winter keeps the grass green and the dust settled. He was sitting on a bench in front of Mawyer's lumberyard reading a book. He was the most beautiful thing I've ever seen, except for you, right after you were born."

"Guess it's downhill for me ever since, huh, Ma?"

Mary smiled. "You're just looking for a compliment, Mac. The fact is that you look a lot like your father. You have his eyes, his build, and his nose. The rest of you is mine."

It was Mac's turn to smile. "So every time I blow my nose, I should think of Pa?"

"Every time.

"He was sitting on the bench bent over a book, his chin perched on one hand like that statue, *The Thinker*. You've seen that, haven't you?"

Mac nodded.

"Well, that's the way it was with your father. He was sitting there, reading his book. I was wondering what enthralled him so. He looked up as though he could read my mind, and then he read me the words:

> *"Shall I compare thee to a Summer's day?*
> *Thou art more lovely and more temperate."*

"That was the first thing he said to me, not 'Hello' or 'Isn't it a nice day?' Sometimes those words come to me at the oddest of times, and then I think of him, wonder what he is doing.

"I found myself going out of my way to walk past the lumberyard, hoping to catch a glimpse of him. Each time I saw him, he would look up and smile at me.

"And one day, when I stepped up to the bench, he took my hand. At that moment I knew I would marry him.

"My father was opposed to it. He didn't think that Alexander had much of a future, but I couldn't . . . I just didn't care. I knew we had to be together.

"He worked at the lumberyard for a year after we were married, and then he blew out of town the same way he blew into it. But then he was carrying me, and I was carrying you.

"He gave me freedom, the kind of freedom that Christ talked about when he spoke of the birds of the air. He said they didn't plant seeds, till fields, or harvest crops, but God provided for them. If he cares so much for birds, Christ said, can we not trust him to care for us, also?"

Mary tipped her head and stared at her son. "Do you remember all the moving we did?"

Mac nodded.

"But no matter where we went, there was always

work for us. We never had anything extra, but I always had everything I wanted—you and Alexander. And then I woke up one day, and he was gone. The pain was so fierce."

Mary dropped her face to stare at her hands.

"Is he ever going to come back?"

She thought about all the afternoons she had spent, taking time from hanging clothing on the lines outside to look toward the setting sun. She knew he would move west, tracking the sun to its resting place.

Mary shook the image from her eyes, focusing on the cards before her. "No, Mac, I don't think we'll ever see him again."

Mac stared at the floor for a long moment. His words were little more than the rustling sound the wind makes as it ripples through long grass.

"Did he leave because of me, Ma?"

Mary stepped around the table and pulled Mac into a hug. "You must never think that. He didn't leave you, and he didn't leave me. He just moved on. I don't think he will ever find out where he is going.

"You know something, Mac?" Mary could feel the boy shaking his head against her breast. "I don't regret anything. He gave you to me, Mac. What mother could ask for anything more?"

14

Nelly was hiding in the room where she kept her establishment's books. He was coming, the sheriff had said. He was coming as her father had come to her as a little child so many years ago. Her fear was pulling the walls of the office in on her, burying her as she had tried to bury herself in the coal bin of her childhood home.

He was coming, as her father had, perhaps singing the little ditty that struck terror into her heart even now.

"Hey, little piggy, no sense to hide,
Papa's coming to take his bride."

Her father had taken her childhood away from her—and maybe her soul. Now this other man was coming to take her life. He would come to her door, and she would try to hide, but there would be nowhere to hide, and . . .

The walls of her office were closing in, squeezing the breath from her, and she swept aside the heavy velvet curtain that separated her office from the rest of the house. She was standing there, willing herself to breathe when the front door scuffed open.

Jack Galt stood there. He was dressed in rough but clean clothing. His boots had an oily sheen. His hair was short, very short and receding, giving him a high forehead and a sense of intelligence. His body was wound tight, and he moved with a certain grace. Most women might find him attractive, but for his eyes.

His eyes were washed out, irises not much darker than the sclera. But it wasn't the lack of color that riveted Nelly's attention. The eyes were opaque, as though they masked something too terrible for mortals to see.

When Galt's survey of the room was complete, he stared at Nelly for a long moment. She wanted to speak, to break his hold over her, but she couldn't. The words wouldn't come. He smiled, then, a smile as flat and opaque as his eyes.

"Hello, Nelly."

Nelly took two steps backward so quickly she almost fell.

Galt cocked his head, and resignation crowded into his voice. "The sheriff talked to you, didn't he? He told you about Sally, and he told you I killed her."

Nellie's hands knotted into fists and darted to her face, her arms pulled tightly to her body as though she meant to hide behind them.

Galt shook his head. "Nelly, I didn't kill Sally. I don't know who did."

Galt took a step toward her, and Nelly's eyes widened in terror.

Galt stopped. "Nelly, I don't mean to frighten you."

Nelly took another step back.

Galt shook his head. "Nelly, you know what it is to be set apart, to have people turn the other way just because they don't want to be seen near you. That's what the sheriff is doing to me. He's turning this community away from me. He's telling people something he heard from the Yellowstone County sheriff. It's not true, Nelly. I'm not what they say I am. If I were like that, I'd be in jail or hanged."

A little moan escaped Nelly's lips.

"Nelly, think about this. I know I'm not a handsome man. I know there is something about me that makes people uneasy, but I've always been decent to you and the girls, haven't I?"

Nelly was staring at the floor.

"I always clean myself up before I come. I have never hurt any of the girls. I have only shown you respect. You have to admit that, Nelly. I'm no different from anyone else who comes through the door.

"Maybe if you and me went up to your room. Maybe I could show you I'm no different."

"No, I don't . . ."

Galt stared at the woman with his dead eyes. "Why, Nelly, you surprise me. You really don't think you're a whore, do you? You think your girls are whores, but you're just their . . . What, Nelly? What do you think you are, Nelly? Their manager? Their provider? A businesswoman?"

Nelly sucked in her breath.

"Businesswoman. That's it, isn't it, Nelly? You think you're a businesswoman? You don't think you're a whore, do you? That's not good, Nelly, a whore should know herself for what she is. Maybe we should go to your room, Nelly, so you know what you are. I won't hurt you, and you'll thank me for that someday, Nelly. You'll thank me."

Nelly screamed, just as she had screamed as a child when her father sought her hiding place in her home on Saturday mornings. She screamed, knowing that it would tell Galt where she was hiding, knowing that it would lead him to her, but she screamed out her pain and her frustration and her anger and the words came. Again and again and again, they swirled through her mind:

"Hey, little piggy, no sense to hide,
Papa's coming to take his bride."

She screamed and screamed and screamed.

Sheriff Frank Drinkwalter was curled around his breakfast in the Stockman Café, absorbing the heat from the sausage and eggs and hash browns Tilly had just served him. He had the paper in front of him. Looking at the pictures, scanning through the long lines of words to find something, anything that made sense to him.

Maybe he could learn to read. Maybe Mac could teach him to remember the words as though each were a picture depicting something. He wouldn't really be able to read, but he would be able to interpret some things, simple things like Wanted posters. He thought he could learn to do that. Names, faces, offenses, and where they were last seen. He could do that.

Drinkwalter swept the paper away with his hand, and then caught it before it slipped off the edge of the counter. Wouldn't do to have someone ask him what he had read that upset him. That wouldn't do at all. Drinkwalter cut the sausage links into bite-size chunks with the edge of his fork. They were good; Tilly's food was always good, but it seemed a little flat this morning. Drinkwalter realized that his own apprehension was seasoning the meal, or rather stripping it of taste. Something was wrong.

He ignored the first tug on his shirtsleeve, thinking someone brushed against him as they moved past, but he turned at the second tug. Beulah was standing behind him. She had no makeup on and her hair was a tangle. That and the rough woolen dress she wore made her seem nothing so much as a farm wife, arisen in the middle of the night to seek the reason for the fuss in the henhouse.

"Sheriff, you've got to come. It's Nelly."

Drinkwalter closed his eyes and drew a deep breath. He stood, reaching in his pocket for a quarter. The tip was too much for a fifty-cent breakfast, but the sheriff liked to show his appreciation for Tilly's special effort.

Drinkwalter took Beulah's elbow, then, and the two stepped toward the door. Sal Carlotta was sitting at a table near the door. He dropped his head and turned his face toward the wall, not wanting to acknowledge any greeting by Beulah. Crazy woman. No telling what she would say.

As the door shut behind the two, Drinkwalter kept his hand on Beulah's elbow, steering her up the street at a faster pace than she was accustomed to.

"Do we need a doctor, Beulah?"

"I don't know. I don't think a doctor could help her now."

Drinkwalter's teeth ground shut. "Tell me what happened. Tell me everything that happened."

"It started last night. Tuesdays aren't very busy as a rule, and the other . . . ladies and I were playing pinochle. Three-handed pinochle. Sometimes we play partners when Nelly or Ole is around, but most of the time—"

"What happened to Nelly? That's what I need to know."

"Well, we were playing. I had just bid thirty-two, and I was having the hardest time—"

"Beulah?"

A sob shook Beulah's body. "Oh, Sheriff, I don't want to talk about it. I don't—"

"I can't help you if I don't know what's wrong."

"We heard Nelly scream. A terrible scream it was, as though her soul were being torn from her body. It scared us. I don't think I have ever heard anything that sounded so helpless. We stood up so fast, we knocked the table over, and the cards fluttered all over the floor.

"We were all standing there all huddled together, and there wasn't another sound from downstairs, not a sound."

Beulah pulled the sheriff to a stop on the boardwalk. "The silence was more frightening than the scream. With the scream, at least, we knew who it was coming from and from where. But in the silence we didn't know what was happening . . . or what had happened.

"I grabbed my shotgun, and the three of us started down the stairs in a knot, both of them hanging on me, and me glad for it. Even if it was something we couldn't handle, it made me feel good that we were together.

"When we got downstairs, the first thing we noticed was that the front door was standing wide open. A cold breeze was pouring through, and we weren't . . . dressed for it. So we all took to shivering. I don't know if it was the cold or being scared or what, but we were all shivering.

"It was totally black outside, and we couldn't tell what was out there, nothing anyway outside that little shaft of soft yellow light that came from the front door.

"And then we saw that Nelly wasn't there. We didn't know what happened. We didn't know what came through that front door and grabbed Nelly and dragged her off."

Beulah stopped, looking up into Drinkwalter's eyes, begging forgiveness for the women's fear.

"We couldn't go outside. We just couldn't. So we walked to the front door to shut it. I heard someone moving around out there, Sheriff. Real soft it was, but I heard it. It took my breath away. I couldn't go outside into that darkness and meet whatever it was that was out there. I just couldn't."

"That's fine, Beulah, but what did you do then?"

"We started looking for Nelly inside the house. Didn't seem to be much sense to it, but it was something we could do. We couldn't just stand there, and we couldn't go upstairs, and—"

"I know, so you went looking."

"Yes," Beulah said, resuming the walk toward her home. We went to the kitchen and opened the door really slow. By that time we were all thinking about what happened to Sally."

Beulah stopped, waiting until the sheriff stopped to look into her eyes. "I don't know what it is about the . . . business that draws people like that, but some people want to hurt us . . . whores. We all know that. We all wonder when someone strange comes through the door if he might be . . . one of those.

"We've all been thinking about that since you told Nelly what that man did to Sally."

Beulah's eyes were asking forgiveness. "We didn't want to step through that door because we were afraid—"

"Because you didn't want to see Nelly like that."

"Yes. We didn't want to see her like that. She's a good woman, Sheriff, she really is. People can't see past what she does, but if they did, they'd see what a really nice person she is. We didn't want to see her all cut up. We didn't want to see her like that."

"But you did open the door?"

"Yes, we did. We stepped through that door. But she wasn't there.

"It seemed awfully cold in the house. I guess it was because the front door had been open, but it felt colder than it was outside, like some Arctic wind swooped down and filled the house with cold and then swept away. So we put some wood in the stove, waiting to see that it caught fire. We hadn't said a word to each other: the three of us moving like we had one mind and not talking at all.

"But after we warmed up a little, we decided that we would look for Nelly. . . ."

"In the house?"

"In the house. Well, we looked in her office. None of us had ever been there before, and we didn't know what to expect. Well, I guess we knew a little something about it. Nelly is a really neat person. She makes all of us clean up after ourselves, and every Wednesday we go through that house from top to bottom. We just make it sparkle, so the . . . gentlemen will have a nice place to . . . conduct their business."

Beulah pulled her elbow free from the sheriff's hand and stared down at the boardwalk. A blush spread across her face.

"Well, I guess we expected it to be clean and neat, and it was, all except for this pile of blankets and sheets in the corner, and we thought it was funny, she left them there instead of setting them out so Ole could take them to the widow McPherson's place.

"We weren't in there all that long before we heard this sigh, like somebody had held their breath for as long as they could and they were letting it go all at once. Then the whimpering started and the words that we couldn't make sense of. Nelly was hiding in that pile of bedclothes, Sheriff, and she was talking gibberish, something about little piggies and wives."

Sheriff Drinkwalter followed Beulah through the front door. Bridget and Jezzie—the sheriff had never known their real names—were standing in front of the velvet curtain that separated Nellie's office door from the parlor.

"She's in there, Sheriff," Jezzie said, pointing into the darkness of the office.

The office was just as Beulah had said it would be, immaculately clean with a place for everything and everything in its place. The pile of blankets in the far corner of the room stood out as a cabin window leaking light stands out on a night-darkened prairie.

"Nelly? Nelly, I've come to talk to you. I just want to know what happened, and then maybe I can help make it better. I won't hurt you, Nelly. I just need to talk to you for a few minutes."

The sheriff leaned over to tug at the top blanket on the pile.

"No, Daddy! No! Please don't hurt me again.

Mommy, Daddy is hurting me. Please make him stop. Please make him stop."

And then in a voice that seemed so strange that the sheriff thought two people must be hidden in the blankets, came the words:

"Hey, little piggy, no sense to hide,
Papa's coming to take his bride."

The sheriff jerked back as though he had put his hand into a den of rattlesnakes.

"Beulah, I'm going to go get Doc Johnson. You ladies lock the doors and don't let anyone in. I'll be back in just a few minutes, and we'll see what we can do."

Doc Johnson stepped from Nelly's office. He pulled a white handkerchief from somewhere within the confines of his three-piece suit and began polishing his wire-rimmed spectacles.

"What is it, Doc? Is she going to be all right?"

The question crossed Doc's face, bringing up one eyebrow into a question mark.

"I don't know. Odd that God didn't give us the brain power to understand how our mind works, but he didn't."

"What happened?"

"Don't know. My guess is that something scared the holy hell out of her."

Doc held his glasses up to the light from the large front room window, and then slipped them on, working them down his nose until he could peer over the top of them at the sheriff.

"Do you remember Clyde Salzbary?"

"Yes, old guy used to live down by the tracks. Died"—the sheriff crossed his arms and leaned back to stare at the ceiling—"two, maybe three years ago."

Doc Johnson nodded. "That's him: old Army veteran. Served in the war under Sherman. Saw a lot of fighting. Saw a lot of things he couldn't forget. Every now and then, someone would come by and tell me Clyde was having one of his fits.

"Well, they weren't exactly fits. Something would trigger his memories of the war, and he would be back there in the war. He and five or six of his mates had been separated from his troop. The Rebs were out looking for him, bayonets fixed. Clyde had squirmed under an old oak knocked down by cannon fire. He lay still as he could while the Rebs found and killed each of the men with him. Said he could recognize them by their screams, and then they came to him, jabbing into bushes with those long bayonets. One soldier was jabbing around the roots of that oak, and a cottonmouth struck at him. He danced a bit, and then killed the snake, everyone coming over to see what he was up to."

Doc hesitated, looking into Drinkwalter's eyes. "Hell of a thing, isn't it, when killing a snake is more of a novelty than killing a man?

"Anyway, Clyde was wondering when they'd started looking again. He was wondering, too, if there was another cottonmouth in that tree. But some sergeant came by and ordered the Rebs away. So after dark Clyde crawled out from under that oak and made it back to his camp, carrying that cottonmouth with him. Made a hatband of it and wore it until he died.

"Anyway, every now and then, Clyde would wake up

and find himself under that oak tree. I would go out there. . . . Well there wasn't anything I could do but order the Rebs away. Then I would tell him that I was Sergeant Corn. Clyde and the other soldiers called their sergeant that because he found corn whisky no matter where they were. So I'd tell Claude I had a shot of corn, and I'd give him a sedative. He'd sleep, sometimes for forty-eight hours. I'd ask one of his neighbors to go in and talk to Clyde, and he'd come out of it.

"Don't know what triggered Clyde. Don't know what got him out of it, but a sedative and a friendly voice were all I could think of.

"That's what I told the ladies, to keep at least one person talking with Nelly all the time. If she isn't better the first time she wakes, they'll give her another dose."

"Do you have any idea when she'll be out of this?"

"None. She might never come out. I know what worked with Clyde, but I don't know if that will work with Nelly. I suspect that her three friends will do more for Nelly than I can."

Doc's forehead wrinkled into another question mark. "What the hell scared her like that?"

"Oh, I know what scared her," Drinkwalter said, "but there's not a damn thing I can do about it unless Nelly comes to and tells me what happened."

"Well, I'll let you know the moment something breaks, Sheriff. That's the most I can do."

15

Mac McPherson tiptoed from the school into the sunlight, testing the day as tentatively as a mother tests her baby's bathwater. Still, the light stabbed into his eyes, leaving him blinking in the shadow while other students spilled past.

A perfect day, a day that lured people into the sun to poke around in their gardens, tending carrots or corn or peas or potatoes. Mac took a deep breath of the spring air. Lilacs at the corner of the school loosed their scent on the air, teasing Mac's nose.

The box elder bugs were out, doing whatever box elder bugs do. Mac was taken with the thought of standing at the south side of the school building until he discovered their secret. The boy had never seen a box elder bug eat or drink, and yet they must. Or perhaps they fed on the sun, absorbing its rays through the red and black patterns on their backs.

Mac leaned against the stone wall. Warm it was from the sun and without hard edges that might have poked into the boy's musings. He thought then that he might lean against the wall and fall asleep, the sun nuzzling his face as a cow nuzzles her calf.

Mac might have fallen asleep but for the click of Miss Pinkham's heels on the walk as she stepped away from school. She stopped beside Mac as she reached the south wall.

"What are you doing, Mac?"

"Thinking about box elder bugs."

Miss Pinkham smiled. "It is a beautiful day, isn't it?"

"Beautiful—even Solomon in all his glory was not arrayed as one of these."

"A Montana day in June?" Miss Pinkham asked.

"A Montana day in June and box elder bugs."

Miss Pinkham smiled, and Mac did, too.

"You work at the sheriff's office, don't you, Mac?"

"Yeah."

"My room is near the courthouse. If you don't mind, I'll walk part of the way with you."

Mac smiled. The two walked slowly, enjoying their time in the sun, and then Miss Pinkham broke the silence.

"Do you enjoy working at the sheriff's office?"

Mac nodded.

"What do you do?"

Mac cocked his head and stared at his teacher for a moment. "Mostly I take care of letters and reports, that kind of thing."

Miss Pinkham was silent for several minutes. "What's the sheriff like? Is he nice to work for?"

Mac beamed. "He's really nice. He's taken me hunting and fishing, and we talk all the time, and—"

"Is that what he does when he isn't working?"

"I don't know. I know he likes to fish. He took me fishing once with Big Jim Thompson. Big Jim is the Yellowstone County sheriff. He's as big as a wall, and he can eat Tilly's sandwiches until—"

"Tilly?"

"Huh?"

"Who is Tilly?"

"You don't know Tilly?"

"No."

"Well, she cooks at the Stockman. Could be that she owns it, I don't know. Anyway, she makes roast beef sandwiches that . . ." Mac shook his head. "I don't know how to say . . ."

Miss Pinkham laughed. "The writer's bane," she said. "How do you explain how something tastes, or why one thing tastes better than another?"

Mac grinned at his teacher.

"Does the sheriff spend a lot of time with Tilly?"

"Just for breakfast and dinner. He either fixes himself a sandwich for lunch or has Tilly fix him one."

"Just a sandwich for lunch?"

"Yeah, I guess so."

"Not much for a tall man like him."

"I guess."

"Well, this is my corner," she said, stepping toward her apartment. She stopped and turned, "Mac, you got an A on your final. I suppose you expected that?"

Mac shook his head.

"Well, you should. Straight A's this year. You're going to make something of yourself, Mac McPherson."

She waved then, and walked off. Mac grinned all the way to the door of the sheriff's office.

The sheriff's door was shut, and Mac hesitated. Anyone could be on the other side. The sheriff might have arrested a murderer, or he might be talking to one of the commissioners about something. Maybe they were talking about Mac, about the five dollars a week that he was being paid. Maybe Sam Goodman was in there arguing that his nephew Sonny Ingram should have Mac's job.

Mac's apprehension battled with his need to know—and lost. The boy rapped at the door.

"Come in."

The sheriff's voice was flat. Bad news lay on the other side of the door. The sheriff was sitting behind his desk, holding a letter from Catherine. The sheriff looked up as Mac entered, smiling wanly.

"How was school today?"

"Fine. Finals week. Most of the farm kids are already home, putting up hay. It's pretty quiet."

Again the wan smile.

"Shut the door, would you, please?"

Mac leaned back and pulled the door shut, taking his seat in the chair before the sheriff's desk.

"Something wrong?"

"Yes, I think so."

The normal stack of official letters was scattered across the sheriff's desk. Ordinarily, the two would go through those letters, and then share the letter from Catherine. But this day those letters held no interest for the sheriff, only the one in his hands.

The sheriff chewed his lip and then handed Catherine's letter to Mac. The boy held the letter to his nose, expecting to catch the faintest scent of one flower or another. Catherine seemed to collect beauty, the sheriff had said, flowers sharing their scents with his beloved.

A question mark crossed Mac's face, and the boy shook his head.

"I don't—"

"No, I didn't, either. Something's wrong. I don't know if I should read it or throw it away."

"But you can't do that."

"No, I can't do that. Open the letter, Mac."

Mac reached for the hand-carved cedar letter opener on the sheriff's desk. The point of the blade slipped between flap and envelope, and the letter hissed open.

" 'Beloved,' " Mac said. "She starts her letter with 'Beloved.' "

"That's good," Drinkwalter said.

Mac bent the folds in the letter so its full face would lie flat on the desk, and began:

> *"Beloved:*
>
> *"I am torn so in the writing of this letter. Death came to Mother Saturday last, and I have been grieving. I remember when death came for my father. My mother's knees buckled, and for a moment I thought that she might fall. But she recovered and set about doing all the duties that are occasioned by a death in the family. Now I must do as she did, and I'm finding how difficult it is to make all the arrangements for her funeral and burial.*
>
> *"I was with her when the doctor told her that he had no treatment that would ease her condition. She died a long death, and there was nothing I could do for her, but try to ease the pain.*
>
> *"I don't know if she awakened before dying or if she fell asleep and simply didn't wake up. I know that she didn't stir in the evening. I have trained myself to listen to her every sound in the night. I know only that when I came in the morning, she was . . . gone. I wish the doctor could have given me something for the pain then.*
>
> *"I have tried to reconcile myself to her death. I*

know that she is in a better place, and I am sure that Father met her with open arms. I've never read anything about heaven reconciling the ages of its residents, but it would be a blessing if she could go to him as she was when he left her.

"I imagine them sitting beside a creek on a picnic blanket, she telling him about us, and he telling her about all that they might see in heaven. She will be giddy as a young girl, and he proud as a king."

Mac stopped reading then, his face stricken. He handed the letter across the desk so the sheriff could see the blurred letters where Catherine's tears had fallen.

"Yes, I see," Sheriff Drinkwalter said, handing the letter back to Mac. "Please read the rest of the letter."

Mac nodded and began again, fighting to get the words past the knot in his throat.

"I've made arrangements for Smith Furniture and Funeral Parlor to handle the arrangements. They came yesterday . . . and took her away.

"The house seems so empty now. In the past few years, Mother has not been much company. The pain was eased only by large doses of a painkiller, and that drained her of consciousness as well as pain. I would read to her some evenings from a book that I particularly liked, and sometimes in the reading, she would smile, so I knew that she was there with me.

"No one is here with me now, and I feel so terribly alone.

"I have longed all these years to be with you in Montana, and now I am filled with doubt. Will you have me still? We have changed over the years, you and I; only my love remains as it did that day when you left Cincinnati.

"I can no longer bear the grief and the doubt. I am writing to tell you, Frank Drinkwalter, that if you will have me, I will settle the estate here, and be on my way to be with you. If you say no, I will love you no less. I will live out the rest of my life here, knowing that I was given someone special in my life.

"Think carefully before you reply, but please don't linger. I have been too long in the waiting to tolerate any more suspense.

"Mac, if Mr. Drinkwalter decides to have me, I expect you to be at the station to greet me. I see you in my mind's eye as a younger Frank, tall and slim. I will know you when I see you, and please bring your mother. I feel as though she, too, is a part of my family.

"I love you, Frank, surely as no woman has ever loved a man before. Please write."

Mac looked up. "She signed it 'Catherine,' just 'Catherine.'"

The sheriff leaned back in his chair, his eyes going to the ceiling. "I'm not going to write her this time, Mac."

Mac's head jerked up. "You can't do that. You have to write to her."

"No, Mac. This time I'm going to send a telegram."

◇ ◇ ◇

Mac edged into the low clapboard building that served at the Eagles Nest depot. The waiting room was empty. Mac shuffled toward the stationmaster's counter, a caged cubicle, poking into the waiting room from the baggage compartment on the east side of the building.

Sparks Pierson was standing at the counter, shuffling waybills. He didn't look up until Mac said, "I've got a telegram."

Pierson peeked over the top of his reading glasses. "No, son. You've got a piece of paper, but you came to the right place if you want that piece of paper made into a telegram."

He took the sheriff's note and rubbed it between his hands as though he were performing magic, stopping only when he brought a smile to Mac's face.

"You're Mary McPherson's boy . . . Mac."

"Yes, sir."

"And you have a piece of paper saying that you will accept the fortune that the president of these United States wants to give you for your past advice, but only if he will stop pestering you about how this country should be run?"

Mac grinned again. "It's from Sheriff Drinkwalter."

"Sheriff Drinkwalter, now there's a fine man. You know, Mac, in their finest tradition, police are the peacemakers. Isn't anyone in town he hasn't helped one time or another, and some of them regular as clockwork. Weren't for the sheriff, Tippins would have been long dead by now, curled up in some snowdrift or another.

Pierson peeked over the top of his glasses. "A person in my position has his finger on the public's pulse, and

I'll tell you that the sheriff is the heart that keeps this community going."

Pierson paused, one eye squeezing shut as he considered what he had just said. "That's not too bad. Better write it down, so I won't forget it."

Pierson pulled a tablet from the drawer in front of him. Let's see . . . yes, he's the heart that keeps this community's pulse beating."

Pierson winked conspiratorially at Mac. "I've been collecting expressions for years. People like to read things like that while they're on the train. People will likely flock to me to see what I have to say about this or that. Could be I'll make a fortune, wind up on some South Seas island, thinking about Montana blizzards."

Pierson winked at Mac, again. "Anyhow, where was I . . . ? Oh, yes, I was telling you about all the things the sheriff does for Eagles Nest. Not long ago a drummer comes busting in here hell-bent on getting a ticket on the 12:20 A.M. Muttering, he was, about his treatment at the Absaloka. 'No two-bit hick sheriff is going to run me out of town,' he said. He was stomping around yelling about what he would do to Frank for libeling him the way he did when a card fell out of his sleeve. An eight of diamonds, it was. Don't know why a man would slip an eight up his sleeve, maybe an ace or two. Anyhow, when he saw me looking at the card, he quieted right down.

"Pete Pfeister told me later that jocko had just about cleaned out Jimmy Tillot before the sheriff came, and Jimmy with a wife just about to have a baby."

"Well, a man can learn a lot if he just listens, and I keep my mouth shut and my ears open, and you'd be surprised—"

"I certainly would."

It was Pierson's turn to grin.

"Well, let's see what the sheriff has to say:

"Catherine Lang at blah, blah blah. Beloved . . . Ah . . ."

Pierson turned to stare out the window. "I wondered about that. Drinkwalter is a fine-looking man and a hard worker, and I couldn't figure out why he . . ."

The stationmaster turned back to the telegram. "Beloved, I grieve for your mother. Stop. Know that you have always had a place in my heart. Stop. Come now and take a place in my life. Stop. Please hurry. Stop. Frank. Stop.

"I want you to come, too. Stop. Mac. Stop.

"You know her?"

Mac shrugged his shoulders and nodded.

"Is she nice?"

Mac nodded again.

"Of course she would be. Sheriff Drinkwalter wouldn't settle for anything less, and now he needs a home for his bride."

Pierson absentmindedly counted the words. "That will be eighty cents. I know it's expensive, but I don't set the prices. You can tell the sheriff that. You can tell him, too, that I'll send it right away. She will have the message no later than tomorrow morning."

Pierson turned to stare out the window.

"And Mac, could you come back sometime this after-noon? I've got an idea, and I might need your help."

16

CLOSED, the sign on Nelly Frobisher's establishment said. The women who worked there were taking shifts caring for Nelly. When she awakened sweating and screaming from a nightmare, one of the women was there to soothe her, a monotone chant of human kindness that Nelly heard in all her waking moments.

She was beginning to edge away from the terror that sent her hiding in the shadows of her past. She talked with the other women now, not much, but a little, and her appetite was returning.

The women were living in self-imposed exile. The interim in their business and the caring for each other was breaking down the shells they had built around themselves. They spent their time cleaning the house and baking great loaves of bread that they would eat fresh from the oven, slathered with slabs of butter from the town's creamery. They were opening up to each other, beginning to see through the facade of caked makeup to the women beneath.

And because each of the women shared similar experiences with Nelly, they began to share those experiences with each other.

Nelly Frobisher's emporium was beginning to heal itself in the early days of June 1912, each woman pulling herself free of the pervasive dread they felt after they found Nelly hiding in a clump of blankets.

A peace settled over Nelly's until that one night when the booming on the front door night brought back the fear, and they wondered if hell itself waited in the darkness outside.

Beulah was upstairs with Nelly, sharing the saga of her life with her companion. Nelly seemed to find the tone, if not the words, soothing, and Beulah talked on. But Beulah didn't tell Nelly about her marriage as a mail-order bride to a homesteader. She didn't tell her about the abuse and the shotgun and the way that the pigs grunted with excitement at the offering of fresh meat. She never told anyone why she refused to eat pork.

Jezzie and Bridget were sitting in the kitchen, sharing reminiscences in hushed voices.

"How did you ever take on a name like Jezzie?" Bridget asked.

"Short for Jezebel," Jezzie said. "My husband was a Bible thumper. He caught me out in the barn with a hired hand we had. He was a pretty little thing and enthusiastic. Really enthusiastic."

Bridget smiled. "Those are the best kind."

"In this business, it seems like the only kind."

The two were chuckling when the pounding began. The door shook from the force of the blows and sent reverberations through the house as the skin on a drum reverberates until it touches the soul. Bridget's eyes widened. She jumped to her feet and drew the shades in the kitchen, but even as she was returning to the table, Jezzie was standing to answer the door.

"Don't go, Jezzie. We don't know who it is."

"What if it's one of our regulars?" Jezzie said. "It

might be Mike Mulligan. He generally comes in Tuesday night. It might be Mike."

"And it might be that dead-eyed son of a bitch who put Nelly in such a state. She's just starting to get better. If he comes through that door, Nelly could sneak back into her mind to hide, like she did that first night."

"It won't hurt to go see. I'll bet it's Mike Mulligan, and he treats me pretty good."

"He treats you like a whore, Jezzie."

"That's what I am Bridget, a whore."

Jezzie stepped past Bridget's protestations toward the front door.

It was dark outside, the lantern not alight as it usually was on business nights. So Jezzie could see nothing but blackness. Mike Mulligan, it would be, Jezzie thought. Shy he was with her, and sometimes he brought a flower as though she were a lady and he a gentleman. Jezzie had a special spot in her heart and in her bed for Mike Mulligan. She would do something special for him tonight, just as he did special things for her.

She opened the door a crack, and darkness leaked into the room. "Is that you, Mike?" she asked, her voice beginning to quaver.

BAM! The blow to the door tore it from Jezzie's hands and sent it crashing against her cheek. She spun unconscious to the floor, leaking lifeblood from a cut on her cheek.

They were drunk, Jack Galt and Leaks Donnan. Donnan came in spraddle-legged, willing his alcohol-numbed body to follow Galt.

The alcohol had left only a flush on Galt's face. He

showed no emotion, not even alcohol lighting a flicker of humanity.

"Where's Nelly?" Galt whispered, his voice dead as his eyes. "Bring her here."

Bridget stood transfixed at the kitchen door. She tried to speak, but she couldn't, standing impaled on Galt's stare.

"Bring her here, damn it! This is a whorehouse and I am in need of a whore. Get her down here!"

"We're closed," Bridget whispered.

"Closed, hell. Who ever heard of a whorehouse being closed? Get Nelly. My friend and me are having a party."

The thump of feet rattled down the narrow staircase like a boulder rolling down a mountain. Beulah burst into the room. Her face was red, eyes squinted almost shut, and in her hands was the Parker double-barrel shotgun. The woman was a force, a strong force, and her entry shoved Galt and Donnan back a step.

"You Galt?"

Galt nodded.

"Going to kill you. No man should do what you did to Sally."

"I was never charged with that."

"No matter, I'm going to kill you anyhow. You, too, Leaks, you slimy little bastard."

Donnan's face was dead white. His eyebrows had crawled up his forehead to make room for eyes round as roller bearings.

A dull red color had come to Galt's face. "Don't you threaten me with no gun. Ain't no whore can threaten me with a gun."

"Bridget, cover your ears. This will make a helluva lot of noise in this little room."

Bridget nodded.

KATHUMP!

The force of the blast rattled every window on the first floor and brushed Jack Galt aside as he lunged for the door. Beulah swung the shotgun's muzzle toward the suddenly sober Leaks Donnan. Donnan dived toward the door as the blast shattered the window, showering him with broken glass. He yowled once, his voice disappearing in the clatter of running feet.

Beulah turned toward Bridget, quivering now in the door to the kitchen.

"Whatever in the hell prompted you two to open that door?"

"Jezzie, I . . . uh . . . Mike Mulligan."

Beulah sighed. "Well, it's done now. You lock the door and get over there and take care of Jezzie. I'll go upstairs and make sure that Nelly's all right. We'll get Ole here in the morning to fix everything up."

Beulah stepped toward the stairs.

"Beulah?" The words were stretched tight.

"Yeah?"

"Were you trying to kill them?"

"No." Beulah said. "Nelly doesn't have any pigs."

Bridget shook her head as Beulah climbed the stairs toward Nelly.

Jim Pratt sat behind his desk in the Stillwater County Courthouse. The office was government utilitarian. A small dark-stained oak desk with a green leather pad built into the top was backed against the windows. Low-backed oak chairs lined the opposite wall.

The office occupied the southwest corner of the second floor of the courthouse, collecting the morning and afternoon sun. Pratt played the sun to his benefit. Visitors to his office could see little more than his silhouette against the bright light, their own faces revealed in minute detail.

But now Pratt didn't want to see the man sitting across from him. Head down, he scribbled furiously at a sheet of paper on his desk, hoping the Stillwater County sheriff would leave his office.

Drinkwalter didn't budge, waiting patiently for Pratt to finish his game. Pratt was a doodler. The scratches on the pad meant nothing. They were window dressing only for the self-portrait Pratt was trying to paint. So Drinkwalter waited quietly, knowing that the game needed to be played out.

The sheriff saw only Pratt's shadow, but he knew the county attorney would be dressed in a three-piece suit, gold watch fob strung across the vest. Pratt had three suits. He alternated the gray and the blue wool suits workdays and wore a black suit to church on Sunday. Which suit would he be wearing today, gray or blue? Drinkwalter bet on the blue—even money.

The sheriff's attention drifted to a calendar hanging on the east wall. Tuesday. Fifteen minutes and the Commerce Club would be staging its noon meeting at the Stockman. Pratt, perennial president, was beginning to fidget. Pratt was a man of habit, and he didn't like his schedule interrupted. He scratched wide, jagged lines on the sheet of paper.

"I really don't know what I can do," he said, elaborately, pulling his hunter-cover watch from his vest and studying it intently.

"You could do your job."

The comment elicited another flurry of doodling at the desk, and Drinkwalter continued. "The man broke into Nelly's with such force that he knocked Jezzie unconscious. Doc sewed up her cheek, but she'll likely have a scar there for the rest of her life."

"Well, we can't flaw a man for being in a hurry to get into Nelly's, now can we?" Pratt laughed, a little nervous laugh.

"The last time he visited the house, he so terrified Nelly that she's been under Doc's care ever since."

"No law on the books about frightening people, is there? If there was a law like that, we'd have to ban Edgar Allan Poe, wouldn't we?"

Pratt looked at his watch again. "Sheriff, I've really got to be going. I can't waste any more time here. . . ."

"Doing your job. Is that it? You can't waste any more time here doing your job?"

"Now look here, Sheriff, I serve the people of—"

"He killed a woman in Billings, and probably Glendive and who knows where else. If we don't stop him, he will kill another. We've got to stop him."

Pratt leaned forward in his chair, his face lost in the light streaming in from the window.

"That's not true. We don't know he killed that woman in Billings or Glendive or anywhere else. We just know that Big Jim Thompson thinks he did."

Pratt leaned back, hooking his thumbs in his suspenders and taking on a professorial air. "If your friend Thompson had any evidence, he could have presented it to the Yellowstone County attorney and asked that the case be prosecuted.

"He didn't have that evidence, Frank. Galt has never

even been charged with one of those offenses. As far as the State of Montana and I are concerned, Frank, he is as pure as the driven snow."

Pratt shook his head. "What do you want me to do: haul Nelly's whores in here and have them testify against an Eagles Nest businessman? What kind of a message would that be? The reputation of this city is more important than one whore being frightened and another taking a little rap on the cheek."

"Eight stitches. That's more than a little rap."

"Whatever," Pratt said, dismissing Drinkwalter with a wave of his hand.

Drinkwalter sagged back in his chair.

Pratt continued, "There's another point here that you haven't thought about in your zest to persecute this newcomer. Nelly operates her business at the largess of this community. This is no longer the Wild West, Sheriff. The good people of Eagles Nest turn a blind eye to Nelly's. But if something should happen that brings that woman into the limelight, there will be a hue and cry to shut her establishment down.

"While you and I might not avail ourselves of the services she offers, she does fill a need within this community. Shutting her down could loose the beast in the men who frequent that place. Our women wouldn't be safe. Now, you wouldn't want that to happen would you?"

Drinkwalter cleared his throat, willing his voice to be level and reasonable. "Jim, this man took a woman out of her office job in Billings and put her on the street as a whore. He let men use her body for whatever they wanted, and he kept the money. Whenever he felt like it, he would beat her up so she would know that he was in full control, that she was nothing more than an animal with no freedom.

"And when she became so desperate that she decided to run, he took a knife to her. No man could do to her what he did with that knife. Jack Galt isn't human, Jim. He started that way, but he is pure evil now. If you don't do something to stop him, he will do the same thing to some woman in our town. How do you suppose they'll feel then when they find out you knew Galt is a killer and you did nothing?"

Pratt leaned across his desk. "You have no evidence that he has done anything wrong, Frank. So get off his back. It's the law, Frank."

"There is a higher law, Jim, and the penalty is much higher for those who break that law or refuse to enforce it."

"I'm a student of earthly law," Pratt said. "That's what I deal with. I have to leave the higher law to people like you. But I will tell you this, Frank Drinkwalter: The law works both ways. So far as the law is concerned, Jack Galt is a model citizen. You seem bent on harassing that man. Rumors are rumors, Frank, and the law is the law.

"Now, I've enjoyed our little chat, but I have more important things to do. The Commerce Club is meeting. We will be discussing means of attracting more businesses to this community. We will also appoint someone to approach Mr. Galt, to ask him to join our efforts.

"I hope I've made myself perfectly clear."

Pratt rose from his desk, donned his hat, and strode out without so much as a look back. Frank Drinkwalter rose slowly from his chair. His eyes squinted almost shut. The law is the law, but there are more ways to access it than through strutting little popinjays.

Jack Galt stood at the forge, shaping a pair of heavy hinges for a rancher. The rancher wanted hinges heavy enough to hold a pole gate. The old man had planted the ends of two heavy logs on either side of the road leading to his ranch house, and then hoisted a third on top. The bark had been stripped off the logs, and he burned his brand into the top log, a sign that he owned the ranch and everything on it. Nobody else would build a monument for the rancher, so he was doing it himself.

Galt was shaping the red-hot metal with his hammer: one tap for the metal, and two for the anvil. Establish a rhythm that beats in your soul, Shorty Gildner had said. Gildner knew everything there was to know about blacksmithing, but he knew nothing about Jack Galt's soul. Still, he taught Galt rhythm, and how to fashion hinges and horseshoes.

The rhythm was running through Galt: *tap . . . tap, tap . . . tap . . . tap, tap*. The metal strap was taking shape, and Galt shoved it back into the coals to collect heat.

Forges's fires had long since burned any sweat from Galt. The heat and the smoke from fires had left his skin tough and dark as tanned leather.

Tap . . . tap, tap . . . tap . . . tap, tap. The beat of the hammer drove consciousness from Galt's mind. He was melded to its heat and the smell of burning coal and coke and the ring of the hammer on anvil and heat-softened metal. The work stripped him of his mind, leaving him in a blissful state of unconsciousness. Work was sanctuary from thoughts about those times when . . . *tap* . . . *tap, tap, clatter.*

Galt shook his head. He had broken his rhythm, allowed those thoughts to break into his work. He couldn't do that. He had to have asylum, one place where he could hide from . . . what had happened before. Remember, now, what Gildner said about the beat that rings into a man's soul. Remember the beat in the nerves and muscles and use it to drive away those thoughts.

Tap . . . *tap, tap* . . . *tap* . . . *tap, tap.*

Jack Galt didn't hear the *click* of boot heels against the ash-and oil-stained floor so much as sensed that someone entered the smithy through the shaft of light that represented the door on the west side of the building.

Set that rhythm until it beats into your soul, Galt sang to himself. Let that rhythm ring in the hollowness of his chest where the soul resides.

"Galt."

The words came soft, but strangely insistent. It was the sheriff, and that meant bad news. Galt bristled.

"Galt."

"That's my name."

"I've got a restraining order for you."

Galt hid his eyes from the sheriff, but they glowed red with the heat of the coals and the indignation of having to deal with people who protected themselves with paper.

"I'm busy. You can put it on the table over there."

"No, I can hand it to you, and you can take it."

The sheriff stepped up behind Galt, and Galt wondered what it would feel like to take the red-hot hinge strap and plunge it into the sheriff's face. The sheriff had no power of his own, only the power given him. Jack Galt could brand the sheriff for his weakness, the hinge strap burning its way through the skin and the muscle and the bone of Frank Drinkwalter's face.

Galt reached into the fire with his tongs. The hinge was hot now, just right for a branding.

"Hold it."

The words were no louder than they had been before, but an edge hung on them, sharp and fine.

Galt stepped back from the forge as though he had been burned by the hinge glowing red in the coals, and the sheriff stepped forward to meet him. Galt turned to face the sheriff, hiding from his memories behind his flat, dead eyes.

The sheriff's eyes were cold, too, but life burned in them, and resolve.

"You are a slow learner, Galt. I told you that it stops here, and you didn't listen. You went out to Nelly's and frightened that poor woman half to death.

"I have a restraining order. Judge Smythe has ordered you not to come within a quarter mile of Nelly Frobisher's place. He says if you set foot inside that quarter-mile limit, he will put you in jail for six months for contempt of court, and put a five-mile restraining order in place. Eagles Nest will be off limits, everywhere in Eagles Nest, including this shop. You'll have to move on, Galt, and nothing could please me more than that."

Drinkwalter gestured over his shoulder into the darkness of one corner. "The restraining order applies to you, too, Leaks."

Drinkwalter stared into Galt's eyes, flat and dead as a snake's eyes. "It stops here, Galt."

Drinkwalter pushed the restraining order toward Galt. Galt stared at the sheriff a moment longer, and then he took the papers.

The sheriff turned to leave, disappearing into the darkness of the smithy for a moment before reappearing in the shaft of light. He turned, stared at the dark shape silhouetted by the red glow from the forge.

Galt listened to the sheriff's footsteps retreating north toward town, his face as cold and hard as his anvil.

Leaks stepped from the darkness of his corner.

"What are we gonna do, Jack?" he whined. "No more Nelly's. We won't have any women at all. I don't think I can go very long without a whore. It's just not fair. I didn't do nothing there. It ain't fair that they should keep me away from Nelly's, too."

Galt's words came in a hiss. "Maybe we'll open a house of our own."

Leaks grinned. "And then I could go there anytime I want, and they'll do anything I want for free."

"We would have to get a woman. What about that Beulah at Nelly's?"

"Uh, no, I don't think she would do that. You know she won't have anything to do with me. She says she'd rather mate with a snake than—"

"Whore ought to know her place."

"Yes, she ought to. She shouldn't ought to take a shotgun to her customers the way she did."

Galt nodded. "Anyone you know who might make a good whore?"

"Well, there's that washerwoman. She's pretty enough, but she's got that boy of hers."

"How old is he?"

"How the hell should I know? I see him with the sheriff every now and then."

"With the sheriff?" A grin crossed Galt's face. "We'll have to look into that, Mr. Donnan. We'll have to look into that."

17

Mac stepped through the Depot door and into the rush of Sparks Pierson's words.

"I'll tell you, Mac, if I've said this once, I've said it a hundred times. The people of Eagles Nest are pure gold. They just shine. They'd build the sheriff and his bride a castle if they had the means to do it.

"First I talked to Mort Jenkins at First International Bank of Eagles Nest. When I told him what was going on, he slapped his desk so hard everyone in the bank looked up. He said Drinkwalter had asked him about that quarter section west of town.

"Bank got stuck on a bad note for it. The land isn't worth much, most of it a hill too steep to graze or farm. But there is a little vale about halfway up the hill and a spring there. I've been there. With the Yellowstone at your feet and the Beartooths on the horizon, it's about the prettiest place around.

"Jenkins said he was going to give the land to Frank for next to nothing anyway, so he'd throw it in the pot for free. Said he owed Frank for stopping a robbery. Not a shot was fired. Nobody was hurt. Most of the customers didn't even know it was being robbed. So Jenkins said he would pitch in the land.

"Went over and talked to Sal Salbador, and he said he'd let the lumber and supplies go for ten percent of cost. Said that was the least he could do after all the sheriff had done for him.

"Pete Pfeister at the Absaloka Saloon said he could round up a hundred men at a moment's notice. Said that many and more owed the sheriff a day or two of hard work."

Pierson was beaming. "Pure gold these people, pure gold. Oh, and Jenkins's wife started in on the women, and they're planning a shindig like this town has never seen. They've already picked out the plans for the house. You run a bit of gossip past that bunch, and they'd see it a dozen different ways. But they sifted through the plans and came up with a dream house. They all fell in love with it."

Sparks cocked his head and stared down at Mac.

"You know how it is that you can look at something a dozen different times and see the same thing, and the next time the shadows or the light is different, and it changes?"

Mac nodded, remembering how the patch of sego lilies had transformed the Keyser Creek pasture.

"Well," Sparks continued. "I've seen Major Stilson a dozen different ways and didn't like any of the views very much. Struts around like the sun rose and set on him, gimping once in a while with his old war wounds when there were ladies present. He has four-flusher written all over him. But he was standing there when I was talking to Sal Salbador about the lumber. He said he would put in the foundation so it would be cured and ready to go by the time the house raising started. He said he would be pleased to do that for the sheriff."

Mac stared at Sparks. "Stilson said he would do that?"

"Said it was the least he could do. Isn't that something?"

Mac agreed. That was really something.

Pierson leaned over the counter and winked. "Mac, this is really going to be something special."

A frown crossed over the stationmaster's face. "There's still plenty to do, but one of the toughest jobs is up to you."

Mac looked up in despair. They left the hardest job to him, a scarecrow.

"You need to tell us exactly when she's coming."

Mac sighed in relief. "That's no trouble."

"No, but then we have to figure out how to get Frank out of town two or three days before she arrives. Think you can help us with that?"

Mac's mind went blank. In all of his young life, he had been at the beck and call of adults. "Cover this story for me, Mac, and I'll give you a quarter." "Spade this garden, and I'll pay you a dollar." "Make sure you get your assignment in." "Wash your hands, Mac."

Sparks Pierson was asking him to switch roles, to bend an adult's will to his own. Mac felt both intimidated and exhilarated. He stood dumbfounded, and then Big Jim Thompson's name popped into his head. Big Jim would know what to do. He would write to Big Jim Thompson, one sorry son of a bitch to another.

"I think I can do that, Mr. Pierson."

"Sparks, Mac. Sparks. I'm the spark, and this good town is the tinder and we're going to set a fire that will warm the cockles of Frank Drinkwalter's and his intended's hearts. That's what we're going to do, Mac."

The door to Sheriff Frank Drinkwalter's office was closed, and Mac McPherson hesitated. Drinkwalter might be talking to one of the people who came to the

sheriff because he was the last resort for settling griev-
ances short of fisticuffs or court.

But Mac couldn't discern the murmur of voices
inside, so he knocked tentatively.

"Come in, Mac." The words came muffled by the
door.

When Mac stepped in, the sheriff was staring out
the window as though the meaning of life were written
on the clouds hanging over the north hills. Mac settled
into his chair, wondering what so preoccupied the sheriff. The minutes stretched on, and finally Mac cleared
his throat.

"Do you want me to go home, come back sometime
later?"

The sheriff jerked around as though he were aware
for the first time that Mac was in the room with him.

"No, Mac. I'm sorry. Let's get to business."

But the letters and stories didn't pull the sheriff
away from his solitary thoughts. The sheriff's mood was
contagious. Mac went through his mind, imagining
what might so preoccupy Drinkwalter. Only Catherine
could touch him so. Something had happened to her.
She wouldn't be coming.

"Can't she come?"

Drinkwalter turned, trying to fathom Mac's words.
Then he folded his arms and smiled, a wan little smile.

"No, nothing like that, Mac. You'd be the first to
know if it were anything like that."

Mac cocked his head, the unasked question stretching between the two, and Drinkwalter nodded. Mac
had become his confidante as well as his Cyrano de
Bergerac that spring. He deserved an explanation.

"Mac, have you ever walked out to the west hill,

where that ridge comes down to squeeze the valley almost shut?"

"I go fishing out there once in a while."

"Have you ever climbed that ridge?"

"Nope."

The sheriff leaned back in his chair. "The first time I did it was one of these fall days when the cottonwoods go gold, and the grass is still green and some of those bushes are red and yellow as fire. The air was so clear I thought I might be able to see to the end of the world, so I started climbing. I found a little swale there, about halfway up. Off to one side there was a big rock, and I climbed it."

The sheriff stopped, his words bringing that day back to him. "The sun was full on my face, and I was damn near dizzy with what I saw. The Yellowstone was low and green and bright as a string of emeralds. It looked like a necklace set in the gold of the cottonwoods. And the Beartooths were blue and white and pure, sapphires and diamonds.

"I thought I might be in heaven. I thought that maybe the strain of climbing that hill had done me in, and I had left my body someplace down below. But I knew it couldn't be heaven without sego lilies. So I climbed off that rock and got down on my hands and knees to go through the grass in that swale. They weren't in bloom, of course, but there are sego lilies up there, the biggest patch I've ever seen. I came back the next spring, and there they were.

"Mac, if music were made from the beauty of each of those flowers, the sound would reach clear to heaven. They are an orchestra fit to play for the angels.

"That place has a special magic to it, Mac, and I

wanted to share it with Catherine. I dreamed about building a home there for the two of us. I would build stairs up to the top of that rock, and we could sit there together, and I would be in the presence of such beauty that the crown heads of Europe would be in envy. I swear God must have made that vale so he could sit there and glory in the beauty of his creation.

"There's a natural seam in the sandstone that goes down to the valley floor. It wouldn't take but a little cleaning up to make it fit for a road. The spring is good water, cold in summer and winter alike, and it tastes like nectar on a hot summer day.

"I wanted to build a house up there, so when Catherine came, she would have a home suitable for her. Us two-legged creatures generally put more value on money than on beauty. I thought I might be able to buy that swale. It sits on just a quarter section, and most of the land is up and down. Not an awful lot of grass except down on the river bottom and in that vale.

"So I talked to Mort Jenkins down at the bank about it. Turns out, it was let go for taxes, and the bank had picked it up. Told him about the vale, and the spring and the lilies. Even sketched it for him, so he could see what I was seeing in my head. He seemed to be interested in selling the piece to me."

Drinkwalter pulled the chair back from his desk and sat down, propping his head up with his arms. "I thought everything was going along all right. I rode out there this morning, just so I could be there again, just so I could think about the kind of house I would put there.

Drinkwalter, eyebrows knitting together, focused his attention on Mac. "Somebody is already building a house there. They're putting in the foundation just where I would have put it. They ran a pipe from the spring down to the house. Whoever has that house won't even have to pump water. They'll just open a valve, and water will come out, pure as can be.

"Nobody was there, so I couldn't ask who had bought it. All I could think about was that Catherine and I couldn't have it."

The sheriff leaned back in his chair and ran his hands over his face and down to his chin, staring up at the ceiling.

"It made me realize how little I have to give to Catherine. That place I rent is good enough for me, but not good enough for her. You should see her house, Mac. It puts any house in Billings to shame, and I can't put her in that place where I live."

Drinkwalter pushed himself back in his chair, straightening his back. "I came out here to build something for us, so I would have something to offer her. I've just come to realize how little I've done. I've got nothing for her. I've worked all my life as hard as I can, and I've always tried to do what's right, and I haven't got a thing to offer her."

"You've got yourself," Mac whispered.

Drinkwalter rolled his eyes and shrugged his shoulders.

"And you've got your friends," Mac added.

"Friends aren't the same as having a roof over your head."

"Sometimes they are."

"I suppose," the sheriff said, unconvinced. "I have half a mind to go down to the bank and ask Mort about that land. But it wouldn't do any good, and I don't know how I would ever have had the money to build a house, anyway. I've been living in a dream world, Mac, made up of a woman I haven't seen for damn near ten years. I built a house for her made of dreams. That's a flimsy place to live.

"When Catherine sees what a failure I've been, she might just step back on the train and go home. At least she's got a roof over her head there."

Mac wanted to tell the sheriff that the people of Eagles Nest were building the home up on the hill for him. He wanted to tell the sheriff that he had laid up a treasure of friendship and appreciation in his time in Eagles Nest. He wanted to say all of that, but he couldn't, not without breaking his word to all the people who wanted to surprise the sheriff.

Mac swallowed, choking down the words he wanted to say. "It'll work out," he squeaked. He left the sheriff's office then, and Drinkwalter rose, leaning against the windowsill, eyes focused on the rims north of Eagles Nest, and mind focused on the failure he was.

18

"I didn't know what to say," Mac said, polishing the dinner plate his mother had just handed him. "I didn't want to leave him like that, but I didn't know what to say."

Mary McPherson finished the last spoon, leaning back, hands on hips, willing the dull ache in her back to go away.

"Mac, would you mind dumping the water? I've been on my feet all day, and I'd like to sit down for a minute."

"Sure, Ma."

Mac took the pan of rinse water, walking as carefully as a man on a tightrope so he wouldn't spill the water on the way to the door. Only after he reached the door did he remember that it took two hands to carry water and one to open the door. He set the pan on the stove and opened the door. Light streamed into the night as though eager to leave the little cabin, and standing in the light, eyes dead as a snake's, stood Jack Galt.

"Hello, Mac," Galt said, his words little more than a whisper. "I've come calling on you and your mother."

Mac dropped the pan; it bounced off the wooden step, sending a spray of steaming water toward Galt. Mac slammed the door then and locked it. He stood at the door shaking, listening to Jack Galt choking as he tried to stifle his laugh outside.

The boy jumped when his mother's hands touched

his shoulders. "What is it, Mac? Who's out there?"

The words jarred Mac into consciousness. The boy ran past his mother's arms to the windows. But as he was drawing the curtain on the window, Jack Galt's face appeared. Galt was laughing, laughing at the boy's attempt to shut him out. Mac ran to the other window, and Galt was there, too. His face lit only dimly by the light leaking through the window. Mac couldn't see Galt's body, only his face suspended like a skull in the darkness. Mac could only hear Galt's laughter.

And then Galt's fists were pounding on the front door, the cabin shaking with the force of the blows. *Crash. Crash. Crash.* Mac could see the hinges tearing loose from the doorframe, yielding to what seemed to be an inexorable force.

Mac ran for the corner of his cabin where he kept his rifle. He could stop Jack Galt with his rifle. But cartridges: Where did he put the cartridges? Max pawed through his shelf, strewn with everything the boy owned. No shells. No shells for stopping Jack Galt, but then he saw the gleam of brass beside the bed. The box of shells had fallen from the shelf, cracking open and scattering the shells on the floor.

Mac scooped up two. He should be able to stop Jack Galt with two shells. His hands were shaking, and he dropped the shells twice before he squeezed them into the magazine. He pulled the lever back and up, and the shell slid into the chamber with a click. And almost as though the click were a summons, Galt burst through the door.

Galt was the devil incarnate, an aura of dull-red evil hanging like mist on his body. He looked at the rifle in Mac's hands and threw back his head and laughed. Mac didn't see Galt pull his knife from his sheath; he saw only its flash as it cut through the air in wide threatening arcs.

Mac squeezed the trigger on the rifle, but it wouldn't move. He pulled on it as hard as he could, but it seemed to be locked in place; he pounded the hammer with his hand, willing it to move forward and strike the firing pin, but it only tore bits of flesh from his hand. Mac screamed and screamed and screamed, the sound of it lost in Galt's triumphant laughter.

"Mac! Mac! Mac!"

Mac opened his eyes. His mother was standing beside him in her bedclothes, holding a lamp.

"Run, Ma! Run for your life."

"Mac, it was only a dream. Just a dream."

Mac sagged back on his bed. "It can't be a dream. It was too real."

"It was a dream, Mac. Just a dream."

"What time is it?"

"About four. I was going to get up early today, anyway. How about I start a fire—"

"Don't go outside, Ma! Don't go."

"I don't have to, Mac. I've got a fine young son who takes care of his mother. Kindling and firewood right beside the stove. You just lay here, and I'll get a fire going. Maybe you'd like some hot chocolate. I've been saving some, and there couldn't be a better morning for it. You just stay here, and I'll be back in a minute."

Mac pulled the covers up to his chin. Then he sat bolt upright in his bed. His rifle! Where was his rifle? He saw the gleam of the rifle's blued barrel, propped in the corner beside his bed. Shells! The boy's eyes darted to his shelf. No shells. His eyes dropped to the side of the bed. The shells were there, spilled from the box just as they had been in his dream.

"Ma!"

Mary McPherson dropped the stick of firewood she had been putting in the stove and darted to the boy. "Mac, what's wrong?"

"Prop the chair against the door, Ma. He's coming."

"No one's coming, Mac. No one's going to hurt you."

"Prop the chair against the door. Please, Ma?"

Mary nodded, shoving the back of a spindly chair firmly beneath the doorknob.

"Is that better, Mac?"

Mac nodded.

Mary McPherson busied herself at the stove, first some paper Mac picked up every Thursday from behind *The Eagles Nest Expository*. Ben Simpkins didn't mind if people helped themselves to his garbage. Every man has some generosity in him; that was the full extent of Simpkins's. Mary stacked a handful of kindling on top of the paper, just so. Lighting the range in the morning was a liturgy. This morning the rite would chase away Mac's dreams.

Mac had filled the boiler on the stove the night before, but it would be an hour or two in the warming, so Mary filled the coffeepot with cool water from the boiler and set it on the range front. The kindling was burning now; the fire talking to itself as it licked at its morning offering. Mary slipped some larger pieces of wood in the stove, and a little coal on top of that. She left the draft open, hoping that the coal would catch. She and Mac had some coal oil for lighting coal, but she didn't like to use it. Coal oil was a luxury.

Mary slipped the lid back on the range and the coffeepot on the lid. She was done now with the morning routine. It had soothed her, given her mind time to fit itself around Mac's screams.

Mac hadn't had a nightmare for years, not since the first year after his father had left them. They had tried to follow him, spending most of their nights in railroad cars or cheap hotels. Danger hides in strange beds in strange hotels with flimsy doors and the sounds of drunken men. Mac had nightmares then, and Mary would comfort him, as much to give ease to her own fears as his.

But now she had to help Mac through this time, talk him away from the night and lead him into the day. She returned to the boy, sitting beside him on the bed.

"What was it you dreamed about, Mac?" she asked, running her fingers through the boy's hair.

"Jack Galt. He was here, Ma. Last night. I went outside to empty the water, and he was there. He was laughing, Ma. It was the most terrible thing I've ever heard. Laughing shouldn't be like that, Ma."

"I wish Sheriff Drinkwalter hadn't told you about Galt. Stories like that get into your mind, and you can't get them out. That's all your dream was, Mac. Jack Galt wasn't here last night. It was just you thinking about what the sheriff had told you."

"But, Ma, in my dream, I couldn't find the shells for my rifle. Then I found them on the floor. The box had popped open when they fell, and some of the shells were scattered on the floor. That's the way they were this morning, Ma. The shells were scattered on the floor just the way I saw them. It wasn't a dream, Ma."

"Mac, you probably saw those shells on the floor before you went to bed. You probably thought about picking them up, but forgot. So they were all ready for your dream. That's all it was."

Mac sagged back into his pillow. "It was so real. . . ."

"Sometimes dreams seem more real than reality. Now, if you think this dream of yours is going to give you an excuse to lay slugabed, you've got another think coming."

Mac smiled. "Ah, Ma."

"Ah, Mac."

The two laughed together and Mac climbed from his bed to begin the day.

Mary had some bacon she had been saving. She fried it, Mac wolfing down the chunks and three fried eggs. How that boy could eat, and yet he never filled out. He might grow up a little, but not out. What kind of mother would people think Mary McPherson was to keep her child so skinny?

Mac thought he would stop over at *The Eagles Nest Expository*. Could be Ben Simpkins would have something for him to do. There wouldn't be much money to show for his labor. Mac could work at the paper all day, and Simpkins would send him away at night with less than a quarter in his hand. But Mac liked the smell of ink, and the sound of the press hard at work. He would go there early. Mac knew he would spend most of the day running errands for Sparks Pierson. There was a lot more to building a house than Mac had realized.

Mac looked over his shoulder at his mother as he stepped through the door into a morning wet with dew. Mary stood in the doorway and watched as he walked through the grass and trees of the river bottom to climb over the rail bed, slipping a bit on the loose gravel. He turned then and waved at his mother before disappearing over the top.

Mary turned to reenter the cabin, stopping when a glint of enameled metal caught her eye. The blue enameled washbasin lay off the corner of the step and when Mary picked it up, she noticed a slight dent in one side. Mac must have dropped it. That's odd, she thought, carrying the basin into the house. Mac wasn't usually so careless.

19

The sheriff sat behind his desk, back stiff as a man awaiting his drop at the gallows. He had wiped the desk clean that afternoon of everything that had gone before, clearing it for everything to come.

Precisely in the center of the desk was a letter from Catherine Lang. The sheriff had been conjuring the contents of the letter, turning it this way and that so the words might tumble out on his desk. But the desk was empty of words. Only the letter was there.

Drinkwalter picked up the missive and passed it to Mac. "Apples, Mac. Just the faintest smell of apples. She's been in the park again, sitting at the same bench she was sitting at when we first met.

"I think she's wondering whether she should come out here. She must be wondering whatever possessed her to stake her future on someone like me who's never made anything of his life."

"She's probably weeping her eyes out," Mac said.

The sheriff's eyes jerked to Mac.

Mac looked the sheriff full in the eyes. "She's probably wondering how she ever hooked her train to a sorry son of a bitch like you."

Drinkwalter's face tightened.

"I figure she's been reading my letters and bewailing all those years she wasted on you when she could have a handsome young lad like me."

The sheriff cocked his head. Then he smiled and chuckled, Mac joining in.

"I have been doing that, haven't I?"

Mac nodded. "Poor Sheriff Drinkwalter has to marry the woman of his dreams. Poor, damn sheriff."

The sheriff hooted. "Yes, I am one sorry son of a bitch."

"Every sorry son of a bitch in the nation holds you up as an ideal that we all strive for."

The sheriff laughed again. "Read the letter, Mac."

Mac wiped an imaginary tear from the corner of his eye and opened the letter.

"Beloved:

"I am in the process of shedding the person I have been. I never imagined all the material things that are necessary to life. Simple things like canceling my milk and ice deliveries, changing the subscriptions of my magazines to Mrs. Frank Drinkwalter of Eagles Nest, Montana. I run that name over my tongue a hundred times a day, and each time it brings a smile to my lips.

"I intend to bring some of my mother's furniture with me. I hope you don't mind. Her family has been in America since its birth, and she has furniture passed along to her from that time. They are beautiful useless things, but I would like to keep them to pass along to our children so that they can have a sense of their roots. Our children: Is that not a wondrous thing to consider? If we should be blessed with a boy, I hope that he is the spitting image of his father. And a girl: She must be as my mother was. How beautiful she was as a young woman.

"Mr. Clavedatcher, my mother's attorney, has been scurrying about to handle the legal details of her passing. And through it all, I think only of you. I awake in the morning with your face clearly before me, and fall to sleep at night pretending that I am resting my head on your cheek.

"Franklin Nicholas Drinkwalter, you are the man of my dreams, and soon those dreams will become a reality. I will be with you in that wondrous place you describe in your letters, and nothing—nothing—will ever tear us apart.

"I've saved the best for last. I've bought my train ticket to Montana. How many times I've dreamed of stepping up to the stationmaster and saying, 'One-way trip to Eagles Nest, Montana, please.' I went to the station Saturday and bought the ticket, and the vendor said, 'Eagles Nest, Montana: whereabouts would that be?'

" 'That would be next door to paradise,' I said. 'Just next door to paradise.'

"He gave me the oddest look, and then he smiled. Isn't it odd about smiles? The more you give, the more you receive. Without realizing it, I've been smiling at everyone, and everyone is smiling at me. I'm so pleased they can share my happiness.

"Beloved, I know this is presumptuous of me, but it has been a tradition of the family Lang since the Revolution to marry off its women on the Fourth of July. Could we please continue that tradition? I will be arriving in Eagles Nest July 2. I'll be bringing my own gown, and the service will necessarily be small. I don't know anyone in

Eagles Nest to stand up with me, but I would like Mac's mother to be there. I've not heard two words about her, but I know that she must be a wonderful person to have raised such a fine young man.

"Mac, please ask your mother to meet me at the station. I hate to be an imposition, but I will need someone to help me get acquainted with Eagles Nest, and I am giddy with excitement. I'm afraid I'll suffer some faux pas in the city of Eagles Nest and embarrass my husband—husband, how that rings in my ear.

"I must go now, beloved. Mac, please take care of my darling for me.

"Forever yours,
"Catherine Lang"

Mac sighed and laid the letter back on the desk. The sheriff took it gently, as though it were a newborn child.

"She wants to have children," Drinkwalter said. "We never talked about it. I've not given it a lot of thought, but I would be pleased to have children, Mac, if they turned out like you."

Mac tried to smile, but he realized for the first time that he wasn't gaining a surrogate mother but losing a surrogate father. Mac hadn't realized how important the sheriff had become to him, and how much Catherine would be a wedge driven between them. There would be no more magic afternoons fishing with Drinkwalter and Big Jim Thompson. He might even lose his job. The sheriff could carry his mail home to Catherine at noon. She could do his correspondence.

Then the boy realized how selfish he was being. The

sheriff was his friend. Catherine was too. He felt close to her even though he had never met her. How could he put his own selfish interests ahead of his two best friends?

Mac turned bright red, and he dropped his head against his chest, feeling revulsion with himself.

"What's wrong, Mac?"

Mac couldn't tell Drinkwalter what he had been thinking. He was too ashamed of himself. His mind skittered around like a drop of cold water on a hot skillet, trying to hide his spitefulness from his best friend.

"Uh, I was just wondering about fox pass?"

"Fox pass?"

"In the letter Catherine talks about . . ."

The boy held out his hand for the letter, skimming through the lines. "Right here, it says: *'suffer some faux pas and embarrass my husband.'*

"What is it about a fox pass that makes it so embarrassing?" Mac sagged limply in his chair, hiding his eyes, hoping that he had said something that would lead the sheriff's mind astray.

"Faux pas, Mac. The word is *faux pas."*

"How do you know that? You can't even read."

The moment the words came from Mac's mouth, he wished that he hadn't said them. He didn't know what made him so spiteful. He dropped his head to his chest, hiding from his friend's eyes.

Drinkwalter's voice was almost a whisper. "Archie's Ice Cream in Cincinnati. People would go there for ice cream, and he would read to them. It was something special, sitting at the counter and listening to him pull the words from the page. I think he must have been an actor once, or wished that he had been. It was almost like watching a play with only one character.

"Archie was reading to us one day, and he said *fox pass*. Catherine interrupted him, so softly that no one but the three of us could have heard what he said. '*Faux pas*,' she said. 'It means "false step" in French.'

"I thought that would upset Archie, but he just beamed. He stepped into the back room and came out with a yellow rose. He gave it to Catherine. 'You gave me the gift of your attention,' he said. 'It is only fair that I should give you something in return.'

"That was when I learned what *faux pas* means, Max. When you can't read, you learn to pay special attention to what other people mean."

"Sorry."

"It's all right, Mac. If I knew how to read, we couldn't have become such good friends. We are good friends, aren't we?"

"Best . . ." Mac said, the words choked off by the knot in his throat. Mac looked up, but the sheriff's face was blurry, disappearing behind the sheen of tears in the boy's eyes. He jumped to his feet and turned his back on the sheriff, his fists tightening as he strained to hold back the tears.

Mac McPherson wouldn't cry. Nobody could make him cry.

"Mac, I have a favor to ask. I was wondering if maybe your mother could come over to my place and see if there is anything she could do to make it a little more . . . well, feminine. Maybe put up some curtains or something.

"I never thought of it as much more than a place to eat and sleep. Now Catherine's coming out, and I don't have anything better to offer her. Maybe your ma could look it over. If she saw something that needs doing, I'll do it or pay her whatever it costs and for her time.

"Do you suppose she'd do that for me?"

Mac nodded and then he stepped out the door. "I'll go talk to her," the boy said, the words dying behind him.

Mary McPherson looked up as her son stepped through the door. Mac's cheeks seemed red, chapped. The wind must have picked up a bit, although Mary hadn't heard it sighing through the tops of the cottonwoods outside.

"Hi, Ma."

"Hi, Mac."

Mary smiled. "Sounds like a vaudeville act, doesn't it?"

"Just me and Ma tripping the light fantastic on the boards," Mac said, but Mary could see that her son's mind wasn't on banter.

"How did your day go?"

"Okay. I did a story for Ben Simpkins: Town Council voted to put in a boardwalk next to the park on the south side of Main Street. He paid me a dime. Nobody gets rich in the newspaper business."

"Some people make their mothers very proud."

Mac dropped the dime into the tin can beside the range and turned to smile at his mother. "Thought maybe we could have an ice-cream cone at the soda fountain. They've got strawberry and maple nut."

"Strawberry for you and maple nut for me," Mary said, smiling. "Did the sheriff find out when Catherine would be coming?"

"Yeah, July second."

"Not much time to finish the house."

"Nope." Mac clapped his hand to his forehead. "Dang it!"

"Mac!"

"Sorry, Ma, it's just that I forgot to tell Sparks when Catherine is coming. I have to get the word to Big Jim, too, so he can figure out some ruse to get the sheriff out of town."

Mac shook his head. "I'm letting everyone down."

"You're not letting me down."

Mac looked up and smiled. "No, I'll never let you down, Ma."

Mac rolled up his sleeves and joined his mother at the stove. She was rinsing her wash, squeezing hot, clear water from each piece putting it in a wicker basket.

Mac gestured to his mother's chair, and she nodded. It had been a long hard day. People were putting their winter clothing away. They wanted it washed, pressed, and folded to hold the scent of the sun through summer and fall. Montanans need the scent of sun in winter to remind them that the season doesn't last forever.

Mac wrung the last piece of clothing, putting it into a basket to carry to the clothesline outside. He cocked his head. "Ma, you'd never guess what the sheriff's real name is."

"His real name?"

"All of it. The whole thing."

"No, I guess I wouldn't."

"Franklin Nicholas Drinkwalter. That's a lot of name to hang on anyone."

Mary smiled. "Parents have the highest hopes for

their children. They look at those wrinkled little lives and see presidents and senators and captains of industry, so they pin grand appellations on them."

Mac's eyelid crawled up. "Did you pin a grand appellation on me?"

"Of course we did—Maximilien."

"Maximilien? My name is Maximilien?"

"That's what it says on your birth certificate, but it never really stuck."

"So I'm never going to be a president or a senator or a captain of industry?"

"No, you're never going to be Maximilien."

"Thank God for that."

Mary laughed.

"Ma, you got to promise you won't ever tell anyone that my name is Maximilien."

"I won't. Actually, your name is Mac. We both looked at you, and we both said Mac. You were Mac as a baby and you're Mac now. I just didn't want you to get on Sheriff Franklin Nicholas Drinkwalter too hard just because his parents gave him a moniker like that."

Mac stared at his mother in disbelief. "Me tease Franklin Nicholas? I'm surprised you think so little of me."

Mary smiled.

Then Mac turned serious. "After I finish the wash, do you suppose I could go to the station and talk to Sparks? I'm sorry about the ice cream, but—"

"Mr. Pierson," Mary interjected.

Mac nodded, impatient to continue. "Do you suppose I could go to the station and tell Mr. Pierson that Catherine—?"

"Miss Lang."

"Ah, Ma."

"Miss Lang."

"All right. Could I tell Mr. Pierson when Miss Lang is coming so we can tell Mr. Thompson in Billings, so he can figure out a way to get Mr. Drinkwalter into Billings so we can build that"—Mac visibly bit his lip—"house?"

"I suppose, Maximilien."

"That's Mr. Maximilien to you, Mrs. McPherson," Mac said, and they both chuckled.

Sparks leaned back in his telegrapher's cage. One eye was squinted shut, and his pencil beat out a *rat-a-tat-tat* on the counter as he thought aloud.

"July second. That doesn't give us much time. The foundation is set up just fine. Major Stilson was in here just yesterday, patting himself on the back. Pete Pfeister says it will take three days, even with the crew he's put together. I suppose we could speed it up a little by having the lumber all picked out and ready to go. We can even haul it up there the night before and have it all set. The ladies will want an early start to get all the food up there. Probably need more wagons for that than for the lumber."

Pierson looked at Mac and grinned. "Pfeister is taking a couple kegs of beer. Nothing like a mug of beer after a long day. Nothing like a mug of beer."

Pierson sucked in his breath as though it were foam from the top of a mug.

"We'll have to get the sheriff out of town from June twenty-eighth through July first. And he can't come back until after dark July first or he'll see the house. Three days. Do you suppose, Sheriff Thompson can hold Frank in Billings for three days?"

Mac grinned. "I suspect he'll do that if he has to sit on him."

"Good. I suppose it would be best to send a telegram."

Pierson leaned over the counter, licking the end of his pencil before he began writing on the form. "James Thompson, Yellowstone County Sheriff, Yellowstone County Courthouse, Billings, Montana."

Pierson leaned back.

"Now what should we say?"

"Need SSOB gone June twenty-eighth at night through July first. Imperative he remain until after dark July first. Sign it SSOB."

"SSOB?"

Mac cocked his head. "It's a code sheriffs use in an emergency."

Pierson nodded. "All right. I'll send it right off. Mac, if you don't mind, maybe you could go to the lumberyard. Sal told Klaus to pick good stock. We'll need nails and paint and windows and doors. Everything all set to go. You do that, and I'll go over and tell Pfeister when we need the men. I better taste that beer. I wouldn't want him to be giving us anything second rate."

Mac grinned. "You're a good man, Sparks Pierson, to be so concerned for others."

"Thanks, Mac. I will drink a toast to your stunning perspicacity."

"What's that mean?"

"It's a two-dollar word that means you're almost as smart as me."

"When I get as smart as you, will I be allowed to drink beer?"

"Can't imagine it any other way. That's how I got so smart."

Mac grinned and stepped through the door.

The Dutchman stood behind the counter in his lumberyard listening to Mac. He seemed to be standing at attention, his back carved stiff by his Prussian ancestors. Two decades in America hadn't rubbed a bit of the old country off Berger. He considered it an affront that Herr Pierson had sent a boy to talk to him about the lumber. Still, the boy was respectful. In these days in this country, you couldn't ask for much more than that. The two had spent the evening sorting through lumber and loading it into wagons.

"Ya, all vill be firsts. You tell dat Sparks he don't have to worry none. Tell him, I got two vagons, but I don't want to tie dem up all day, so would be good he get me anudder one."

"Yes, sir."

Berger smiled. Respect: That was good.

Mac walked away from the lumberyard into the night. His mother was fixing salmon loaf. Salmon, or any fish that Mac didn't catch, was a luxury, but with the five dollars a week Mac was bringing home, they could afford a little luxury now and then.

The boy could smell the salmon thirty feet from the cabin door, and his mouth watered. He was hungry, not hurting hungry, but hungry nevertheless, and salmon was a treat.

The boy was about to step into the cabin when something moved through the dark shadows to the north of the McPherson home. It slipped away before Mac's eyes found it—a deer probably. Probably a deer going to the river to drink. The boy stepped into the cabin and his mother's smile.

Jack Galt waited until the door closed, and then he eased toward the railroad. Wild rose tugged at his pants as he passed. Damned roses. Not good for one damn thing except tearing clothes and sticking passersby. If it were up to him, he would pile all the roses in the world in one big heap and set them afire.

What a fire that would be, its flames roaring to the heavens. All those timid little souls who spent their summers on their knees worshiping at the altar of roses would wail and gnash their teeth. Galt grinned, light glinting from his teeth.

The thought eased Galt's temper. He had caught only glimpses of Mary McPherson as she fussed around the stove fixing dinner. He wanted to know more about her. He needed to know more about her. He might be wrong about Mary McPherson, but Jack Galt wasn't wrong often. If he watched the woman long enough, his mother would appear from her hiding place in the McPherson woman. It had always been that way.

Galt scrambled up the gravel bank to the track north of the McPherson shack, pausing to see if anyone was watching. Then he stepped over the track and walked toward Main Street. The sun was fading behind the hills to the west. That was good, Jack Galt thought as he walked toward the Absaloka Saloon. Darkness was always better than light. Maybe he would stop for a beer before he went back to his place.

20

Sheriff Frank Drinkwalter stared at the telegram in Mac's hand and shook his head. "It never rains, but it pours." He stood, peering through the office's dusty window at the lilac bushes north of the jail.

"I'm out here for years, and nothing happens. Once a month I fetch Tippins from the Absaloka. Once in a while I go tell Milt Jenkins's wife to stop beating on her husband. Every now and then I shake Leaks Donnan down for one petty theft or another. And once in a blue moon I go to school because a bunch of kids get together to beat up on one.

"But now, just when Catherine is coming, the whole thing falls apart. Jack Galt and now this."

Drinkwalter shook his head, turning to stare at Mac. "Don't read the telegram again: Just tell me what it means in your own words."

Mac cleared his throat. "Yellowstone County Sheriff Big Jim Thompson requests your presence in Billings because one of his deputies is in cahoots with a known crook. The miscreants are plotting to have his preeminence booted out of the sheriff's office. Thompson knows one deputy is involved, but he doesn't know if anyone else is. So he wants you to go to Billings and . . ."

Mac glanced again at the telegram. "And stake out the building where the crook lives. He has to know who the other traitors are. He says he'll pay your expenses

227

on the milk run. You can stay with him, and he promises to take you out to dinner at the Northern Hotel one night."

"One night? He's dragging me to Billings just before Catherine comes to Eagles Nest, and he's willing to take me to the Northern one night? I buy Tilly's sandwiches by the ton every time he journeys up the Yellowstone to visit his preeminence on me. And he will take me out to dinner one night at the Northern Hotel? He is the cheapest son of a bitch in the whole state of Montana and beyond."

Drinkwalter shook his head. "One damn dinner. That son of a bitch!"

Mac cleared his throat. "It might not be so bad."

Drinkwalter's eyes jerked to the boy.

"You said you wanted Ma to go through your place and put a . . . uh . . . feminine touch to it. She can't do that while you're banging around in there, so maybe while you're gone, she could go in and put up some curtains and things like that."

Drinkwalter rubbed his chin with the palm of his hand. "That's true. It wouldn't really be a total loss of time, and it would give me something to do so I wouldn't be worrying so much."

Drinkwalter peered down at Mac. "You asked your mother yet?"

"I talked to her, but—"

"She say no?"

Mac shook his head.

"Well, how about I walk home with you. I'll ask her myself. She can tell me what it'll run for curtains and towels and stuff like that, and I'll make sure she's got enough. That all right with you?"

Mac nodded, his mind forty miles away in Billings: crooked deputies and a plot to unseat the Yellowstone County sheriff? How could a fisherman foist such a feeble lie off on people who had heard him tell masterpieces?

"I'll tell you, that was the biggest damn fish I've ever seen. Saw him rise, but I didn't have fish line, so quick as could be, I braided my horse's mane into a line. It was strong, but I didn't know how long it would hold a fish like him. I'd been fighting him for near an hour and had him skittering along the top of that pool when this really humongous bull trout came up and swallowed him in one bite. Well, I'll tell you I had a fight on my hands, then . . ."

That was a lie a man could be proud of, but nudge Big Jim out of his genre, and he comes up with a story a two-year-old kid wouldn't believe, and Drinkwalter falls for it.

Mac's faith in the sheriff was shaken. Drinkwalter must be the most gullible son of a bitch in the Pacific Northwest. Telling lies was an honorable profession, but believing them . . . Mac shook his head.

"Something wrong, Mac?" Drinkwalter reached to take his hat from the tree beside the door.

"Think I'm getting a headache."

"Oh," Drinkwalter said.

Mac shook his head and followed. Now the headache was a lie, a nice easy irrefutable sort of lie. It didn't stretch anyone's imagination. It didn't have crooked deputies and a crook trying to unseat the Yellowstone County sheriff. Next time that sorry son of a bitch came to Eagles Nest, Mac would have to give him a remedial course in lying. A man shouldn't be so awkward at it; it was an embarrassment to him and to his friends.

Mac stepped ahead of the sheriff at the cabin, opening the door only wide enough for him to slip through. "Ma, Sheriff Drinkwalter's here."

Mary McPherson looked up from the rinsing tub steaming on the stove. She picked the last piece of clothing from the water to wring it dry and hang it on the line outside, but then she realized that it was a woman's undergarment. It would not be proper to handle a woman's undergarment while the sheriff was in her home. She threw the piece back into the water and smiled at Mac. "Invite him in."

She reached for a towel, blowing back a wisp of hair that fell across her eye. She smiled at the sheriff as he stepped through the door, but the effort seemed to exhaust her.

Drinkwalter removed his hat and smiled at Mary McPherson. The woman was tired, as well she might be. Mary and Mac had hung clotheslines from every available tree outside the cabin, and each of the lines was laden with clothing, drying in the soft breeze and warm sun. Drinkwalter had caught the scent of sun-dried clothes as he neared the cabin, and for a moment he envied Mary McPherson. Not many people could capture the sun, however briefly.

"Ma'am, you're busy now. Maybe I could come back tomorrow?"

Mary smiled. "Please sit down, Sheriff. I put a roast

on this afternoon, and it should be just about finished. We would be pleased to have you join us."

"I don't want to intrude."

Mary smiled. "It would be especially nice for me to talk to another adult. Mac has gotten much too smart for me."

"He's been pretty smart with me lately, too," Drinkwalter said.

"Sit down, Sheriff. Mac, could you set the table? I'll check the roast."

Mary bent over, bracing her back with one hand on her knee as she pulled open the heavy oven door. She lifted the lid from the roaster. The meat was done to a golden brown and the potatoes soft to the fork and brown from the meat's juices. The smell of the meal washed over her, and she almost fainted with the scent of it, but she didn't know how she would get the roast from the oven. She couldn't lift the roaster one-handed, and she couldn't kneel on the floor as she did when she was alone. She didn't want them to see how much her back ached.

Mary pushed herself upright with her arm.

"Mac, could you get the roast, please? I forgot to wash my hands."

Mac cocked his head and studied his mother. Her hands were almost bloody with washing, but he nodded and stepped toward the stove.

"Use those towels, so you don't burn yourself," Mary said. "Maybe you could cut the roast into slices for me."

Mac nodded, reaching for the family's only knife: bread cutter, meat carver, and vegetable slicer. The meat was done to perfection. Mac's mouth watered as he cut slice after slice from the roast. He was thinking how the meat would taste tonight and how it would taste in sandwiches later. They would be as good as Tilly's sandwiches, better because his mother had made them.

Today was special in the McPherson household. Roast beef was a rarity.

Mary offered her hands to Mac and the sheriff, wincing a little as they took them.

"Dear Lord, thank you for the bounty you have given us. Thank you for our health, for the beauty of your creation and the time you have given us to share in it. Please give us the wisdom to see the path you have set for us and the courage to follow it. Amen."

"Amen."

"Amen."

"Sheriff, would you please serve yourself?"

Drinkwalter nodded, taking a piece of meat and a potato as though he were taking the sacrament in church. And when each had been served, they began to eat. The meat was excellent and the potatoes heavenly.

Each time Mac took a bite, he closed his eyes as though transported by the epicurean delight.

"Ma, this is so good."

"Thank you, Mac."

The boy cocked his head. "Why did you fix roast tonight?"

Mary stopped eating, hesitating before she cleared her throat. "Today is our anniversary, your father's and mine. He loved roast beef, so I try to serve roast beef on our anniversary."

"Happy anniversary," Drinkwalter said.

Mary smiled. "Thank you. Now you have to tell me about Catherine."

Drinkwalter hesitated.

"You are among friends, Sheriff."

Drinkwalter shook his head in exasperation. "I can't bend my words around Catherine. They're too brittle, and she's . . ."

Drinkwalter sighed. "I can't for the life of me understand why she would have me."

Mary smiled. "It's no different for her. She's wondering if you will still be attracted to her, or forget the wedding or perhaps marry someone else. She will be wondering how someone like you could possibly be interested in someone like her."

Mary leaned across the table toward the sheriff, wincing a little at the pain in her back. "You aren't the first two people in the world who have gone through this. It's the same with all of us. If you want me to, I'll look through your place and soften the edges for you. But I won't hang curtains or do anything like that. Catherine will want to do that. It's up to her to build a nest for the two of you."

Drinkwalter sighed and stood. "You know she wants you to stand up with her at the wedding."

"No, I didn't."

"Mac didn't tell you?"

Mary shook her head. "Mac?"

"What's so important about standing up with someone?"

"It's important," Mary said, wondering where she would ever find a dress for the wedding.

"Ma'am?"

"Mary. Please call me Mary."

"Mary, I noticed that your hands seem awfully sore."

"It's the lye in the soap."

"I've got just the thing for that. It isn't fancy, but it works like a charm. Would you mind if I bring you some?"

"You don't have to do that."

"You didn't have to share your dinner with me, either."

Mary nodded. "I would be pleased to try your magic elixir."

Drinkwalter grinned. "Well, I'm no Merlin, but I think this will work.

He stepped to the door and then turned back. "Thank you, ma'am, I appreciate what you said."

"Mary."

"Yes, Mary."

The sheriff tipped his hat and stepped out into darkening shadows.

Sheriff Drinkwalter pawed through the contents of the upper drawer of the three-drawer chest, slouching beside his bed in his two-room house. The single bulb hanging from the ceiling lighted little more than a dim ball of yellow reaching down from the ceiling in the center of the room. The contents of the drawer were hidden in shadows, and the sheriff's fingers probed the drawer as a raccoon feels along the bottom of a river for freshwater clams and crayfish. A jar, wider than a silver dollar and about three inches tall. There it was.

Drinkwalter held up the jar to the dim light. That's it: Uncle Saul's Bag Balm. Guaranteed to heal a milk cow's bag. The balm filled that promise and more. Montana's winter wind wrings the moisture from man and beast. The bag balm healed cracked lips and chapped hands. It would work wonders for Mary McPherson.

He slipped the jar into his trousers and looked around his room. Spartan, some might call it, more army barracks than home. No pictures representing his view of life hung from the walls. No family photographs decorated his single dresser. The wardrobe held only uniforms and fishing clothes. Two pairs of boots poked their toes from beneath the bed, one for work and the other for rare days when he took time off to go fishing or hunting. Not a single book lay propped open on a chair beside the bed. Nothing in the room said Drinkwalter lived there.

The sheriff stepped out the door, shutting it behind him. Maybe Catherine could turn his little rental into a home. Mary and Mac lived in a shack. There was no other word for it. Most north winds would blow through it, not around it. But for the shade of the giant cottonwoods along the river, the place would be baking hot in summer.

Still, the McPherson home glowed with life. It had a sense of warmth that went beyond the huge range. Maybe Catherine could bring life to the Drinkwalter shack. Drinkwalter knew that she would bring light and warmth and laughter. Maybe he was worrying too much.

Drinkwalter's step slowed. It was a wonderful night, stars clear in a black sky. The Little Dipper hung from the North Star, like the dipper hanging from a nail in the McPherson shack. Most of Eagles Nest was buttoned up for the night. He glanced across the street to the Baldrys' place. It was the Baldrys' turn to host the whist game. Sometimes they asked the sheriff to sit in.

He enjoyed those nights: quiet talk, good coffee, exasperation and triumph, all without leaving a table.

The railroad tracks shone pure white starlight as the sheriff neared. He climbed the roadbed carefully, not wanting to slip and bang his head against the track or the oaken ties. Creosote, always the smell of creosote around the railroad track, and the gravel, warm still from the afternoon sun, kept the creosote warm and redolent far into the night.

Over the track the sheriff's feet found the path Mac used on his way home from school. The scents along the river pulled the sheriff into the night. He wondered whether the heavy dark air pulled the scent from the roses, the river bottom grasses, and the wild mint, or if being partially denied the use of one sense, his sight, that his olfactory senses grew sharper in the darkness.

Drinkwalter might have seen the man sitting on his haunches along the path if the light from the McPhersons' cabin hadn't pulled the sheriff's eyes to it, dulling the darkness. Drinkwalter might have seen him before he bumped into him.

"What the . . . ?"

The man, surprised as the sheriff, jumped to his feet, knocking Drinkwalter off balance. The sheriff stumbled backward. He caught himself and leaned forward, his arms seeking the dark shape he had stumbled across. And then he felt the coming blow.

Frank Drinkwalter had been a fighter in his youth. Other children pecked at him, as chickens peck at any wounded pullet in their flock. They pecked at him until he thought they would peck him to death, and then he struck back.

He didn't learn to fight so much as open his mind to

it. One has to fight below the cognitive sense, in the deep recesses of the brain that govern other animals that stalk this earth.

Drinkwalter's lower brain felt the blow coming at him from the darkness. His lower brain sent his left arm to brush aside the blow. His lower brain computed at a speed imaginable only by the stars above that if the blow was coming from that direction, then the man's nose must be . . .

Drinkwalter's consciousness sent no message to his right arm to send his fist crashing into the darkness where his assailant's nose should be. The fist simply flew its way with incredible speed and certainty.

The hard bones of the fist crashed through the soft cartilage and then the bony tissue of the nose. The fist continued its crushing blow to the hard bones of the man's face. Blood sprayed into the night, and the man was driven back into the darkness.

Drinkwalter's brain switched levels, edging back toward consciousness and reason. He heard the body of his assailant crashing through clinging branches. Drinkwalter heard the man's breath leave him in a loud *WOOF* as he fell, and then the scrambling sounds of a man seeking his feet. He heard the beat of feet against the earth. Little yowls of pain marking thorny patches of rose and thumps the occasional collisions with trees.

And then the noise was gone, and the adrenalin drained from Drinkwalter. He took a deep breath, wondering what he had done.

Drinkwalter felt exhausted as he walked toward the McPherson cabin, consciously lifting each leg, consciously taking each breath.

* * *

Mary had spent the sheriff's absence doing the dishes and straightening the house. She considered sweeping the floor again, but since there was no foundation, sometimes a broom stirred up more dust than it cleared.

Mac was sitting at the table reading Herman Melville's *Moby Dick*, wondering at a sea so vast it must match Montana's prairies, when the knock came to the door. He looked up to see if he should answer it, but his mother was already on her way, brushing back a stubborn wisp of hair that defied the severe bun she wore most of the time.

She opened the door and gasped. Sheriff Drinkwalter stood in the light from the cabin, pale as a ghost, his shirt sprayed with blood. She reached out and grabbed the sheriff by the elbow, dragging him into the cabin.

"Whatever happened to you?" she asked, her eyes seeking the wound that would leak so much blood.

Drinkwalter shook his head. "Nothing. I'm fine."

"Mac, get the sheriff a chair."

Mac scrambled to bring his chair from the table. Mary dripped a cloth into rinse water still steaming on the stove, then wiped the sheriff's face, still seeking the wound.

Color was coming back to Drinkwalter's face, and he tried to rise, but Mary held him in place with her hand on his shoulder.

"Just sit still. We'll clean up the wound and get a bandage on it."

Drinkwalter waved her hands away. "It's not me, I'm not hurt. I . . ." he said, shaking his head.

Drinkwalter didn't want to tell Mary and Mac that someone had been hiding in the darkness outside the cabin watching the McPhersons. He didn't want to tell them that the man in the darkness was likely Jack Galt. He didn't want to frighten them, but he didn't want them hurt, either.

"Ma'am, uh, Mary, I was bringing you some balm for your hands." He fished through his pockets, finding the elixir in his shirt pocket. "I know this isn't meant for people, but it really works. I use it all the time, and I had this extra, so I'd like you to have it. Put some on now, before you go to bed, and your hands will feel better tomorrow. I know they will."

Mary took the balm, nodding.

"Rub it in, but not so it hurts, just real gentle."

The sheriff's sleight of hand to draw Mary's attention away from the blood on his shirt didn't work.

"What happened out there, Sheriff?" Mary's voice was tight, insistent.

"I don't know. I was walking up the path toward your place, and I stumbled across someone squatted down out there in the bushes. I startled him. He startled me. He took a swing at me, and I . . . swung back. He ran off."

"Do you know who it was?"

"It was dark. I don't know for sure."

Mac stepped between the two. "It was Jack Galt, wasn't it?" he whispered.

The sheriff stared at the ceiling for a moment and then shifted his attention to the boy. "I think so, Mac. I think maybe it was."

"He's coming for me and Ma?"

"Maybe, Mac. Maybe. But tomorrow we'll fit your door with a lock. We'll put on a lock so nobody can get in here if you don't want them to. You folks just stay close to hand. Don't go out, one without the other. I'll go down and roust Galt tonight, see if he was the one, and if he is, I'll talk to Jim Pratt tomorrow, see what we can do."

Drinkwalter looked down at Mary. "Don't worry about it, Mary. I'm not going to let anyone hurt you."

Drinkwalter stepped to the door. "Be sure to lock this now, and keep the curtains drawn."

As the sheriff stepped through the door, he could hear Mary's voice, low and insistent: "Who is Jack Galt, Mac? Tell me everything you know about Jack Galt."

"He's the devil, Ma. Jack Galt is the devil."

21

"No! I damn well will not do that!"

Jim Pratt, Stillwater County attorney was leaning across his desk both arms thrust forward to support the heat of his anger.

"Listen . . ."

"No, you listen!"

Pratt's face was glowing a dark, dull red, and the veins and sinews of his hands stood out as he leaned again across the desk to storm at Drinkwalter.

"I don't know what you have against Mr. Galt, but I will not be party to your continued harassment of him. I will count this my lucky day if he does not file suit against you and the county. Any judge, except for that old reprobate that sits on the bench here, would put you in jail for what you've done."

A growl edged into Drinkwalter's voice. "That's what this is about, isn't it? You wouldn't give me a restraining order to keep Galt away from Nelly's, so I went to Judge Smythe. That's what's really rattling around in your craw, isn't it?"

"Rattling around in my craw, as you so colorfully put it, is your total misapprehension of the law you are sworn to uphold. Rattling around in my craw is the fact that the sheriff of Stillwater County has viciously assaulted a man for no reason whatsoever."

"I defended myself."

"You defended yourself." Pratt stood upright, assuming the stance and manner he used for especially recalcitrant witnesses. "And when did this alleged attack take place?"

"Last night. I told you, last night."

"And what were you doing?"

"I was walking to the McPherson place."

"And it was dark?"

"Yes, very dark."

"And what happened?"

"I stumbled into Galt. He was watching the McPherson home."

"And what happened then?"

"He took a swing at me, so I swung back."

"He hit you, then?"

"No, he didn't hit me. He just swung at me."

"You said it was very dark. How did you know that he swung at you?"

"I could feel it."

"You could feel it. What a remarkable person you are, Sheriff, to be able to feel other people's movements. How long have you had this gift?"

"It's no gift, I—"

Pratt sneered. "And what did you do then?"

"I swung back."

"And you hit your 'assailant,'" Pratt said, sarcasm dripping from his voice.

"Yes. I hit him on the nose."

"You said it was very dark. How do you know that you hit him on the nose?"

"The way it sprayed blood."

"Is that what noses do when they are struck?"

"Yes."

"And how do you know that?"

Drinkwalter's eyes dropped to the floor. "I've seen it before."

Pratt's dripped dripped sarcasm. "So you are in the habit of driving your fist through the cartilage and bone of another man's nose?"

Drinkwalter jerked to his feet, words rumbling ugly from his throat. "That's the way it was. I'm not like that anymore."

"You were 'like that' last night, weren't you, Sheriff?"

"The son of a bitch attacked me."

"You bumped into a man in the dark. You 'felt' him swing at you, so you broke his nose. You are one hell of a peacemaker, Sheriff. I'd best watch out that I don't bump into you on the street."

Drinkwalter gritted his teeth, cutting off the words he wanted so badly to say.

"So you bumped into somebody in the dark, and you hit him, you think, on the nose, and you have twisted this around to some bogus charge that Jack Galt was prowling around the widow McPherson's place."

"I know it was Galt. I went to his place last night, and he was nursing a broken nose. So I *know* he was outside that cabin last night. I *know* what he was doing, and if you were more county attorney and less chairman of the commerce committee, you would know that, too."

Pratt raised both fists and crashed them against the top of his desk, a pencil lying near the edge skittering off to the floor.

"You will keep a civil tongue in your head when you are talking to me, Sheriff!"

The county attorney drew a deep breath, willing himself to bring his temper under control. "And what did Galt say when you asked him about his injury?"

"He said he fell out of bed."

"Is it not more likely that he fell out of bed than that he was sitting in the dark outside a woman's cabin and you happened to stumble on him, and you happened to feel him swing at you and you happened to hit him on the nose on a night so dark that you couldn't even identify the man?

"No court in the world would pay any attention to your ranting, Sheriff. And I see no reason why I should. But I'll tell you this. You leave that man alone. I will not have you harassing him. Now, run off to Judge Smythe and get another one of his *restraining orders* that won't stand up in a court of law.

"Get the hell out of my office. You can be sure that I will do my damnedest to get you booted out of office at the next election, or before, if I can find any reason at all. Do I make myself clear?"

The sheriff's eyes squinted almost shut. "Crystal clear. You know this: Doing your 'damnedest' doesn't amount to a puff of dust to me or anyone else in this town."

"GET OUT! Get out, you, you, you . . ."

Drinkwalter stepped through the door, closing it on Pratt's ranting. He tried to smile at Pratt's secretary, but his anger drove the smile away. Liz stared wide-eyed as the sheriff stomped out of the office, heels ringing on the granite floor of the courthouse proper.

Mary McPherson's back stiffened at the knock at the door, and Mac's eyes traveled to the corner by the front door where his rifle was propped.

"Won't be him, Ma. I'll get it."

"Block the door with your foot, Mac. The way I showed you."

Mac nodded and stepped to the door. The house key was in the lock, and Mac turned it. *Click!* The sound grated on Mac's ears, and the boy winced. He turned the latch and opened the door, bracing it with his foot.

Sheriff Frank Drinkwalter was standing on the step, an official-looking envelope in one hand and a gunny-sack in the other. A four-foot length of two-by-four extending from the sack's opening.

"Hey, Mac. Can I come in for a minute?"

Mac nodded and opened the door. The sheriff stepped through.

"I come bearing gifts," the sheriff said, but his smile seemed strained.

"First, we have a restraining order from Judge Smythe forbidding Jack Galt from coming within a quarter mile of your place. That will stop him from crossing the Absarokee road to the west of his place. It will ban him from most of Eagles Nest. I've talked to Bert, and he's promised to swing past here every night just to make sure everything's all right."

"Next from my bag of gifts . . ." The sheriff pulled a couple of steel straps from the sack. They were bent in the shape of a U, but with one side longer than the other. Holes had been drilled through that side.

"See, Mac, you just mount these in the two-by-fours on either side of the door. I've got some lag bolts in the sack, and a wrench in case you don't have one. Then you drop the two-by-four in, and it's Katy bar the door."

The sheriff tried to smile, but again the smile died.

"Look, I don't want to scare you, but I don't want anything to happen to you, either. I don't think he'll try anything, not with Bert around and the restraining order, so this is just a little extra. Just something so you'll sleep a little better . . . and so I'll sleep better, too.

"You two all right with this?"

Mary and Mac nodded.

"Now, Mac, if you could spare me a little time?"

Mac's eyes jerked to his mother. She nodded. "I'll be fine. I don't think that Jack Galt poses much of a danger in the daytime."

The two stepped out into a glorious morning. A little breeze whispered through the trees, drying the dew that held still to the shadows. Drinkwalter walked north on the trail to the railroad, eyes down, studying the grass.

"See there, where it looks like a deer bed in the grass?"

Mac nodded. That must have been where he was sitting, close enough to the trail so he could find his way out in the dark.

"Here's where we scuffled." The sheriff was pointing at broken grass and chafed soil. "When I hit him, he flew off there."

Drinkwalter stepped off the path toward a little copse of cottonwoods. "Here, Mac. See this?"

Mac squatted by the sheriff. There was a fine spray of brown on some of the grass, and here and there bright red where the blood was kept cool and moist by the dew.

"And there, where the branches are broken on those saplings. Do you see that, Mac?"

Mac nodded.

"Now, get this all straight in your mind. Look at it so you remember exactly how it looks. After I hit him, he fell back, roughly southwest. And where did he hit that copse of trees?"

"Just south of that rosebush."

"Good. Get it all in perspective. You might have to back me up in court. Jim Pratt's got a burr under his saddle. Says I'm picking on one of his precious businessmen. Fact is that I stepped into a squabble between him and Judge Smythe. Neither one has much use for the other.

"Now, you get into court, they'll try to twist everything you say, trip you up any way they can so they can use you to their own advantage. You be sure you understand how this happened, Mac. Make sure that you've got it straight in your mind."

Mac nodded again.

"Okay, see here where he fell, the blood? Then he got up and started to run. He had to run toward his place. He was there when I got there last night, nursing his broken nose and concocting that cock-and-bull story about falling out of bed.

"So we know basically which way he was running, Mac, almost due east. We should be able to find his tracks and a little blood here and there if we look really close. Places where there's still dew, we should be able to see his tracks in the grass. But where the sun is on it, it won't be so easy. So watch for broken twigs and leaves torn from trees."

"There," Mac said, pointing to a sunflower snapped off at the base.

"Good, and see this speck of blood? We're on to him."

The two followed the trail then, picking up clues as they went. Each time the sheriff stopped, he asked Mac to memorize this clue or that. About two-hundred yards from the smithy, their quarry had stumbled over a log. After Big Jim told them about Galt, Mac had occasionally hidden behind that log, watching the black shape of Jack Galt silhouetted against the red glow of the foundry. There was more blood there, Galt apparently having reinjured his nose in the fall.

And then they were at the smithy. The door was open and a shaft of light stabbed into the darkness there. But it died, dust motes dancing out its death in the cave-like darkness of that building. Inside, Mac could feel bodies moving in the darkness, but he could not see them.

And then something darker even than the darkness of the smith stepped between them and the forge, black, absolute light-killing black, against the red glow of the forge, and Mac felt a shiver run down his neck.

The shadow said nothing, motionless as a statue forged in the heat of the fire.

Sheriff Drinkwalter stepped into the shaft of light, casting his own shadow on the darkness inside.

"Another restraining order, Galt."

"Din't do nudding," Galt said through his broken nose.

"You're not to go within a quarter mile of the McPherson cabin. That means you can't cross this street. Downtown, you can go to the bank, the store and Black Jack Jim's bar. That's it. Everything else is out of bounds."

"You cad do dis to me. I got my rights."

"Step out here, Galt. Got somebody I want you to meet."

Galt shuffled, blinking toward daylight. "This is Jack Galt, Mac. You see him. You hear him. You suspect he's anywhere near you, you get me or Bert, and we'll toss him in jail."

The sheriff leaned toward Galt. "It stops here, Jack Galt. It stops here."

22

"He hissed." The words leaked into the darkness of the McPherson shack.

"Mac?" The word came fuzzy, from the edge of sleep, and Mac's eyes squinted shut. He hadn't meant for his mother to hear. He didn't want her to know.

"Mac?"

"Yeah, Ma."

"What were you talking about?"

"Nothing."

His mother's voice came clearer, now, concern chasing sleep from her brain.

"Mac, what's bothering you?"

Mac lay wide-eyed in the dark staring at the ceiling, dark shadow on light. "It was nothing, Ma. I must have been dreaming."

"Tell me, Mac."

Only the silence spoke.

"Mac, we don't have any secrets. Remember?"

Mac lay in the dark, trying to put words to his fear. "It's Galt, Ma. The sheriff took me down to Galt's smithy today to serve the restraining order . . . so he wouldn't hide around our cabin at night.

"He hissed, Ma, like all those words and the court order and sheriff didn't mean anything to him. All the time he was looking at me. His nose was broken and both his eyes were black. He looked like a skull, Ma, with a snake's flat dead eyes.

"He said he was going to see a lot more of me. I think he will do whatever he wants to. I don't think anyone can stop him. I don't think he's human, Ma."

The boy's words crept into the room. "He was the one I saw standing on our step the other night, Ma. It was him. I could tell even with the broken nose. It wasn't a dream, Ma."

After what seemed forever, his mother spoke. "Mac, we have the sheriff and a barred door. Mostly, we have each other. I won't let him hurt you, Mac."

"I won't let him hurt you, either, Ma—not if I can help it."

"Good, now you go to sleep. We'll have some busy days ahead of us if we're going to get that new home built for Mr. Drinkwalter and his bride."

"G'night, Ma."

"Good night, Mac."

Mary lay awake, now, staring at the ceiling. Danger was no stranger to the river bottom. Fate could set a Rocky Mountain fever–bearing tick on Mac or her. They probably wouldn't even notice the bite until the sickness came upon them.

In August, rattlesnakes fled the dry hills for the river. They were hard to see in the grasses along the Yellowstone, and sometimes when they buzzed, she didn't know if they were poised six inches from her ankle or a safe yard away.

Always, there was the Yellowstone River. Whenever Mac was late coming home, she worried that he had fallen into the river, disappearing downriver until the Yellowstone spit him out on a gravel bar. That thought lay like an abscess on Mary's mind. She would be left alone, wondering if he were dead or injured or if he had just gone away, seeking the place where the sun set.

Those dangers lived in Mary's mind. They were old acquaintances if not old friends. But now a man was stalking them for some reason Mary couldn't fathom. Darkness drew this stranger to the bushes outside their cabin. Darkness was settling over the McPhersons'. The shades were always closed in their little cabin now, and Mary suffered the lack of light.

Mary lay awake well into the morning hours, jerking each time a cottonwood creaked as it twisted in a passing wind. Then she heard the creak of the step, protesting a man's weight. Mary couldn't breathe. She pulled her covers tightly to her neck, hiding in the safety of her blankets, pretending she hadn't heard the sound. But the sound was real. Another squeak and then a voice.

"Mrs. McPherson? Mac? It's me, Bert Edgar. Sheriff asked me to check every so often to make sure you're all right."

"We're fine, Mr. Edgar. Thank you for stopping by."

"You sure there's somebody in that old house?" Sheriff Drinkwalter said, speaking around a really good cut of New York steak.

"Don't like to talk business while I'm eating," Big Jim Thompson said, shoving away the remains of his first steak and signaling the waiter to bring him another.

"You don't like to do anything but eat."

"True enough," Thompson said, fidgeting a little as he watched the door where the waiter had disappeared. "Hell, it shouldn't take so long to cook a piece of beef. I didn't ask him to scorch it or nothing."

"It hasn't been thirty seconds. You can't broil a good piece of beef in thirty seconds."

"Maybe I should go speed him up a bit. You know those guys get a little lazy if you let them."

Thompson threw his napkin on the table and rose from a chair that looked like a child's toy under his bulk. "I'll just go rattle his cage a little. No sense dawdling over a meal."

At that moment Walt, the waiter, burst through the door to the kitchen, carrying a plate of steak, baked potato, and asparagus strips. Thompson backed into a chair that squeaked in protest of his weight.

"Took you long enough," Thompson growled at the waiter.

"Damn near a minute."

"Don't suppose you expect much of a tip for this?"

"Don't expect anything from you. About the best thing anyone says about you is that you're a cheap son of a bitch. I always tell them, they're too kind. Anyhow, we don't like you banging around in the kitchen like you did last time."

"I never hurt anybody."

"You scared the chef so bad that he took the next two days off."

"Well, he deserved a few days off. He serves a fine steak. A man ought to get something a little extra for being good at what he does."

"What, did they cut your pay again, Big Jim?"

Thompson growled. "Damn, when's this restaurant going to get some decent help?"

"About the time Yellowstone County gets a good sheriff."

"Well, I guess you'll have to do, then," Thompson said, and both men laughed.

"Walt, this is Frank Drinkwalter. He's sheriff in that

little Podunk town west of here." Thompson leaned back in his chair. "What's it called? Sparrows Twig. Yeah, I think it's called Sparrows Twig. Anyhow, he's sheriff up there."

"Do you suppose we could get him to run for sheriff down here? We sure as hell could use a good sheriff."

"You could use a good cuff. You tell that chef not to waste so much time on the next steak."

"It's broiling as we speak."

"Well, get to it. I haven't even started, and I've damn near finished this steak already. Get moving, Walt."

"Go to hell, Sheriff," Walt said.

"Not bad food, but the service is slow," Thompson said to the waiter's back.

Drinkwalter waited until the waiter disappeared behind the door to the kitchen. "You don't need anybody to conspire against you, Thompson. You conspire against yourself."

Thompson paused, fork halfway to his mouth. "You mean Walt?"

Drinkwalter nodded.

"Walt's okay. He's one of my best informants. People say things over dinner and a few drinks that they won't say in public."

"Like the conspiracy to boot you out of office?"

"Yeah."

"Well, it isn't much of a conspiracy, not if today is any measurement."

"Quiet around the house?"

"Dead closer to it."

"Word is that's where they're meeting."

"You trying to put the shuck on me?"

Thompson looked hurt. "You think I'm lying to you?"

"Hard to tell, but you sure as hell haven't worn out the truth since I've known you."

"I'm surprised that you feel that way. I thought we were friends."

"Friends tell each other the truth."

"Like that part rainbow, part alligator you caught on the Stillwater?"

"That wasn't a lie. That was fishing."

"Fishing? What you know about fishing I could write on the corner of this napkin. If I had gotten to Mac earlier, he would have landed that big rainbow."

"He was doing fine until you showed up."

"Well, maybe." Thompson leaned back in his chair. "What makes you think I'm lying about the conspiracy?"

"Hell, they wouldn't dare boot you out of office. Only thing you've ever done is law enforcement. If they gave you the boot, you'd be on the county dole. Yellowstone County hasn't got enough money to feed someone like you."

"S'pose not."

"You going to tell me why you dragged me down here?"

Thompson sighed. "Well, I didn't want to tell you this, but I haven't been feeling too well. So I went to see the doc, and he told me . . . Well, he told me that I didn't have long. I didn't want to tell you, 'cause it might spoil your summer, but I wanted to see you before—"

"That's pathetic," Drinkwalter said, shaking his head. "You are maybe the worst liar I have ever seen. Can't you come up with something better than that?"

"Don't see why we have to chatter so. A man sits

down to eat, he wants to eat. He doesn't like having his lying criticized. I'm pretty damn good at it: You can ask anybody. It's a hell of a thing to call a man a pathetic liar, and you a sorry son of a bitch, too."

"Hell, I didn't mean to hurt your feelings. You eat your steak. Then we can talk."

The Yellowstone County sheriff nodded, burying himself in his meal, raising his eyes occasionally to glower at Drinkwalter.

When the last bite of steak disappeared down Thompson's maw, he sighed, too soft an expression for a man like him, but appropriate for the end of a really fine meal. Walt the waiter appeared at the table, and Thompson looked up.

"Just half an apple pie, Walt. You tell the chef that his apple pies are the only fit ending for a dinner like this. You tell him that for me, will you?"

Walt smiled and nodded and headed for the kitchen.

Drinkwalter growled, "Now, can we talk?"

"I've got enough food in me now that I could tell you a really good lie. Not so good a lie as I could tell you after the apple pie, but a good lie, good as anybody's. But I'll tell you the truth straight out, if you'll promise me one thing."

"What's that?"

"That you'll stay down here in Billings for the whole three days."

"Hell, I can't do that. Not with Catherine coming, and Galt up there. He's been after Mary McPherson—"

"No, he's been watching her."

Drinkwalter cupped his chin in his hand. "Yeah, he's been watching her. How'd you know about that?"

"That's the kind of thing us big-city sheriffs know

about." Thompson leaned across the table. "We've got a whole file on him, reports we've gotten from other sheriffs. He spends some time picking out who he's going to . . ."

Thompson left the words hanging in the air like an ax. "When he makes up his mind, and we don't know what makes him do that, then he comes in nice as can be, a real gentleman suitor. Then he drags the woman through the mud and . . . kills her.

"You've got Bert watching the McPhersons, don't you?"

"Yeah."

"And Mac's there most of the time now that school's out?"

"Sure, but he's just a kid."

"I think the kid in him wore out some time ago."

"Yeah, maybe."

"Mac and Mary are okay. You don't really have to be up there the next three days."

Realization spread across Drinkwalter's face. "That's it, isn't it? Mac wanted me out of there so his mother could clean up my place and put some curtains and things in it. He even said that the three days would give his ma the chance to do that. That's what it is, isn't it? They want me out of there so they can get the place ready?"

Thompson shook his head. "I couldn't have said it better myself."

23

"Ah, Ma, that looks beautiful."

Mary McPherson looked up from her roaster pan filled with potato salad and smiled.

"The way you put those sliced eggs around the outside, and the cluster of them in the middle, it's just beautiful, Ma."

"No, Mac."

Mac, all innocence, looked up at his mother in surprise. "No what, Ma?"

"No, you can't have any potato salad now. Come noon, you'll have more food to eat than you've ever seen."

"Wonder if Tilly's going to bring some sandwiches?"

"Probably. I'm looking forward to that. I'd like to know what she does to make them so special."

"It's a secret, Ma. I don't think she'll tell you her recipe. Some day it will be worth a fortune."

"It's about time someone shared a fortune with me."

"Wonder why Sparks isn't here yet."

"They're probably still loading his wagon at the lumberyard. You can't very well criticize someone for being a little late when he's been nice enough to offer you a ride."

"It's going to be fun, isn't it, Ma."

Mary stopped fussing with the potato salad. "Yes, Mac, it's going to be fun, more fun than we've had in a long while. It's always fun when good people get together to do something for someone."

"I'll bet the sheriff will be surprised when he sees his new house."

"*Flabbergasted* would probably be a better word," Mary said, and the two laughed.

"I can't wait to see her, Ma."

"I can't, either, Mac. She must be special to hold someone like the sheriff for so long. How long did you say they've been apart?"

"Ten years, the sheriff said ten years."

"That's just about how long it's been since your father left."

"You're still hanging on to him, aren't you, Ma?"

Mary cocked her head and looked at her son. "Yes, Mac, I suppose I am."

The jingle of a harness pulled their attention to the door, and a moment later the door rattled with a decisive knock. Mary glanced around their single-room cabin. It would never look nice, but Mary wanted to be sure everything was in its place, and then she opened the door to Sparks Pierson.

Pierson, who labored daily in a stiff white shirt, was wearing a pair of bib overalls, stiff still with starch that marked them as just off the rack.

"Madam, your chariot awaits."

Mary smiled, and Pierson grinned. "Well, not exactly chariot."

They both grinned and stepped into a beautiful spring day. The air was clear and sweet as wine, and it was early enough for stillness yet to rule. Mary's roses were blooming, red and white and yellow, sharing their scent with the day.

Pierson helped Mary take her seat on the wagon, and then he and Mac climbed up. Mac found a perch on a barrel of nails standing in the wagon bed. Lumber, good lumber, most of it clear of knots and blemishes and smelling of high mountains and tall trees, occupied the wagon bed.

"Back, now, back," Pierson said, urging the horses to back away from the cabin so he could turn them around in the narrow track. The horses swung wide in the turn, pulling the wagon free of the riverside shadows.

"Beautiful day," Pierson said.

"Beautiful."

"County crew was out there almost all last night. There's a natural seam of sandstone that leads right up to the building site. They've been cutting into the hillside a little, clearing off the track. Chuck Gilson was in this morning. He said it was probably the best road in the state of Montana."

The wagon clattered over the railroad crossing, steel shoes and wheels bumping against steel track. Then Pierson pulled the team west down Main Street. It was early still, but the street teemed with people loading picnic lunches and tools into wagon beds. They looked up and waved as Pierson's wagon passed. "Be out there in a minute, Sparks." "Don't build it all until we get there." And each time someone called, Pierson thrust his arm into the air, waving a thumbs-up at the people of Eagles Nest.

"Good bunch of folks," Pierson said. "Couldn't find any better."

"Mac was saying that you put it together."

Pierson shook his head. "No. I might have talked to some people, but they took over. They just want to do what's right for the sheriff, and they want to meet his intended. You'd think the Queen of Sheba was coming right here to Eagles Nest, Montana. Guess I'd have to count myself in that bunch."

"And me," Mary said.

"And me, too," Mac added.

The horses tugged the wagon up the little hill on the west edge of Eagles Nest. Nelly Frobisher's place, freshly painted, stood out beside the road. Both Sparks and Mary averted their eyes, looking down from the bench to the river bottom and the Yellowstone glowing green in the morning light. Here, the road edged around a slough, once a loop in the river, but cut off now by the Northern Pacific track. The slough was filled with cattails and blackbirds, some with bands of red across their wings, and a few even with yellow heads.

The birds set up a clatter as the wagon passed, each warning the others to guard their nests from the passing two-leggeds.

And then the road dipped down to a bridge over Keyser Creek.

"Saw this run bigger than the Stillwater one time," Pierson said. "Big summer thunderstorm and hail out north and all the water collected in this creek and roared downstream. It ran over this bridge, well over it, and we figured it would be washed out. Never saw anything like that. More water than the Stillwater: I'd bet on that."

Mac piped up from the wagon box. "Out on the west side of the creek, about there," the boy said, pointing with his finger. "There's a whole bed of sego lilies. They're beautiful, just beautiful."

"Segos are beautiful," Pierson said, and then he gestured toward the river. "Good fishing along that stretch. Not now with the water up, but in early spring, it's good fishing."

"In the fall, too," Mac said.

"You a fisherman?"

"You bet, had one on this spring that was as long as my leg, but he shook himself loose."

"Yeah, you're a fisherman all right," Pierson said, and all three laughed.

Ahead, they could see the county road crew putting the finishing touches on the road. Pierson nodded at them. "Came out here on their own time. Worked half the night so we could get the lumber up for the house. Good people in this town. Really good people."

The wagon jolted, horses' hooves clicking and wheels ringing as the wagon pulled up the hill toward the dale where the house would be. And then they were there; Mary gasped. It was beautiful, the Yellowstone stretching off east and west and the Stillwater twinkling to the south. And south, at the edge of the world, the Beartooths, snowcapped still, poked into the sky. Blue they were, blue scraped from the belly of heaven by rough crags.

Tables were lined up along the southern edge of the dale, and Mac could smell fried chicken and potato salad and baked beans and fresh biscuits. At the end of a table a whole side of beef rested on a spit over hot coals. All night it had been broiling. About noon it would be just right. Horace Bumgartner would see to that.

The German immigrant stood in the smoke of the coals and the scent of the roasting meat, his weariness marked in his movements. He would serve this congregation the best beef they had ever had. That was the way Horace Bumgartner did everything, the best way he could.

Mac looked at the growing repast, and his mouth watered.

Pierson pulled his attention back to the tasks at hand. "Mac, might be you could give your mother a hand and carry the salad over to the table. By then I should have the wagon backed up somewhere in the vicinity of that lumber there. Maybe you could give me a hand unloading it."

Mac nodded.

"Brought an extra pair of gloves, just in case I could recruit some slave labor," Pierson said, handing a new pair to Mac. "You can get a handful of slivers from handling lumber without gloves, even good lumber like this."

Mac nodded, turning to climb down from the wagon. The boy gasped, "Ma, look at that."

The track they had just traveled was filling with people from Eagles Nest. It seemed that someone had pulled a plug, and the town was draining, spilling toward the west. On they came from the morning sun, wagons, horses, and even a few pedestrians carrying shovels over their shoulders. They were nodding and waving to one another. Occasionally a shout, too faint to be understood, would ride the clear morning air.

"Almost the whole town," Sparks said. "Few curmudgeons left, but there's always a few curmudgeons. I suspect we'll have this house up today. Tomorrow we'll be painting and finishing.

"Reverend Peabody said he would hold services out

here for anybody who wanted. Tried to talk him into putting them off until afternoon. His sermons would dry the paint on this place faster than a desert wind."

Mary grinned as Pierson helped her down off the wagon.

The stationmaster bowed his head slightly, an unconscious gesture that made Mary smile again.

"Ma'am . . ."

"Mary."

Pierson nodded. "Mary, those ladies in the circle over there are working on curtains. Gladys Johansen said she could sure use the help, if you don't mind."

"I would enjoy that."

"Good, now come along, Mac. Let's get this house built."

Mac was leaning back on the grass, watching the clouds float by. He was stuffed, two days of eating whenever he wanted. The roast beef was wonderful. Horace Bumgartner took the compliments formally in the German way, nodding and saying *danke*, but Mac could see the old man smile occasionally, when he thought no one was looking. His mother's potato salad was wonderful, everyone said so, and each time they did, she blushed. And each time she blushed, Sparks Pierson looked at her in an odd, gentle sort of way.

Everywhere there was laughing and joking and food. Everywhere people would stop for a moment to look into their neighbor's eyes and laugh for the sheer joy of what they were doing.

And now only Mort Timpkins remained in the house. He inched backward toward the door on his hands and knees, rubbing oil into the oak. As his haunches appeared at the door, a roar went up from the crowd. The home was finished. In two days the people of Eagles Nest had come together to build a home for Sheriff Frank Drinkwalter and his bride. For two days the people of Eagles Nest had come together.

Pierson stood and threw his hat in the air, and a moment later everyone's hat and bonnet sailed up, riding a chorus of hurrahs into the heavens.

Sheriff Frank Drinkwalter rattled toward Eagles Nest in a cloud of despair as dark as the heavens outside the train. Not long now until he reached town. Not long now. The sheriff shook his head and sighed. He would reach the culmination of his life, tomorrow morning when Catherine Lang stepped from the train.

She would emerge as a crocus emerges from the barren ground of winter. She would be a spot of color and beauty in his life, and he would take her over to his home, and drag that color and beauty into icy despair.

Catherine's face was never far from Drinkwalter's mind. It merged into his consciousness at the oddest of times. Sometimes when he was watching a sunset, he would see her eyes, sun and sky creating just the right mix of clarity and color. Sometimes he would see her smile on another woman's face, disappearing a moment later. Once in Billings he had seen a woman two blocks away. There was something in the way she carried herself that made him think Catherine might have come early, hoping to surprise her beloved. But the stranger wasn't Catherine, only a woman who walked a little as she did.

He knew that he appeared to Catherine that way, too, little hints of him in other men she might see. But tomorrow morning she would see him as he was, a failure in a world where one's value is judged by his possessions. Tomorrow, she would see what he had made of himself, and she would be mortified.

The train lurched, the engineer setting the brakes for the slow approach to Eagles Nest, the clatter of steel wheels against steel track, easing a bit. The sheriff rose, taking his valise from the seat beside him. He walked to the back of the car, nodding to the conductor as he stepped past him to the loading platform.

There was a light inside the depot. Sparks Pierson must be doing some late work. Good man, Sparks. A real community leader, not like that self-anointed, strutting little peacock Jim Pratt. The sheriff stepped down stairs to a walk and made his way toward Main Street, watching for any lines on the sidewalk revealing a snake curled there on the warmth of the concrete.

Lot of racket coming from the Absaloka. Pete must be having some kind of party. Drinkwalter thought about walking down to the saloon. Usually that's all he had to do, stop in so the men there would remember that reality lay just outside the saloon doors. But Bert was in charge now, and the sheriff wanted to get back to his place.

The sheriff turned the key to his home and stepped inside. The place was stuffy. He would leave all the windows open tonight, freshen up the place a little. That was something he could do. It wasn't much, but it was something.

The sheriff's hand found the string hanging from the overhead light. The bulb didn't do much to light the room, but it provided enough light for the sheriff to see that nothing had changed very much.

And then he saw something out of place on the table. A bouquet of flowers, a collection of tulips and lilacs and roses were together in one big bouquet. And his suit, his only suit, hung freshly cleaned and pressed from the door to his bedroom. His shirt was starched and ironed. And a tie, a new tie, was draped around the collar.

The McPhersons had done what they could. He would thank them for that. They said they would go to the train with him to meet Catherine. He hoped they would be there. It would be easier if there were more people there. Then Catherine's attention wouldn't be focused only on him. Then she wouldn't see what a failure he was, at least not right away.

The sheriff stepped into his bedroom and pulled off his boots. He undressed and pulled back the covers. Fresh sheets. Mary McPherson had done everything she could.

He lay back in bed, his head cradled in his hands and eyes open, staring through the dark at the ceiling. Not much sleep tonight, he thought. Not much sleep the night before the most important day of his life.

24

Mac sat on one of the two chairs in the McPherson shack, rubbing bootblack into shoes long past resurrection. His mother stood at the range, her hair cascading into a basin as she rinsed it with rainwater for the third time.

"S'pose the ten forty-two will be late?"

Mary shook her head, squeezing the water from her hair as she straightened.

"No, the ten forty-two is never late. Never on a day when you want it to be, anyway."

"I don't want it to be late. I want it to be early."

Mary smiled. "I want to meet Catherine, too. It's just that we have so much to do. . . ."

"To make ourselves presentable?"

Mary stopped running a towel through her hair to stare at her son. "Mac, I didn't mean that. I suspect Miss Lang will accept us as we are. I just want everything to be perfect this morning."

"Like it was with you and Pa?"

Mary smiled again. "Yes, like it was with me and your father."

She shook her head, little droplets of water sputtering as they fell on the stove. "I don't know what I'll wear."

Mac jumped to his feet. "Well, what in the world is that?"

Mary jerked, knocking the basin to the floor. Galt. Mac must have seen Galt, but Mac was looking at his bed. Something had slithered into their home. Another mouse? Or maybe a snake. Maybe a rattlesnake had crawled into the warmth of the shack.

Mary drew back, willing whatever it was not to be a rattlesnake, but Mac didn't seem to be frightened. The boy stepped to the bed, dropped to his knees, and reached under, hand groping for something.

"Careful, Mac! Be careful!"

Mac turned to his mother. "Ma, we chased the bogeyman away some time ago. I was just wondering what this was." The boy pulled a box wrapped in shiny pink paper from beneath the bed.

"Well, look at this, Ma. A box." He studied the card as though it were a clue in a Sherlock Holmes murder case. "It's for you, Ma."

Mary took the package. A secret admirer, the card said. She looked at Mac. He was struggling to conceal his grin. "Why, someone must be taken with my feminine wiles," she said.

"Don't see how it could be any other way," Mac replied.

She stripped the paper from the package and opened the pasteboard box inside. A dress! A pretty pale blue dress with long sleeves and white trim. On one lapel was a pink embroidered rose that distorted and then disappeared behind Mary's tears.

"Sheriff gave me a raise to six dollars a week. I didn't tell you so I could hold back the dollar. Mrs. Harris helped me pick out the dress. She was real nice. She embroidered the rose on it. I told her I'd like to have a rose on it because I know you like them so. Do you like it, Ma? Is it okay? Mrs. Harris said it would fit you to a T."

But then Mac saw the tears streaming from his mother's eyes, falling *splat* on the floor. The excitement disappeared from Mac's voice, leaving it flat and dead. "I'm sorry, Ma. I should have asked you before I bought it. Maybe Mrs. Harris will take it back."

Mary bridged the space between her and Mac in two steps. She wrapped him in her arms, her tears falling into his hair. "Mac, it's the prettiest dress I ever saw, and I'm the proudest mother ever."

Mac and his mother stepped into a beautiful day. The sun trickled through the leaves of the cottonwood trees, lighting the trail. They walked single file to the street, but as they stepped out of the trees, Mary reached to take Mac's arm.

"Guess we're the highfalutin McPhersons on their way to the biggest social affair of the season," Mac said.

"Just Mac and me stepping out on the town."

Both laughed.

"Ma?"

"Yes."

"You know how it is when you think something will be the best thing in the world and then when you have it, it doesn't seem like so much?"

"Yes."

"Do you suppose it will be like that with Catherine?"

"You mean will you think less of her when you meet her?"

"Yeah."

"I think she must be someone special, Mac. You can see that reflected in the sheriff's eyes when he talks about her. I think she must be something special."

The morning sun was high enough to warm the day,

and it reached down to kiss them, welcoming them into its light and warmth. The sheriff stood on the depot landing. He was wearing the blue serge suit Mary had cleaned and pressed, and he held the bouquet of flowers as though in salute.

"Ma, he's wearing the tie we bought for him."

"Yes."

"He really looks sharp, doesn't he?"

"Yes."

Mary thought about her first meeting with the sheriff, how flustered she had been. Sheriff Drinkwalter's tall, rangy good looks were part of that. But Mary had been drawn to his eyes. They were clear and they invited people to peer within. That afternoon on the doorstep, she was afraid that if she looked too long into the sheriff's eyes, she might not find her way out.

Drinkwalter nodded and smiled as Mac and Mary drew near. "You look very nice today, Mary. The dress becomes you."

Mac smiled as though the compliment were meant for him. He looked at his mother, pleased to see a blush spreading across her face.

The sheriff's attention turned east again, peering at the hill where the track swung loose from the river. So focused was the sheriff that he didn't notice the little knots of people gathering at the depot. They came in flutters of color as though bouquets of flowers had taken to walking the streets of Eagles Nest. First one bunch appeared and then another, whispering greetings and sharing excitement. They filled the depot and spilled over to the gravel beside the track, each maneuvering for the best place to see Catherine.

The sheriff was oblivious to the fussing and whispers of the people hiding in the shadows of the depot. His entire being focused on that tiny point where the two tracks became one and the river raged at the railroad.

Mac's eyes ranged over the crowd behind them and then jerked back. Yellowstone County Sheriff James Thompson was marching up to the landing with a covey of deputies. They were dressed to the nines, uniforms pressed and boots polished. The men might have been a contingent from a military academy, so straight were their backs.

They came to a halt and then parade rest without a word from Thompson. So disciplined were they that Mac imagined they would stand at attention on the track until a train swept them away if Thompson ordered them to.

Imposing as the deputies were, they stood like toys next to Big Jim. He stood at attention, eyes focused on something only he could see. The people of Eagles Nest shifted back, giving the law-enforcement officers room.

Thompson must have come up on the milk run and hidden out until this moment, Mac thought. But how could that bunch hide in a town the size of Eagles Nest?

Drinkwalter stiffened. Mac felt it more than saw it. Light flashed as the train pulled into sight at the east hill. Puffing smoke it was, sending up its own clouds into that bright blue sky.

Mac heard the sheriff inhale. The boy felt his back stiffening, as though the sheriff's breath had sucked the air from his own lungs.

Seconds stretched into days as they waited for the

caboose to pull free from the hill, but the train seemed to pick up speed once it reached the valley floor. Now it was coming too fast, as though the engineer had forgotten the stop in Eagles Nest, but then he set the brakes. Sparks sprayed as the immovable object of the tracks met the irresistible force of the steel wheels.

Mac's chest swelled. That was the way for Catherine Lang to come to Eagles Nest, sparks flying.

The train rolled to a stop, chuffing as though to catch its breath after a long run.

James Thompson and his men marched up the wide steps to the landing, boots beating a rhythm to match the chuffing of the train. The conductor poked his head out, saw Thompson, and nodded. While the conductor set up the step on the landing, the deputies formed an aisle leading from the door of the car.

Catherine Lang stepped from the train, and the crowd sighed.

She was wearing a green dress, a soft green, like the first leaves of spring but softer. Mac strained to see her face, but it was hidden in the shadow of a hat tied under her chin. She turned and saw the sheriff.

The crowd, the train, the depot disappeared then. In all the world, there was only Catherine Lang and Sheriff Frank Drinkwalter. It wasn't that the crowd had been excluded from the meeting, but that they had been pulled into it, that they were part of it.

Thompson offered Catherine his arm, and she took it, and the two of them walked toward Drinkwalter. Mac thought that if the Queen of England had followed that pair from the train, no one would have noticed.

Catherine didn't seem bound by gravity or the awkwardness that afflicts lesser creatures. She glided toward Drinkwalter. As she neared, Mac could see that she was crying, tears cutting little rivulets down her face.

A step away from Drinkwalter, she dropped her arm from Thompson's. Thompson seemed stricken to lose her, but when she and Frank Drinkwalter came together, he smiled, and Mac thought he saw a tear in Thompson's eye, too. Mary's face was shining and her eyes were leaking tears.

Every man in that crowd took Catherine into his arms at that moment, and every woman stepped into Frank Drinkwalter's arms. They came together like two pieces of a whole, each special, but together, they were . . .

Mac shook his head, his words unable to describe his feelings. He understood then what the Reverend Eli Peabody had meant when he said that God was more likely to speak to people in feelings than in words.

The embrace may have taken an hour or a day or a week. Mac didn't know, and he didn't care. He was pleased simply to be that close to it. When the two stepped away from each other, the crowd roared.

For the first time, Drinkwalter seemed to notice the people around him.

Thompson clapped his hands, and his deputies formed ranks marching through the crowd to Mort Timpkins's carriage, making way for Frank and Catherine. They stood at attention while the sheriff and Big Jim helped Catherine into the carriage. Drinkwalter waved Mac and Mary to the carriage, helping Mary in and then waiting until Mac boarded before he took his place beside Catherine.

Timpkins clicked his horses into movement, and the

carriage set off toward the west hill, leading a parade of wagons.

The sheriff's face curved into a question as they rattled up the sandstone road leading to the house. When he saw the steps leading up to the top of that big flat rock, his eyes jerked to Mac. Mac was the only one he had told about that rock.

The carriage pulled to a stop beside the house. Beautiful the house was, white as a cloud with blue trim, just like the peaks of the Beartooths to the south were blue where shadows lay across the snow. The house had two bedrooms toward the back, one larger for the Drinkwalters, and one for their child or children. A formal entry just inside the front door opened into a hall that led to a front room, a kitchen, formal dining room, and sitting room with shelves for books. Outside, a porch shouted for rocking chairs so the Drinkwalters could sit there and watch the rivers and the mountains. They had even built stairs to the top of the cabin-sized rock. During the construction of the building, one or another of the people had climbed those steps to take deep breaths of clear air, to see the beauty of the place and the work they were doing.

Frank and Big Jim helped Catherine and Mary down from the carriage. Thompson spotted the tables piled high with food. He winked at Mac, took Mary's arm, and charged the tables.

Sparks Pierson stood on the porch yelling "Your attention please" until he had it.

"Sheriff, you might say this house is a monument to you and the people you serve in Stillwater County, and you would be right. You might say, too, that this house is a monument to the good people of Eagles Nest, and you would be right there, too. You might say, too, that . . ."

A voice floated out of the crowd. "You might say you're a little windy, Sparks."

Sparks grinned. "I guess I am at that. Anyway, Sheriff, we have declared July second Frank Drinkwalter and Catherine Lang Day, and I would like to present you with the deed, free and clear, to this home. May you always be happy here."

The crowd cheered, and the same voice floated up again. "The best part of Sparks's speeches are always the end."

Pierson opened the door to the house, handed Drinkwalter the key, and ushered them through. The crowd pushed up to the windows so they could watch the two examine their handiwork.

"Oh, she likes that couch. I knew she would. She's got taste. You can just tell she's got taste." "Did you see the look on her face when she saw the kitchen? I think she was looking at that Majestic stove." "No, it wasn't the stove; it was that table and chair set. Sam Gibbons made that out of walnut, and it's just beautiful." "They could entertain the governor in that sitting room."

Sheriff Frank Drinkwalter and Catherine Lang sat together on the couch in their front room. Mac and his mother sat on spindly, stiff-backed chairs, and Yellowstone County Sheriff Big Jim Thompson sprawled in an overstuffed chair, comfortable as a cat.

Thompson yawned. "S'pose I should go into town and get something to eat."

"Eat?" Drinkwalter said. "You ate half that table this afternoon."

"Did not," Big Jim said. "Just gnawed a little at one of the corners. Besides, a man's got to keep his energy up."

"Keep your energy up? If you had any less, you'd be hibernating."

Both men grinned.

Drinkwalter shook his head. "I didn't know how to thank them. The words just wouldn't come."

"You got that twisted," Thompson said. "All this is a thank-you for things you've done for them. They're grateful, just like the people in Billings are grateful to me. It's just that the Billings bunch is not so . . . demonstrative."

"Yeah, they hold it in really well," Drinkwalter said, and both men grinned again.

Drinkwalter sighed. "Mary, I know this is a lot to ask, but I would really appreciate it if you and Mac could stay here at the house until the wedding. I don't want to leave her out here alone."

Catherine broke in, "I would like to go into Eagles Nest tomorrow to see the town, learn my way around. I'm more than a little curious about this place where I will spend the rest of my life."

Mary smiled. "We would be pleased to show you around, but there isn't all that much to see."

"From what I saw today, I know I'll love it."

A frown crossed Catherine's face as she turned to Mary. "I know this is terribly unfair to be asking so much of you, but would you please do us the honor of standing up with us at our wedding?"

"I would be pleased to," Mary said.

Drinkwalter broke in. "Mac, would you be my best man?"

Mac blinked. "You want me to be your best man?"

"Yes."

"Yes," Mac whispered.

"And Jim, would you give Catherine away?"

Thompson shook his head. "No, no way in the world I'd ever give her away. She's a keeper."

Drinkwalter stared at his friend, and Thompson sighed. "I would be honored to do that for you," he said. "I'll have to go back to Billings tonight—that is, if I can get Harold away from that Miss Pinkham. He went all starry-eyed. But I'll be back in time for the wedding. There isn't anything in this world that could make me miss that. "

"It's settled, then. We've got everything taken care of."

"Everything except Galt," Thompson whispered.

"Yes, everything but Galt."

25

Jack Galt peered through the heat of the forge at Leaks Donnan, cringing in a dark corner. Galt smiled. That's where Donnan belonged, in a corner in the dark.

Donnan was a sycophant, a miserable little man with no power. Still, he had his uses. He was a skulker, a man who hid in shadows. If he saw something of value untended, he took it. If he saw a woman preparing for a bath, he watched. If a drunk were passed out in an alley, Donnan would take his money and put his boots to playing a tune of his own weakness on the drunk's ribs.

Donnan knew things other people didn't know, and he shared that information with Galt. So Galt let Donnan sit in the shadows of the smithy.

Donnan coveted the blacksmith's power. Galt knew that, but the little man might as well want the moon. If he transferred even an infinitesimal bit of his power to that pathetic little man, Donnan would puff up like a balloon and explode, raining blood and guts on unknowing passersby. The thought made Galt grin, his teeth reflecting the red heat of the fire.

Donnan cringed in his corner. Galt's grins were feral at best, and lighted by the forge, his mouth seemed filled with raw meat. Donnan didn't want to think about that. Donnan didn't want to think about anything, so he spoke. "Not much business today."

"No. They must be up to something."

"They're over at the railroad station. Sheriff's waiting for his bride, and they all want to get a look at her."

Galt's head jerked up. "The sheriff's bride?"

"Yeah, from back East someplace. Must be a mail-order bride. No woman who knew the sheriff would marry him." Donnan laughed at his own joke, the sound irritatingly like the squeaking of a rat.

"A whore would. A whore would marry the sheriff."

"I s'pose."

Galt pulled a bar of steel from the fire, the metal glowing red with heat. "I can finish this later. Let's go see this whore."

Donnan scrambled into the light. "Yeah, let's go see this whore."

Galt dipped his hands into a bucket beside the forge, washing smoke from his face and neck. The two stepped into the sunlight then, both blinking against the sharp morning light. Galt didn't like the light. The sun scratched at his skin, and he didn't like being in places where he might be seen. He plunged across the street into the shadows of cottonwoods beyond.

Galt and Donnan broke free of the trees just as the train shuddered to a stop at the depot. The two scrambled over the rail bed, slipping a little as they reached the top. But the crowd didn't hear the clatter of cascading rock. The crowd's attention was fixed on the train.

Galt and Donnan scrambled into the shadows beneath the water tower, hiding themselves from the sun's bright light and public scrutiny. Galt could see the sheriff standing on the landing, holding a bouquet of flowers.

Galt chuckled despite himself. Carrying flowers to a

whore: that was Sheriff Frank Drinkwalter, all right. The grin fled Galt's face. Big Jim Thompson was leading a bunch of deputies up to the train. Galt shrunk back into the shadows.

"Whooee," Donnan croaked. "Whooee, she's a beauty, ain't she, Jack?"

Donnan had climbed several feet up the water tower. Galt joined him. From that perspective, they could see over the crowd. From that perspective, Jack Galt could see Catherine Lang. She was wearing a green dress, one of those fancy ones from big stores like they had in Billings. Her hair was honey-colored and it shone in the sun. He could see her face. She was pretty, beautiful even for a whore.

Silence nagged Mac awake. The boy stirred, looking around the room, trying to fathom where he was and how he had come to be there. The freshly painted walls were disconcerting, and the silence rubbed at his senses.

The trees whispered constantly around the McPherson cabin, spreading cosmic rumors. Beneath that sound, beneath all sounds, was the river. The Yellowstone raged at the rocks that tried to block its way, throwing spray like epithets into the air as it coursed through the rapids upstream. But it regained its temper outside the McPherson cabin, slowing to consider the nature of rocks and river. The channel was deep and contemplative, epiphanies appearing as eddies and then disappearing into the depths for reconsideration. To live near the Yellowstone is to be constantly aware of it. The river feeds, cleanses, slakes the thirst, and soothes the souls of those who live on its banks, but it kills, too, depending on its mood, so always Mac listened.

Silence crept into this room, silence broken only by the faint caw of a magpie. Then the boy remembered the train and the sheriff and Catherine Lang.

Mac had makeshift quarters on a makeshift cot in the pantry. The boy climbed from his cot, shivering a little in the cold air. He pulled on his clothing, double knotting his shoelaces. Easy to stumble in the dark, easier still to step on an untied lace and fall into the darkness.

He opened the pantry door and stepped into the hall, stopping to stretch and yawn before tiptoeing past the two bedrooms to the front door. He hadn't slept well that night. Every time he closed his eyes, he saw Galt's face, blackened by the smoke of the forge. Each time he started to drift toward sleep, he heard Galt hiss.

He stepped tentatively to the front door, hoping the floor wouldn't squeak, but it was solid oak over pine. It didn't yield to the boy's step and give him away.

Stars gave some shape to shadows outside. Mac stepped around the vale, hoping he wouldn't surprise a rattlesnake, hoping that he wouldn't see Jack Galt. The sheriff had picked a good place for his home. Steep slopes and cactus and yucca and unstable footing barred the way to intruders. Only the new road offered access.

If Galt came, he would have to come up the road, and the stars and the moon painted the fresh-cut sandstone gold. Galt would stand out on the road like tar on a cement sidewalk.

Still, Mac wasn't satisfied. He stepped down the road, eyes watching for any rock that might roll and pitch him off the side, ears listening for the *buzz* of an irritated rattlesnake.

Down the hill, the boy picked up his pace, stopping occasionally to peer into the darkness ahead, to check shadows that seemed to move as a man might if he were up to no good. Cold, the night was, cold enough to send shivers down the boy's back, but as he walked toward town, his heart pumped faster, warming the boy with blood.

As Mac passed the slough beside the road, a band of blackbirds took flight, fleeing this two-legged creature. The birds seemed to awaken mosquitoes that descended on Mac in a cloud. He swatted at the insects, and they exploded, leaving patches of his own blood drying on his face and neck.

Mac left the mosquitoes behind as he climbed the little hill where Nelly's place perched, a red light on the porch giving away the nature of Nelly's business. Tonight the light attracted nothing but a cloud of moths.

He slipped down the hill, leaving Nelly's behind him, slowing before he crossed the railroad bed. He hesitated for a moment in the shadow of the trees that lined the river bottom, and then stepped on the path he had walked every day of his life in Eagles Nest. A breeze rustled the leaves overhead, and Mac heard hiding men and stalking cougars in that. But it was only the leaves, welcoming him home.

He stepped softly down the trail, stopping often to listen to allow his eyes to probe the darkness. No one. No one was hiding in the shadows, but what about the cabin?

Mac eased toward the cabin, hesitating before stepping into the little clearing that marked the McPhersons' yard. No groomed foreign grass was this to be cut every Saturday. This was native grass, and it whispered to Mac as he passed.

The boy eased on the step outside the cabin door, freezing when it squeaked. But there was no movement in the cabin announcing an ambush discovered, and Mac opened the door. Nothing was different. Nothing taken. The long blue barrel of his .25-35 rifle winked at him from beside the bed, and Mac felt better knowing it was there.

He left the cabin, slipping along the path following the river east and then south. He wanted to cross the road south of the smithy where the lights of town wouldn't betray him. It was a pretty night, quiet but for the rustling of leaves and the faint sound of men at the Absaloka saloon, telling and retelling the surprise on the sheriff's face when he saw his new home. They whispered, too, about how pretty Catherine was, and how lucky the sheriff was to have her, but those whispers were only a murmur on the river bottom.

Mac paused in the shadow of the trees, holding his breath so he could hear any movement he couldn't see. The roadbed was covered with rock and dust, and the boy placed each step carefully, willing the gravel not to crunch beneath his feet.

The evening zephyrs carried the scent of an irritated skunk. Probably the Johansens' dog. People made way for that dog, crossing the street half a block ahead of the animal to avoid meeting him. Always he smelled of skunk. The dog lived to kill skunks. Mac had seen him as far as the west hill, tracking the black-and-white-striped animals along the river bottom.Smart dog, Mac thought, to hide his scent behind the scent of his prey. But always Mac wondered what drove the dog to kill skunks.

Mac walked north now, stopping in every shadow to be sure that he wasn't seen. As he neared Galt's smithy, his heart beat faster and his throat closed as though Galt had his hands around it and was choking the life from Mac.

Dread put the hairs up on the nape of Mac's neck. He wanted nothing so much as to walk far enough away from the smithy so he could breathe again, but he had to know that Galt was there and not stalking his mother and Catherine.

The dull, yellow light of a kerosene lamp appeared in the window of the lean-to attached to the back of the shop. Galt was there, all right, and awake. Mac willed his eyes not to look at the window. The lot was strewn with old rusting iron and gravel. If he looked into the light, he wouldn't be able to see into the darkness at his feet. If he stumbled and fell, he would be at the mercy of a murderer. Mac had seen Jack Galt's eyes. He hadn't seen any mercy there.

Mac inched toward the window, peering in. Galt was lying in his bed still, but he was awake. Suddenly a grin crossed the blacksmith's face, and he began laughing.

The laughter was evil. The force of it pushed Mac backward. He stumbled over a piece of metal, and the clatter was enough to awaken the dead. Mac didn't care about the noise. He ran from the insanity, toward the west hill and his mother and Catherine.

Galt had awakened that morning in a sweat-drenched bed to the sounds of his mewling. "No, Mamma. Please don't make me do it, Mamma."

The dream had carried him back again to a tiny shack at the edge of a Missouri railroad town. Always the dream was black, black as the lean-to. Slivers of light streaming into the lean-to from cracks in the walls and ceiling only sharpened the contrast between black and white.

Galt whimpered as he remembered the dream, how she would dress him in his good clothes, and how he would cry, "No, Mama. Please no."

She would smile at him then, but the smile stung like the blows from her fists. So he would stand still and let her dress him and save his tears until she locked him in the lean-to again.

He couldn't see anything from the lean-to at night. There was only the blackness outside, and the blackness inside and the blackness in the little boy's chest where his heart should be. He would sit in that darkness and listen for the sound of the door opening and the *clink* of bottle and glass and the whispers between his mother and her guest. Always she called the men guests.

More clinks and whispers and then Mama would stagger to the lean-to's door. "Here he is," she would giggle. "Here's the whore."

If he had wind enough, he would squeal, "No, Mama, you're the whore!" But usually he had no breath. Usually he couldn't breathe or speak or run, and then the doorway would fill with the shape of a man.

Galt the child would stand in the shaft of light from the shack, arms pinioned across his chest in fear. Galt's tiny fists would flail against the man's chest and face, and the man laughed with the sport of it. And then there was the pain, that terrible pain, and his mother's laughter.

A tear trickled down the side of Jack Galt's face. Why did he dream that dream on July 2, 1912, in Eagles Nest, Montana? He only dreamed that dream after he found his mother hiding in the body of another woman.

He thought he had killed her in that little shack beside the railroad track, but she kept coming back. She tried to hide from him, but always he found her. Galt grinned as he stared at the ceiling. Sometimes a wink gave her away, or the way she walked, or the way that she said hello on the street. Always Jack Galt knew.

And when he found her, he stripped her of the illusion that she wasn't a whore. When she knew that, when she knew it deep down in her soul, he would take his knife to her. The dreams told him exactly how to cut his mother out of her hiding place in other women. How his mother screamed. Such fierce joy he took in the killing.

Galt's grin collapsed into a question: Why the dream now?

Always the dream came when his mother had revealed herself to him, but he hadn't seen his mother in Mary McPherson or any of the women at Nelly's. It couldn't be the sheriff's whore. Galt had stared at Catherine while she stood on the depot platform. Nothing in Catherine Lang reminded him of his mother. He knew he could watch Catherine Lang forever and never see his mother in her.

Galt's eyes widened as the revelation struck him. It came suddenly and startlingly clear. He had killed his mother's body in bits and pieces. Only her soul remained. Her soul was hiding in Catherine Lang's body. Galt had only to kill Catherine Lang to forever banish his mother's soul to hell. He would be free forever from the she-wolf that had whelped him.

Jack Galt felt like shouting his revelation to the world, to tell them that his trek had ended in Eagles Nest, Montana. That stupid son of a bitch Drinkwalter had been right. "It ends here," he had said. "It ends here."

Jack Galt laughed. He clamped his hands over his mouth to stop the noise, but it forced its way through his fingers. He laughed and laughed and laughed.

Then he heard a clatter of metal banging against metal. Leaks Donnan was stirring in the smithy.

Galt climbed from the bed. He cocked his head as he stared toward the door to the smithy. Yes, that was it. Donnan would be useful for the first and only time in his pitiful life.

Galt grinned. Police were no match for him. They were mere mortals hanging on the strings of laws and regulations. Jack Galt was bound by nothing but his mission to kill his mother. Tomorrow it would begin. Tomorrow he would tip the dominoes so that they went clattering toward the inevitable conclusion. Tomorrow he would begin killing Catherine Lang.

26

Mac McPherson had run into the morning. The sun was still hiding behind the eastern horizon, but the Beartooth peaks were already tinged with light. The boy stood gasping at the top of the road to Frank and Catherine's new home.

"Mac."

Catherine Lang was sitting in a chair on the flat rock. Mac couldn't imagine how he had missed seeing her.

"Mac, would you please join me?"

The boy climbed the stairs to the top of the rock just as the sun edged over the east hills, setting the world on fire. Catherine was so enthralled with the view, she didn't notice Mac's rasping breath or the ring of sweat around his collar.

She pointed to the south. "Those mountains. What are they called?"

"The Beartooths. They call them the Beartooths."

"Have you ever seen anything so beautiful?"

"No. Some people say seeing the Beartooths is like going to church, the mountains making us realize how . . . small we are."

Catherine smiled. "And the rivers?"

"The Yellowstone down there," Mac said, pointing with his chin. "And that's the Stillwater coming in from the Beartooths over there. The Rosebud runs into the Stillwater at Absarokee."

"I would have called it the Silver River," Catherine

said. "It shines so in the sun. And the trees along the river?"

"Cottonwoods, mostly, and cedar and ponderosa pine on the hills."

"What's that spiked plant there on the hill, the one with the huge flowers?"

"We call it soap weed. You can use the roots for soap. But I guess most places, they call it yucca."

"Yucca is such an ugly name for such a pretty plant. And the cactus with those beautiful yellow flowers?"

"Prickly pear."

"They're prickly, all right."

Mac smiled. The place and Catherine and the morning pulled the dread from him.

"Frank tried to tell me about this place. He has a touch of poet in him. Did you know that?"

Mac nodded. "When he talks about sego lilies . . ."

"Yes, sego lilies. Are there any nearby?"

Mac pointed toward the edge of the hill. "Might be one or two left."

"Would you show me after breakfast?"

Mad nodded.

"He tried to tell me about this," she said, sweeping her arm from horizon to horizon. "But it's beyond words."

"Yes. Sometimes I try to describe it, and I can't."

Catherine smiled. "He thinks the world of you, you know."

Mac stared at the rock.

"Well, he does."

"He's the best man I know."

"We're going to be great friends. You, your mother, Frank, and I."

Mac grinned. "I'm glad you came. I'm really glad you came."

"Me, too, Mac."

Catherine stood, steadying herself with a hand on Mac's shoulder. It was damp and cool with the sweat of his running.

"Where did you go this morning, Mac?" she asked.

"Just for a walk. I just went for a walk."

Mac couldn't tell Catherine what he had seen that morning. He couldn't tell her why he had felt compelled to check on Jack Galt. He couldn't tell her why Galt's laughter had terrified him so.

Jack Galt stepped through the door into the smithy. Leaks Donnan rose from the shadows and stepped into the light streaming through one of the windows.

Galt smiled. This would be so easy. "You've been a good friend, Leaks, and I'd like to do something for you. You said once that somebody in town has a pistol you'd really like to have."

"Charley Remmick's got a nice Smith and Wesson he wants to let go. It's real pretty. It's got ivory handles, and—"

"What's he want for it?"

"Thirty-five dollars, and he'll throw in two boxes of cartridges."

"What would you say if I bought that pistol for you?"

Donnan looked like a cocker spaniel that had just been told that his master would take him for a walk. "Well, I've always wanted one. Never could seem to get the money together. Hell, yes, I'd like that."

"Tell you what I'll do. I'll give you the thirty-five dollars and an extra two dollars for a bottle of whisky. You take that pistol out and start practicing with it. Pistol ain't worth a damn if you can't hit what you aim at. So you practice. Take a coffee can, and you shoot until you can hit it every time from about six steps. That's about all a pistol is good for, six steps.

"Then you stop at the Absaloka, and you have a drink on me. Not every day a man gets a new pistol. Might be you'd want to show some of the other fellows them ivory handles."

Donnan's face was shining.

"Hell, I can hit a can at six paces. I could do that right now."

"Well, it sounds easier than it is. You just have a good time and come back and see me tonight. I got something cooking that will make you cock of the walk. You got that, Leaks?"

"Hell, yes, I got that," Donnan said. "Hell, yes, I do."

"Just have a nice time, and don't tell anyone that I gave you the money for the pistol. Okay?"

The admonition was a formality. Galt knew Donnan wouldn't tell anyone the pistol was a gift. For a pathetic creature like Donnan, a pistol would represent the only power he ever had. To admit the power had been given to him would diminish it.

Already the pistol had Donnan in its grip. Galt could read that in the little man's eyes. Donnan could see himself strutting into the Absaloka, packing that pistol and tossing two dollars down on the bar. Donnan was already seeing the newfound respect in the eyes of the regulars at the Absaloka. They would see him shaded with the power of the pistol. A crooked grin was wrestling with Donnan's need to keep this moment solemn.

"You got it?" Galt repeated.

"Hell, yes, I got it."

Donnan took the money and stepped toward the door. He stopped and turned back. "You're the best friend I ever had, Jack."

Galt sneered at Donnan's back. That pathetic little man wasn't worthy to be Jack Galt's friend. No one was. Galt began putting away his tools. He had important work to do. It would require his entire attention.

Galt stepped back into his room, bending over a trunk. It was just as he had left it. Each shirt was impeccably folded and fitted into the space allotted to it; each pair of socks rolled tightly enough to bounce had they been dropped to the floor. Galt removed each piece of clothing and stacked it carefully on his bed.

When the trunk was empty, he pulled at a scrap of leather that seemed to have caught in a crack between the bottom of the trunk and the sides. The false bottom of the trunk rose, scuffing against the sides.

Galt's secrets were safe there. The trunk had been searched before, but no one had found the hiding place.

The knife came gleaming into the light, its oiled blade shining like silver. Galt's hands were trembling as he rubbed the cloth over the blade, ensuring that the oil was spread evenly. Too much oil and a knife picked up dirt and lint. Too little and rust would pit it. Galt kept this knife in perfect condition. The knife was sharp enough to shave with, but Galt would never commit such a sacrilege. Galt had killed his mother with this knife. It was his only defense against her reincarnations.

Galt's thoughts swirled back to Billings and Sally Higgins. His mother had clung tenaciously to that disguise. Sally wouldn't admit she was a whore, not even when Galt was selling her on the street, and Galt had been afraid that he wouldn't be able to touch her soul. Then he had found the train ticket. She meant to run from him. He couldn't allow that.

He had come to her as he always did. But this time he carried the knife. She had screamed when she saw the blade, but he cut the scream short. While she was struggling with death, Galt was doing his work with the knife, cutting his mother from her as his dream had told him to.

Now he had found his mother's final hiding place. Killing Catherine Lang would be more complex than the others. Sheriff Frank Drinkwalter complicated matters, but Galt had plans for Drinkwalter.

Galt was a perfectionist. He left nothing to chance. Planning made him strong, stronger than the men who had hunted him. He had taken their beatings and their accusations, but always he had walked free.

A chuckle rattled Galt's throat. He was so strong, and they were so weak. Pathetic little mewling creatures who needed to hide behind law for their killings.

Galt stood by the forge thinking about the knife and Catherine. His mother would be so surprised that he had found her. He could imagine the look on her face when she saw the knife. He would laugh and laugh and laugh then, the sound of his laughter louder even than her screams.

This would be a good day for Jack Galt. Tonight would be even better.

Sheriff Frank Drinkwalter and Catherine Lang sat atop the boulder in the yard of their new home. The day had been glorious, a warm sun softened by a breeze.

Trees had rustled their leaves as though they were talking to each other, and everywhere Catherine and Mac and Mary were greeted with smiles and soft sighs. It was springtime, and it seemed that the whole community's thoughts had turned to love.

The sunset was the only fitting conclusion to the day. The sun painted the sky violet and red and blue and yellow and orange. The two lovers sat enthralled in its light.

Catherine turned to Frank. "This is so beautiful, I feel guilty sitting here."

"While Mary and Mac do the dishes?" Drinkwalter asked.

"Yes."

"Mary said she wanted to. I think once she sets her mind on something, it's best to step out of the way. What did you think of Eagles Nest?"

Catherine smiled. "I think it's a beautiful place to spend a lifetime."

"What did you do?"

"Oh, we stopped at nearly every shop. Mary has her mind set on buying Mac a suit. She's been saving money so he can go to college. But she broke into the piggy bank to buy him a suit. I don't think they were more than at arm's length all day."

"They're a pair to draw to," Drinkwalter said. "I can't see how Mary's husband ever left her."

"Is that what happened?"

"Yes, Mac told me a little about it one day. He said his father went off to see where the sun sets."

"Isn't that strange?"

"I guess he was a wanderer. He stayed around until Mac had a few years on him, and then they went roving. They were never in one place long enough to get roots. One morning they woke up, and he was gone. They followed his trail to Eagles Nest and settled in here."

"Do you think he'll ever come back?"

"No."

"Why would he ever leave his wife and child?"

"I don't know. I can't for the life of me figure that out."

"Are you going to leave me, Frank? Are you going to go off to discover where the sun rests at night?"

"Catherine, I know where the sun goes at night." Drinkwalter pointed upstream on the Yellowstone. The sun was spraying golds and violets and purples and pinks across the horizon.

Catherine smiled, and Drinkwalter leaned over and kissed her, forgetting everything but her lips. He pulled away, cupping her face in his hands. "You are my sunrise and my sunset and my noonday."

Drinkwalter stood, pulling Catherine to him in a long embrace. When it seemed that they had fused, become one with themselves and the rock and the setting sun, Drinkwalter whispered, "Catherine, will you marry me and come to live with me in this place where everywhere you look there is beauty and friends and love and God?"

Catherine pulled Drinkwalter's face down for a long kiss.

Drinkwalter nodded, and helped her off the rock. He stood looking at her then, as though he had to frame her picture in his mind for all eternity. He turned his back then, to climb into the buggy, and urged the horses down the hill.

Mac had just stepped out onto the porch. He watched the sheriff until he was little more than a speck on the seat of the buggy as it disappeared into town. Mac would never forget that moment.

27

Mac followed Catherine into the house. His mother was polishing the counter in the kitchen. She looked up and smiled at the two. Catherine smiled at Mary and then disappeared into her room.

Mac sighed and sat down at the kitchen table. "This has been some day."

"Like none other," Mary replied.

"Will it always be like this?"

"Do you mean: Will they always be this happy?"

Mac nodded.

Mary shook her head. "I don't know."

She reached down to polish the counter again, then she stopped, sitting down beside Mac.

"Sometime you will see a girl and she will be the most beautiful thing you've ever seen. Her voice will send shivers up your back, and you'll think the heavenly choir is singing."

"Pretty as Catherine?"

"More beautiful."

"Pretty as you?"

"Of course not, Mac. You know that your mother is the siren of the Nile."

"Ah, Ma."

"Ah, Mac."

They laughed, but Mary turned serious. "You will see that girl, and you'll believe that you cannot live without her. You will believe that the sole focus of your being is to be with her. Most likely, you'll marry her."

Mary stared into her son's eyes, willing him to understand. "Your lifetime will temper that love and make it stronger, just as a blacksmith tempers fine steel."

"Not Jack Galt."

Mary whispered, "Listen to me, Mac. This is something I've been thinking about since I saw those two come together at the depot.

"Catherine's been in Cincinnati caring for her mother. Frank has been out here, trying to make a life for the two of them." Mary cocked her head. "Their love has already been tested. It is tempered until it rings so loudly, everyone can hear it.

"Do I sound silly, Mac?"

"No, Ma. I know what you mean."

Both turned to the sound of an opening door. Catherine stepped into the kitchen carrying a dress. She held it up as best she could so they could see it. "I know this isn't in style, but my mother and my grandmother and my great-grandmother were married in this dress. I . . . would like to carry on that tradition."

"It's beautiful, Catherine. Absolutely beautiful."

"Perhaps you could help me into it. I may have to alter it."

Mac sat at the kitchen table, wondering why the image of Drinkwalter disappearing into Eagles Nest so persisted in his mind. He was thinking about that when Catherine and his mother stepped back into the kitchen.

And when he saw Catherine, he forgot how to breathe.

The dress was white satin, with a wide skirt favored

in the Victorian Age. An overdress of Brussels lace adorned the dress from the waist down. The overdress was scalloped on the bottom, with rows of pink silk flowers ascending to the waist. The sleeves were Brussels lace, too, and they covered the wrists, and at each shoulder where the satin stopped and the lace began, there was a bow. A circlet held the veil in place.

"It's beautiful."

"Thank you, Mac."

Catherine turned to Mary, and Mac knew the evening belonged to them.

"Going down to the river, Ma."

"Be careful, Mac."

Mac nodded and stepped out into the evening. He walked over to the edge of the hill, eyes seeking the Beartooths to the south. He took a deep breath and plunged over the edge, letting the hill carry him down, watching only to avoid bushes that might hold rattlesnakes. He reached the bottom in a cascade of little rocks and breathed the smell of creosote as he crossed the track to the river.

The river was high and muddy and yelling at its banks. Cottonwoods swept past, turning and twisting in the current, waiting for the river to decide if they would look better on this sandbar or that.

Every year the river remodeled its home, shifting meadows from one side to the other, replacing a copse of cottonwoods with a stand of willows. Always the river demanded change.

Being around Catherine and Frank and Galt was like being carried along by a hundred-year flood. He didn't know where he would find safe waters. Mac was frightened. He couldn't define the dread he felt, so he sat beside the Yellowstone River and looked for answers in those raging waters.

Jack Galt stepped back from the forge, shrugging his shoulders against the ache. He stepped to a washbasin on his way to his room, filling and emptying the basin with water several times as he scrubbed himself free of the dirt and sweat that had accumulated during the day. He put on a fresh shirt and pair of trousers, straightening his back as he walked back into the smithy.

"You ready, Leaks?"

Leaks stepped into the soft glow of the forge.

"I'm all ready, hell, yes, I'm ready."

"Where's your pistol?"

"I . . . uh, I left it over there in the corner."

Galt shook his head. "Leaks, you take that pistol and stick it in the front of your trousers. You're going to be a big man in Stillwater County after tonight. Could be some dime novelist will come out here and write about the exploits of Dangerous Leaks Donnan."

"Dangerous Leaks Donnan?" Donnan whispered, a grin flickering across his face.

"Dangerous Donnan, might be it. Could be they'll stop calling you Leaks, and just start calling you Dangerous."

Donnan glowed.

"How'd you get the name Leaks, anyway?"

The smile fled Donnan's face. "It was . . . uh, when I was a kid. I couldn't always . . . Uh, sometimes, I . . . uh, wet my pants."

"Dangerous Donnan it is, then. No more Leaks Donnan for you, Dangerous Donnan."

The glow came back to Donnan's face. "I'll get that

pistol now. Hell, yes, I'll wear it in the front of my trousers so people will know how I've changed. So people will know I'm Dangerous Donnan now."

"You practice like I told you?"

"Hell, yes, I did. I shot up most of those cartridges."

"You hit that tin can every time?"

"Hell, yes. Well, most of the time. Almost all the time."

"Well, your target tonight will be a hell of a lot bigger than a tin can."

"Hell, yes, it will be. A lot bigger than a tin can."

Galt shoveled coal on the forge. "This should be burning good by the time we get back. I'll use the bellows to stoke it up, so you'll have plenty of light."

"Hell, yes, I'll have plenty of light. Hell, yes."

Nelly Frobisher had her coming-out party a week ago. Beulah and Bridget and Jezzie had nursed her through those dark times when she hid in the shadows of her childhood. Their soft words and gentle care pulled her back from her nightmares.

Nelly told the others her story, then, a story she had never told anyone else. Every Saturday, she said, she would try to hide from her abusive father. Every Saturday he tracked her home, making a child's game of the violence he was about to visit on his tiny daughter.

"Hey, little piggy, no sense to hide,
Papa's coming to take his bride."

Their words began to flow, then, as their tears had. Bridget and Jezzie talked about their childhood and their first "lovers" and what had brought them to the life. Beulah was the last to talk because she had the most to lose. She talked about how she had been used by the lord of the manor where she worked back East. She had seen the advertisement in the paper. A farmer in Montana was in need of a wife. The advertisement said he was an honest, God-fearing man. But when he realized she was not a virgin, he raged at her. When she asked if he was, he struck her.

Beulah had been knocked unconscious, and when she awoke, she was in a feed shed that backed into the pigsty. That was her home, a hard-scrabble bed she built of boards so she wouldn't have to sleep on the floor. She covered herself at night with burlap sacks and the stink of the pigsty. The stench permeated her pores, until she thought that she would never be shut of it.

She had almost come to believe that she was a pig. She ate scraps. She slept next to them, imitating their grunts and squeals, trying to learn their language. She needed to tell someone that her back ached or that the sun was burning her or that the cold had seeped into her bones and would never come out.

Her husband spoke to her as much with his fists as with his words. His words were limited to telling her what her work would be that day. When he had butchered that fall, Beulah had in her mind that he intended to butcher her, too, to hang her hams in the smoker behind his cabin so he would have meat in the cold winter months. It was then that she had gone into the cabin and taken the shotgun from the wall.

When he came back to the sty and found that she was not at work, he had raged at her, shouting for her to come out where he could see her. So she did come out, and when he saw the shotgun, he glared at her. She was too stupid even to cock the hammers, he said. So he strode toward her, his face livid with rage while she tried with her tiny hands to cock the weapon.

She still remembered the look on his face when the buckshot tore through his gut. He was surprised, Beulah told the other women. He was so very surprised. She had dragged his body into the sty with the pigs so that they might have meat for the winter. When they were finished, she carried the bones into the cabin. She sloshed kerosene over the floor and stepped outside, tossing a lighted match through the door. She opened the gate to the sty then, and to her shed where the feed was kept.

The pigs had followed her for a while, she striding along with the shotgun under her arm and the towering fire at her back, but eventually they went back, the sty being the only home they had known.

The stories brought the women together and made them stronger. And that was the reason that when Jack Galt and Leaks Donnan stepped through the front door of Nelly Frobisher's establishment that night, it was much different from the first time they terrorized the women.

Nelly was sitting in her little office, going over her books. When she heard the front door open, she stood, sweeping aside the green velvet curtain that separated her office from the front room.

Galt watched her, anticipating the panic that would cross her face as it had before. But there was no fear in her face.

Nelly walked to the stairs leading to the second floor. "Beulah," she called. "It's time to slop the hogs."

Beulah's laughter preceded her down the stairs. Galt and Donnan heard the ugly *snick* of one hammer being pulled back to full cock, and then the *snick* of the other hammer.

Galt stepped back. It shouldn't be like this. They should be terrified. They shouldn't be so sure of themselves. He was Jack Galt, a man of great power, a killer of whores. Nelly Frobisher should be terrified, but she stood as confidently as she might when welcoming an old customer.

And then from the stairs: "*Sooee Sooee!*" Nelly took up the call: "*Sooee, sooee!*" Bridget and Jezzie's voices floated down from the second floor: "*Sooee, sooee!*"

Terror edged into Donnan's voice. "Why are they calling the pigs, Jack? They ain't got any pigs. Why are they calling the pigs, Jack?"

Galt's voice cracked. "You whores best be careful. I've got Dangerous Donnan here, and he's armed with a new pistol. You whores best learn your place."

But the only reply to the threat was another *sooee!* from the staircase. Closer, now. Too close, and then Jack Galt thought about his mother coming to get him. "He's the whore," she had said. "He's the whore, not me." Terror coursed through Galt.

"Run, Leaks. Run. These whores mean to kill us."

Both men burst through the door just as Beulah turned the corner at the bottom of the stairs. A blast of buckshot followed them into the darkness of the night.

28

Sheriff Frank Drinkwalter lay in his bed, staring at a ceiling he couldn't see in the darkness. Tomorrow, on Thursday the Fourth of July in the year of our Lord 1912, he would stand at the altar with Catherine Lang and become one with her in God's eyes and his own.

Her image had come to him so many times in his dreams that the dreams seemed real and tomorrow a dream. Her arrival, their new home, the community's generosity all seemed more dream that reality.

He was going over each moment now, remembering the tilt of Catherine's head, her laughter, her awe at the beauty of the place where they would make their home. She teased smiles from Mac, and that pleased the sheriff. He was surprised at how quickly Catherine and Mary had become friends. Their lives had been so different, but they shared something that made their friendship special. Still, the sheriff stood guard over his happiness, his mind tripping over everything that could go wrong.

The rap at the door was an intrusion, breaking into his thoughts. For a moment he ignored it, but it persisted. The sheriff pulled back the covers and rose from the bed, pulling on a pair of trousers.

Pete Pfeister was at the door. "Sorry to bother you, Sheriff."

Drinkwalter nodded. "Come in."

The sheriff led Pfeister through the darkness to the table in his kitchen. He pulled a match from the box on the shelf above the stove and lit a lantern he kept in the middle of the table. Even as he put the flickering match to the wick, he realized that he might have pulled the string on the single lightbulb overhead. But Drinkwalter was more a man of kerosene lamps than of electric lights. He wasn't at ease yet with flipping a switch.

The lamp lit Pfeister's face from the bottom up, cheekbones casting dark shadows in eye sockets, his soft, round face drawn stark and sharp-edged. For a moment the sheriff's sleep-addled brain painted that face as death, death come for Stillwater County Sheriff Frank Drinkwalter. He shook his head, trying to clear his mind of that image.

"What happened?"

"Well, I was tending bar and Beulah came in." Pfeister cocked his head, willing the sheriff to understand. "She works out at Nelly's. She's kind of heavyset . . ."

"I know Beulah."

"Anyhow, Jack Galt and Leaks Donnan showed up at Nelly's."

Pfeister shook his head. "Thought I knew everything that happened in Eagles Nest. Didn't know about the restraining order. Did that have something to do with Nelly's place being closed?"

Drinkwalter nodded.

Pfeister shook his head. "I'm not sure I understand this, but when Galt and Donnan came in, Nelly yelled it was time to slop the hogs. What the hell do you suppose she meant by that?"

"Tell me what happened, Pete."

"Well, Beulah came down the stairs with a shotgun.

Now, Leaks Donnan ain't spit, but Galt looks mean as a rabid dog. Didn't bother Beulah. She was set to go head to head with both of them."

Pete shook his head. "I don't think Beulah was bluffing, and Jack Galt didn't think so, either. They lit out. Beulah hurried them on their way with a blast from her shotgun. She doesn't think she hit anyone.

"Anyhow, she said you had asked Nelly to tell you if Galt ever showed up there again. Well, he did, so she told me, and I'm telling you. I suppose this could wait for a couple of days, what with the wedding and all, but she told me to tell you. . . ."

"Thanks, Pete. Appreciate your telling me."

Drinkwalter stared out the window. "Who's tending the store?"

"Harry Goetz. He fills in for me sometimes."

Drinkwalter turned to Pfeister. "I have a favor to ask. Bert's out at the house with Catherine and the McPhersons. I'll be hauling Galt and Leaks in. I'd like to have you at the jail—just in case."

Pfeister nodded. He reached the door, before turning back to the sheriff. "Best watch your back. Leaks is carrying a pistol now. He was showing it off at the Absaloka today. Thinks he's some desperado or something. Kept telling people to call him Dangerous Donnan."

"He's dangerous, all right—to Leaks Donnan," Drinkwalter said. "Funny he hasn't shot his foot off."

Galt stood in the shadows, watching the railroad track.

"He's coming, Dangerous. He's coming. You ready, now?"

"Hell, yes, I'm ready."

"You cock that pistol, now. So he doesn't hear it when he comes in."

Snick. Snick. The pistol's hammer slid past half cock to full cock.

"You sure this is going to work?"

"Can't fail. He comes in here blasting. You pull your pistol to save your life and mine and shoot him dead. You're going to be a hero, Dangerous. You'll be the man who gunned down Sheriff Drinkwalter in a fair fight. You'll be the man who saved a friend from that wild-eyed son of a bitch."

"What if they charge us?"

"Our word against his, and he'll be dead. When you get right down to it, the law is a weak sister. You can bend it around your finger anyway you want. Won't be any trial, and when the rumbling cools down, we'll set up a whorehouse with that new bride of his. We'll auction her off the first time. Not often men get to buy a whore who's still a virgin. We'll make us some money, and you'll get a new name, Dangerous Donnan."

Donnan's voice took on a whine. "I don't really have to shoot it out with him, do I? He's a hell of a shot. I seen him shoot."

"Hell, no. I don't want to risk a good friend like you. All you got to remember is to shoot when I say shoot. All you got to do is hit the tin can in the center of his chest."

"I can do that. Hell, yes, I can do that."

"Quiet, now, he's almost here. Just stay quiet until I say shoot."

"Hell, yes. Hell, yes, I can stay quiet until I shoot him."

"Good. Now, hush."

Galt stepped behind the forge, pumping air on the hot coals so they would glow with light, so they would give Leaks Donnan an easy shot when Sheriff Frank Drinkwalter stepped through the door.

It was a beautiful night wrapped in stars. The sheriff almost tripped over the tracks as he watched a falling star streak through the sky on some cosmic mission. There was light in Galt's smithy, and it flared a little brighter as the sheriff watched. He took his eyes from the light, focusing them on the darkness at his feet. If he lost his night vision, no telling what he might step on. Shouldn't be any rattlesnakes out now, but you never knew. Sometimes they came out of the long river grass to lie on the road, absorbing the heat it held during the cool of the night. It wouldn't do to step on a rattler tonight.

More pressing was the arrest of Jack Galt and Leaks Donnan. Each arrest was different. Drunks were likely to believe they had the power to shape the law with their fists. Wife beaters railed at the law, unwilling to face their own inadequacies. Most arrests were peaceful, though, the people recognizing that they had done something wrong and regretting it.

Always before arrests, Drinkwalter tried to appraise how people would react. Doing that had kept him out of trouble more than once. But Galt was strange. He was a man without remorse.

The light from the forge temporarily blinded the sheriff as he stepped into the smithy. He blinked, trying to bring his eyes into focus, and the shape of a man emerged behind the forge.

"Galt? That you, Galt?"

The man didn't answer. The sheriff stepped closer to the forge. It was Galt, all right, and he was grinning. The grin was evil, pure evil. He must know that he would be arrested: Why was he grinning like that?

"Galt, you're under arrest. You'll have to come with me tonight."

"Don't think I'll do that, Sheriff."

"Don't think you have any choice."

"No, I think maybe I'll celebrate tonight. Going into a new business."

"You're going to jail."

"No, I'm going to start a whorehouse. Minute I saw your bride, I said to myself, now, there's a whore to build a whorehouse around. So that's what I'm going to do. I'm going to start a whorehouse."

"Hell, yes. We're going to build a whorehouse. Hell, yes."

The sheriff's eyes probed the darkness. "That you, Leaks?"

The smile left Galt's face. "Leaks, you stupid son of a bitch. I told you to keep your mouth shut."

"Hell, yes, I can keep my mouth shut."

And then Drinkwalter realized what he had stepped into. Donnan was carrying a pistol, and Galt was shouting, "Shoot. Shoot, you stupid son of a bitch."

"Hell, yes, I can do that. Hell, yes, I can."

Drinkwalter saw a yellow ball with a black dot in the middle just as the *thump* of the pistol reached his ears. The slug hit him like a fist in the center of his chest and threw him backward, he hit his head on something hard as he fell, and then there was only darkness.

Galt stepped quickly around the forge. The sheriff was flat on his back, his head twisted to one side, his shirt red with blood. The blacksmith bent over the body, pulling the sheriff's pistol from his holster.

"Dangerous, you drilled him dead center, and he's got a wad of cash on him. You not only got the sheriff, but a wad of cash, too."

"Hell, yes. Hell, yes. I got the sheriff. Hell, yes, I did." Donnan stepped around the forge and leaned down to look at the sheriff's wad of money, but all he saw was the muzzle of the sheriff's pistol. Now, why would Galt be . . .

Thump!

The bullet turned Donnan's brain to a fine pink mist and sprayed it out the back of his head.

"You can bend the law to your own purpose," Galt said to his victim, "but not with a brainless fool like you on the witness stand."

Brainless, that's what Donnan was now, brainless. The thought tickled Galt, and he almost laughed, but he had more important things to do. The laughter would come later, when he showed Catherine Lang his knife. He would laugh then. Laugh and laugh and laugh.

The blacksmith pressed the sheriff's pistol to his side, aiming the muzzle so the bullet would tear his skin and bounce off a rib before hitting the back of the smithy. *Thump.*

The blow hit Galt like one of Sheriff Thompson's fists, knocking the wind from him. He bent over, grasping his knees and trying to suck breath back in his lungs. Then came the searing pain. Galt's eyes squeezed shut. For a moment he thought he would faint. He pulled back the hammer on the sheriff's pistol *snick, snick.* Then he put the muzzle against his thigh, so the bullet would only cut through his skin on its way to the south wall.

Thump! Again searing pain that almost snatched his consciousness away, but Galt gritted his teeth and stood. He dropped the pistol just beyond the sheriff's fingers and turned toward the door. Every breath sent pain shrieking through his chest.

It was dark outside, very dark, and that was good. Jack Galt drew strength from the darkness as plants draw strength from the sun. He stopped once at the railroad track, trying to suck air into his lungs in little bits to limit the pain. That was how he made his way to the Absaloka Saloon, stopping every minute or so to catch his breath.

Galt staggered on, leaving a trail of blood on the walk. He burst through the batwing doors of the Absaloka. The bartender looked up, his eyes widening as he saw Galt's blood-drenched body. All noise stopped; only Galt's wheezing breath could be heard.

"The sheriff came shooting," Galt wheezed. "He shot Donnan and me, and Donnan shot him." Galt fell then to the floor, a wave of darkness opening to embrace him.

Mac came awake with a jerk. It was dark still in the pantry, but something had awakened him. Someone was moving around in the parlor. Dread, dark as the pantry, filled the boy. Somehow Galt had gotten past Bert, and now he was in the house, seeking Catherine and his mother.

Mac's hand was shaking as he reached for the door handle. Galt was too strong to handle straight on. Mac would have to be very quiet, come up behind him

with . . . with what? He had no weapon. He turned the
door handle slowly, willing it to be silent. He opened
the door an inch. A soft light filtered into the pantry,
and Mac's eyes searched it frantically for a weapon of
some sort. There! On the shelf. A rolling pin. That
would be perfect.

Mac grasped one end of the pin and eased into the
hallway. The scuffing noise again! Galt was in the parlor. The boy edged to the doorway and peered around
it, slowly so he could see without being seen. Mac
charged into the room, rolling pin raised high and a little squeal whistling from his lungs, only to come face to
face with his mother and Catherine.

Mac was simultaneously shaken and embarrassed.
Bert Edgar was standing on the step with his hat in his
hand. His face was twisted as though he were going to
cry. Catherine invited him into the kitchen, and Mary
set about making some coffee. Bert took a chair at the
table, wrestling between his attempt to speak and his
attempt to hold back his tears.

Mac watched the struggle, both dreading and need-
ing to know what had upset the deputy so. Bert took his
cup of coffee as though it were the Eucharist. He raised
his eyes, then, to Catherine and told her with stark simplicity: "Frank is dead."

Mac thought Catherine knew what Bert was going to
say before Bert did. She and Frank were so much a part
of each other that she must have felt his passing. But
when the words came, she just wilted.

Mary grabbed Catherine's shoulders, helping her to
a chair.

"How did it happen, Bert?" Mary asked.

"There was a shootout in Galt's smithy. Frank and

Leaks Donnan are . . . dead. Galt was shot in two places, but he wasn't hurt bad. Doc stitched him up and sent him home.

"I talked to Galt. He said Frank came into the smithy shooting wild. Frank shot Galt twice, and then Leaks stepped out of the shadows. They both fired at the same time . . . and killed each other."

"No!"

Mac's face twisted into a mask of pain. "No! Frank Drinkwalter wouldn't have done that. No!"

Bert looked up at Mac. "I don't believe it, either, but Galt is the only one alive. That was the story he was telling. There isn't anything much we can do."

Bert turned to Catherine. "They have Frank down at the furniture store."

She seemed strangely calm. "I want to go to him."

Mary nodded. "I'd like to go, too."

Bert stood. "Peter Pfeister figured that. He brought a buggy out and walked back to town. Plenty of room."

The three stepped into their rooms to dress. Mary and Mac returned first. It seemed hours to Mac before Catherine came from her room, carrying a suitcase.

Mac cocked his head. Catherine wouldn't leave now. There were too many things that needed to be done. Catherine didn't say why she had her suitcase, and Bert didn't ask.

Bert carried the suitcase to the buggy. Catherine and Mary and Mac settled against the buggy's cool leather seats. Bert snapped the reins, and they set off into the black of a false dawn.

Mac could see the road, but only barely. Only the light from the depot beckoned them toward Eagles

Nest. The rest of the town was as dark as their thoughts.

Frank died and the light went out in Eagles Nest, Mac thought as they rode through the cool morning air. Frank died and the light went out in me.

Mac hadn't thought about how important Frank Drinkwalter had become to him, but memories flooded into him. When they crossed the Keyser Creek Bridge, he thought about the patch of sego lilies. That thought carried him to their hunting trip and the ride through town afterward. The day had been sunny and warm, and Mac wanted people to look at him for the first time in his life. Now he was going to town in the black of night, and he didn't want anyone to see him.

Mac craned his neck back. Never had the stars seemed so far away.

Bert was trying hard to be a rock the other three could cling to, but occasionally he would *chuff*. Each time he did, Mac could feel his mother jerk as though somebody had slapped her. Catherine was just a shape in the darkness.

The buggy pulled to a stop at Timpkins Furniture Store. Bert jumped off the seat and helped Catherine and Mary down. He opened the door, and standing in the rectangle of light was Sheriff Thompson.

Thompson looked at Catherine. The two of them didn't have enough color in their faces to put the blush on a rose petal. Thompson shook his head. He was apologizing to Catherine, Mac thought, without saying a word.

"I . . ." Thompson said, and then his chin dropped to his chest. The death of Frank Drinkwalter had fallen on his shoulders, and the look in Catherine's eyes tore his heart out. Thompson stepped over to Catherine. He held both her hands in his, his face wrinkled, and then he choked and tears streamed down his face.

Mac remembered his pledge that nothing would make him cry. He broke his pledge that night.

Thompson stretched out his huge arms and pulled all of them to him. Mort Timpkins and Bert joined them. They cried, too.

When the sobbing stopped, Thompson opened his arms. Tearstains marked the places on his shirt where Catherine and Mary had laid their heads.

Catherine stepped over to Frank. She took his hand in hers and kissed him on the forehead. She turned then to ask Mort if she could pick Frank's coffin. He showed her everything he had, and she picked one made of oak. That done, she turned to Bert. "Could you bring me my suitcase, please?"

Bert nodded. He was pleased to step out into the cool darkness of that Montana morning. He was pleased to be standing by himself drinking great draughts of morning air. When he thought he had his emotions under control, he reached into the buggy for the suitcase. He carried it inside and placed it on a chair.

Catherine opened the suitcase. Her wedding dress was there, all silk and Brussels lace and pink roses. Her ma and her grandma and her great-grandma had worn that dress at their weddings. Catherine had intended to wear the dress to her own wedding, but there would be no wedding, and she would have no child to pass the dress to.

She fluffed it, and then picked it up and carried it to the coffin. Mort Timpkins lifted the lid, and Catherine spread her dress across the bottom.

"That's where I want it to be," she said. "I want it to be with Frank."

Thompson choked as though someone had hit him in the throat. Mary smiled just a little. She knew what it was to be a one-man woman. She knew about that.

Mac's shoulders were shaking. He knew he would never forget that moment any more than he would forget sego lilies or the Beartooth Mountains or the Yellowstone River on a fall day.

The people of Eagles Nest didn't celebrate the Fourth of July 1912. Instead, they lined up outside Frank Drinkwalter's home, carrying casseroles and condolences with them. They popped in and popped out. They were terribly sorry, they said during their brief stays, and they would do whatever they could to help Catherine through these difficult times.

Mac stayed in the home. He answered the door, ushering the visitors into the kitchen where Catherine and Mary met them, thanking them for their consideration, answering any questions they could.

Yes, the funeral was tomorrow. No, Catherine didn't intend to stay in Eagles Nest. No, she hadn't decided yet what she intended to do with the house. Yes, she very much appreciated their concern and the welcome they had shown her.

Big Jim Thompson spent the day at the smithy and asking neighbors what they had seen or heard the night of the shooting.

The days moved on and the nights, running together. Mac saw them pass, dark colors through tear-filled eyes.

⋄ ⋄ ⋄

Bert Edgar sat at the judge's bench like a sinner at the altar. Stillwater County Attorney Jim Pratt strutted around the court, winking at this member of the audience, stopping to talk to that one. The court was Pratt's stage. He intended to strut and fret his piece on it.

Edgar called the coroner's inquest to order, reading instructions Pratt had given him. The inquest would determine the nature of Sheriff Frank Drinkwalter's death, and whether further investigation was necessary.

Pratt nodded to Edgar and called Jack Galt to the witness stand. Galt swore that he would tell the truth, so help him God, but he couldn't hide the smirk on his face.

Pratt approached Galt as he might have approached a friend on a street corner.

"Mr. Galt, would you tell the court what you were doing late in the evening of July third."

"Working. I was trying to finish some work I had scheduled. I try always to get my work done on time."

Galt turned to the jury. "I commend you for that. The businessmen of Eagles Nest are known for burning the midnight oil on behalf of their customers, or their clients."

Advertisement delivered, Pratt turned his attention back to Galt. "Did anything unusual occur that night?"

Galt leaned forward in his chair. "It sure as hell did. Sheriff Drinkwalter came in yelling like a banshee and shooting."

Galt reached over to touch his ribs and his leg. "He shot me twice before I even knew what happened. If it hadn't been for Leaks Donnan, the sheriff would have killed me."

Galt dropped his eyes to the floor. "My friend Leaks

Donnan stepped out to save me and it cost him his life. Drinkwalter shot him down as though he were nothing more than a dog."

"Do you have any idea what prompted him to do this?"

Galt shook his head. "I have no idea what caused him to shoot me and Leaks Donnan. I didn't ever do anything to him or anyone else in this town. I'm an honest businessman. I've never been charged with a crime, not here or anywhere else, but he's been spreading stories about me, stories that were completely false."

Galt dropped his eyes. "Donnan was my friend, trying to save my life, and the sheriff shot him to death."

"Bullshit!" The word rattled the windows in the courtroom, and Big Jim Thompson marched to the front of the courtroom. Pratt turned twenty shades of white, and Galt seemed bent on slithering out of the courtroom on his belly.

"Bullshit!" he roared again, and there wasn't a soul there who didn't know Big Jim was in charge.

Thompson stood in front of Bert Edgar, gripping an old flour sack so tightly that his knuckles glowed white.

Thompson's face pulsed red and purple. Lightning flashed from his eyes. He stood there like God's right hand, and his voice rumbled like thunder.

"I will not let this little pipsqueak demean the most honorable man I've ever known."

Big Jim tapped Pratt on the chest with his index finger and knocked him back three steps. Then he stomped over to the chair where Galt was sitting. The room shook with the force of his steps.

He leaned down until he was nose to nose with Galt. Galt squirmed, trying to get away from Thompson's eyes, but they were too strong, and he was too weak.

"This outstanding businessman your county attorney praised so mightily is a murderer, a man who takes knives to women. He cuts them up in ways that would shame the devil. He did that in Billings. He did that in Glendive. Everywhere he goes he leaves some woman dead and mutilated.

"This son of a bitch killed Sheriff Frank Drinkwalter, and I can prove it."

Pratt was standing beside the judge's bench gulping. Finally he found his voice.

"I will not have this legal proceeding interrupted by a man who has obviously lost his mind."

Thompson swiveled around, putting the full force of his glare on Pratt.

"You going to throw me out, Pratt?"

Pratt shook his head and collapsed into a chair.

"You gonna throw me out, Bert?"

Bert Edgar, wide-eyed, shook his head.

Sheriff Thompson turned his attention on the crowd. "Any yahoo in here fixing to toss me out?"

Not one man moved. Not one sound issued from the courtroom.

Thompson took a deep breath. Then he took another, and the color dulled to a soft, hot red, like the coals in Jack Galt's forge.

"Do you remember what this piece of dog puke said about Sheriff Drinkwalter coming into the room shooting?"

One of Thompson's eyes squinted shut as he stared around the room. "Damn it! Nod if that's the way you remember this lying little weasel's story!"

Heads bobbed in unison.

Thompson turned to the coroner's jury. "That the way you remember it?" he said, his voice softer. The jury nodded.

"Now, what I'm going to show you will upset some of you. It sure as hell upset me, but I don't know any other way."

Thompson put his sack on the table. He opened the top and reached inside.

"This," he said, holding a shirt by the shoulders, "is Sheriff Frank Drinkwalter's shirt, stained with his own life's blood. You'll notice there isn't much blood on it. That's because the bullet shattered his heart. There was nothing left to pump blood out of his body.

"Now, I'll tell you what isn't on this shirt—powder burns. Doc and I went over it together with a magnifying glass, and there isn't one speck of powder on it.

"You'll have to take my word for this. If this was a trial, I'd bring in Doc, and he'd swear to it. But this isn't anything but a foul-hearted attempt by that little bit of chicken droppings"—Thompson pointed to Pratt—"to besmirch my best friend's good name and to mislead the good people of this community."

Thompson sneered at Pratt. "Not that evidence has ever intruded on the workings of your little mind, but there were lots of powder burns around that hole in Leaks Donnan's head. Doc and me, we did a little testing, and that muzzle wasn't more than three or four feet from Donnan's head when the trigger was pulled.

"That means that Frank would have had to walk up to Donnan, shoot him at point-blank range in the head and then walk over to the other side of the forge to wait for Donnan to arise from the dead and shoot Frank in the heart. But that didn't happen. That couldn't have happened, and I'll tell you why."

Thompson took a deep breath, trying to put a damper on his anger.

"Any hunter knows that a bullet carries blood and tissue out the exit wound. The blood from Frank's wound sprayed on the smith's west wall. That proves he had just stepped in the door when he was shot to death.

"Donnan was shot in the head at close range. His brain tissue sprayed against the ceiling over the forge. He had to have been leaning over a mortally wounded Frank Drinkwalter when he was shot between the eyes. Remember, Frank died instantaneously. Remember, he had no powder burns on his shirt. He was shot from some distance. So Frank couldn't have shot Donnan.

"There's something else about this little game that you should know."

Thompson leaned toward the jury box. "Now, where do you suppose it was that Doc found the most powder burns?"

Jurors shook their heads.

"Well, I'll show you where the most powder burns were."

The Yellowstone County sheriff reached into the sack and pulled out a bloodied pair of trousers and a shirt.

"Jack Galt's shirt and trousers were thick with powder burns. That's because this sniveling little son of a bitch shot himself. Not bad enough to cripple him. Just bad enough to sell his lies."

Thompson's eyes squeezed shut as he turn to face Pratt. "A real county attorney wouldn't have bought this story from the get-go, but you people don't have a real county attorney. All you have is a lawyer on the public dole."

Thompson scowled and stalked over to Galt.

"Now, those clothes are proof of what I just said. I can't prove the rest, but I'll tell you what I think. There is on file a legal restraining order prohibiting Galt from going near Nelly Frobisher's establishment. Sunday night he went to Nelly's, knowing that Frank . . . Sheriff Drinkwalter . . . would be after him about it. Then he set up the ambush in the smithy. Donnan shot the sheriff. Galt took the sheriff's pistol and shot Donnan as he leaned over the sheriff's body, and then he shot himself. There is no other explanation for those powder burns.

"This . . . this coroner's inquest"—Thompson looked as though he wanted to spit—"was set up so that little popinjay could strut his stuff and malign an honest man's character."

The sheriff turned to Bert Edgar. "Bert, I know this is your first coroner's jury, but is it serving any purpose whatsoever?"

Edgar shook his head.

"Then I suspect you should adjourn it."

Bert nodded.

"The gavel, Bert. Rap the gavel and say this jury is adjourned."

And Bert Edgar did.

29

Dinner was a farce. The table was piled high with food, but no one could eat. The four sat at the table, avoiding one another's eyes. Finally Mac and Big Jim Thompson fled to the porch.

"What's going to happen now?" Mac asked.

Thompson leaned back in his chair, twisting his neck to relieve a kink. "Pratt won't do anything. If he did, he would be admitting he did something wrong. Everybody knows he screwed up, but he isn't about to admit it.

"Most of the men will be in the Absaloka, telling stories about Frank and what happened at the courthouse today. Another hour or two, some drunk will shout: 'Let's lynch that son of a bitch.' That's all it will take, just the one shout."

Thompson looked west along the Yellowstone, watching the last sliver of the sun sink behind the horizon. "But I have five deputies posted at the Absaloka. They'll send the crowd home. The good people of Eagles Nest will go, muttering about what a hell of a thing it is when the law has no respect for justice. But inside, they'll be glad they were stopped. It's a hell of a thing to take a life, Mac. Nobody wants to do that."

Big Jim's chair creaked under his weight as he turned to Mac. "You know why I'm not there, Mac, waiting with my deputies to meet that mob?"

Mac shook his head.

"Because I'd be the one yelling for the lynching. I'd be the first one out of that bar, hoping to put the rope around Galt's neck. A sheriff can't do that, can't kill somebody in cold blood like that. But if Galt comes out here to get at your mother or Catherine, I can kill him."

Thompson leaned over to spit off the rock, to rid himself of the bitter taste in his mouth.

"I should have killed him before, Mac. I should have killed him when he took that knife to the woman in Billings. But I didn't want his rancid soul hung around my neck when I went to meet my Maker. So now I have Frank Drinkwalter's soul hung around my neck. He was my best friend, and I let that son of a bitch Galt kill him."

Mac's voice scratched from a throat squeezed shut with emotion. "You didn't know he would kill Frank."

"No, but I knew he would kill somebody. That's the hell of it, Mac. To stop him from killing someone else, I had to kill him. So I would damn myself to hell for someone I didn't even know. So I did nothing, and now Frank is dead, and it's my fault."

"What will Galt do now?"

"He'll try to run, but it won't be easy. I've got another deputy at the depot. So Galt will likely sneak out of town and wait for the milk train at one stop or another. I figure he'll go east. I figure he'll try to get at Catherine. I think he killed Frank so he could get to Catherine."

The words blew over Mac like a cold wind.

The boy spoke in a whisper. "Before the inquest, he asked Sparks for Catherine's address. He said he wanted to send her a letter saying how sorry he was about Frank."

Thompson spat off the rock again. "I tried to talk her into staying, but she said she couldn't spend the rest of her life seeing Frank in the eyes of the people she passed on the street."

The Yellowstone County sheriff stirred in his chair. "I'm going inside and pray to God that Galt comes at me with that knife."

The sheriff rose and gripped Mac's shoulder. "You coming in?"

"No, I think I'll go down and sit by the river for a while."

"That's good. You see him coming along the track, you let me know."

The sheriff turned back as he reached the door. "Mac, knock three times before you come in so I'll know it's you."

Mac nodded, the gesture lost to the growing darkness.

Jack Galt bustled around his shop, packing for his trip to Cincinnati. He would have to leave most of his tools. They were too heavy to take with him. He had his trunk packed and his knife. That was really all he needed—his knife.

Galt surveyed the shop, grinning a little as he looked at the dark stain on his floor where Frank Drinkwalter had fallen. Drinkwalter said it would stop here. The sheriff was right; it did stop here—for him. Galt laughed, an ugly, evil laugh.

Petty damn people thinking they could stop Jack Galt. Galt frowned. It looked bad when the Yellowstone County sheriff stepped into the courtroom. It looked real bad then, but the law had prevailed and Jack Galt had stepped free. There would be rumblings now in the bars about lynching Galt, but Thompson and his men would put a stop to that. That son of a bitch Thompson would protect Galt so he could make his getaway. Galt laughed at that joke, a high maniacal laugh that set the dog across the street to howling.

One of the doors to Galt's smithy opened, and the blacksmith squinted into the night. "You can't be here," he gasped. "You're d—"

The blow caught him in the belly, tossing him into the air. He twisted like a fish fighting the sting of a hook and fell belly first on the forge. The coals sizzled with pleasure as they ate into his flesh.

Mac stirred to the sound of voices outside in the kitchen. He lay a few more minutes on his cot. It must be daylight. The pantry was dark still, but there was a band of pale light under the door.

The boy rose, pulling on a pair of trousers and slipping into his shirt. He dropped to his knees then, fingers probing the floor for his socks and shoes. He tugged them on, fingers feeling for laces and pulling them snug. He pushed open the door and stepped toward the kitchen, stopping to take a deep breath before he stepped into the harsh electrical light.

Mary was by the sink, fussing with the coffeepot. Sheriff Thompson and Bert Edgar were at the table, hunched over and whispering to each other. Mac caught Bert's words: "Damnedest thing I ever saw."

Thompson looked up as Mac entered the room. "Galt's dead, Mac."

The boy braced himself against the back of one of the chairs.

"Dead?"

"As a doornail," Bert said.

"How?"

"Don't know. Charley . . . what did you say his name was, Bert?"

"Ismay. Charley Ismay."

"Charley Ismay was bringing in some cream and eggs this morning. Said he smelled something burning at Galt's place. He peeked in through the door. Galt was pitched over the forge. The top half of him was pretty well burnt up, but his head and legs were okay."

"Looked like he was grinning," Edgar said. "Looked like he had played a joke on somebody."

Mac collapsed into a chair.

"Mort took him to the funeral chapel and put him on ice. Hell, he was still smoking when we slipped him in there."

Mac gagged and ran for the front of the house, dropping to his knees on the edge of the porch and spewing the contents of his stomach on the prairie grass. When he returned to the table, his face was ashen.

"Maybe you'd best not listen to this, Mac."

"No, I want to know."

Mary set three cups of coffee on the table. Mac looked up at his mother. Never before had she offered him coffee. She nodded. "It might help settle your stomach."

Bert continued. "Couldn't find anything in there out of the order, just scuff marks where he . . ."

"You bring a buggy, Bert?"

"Yup."

"Why don't we go down there and take a look."

Mary turned to face them. "Aren't you going to

have breakfast? I was just about to put some eggs on."

"Might be better if we didn't," Thompson said.

Mac stood. "I want to go, too."

"Mac, I don't think that's a good idea."

"I've got to go, Ma. I got to."

Mary nodded, and the three rose and left the table, silent as wraiths.

A crowd had gathered at the smithy, some with handkerchiefs over their faces to kill the stench of burning flesh. Little circles had been rubbed in the dust that covered the windows, the crowd trying to peer into this mystery.

Thompson stepped down from the buggy, and the crowd parted.

"What do you figure happened, Sheriff?" one man called out from the back of the crowd.

"Don't know yet. Haven't had a chance to look around. Why don't you all go home. Bert, here, will let you know what happened."

Edgar had locked the main door to the smithy. He drew a key from his pocket and unlocked it, pulling open the double doors and sending a shaft of light into the building. A murmur sifted through the gathering, and they pushed toward the door.

Thompson said only "Bert" and nodded toward the crowd. Bert stepped back, whispering to little knots of people, telling them he would let them know as soon as he had any information. They were reluctant to go, mysteries being rare in Eagles Nest, Montana. Galt's death would be hashed and rehashed for months to come.

The stench of death was even stronger inside the smithy, and Mac thought he might gag again, but he choked the reflex and forced himself to look at the forge. The fire had sapped Galt's body of its fat and muscle and bone, but in return, Galt's body had sapped the fire of heat, leaving a discernible outline across the coals. Thompson stared at the forge, seeking clues to the mystery, brushing a burnt piece of Galt's shirt on the floor.

"Lying faceup or -down?" Thompson asked Bert.

"Facedown."

"But his head was on the other side of the forge?"

"Yeah, it was burnt up to about the bottom of his neck."

Thompson cocked his head. "Doesn't make sense."

The sheriff cradled his chin in one hand. "Bert, you're about the same height as Galt was. Come over here for a minute."

The sheriff took Bert by the shoulders, turning him this way and that. "See, that's what I thought. If you slipped and fell into the fire, you'd be burned from the face down. You'd have to jump to put your head on the other side of the forge."

"Guess so," Bert replied.

"I suspect Galt wouldn't have jumped across the forge and then lain there while the fire burned his guts out."

"Maybe somebody pushed him."

"But if they pushed him, he would have been burned, but he sure as hell wouldn't have stayed on those hot coals. He'd be down at Doc's now, being treated for burns, but he wouldn't be dead."

Mac's voice poked into the conversation. "Maybe somebody hit him on the head and threw him on the fire."

Thompson nodded. "Maybe. Bert, you just stand there for a minute."

Thompson walked around the forge, considering that possibility.

"Mac, I don't think he was hit and thrown across. He was a heavy man. I could probably toss him across the fire, but there aren't many others who could. They would have had to drag him across the coals.

"Skin peeled off his face, Bert?"

"Nope."

"If he was pulled across the fire, his face would have been burned, and look here, Mac."

Thompson pointed to the floor beside the forge. "No coals were pushed out on this side. If his body was dragged across, you'd think that it would have pushed some coals. See what I mean?"

"Yeah."

"So he had to have jumped. But what in the hell would drive a man to jump across a forge? It doesn't make any sense."

"Maybe he was sorry for what he had done," Mac whispered.

"Nah, Galt didn't have a conscience. He had that drummed out of him a long time ago, and even if God had given him a fresh batch of remorse, he wouldn't have decided to do himself in by lying on a bed of hot coals."

Thompson turned back to Bert. "He ever have any seizures that you know about?"

Bert shook his head. "Didn't know much about him, though."

Thompson turned to Mac. "He lived in the back room?"

"Yeah."

"Let's go back there, while I let this simmer in my head for a while."

The three stepped into the lean-to, Thompson ducking his head under the low ceiling. "Not much here."

Thompson shook his head. He sure was a neat son of a bitch. "Well, what do we have here?"

Thompson knelt before a trunk, knuckles turning white as he twisted off the lock that held it shut.

"Not much in here that I can see."

Thompson pawed through the clothing, his fingers feeling along the bottom of the trunk.

"Well, look at this," he said, more to himself than to Mac.

"What is it?"

"A little slip of leather. Wouldn't be surprised if there's one on the other side, too. Yeah, here it is."

The bottom yielded to Thompson's strength, and he lifted it out, Galt's carefully packed clothing cascading to the floor. "I'll be damned."

Inside was Galt's killer knife, oiled blade gleaming in the soft light from the window. Inside, too, was a map.

Thompson spread the map on the table. He took one look at it, then backed away, turning to stare out the lean-to's dusty window.

"Take a look at that."

Mac stepped up to the table.

"See, Glendive and Billings are circled in red. A lot of other towns are circled in red. Eagles Nest isn't circled, though. You know why, Mac?"

"No."

"Because he didn't kill any women here. He only circled cities where he killed a woman. I'd bet my life on it. You notice anything else about the map?"

"No."

"It tracks him west. From Missouri north and west. Just a single line, ending in Billings. But there's something out of place, Mac. Do you see it?"

Mac leaned over the table. The discrepancy was obvious. "Cincinnati. He circled Cincinnati."

"Yeah, Mac. He was going after Catherine. No doubt about it."

Thompson turned to Bert. "How about you go to those houses across the street and see if they saw or heard anything out of the ordinary. Mac and I will finish in here."

Thompson folded the map and put it into his pocket. "Think I'll check this out." Then he pulled the knife from the trunk, carrying it with two fingers into the smithy. Thompson lifted one anvil, muscles straining with the weight, and placed it about six inches from another. He laid the knife across the chasm and picked up a hammer. The blow sent the fragments of the blade spinning off, cutting slices from the pale light in the room. Thompson picked up shards from the handle and threw them into the forge where they smoked for a moment and then burst into flame.

"Now, Mac, let's see if we can figure out how this son of a bitch died. He wasn't slugged and dragged across the fire. We know that. So he had to have been pushed, but how?"

Thompson stared at the coals glowing still with heat, and then he whispered, "He was shot, Mac. The shock of a rifle bullet would have thrown him across the forge. That's got to be it."

Thompson swiveled his head. "Most likely the bullet would have gone through him. Should be able to find a hole over there on the wall."

The two spent most of the next ten minutes examining the wall opposite the smithy's main door, seeking splintered wood where the bullet passed through.

Thompson stopped, hands on hips as his mind worked through the possibilities.

"Small bullet," he muttered. "Small bullet at high velocity would have shoved him across the forge, but it might not have gone through the body. That's got to be it.

"While Galt was cooking, the bullet dropped into the forge. But we won't find it. Those high velocity bullets explode when they hit. Whatever else was left of it would have melted into the coals."

Thompson took a poker from beside the forge and stirred through the coals where Galt's body had been found.

"Small caliber. Something like that .25-35 Deak used to have."

Thompson jerked upright. He turned to stare Mac full in the eye.

"Nothing there," he said. "Guess we might as well call it quits. No one is ever going to find out what happened to Galt. You can bet your life on that, Mac."

Thompson stared at the floor. "I should have killed him when I had the chance. All of this is my fault, Mac. Do you understand that? All of this is my fault."

Mac sat on a rock beside the Yellowstone River. He was watching a cottonwood rolling in the current. The tree twisted and turned as though to free itself from the river's grip, but the Yellowstone rolled on, carrying the tree with it.

It was a year since Frank Drinkwalter had been killed and Catherine Lang had moved back to Cincinnati. She had written to Mac and Mary over the year, trying to hide the pain she felt, but it had shone through her letters.

Now someone else was writing for Catherine. Her attorney, Murray Clavedatcher, had written to inform the McPhersons of Catherine's "untimely passing." Doctors were unable to determine the cause of her death, the letter said.

Mac stood. Catherine had died of a broken heart. He knew that. He didn't know why the doctors didn't. For some time he thought he might die of the same affliction. He walked toward home then, the letter rustling in his pocket.

He passed Nelly's house. It was closed now, the people of Eagles Nest needed to find someone to blame for the tragedy, so they had sent the girls packing. One of the Jones boys had married Beulah. They had a hard time until all the preachers in town got together and unloaded two Sundays of Mary Magdalene sermons. The two had a baby on the way, and the town's ladies had gotten together to do a shower for her.

Blackbirds had reclaimed the cattails in the swamp just west of the house. They chattered at Mac as he passed. *"Intruder. Watch out for the two-legged intruder."*

Mac paused at the bridge over Keyser Creek. He turned then, walking north on the west bank above the stream. The sego lilies were there, nodding at him in the gentle breeze as though to welcome a good friend.

He knelt at the flowers, remembering what Frank Drinkwalter had said that first day when they were sighting in their rifles.

"You'll do, Mac. You'll do."

A tear fell from his eye into the gold center of the lily, shining there. Mac jerked back, not wanting to sully the flower.

After Mac had hit his first target dead center, the sheriff had said that Mac was a natural. Mac stood, shaking his head as though to free himself of that thought. He walked toward the west hill, walking into the sun until he reached the hill's shadow.

He stepped up the sandstone road then. It was a beautiful road, just as the sheriff had said it would be.

His mother was sitting on the porch, a swath of wool taking shape as a shirt. She smiled as Mac stepped on the porch.

Mac dropped his gaze, staring at his shoes as though he had never seen them before.

"I . . . her attorney . . . I . . ." Mac stood unable to speak. Mary jumped to her feet, her project falling to the floor.

"What, Mac? What happened?"

"Catherine died."

Mary's face twisted into disbelief. "No. No."

"The doctor said he couldn't determine the cause of death, but we know, don't we, Ma."

Mary wrapped her arms around her son. Her words squeezed between sobs. "Yes, we know, Mac. We know."

When the shuddering stopped, Mac stepped back from his mother and handed her the letter. "She left us everything, Ma. It's . . . college and . . . whatever else we want it to be. Why do you suppose she did that, Ma?"

Mary's eyes widened as she looked at the letter. "I don't know. I don't know."

Mac took his mother's hand then and led her to the top of the rock beside their home. They sat down on the bench. The Yellowstone, muddied now with the spring runoff, ran through cottonwood trees adorned with the soft green leaves of spring, the soft green of the gown Catherine had been wearing when she had stepped off the train.

The Stillwater ran sparkling into the Yellowstone. What was it that Catherine had called it? The Silver River; she said she would have named it the Silver River, Mac thought of it as a string of diamonds, running into the string of emeralds that the Yellowstone would be later this summer.

Mary reached over and took Mac's hand. "You don't remember your father, do you?"

Mac shook his head. "Sometimes I think of something, but . . ."

"I hurt terribly when he left. I felt as though someone had pulled my heart from me. Do you know what that hurt is like, Mac?"

Mac nodded, turning his face away from his mother so she wouldn't see his tears.

"Does it hurt so bad that you wish you'd never known Frank and Catherine?"

Mac's head jerked around. "No, they were the best. . . . No."

"That's the way it was with me. When your father left, I hurt so bad I thought I might die, but if that was the price I had to pay for knowing him, I was blessed with a bargain. Is that the way it is with you, Mac?"

Mac nodded, his attention pulled away by the clatter of wagon wheels on the sandstone road leading to their home. "Looks like Sparks is coming out again to check on his shirt."

Mary blushed. "Ah, Mac."

"Ah, Ma."

Mac took his mother's hand and led her down from the rock, and into Sparks Pierson's smile.

Visit the
Simon & Schuster Web site:
www.SimonSays.com

and sign up for our
mystery e-mail updates!

Keep up on the latest
new releases, author appearances,
news, chats, special offers, and more!
We'll deliver the information
right to your inbox — if it's new,
you'll know about it.

SIMON & SCHUSTER
A VIACOM COMPANY
www.SimonSays.com

POCKET BOOKS

POCKET STAR BOOKS

2350-01